Correspondence Course:

THE BATHSUA PROJECT

Correspondence Course:
THE BATHSUA PROJECT

A Novel

—ɯ—

Rhoda Trooboff

STILL POINT BOOKS
AN IMPRINT OF TENLEY CIRCLE PRESS, LTD.
WASHINGTON, D.C.

Published in the United States by Still Point Books, an imprint of Tenley Circle Press, Ltd., Washington, D.C.

www.tenleycirclepress.com

LIBRARY OF CONGRESS CATALOGING-IN-PUBLICATION DATA
Trooboff, Rhoda M.
Correspondence course: the Bathsua project

IBSN 978-0-9773536-8-2
Library of Congress Control Number: 2014934018

Still Point Books/Tenley Circle Press, Ltd.
P.O. Box 5625, Friendship Station
Washington, D.C. 20016

Manufactured in the United States of America by Beacon Printing Co. (Waldorf, MD).

BOOK DESIGN: *J.A. Creative*
COVER DESIGN: *Anna Nazaretz Radjou*
PHOTOGRAPH: *Margaret Adams Parker: "In Communion V—At the Table." Terracotta, 1991. Private collection.*

For my late parents – Sylvia Woolf Morss and Sumner Melvin Morss

That things are not so ill with you and me as they might have been is half owing to the number who lived faithfully a hidden life, and rest in unvisited tombs.
– George Eliot. *Middlemarch.*

—⁓— *One* —⁓—

Subject: Hello again, my love
Date: 7/22/2002 02:27:04 A.M. EDT
From: dndyoung2@owl.com
To: dndyoung1@owl.com

Dearest Dan,

Remember the sounds the house makes late at night? The ticking of the clock, the kick and groan of the water heater refilling, that *thunk* in a bureau drawer – is it yours or mine that lets out a random sound every now and then for no apparent reason? A few minutes ago the mantel clock let loose its winding-up-into-readiness-to-chime at thirteen minutes past the hour, its spring engaging, *fah-chitz*, just before it sounds the quarter hour.

I know it's late, Dan, later than I was ever up when you were here. Now when I wake up in the middle of the night, I can't fall back to sleep. I leave our half-warm bed – or better put, my warm half-bed – and come in here to the study and turn on the computer.

Thank goodness for this computer. Most nights I leave it on standby when I go to bed. It's like having another living thing in the house. With just a finger's touch the gunmetal gray screen starts to glow companionably. The best part, Danny, is the desktop wallpaper. I've got all my little icons surrounding the picture I'm growing to love, the last family photo we took before you died.

Remember that picture, Dan, from last Thanksgiving? Zoë and Jack are standing behind you and me, and Papa's seated to my right. Zo's right hand is on your shoulder, and Neddy and Gracie are sitting on the floor at our knees. We're all together, the seven of us. If you put your glasses on and look closely (squint, Dan, the way you used to through those never-clean glasses of yours), you'll see the camera flash glinting off the braces on Gracie's front teeth. Maybe it's my distorted eyesight, that worn, hot feeling

I get nowadays in my eye sockets. Or maybe what I think is light glinting off Gracie's braces is a psycho-optical mirage from those tears I haven't shed for the last month. Or the ones I didn't shed when Papa died in January, or those left over from all those years ago when we lost Nate. But there we are, you beside me to look at whenever I turn on this computer.

I look at that photo again and again every day. There we are, four generations, most of us half-smiling even. Our faces, Dan, yours and mine, are turned toward each other. We seem to be devouring each other with our eyes. Your profile – how waxy and drawn it is, your nose more like an eagle's beak than ever. You're wearing an Orioles cap to hide the chemo baldness. Thank goodness for Gracie and Ned. (He wants to be called *Ned* now, not *Neddy*, he announced after the funeral.) They're in front of us, so you can't see you're in a wheelchair, or how skinny you are in that extra-large tee shirt.

This morning at breakfast I found myself laughing out loud for the first time since you died. (It was yesterday actually, since it's Monday morning already.) I was eating a bagel, drinking coffee, reading *The Times* Sunday Style section. Something about the Wedding of the Week struck me as awfully funny. I surprised myself by laughing all of a sudden, and tears started rolling down my cheeks. I longed to hear your laughter, Dan, wrapping itself around mine. Then I got the hiccups. I wanted you to share the joke with me there at the breakfast table. Is that crazy? I almost saw you looking up from the News of the Week over your reading glasses. Could almost hear your voice.

I'll try again to fall asleep now. Maybe I'll dream of you and wake up laughing. No need to reply, my love. Rest well.

Yours, ever,

Dee

Subject:	I thought you ought to know . . .
Date:	7/22/2002 06:35:40 A.M. EDT
From:	dndyoung2@owl.com
To:	dndyoung1@owl.com

Dearest Dan,

I'm planning on going out for the evening for the first time in a while.

Remember that Gen X Book Club some of our old students started last winter to distract me from your *Condition*, as we so subtly called *It*. Remember when I'd go out once a month to some apartment in Adams-Morgan for a discussion over pizza and beer of what they had learned in college to call *texts* instead of *novels*? It was Jess Hall's brain child. She recruited the others, her pals who've come back to DC after grad school and landed cooler jobs than you and I ever dreamed of. They send out endless "Reply to All" emails to decide on books and dates and hosts for their meetings. What time they must consume at their desks "working" to fine-tune their social lives! They started out re-reading stuff they studied in class with me years ago at Remington, just to see how those novels, err, *texts*, hold up to sophisticated adult re-readings. Remember, they called it *Ms. Young's Old Pupils' Inquiry Association*, MYOPIA for short, in honor of those little fold-up half-lens reading glasses I wore those last years of teaching? We did some Salinger and Kerouac and Hurston in the winter, then took a breather in the spring. They blamed taxes and wacko work schedules, but I think it was in deference to my preoccupation with you and *It*. Jess emailed me a couple of weeks ago – a month or so after the funeral – to announce the book club's resumption with a new plan – to read what I couldn't have them read in high school, things like *Lolita* and *Lady Chatterley's Lover*, for goodness sake.

To get MYOPIA rolling again, Jess said we'll start with Flann O'Brien's 1939 *At Swim-Two-Birds* for the first meeting they could respectfully get me to attend. The date is set for next Monday night. It's been over a month now. Zoë says I should go, that getting out of the house will do me good, being with young people. I'd never heard of Flann O'Brien or *At Swim-Two-Birds* until Jess's email, but of course I found a copy on your bookshelf. Between Jess's urging and your having a copy (what haven't you read?), how can I resist?

Remember Jessie as a gangly sophomore with braces and glasses, babysitting Neddy that summer when Zoë and Jack stayed with us? Her email is a classic. Here it is for your delectation:

Subject: Reading Assignment
Date: 7/11/2002 10:28:25 A.M. EDT
From: hallj@apr.org
To: dndyoung2@owl.com

Hey, Ms. Young –

Am thinking of you – and Dr. Young – every day in all the little time crevices. Here at work when I should be working. Standing on the Metro. Flossing my teeth, even. (Speaking of little crevices.) I wish I could give you both those daily goofy after-class "see ya's" from long, long ago. But maybe you can start to imagine that life really does go on:

Who: MYOPIA

What: Flann O'Brien's *At Swim-Two-Birds*

Where: My place on Ashmead Place

When: Monday, July 29, 2002 at 7:30 P.M.

Why: Just because!

Remember when you used to nag us to do our reading? Here I am nagging you to read what the cover says is a "a wildly comic send-up of Irish literature. . . . O'Brien opened up a whole new world of possibilities for fiction [based] on his zany . . . idea that characters in fiction have earned the right to be 'recycled' – not retired once their stories are finished." Hey, Ms. Y, join us, please. Pullleeeeze?

Love,

Jessie

All of this to tell you, Dan, that I'm going out next Monday evening. The first time since You Know What. I'm afraid, actually.

Yours, ever,

Dee

Subject: [No Subject]
Date: 7/23/2002 02:08:26 A.M. EDT
From: dndyoung2@owl.com
To: dndyoung1@owl.com

Dan, dearest,

    I stayed up reading the whole Style Section over and over, hoping to find what it was that made me laugh at breakfast. Couldn't. At least, though, my eyeballs are now all hot and oogly from all that reading. Maybe I can sleep. So to bed. To our bed. To sleep. Perchance to dream.
Yours, ever,
Dee

Subject: *Ἐξίσταται γὰρ πάντ' ἀπ' ἀλλήλων δίχα*
Date: 7/24/2002 07:03:19 A.M. EDT
From: dndyoung2@owl.com
To: dndyoung1@owl.com

Dearest Dan,

    I wish I could remember my dream. You were in it, and it was lovely, even though it involved gutter repairs. They need tending to. So does this mountain of paper work. And your bureau and closet and study.

    I'm going down to the Library in a little while to solve the Mystery of the Greek Epigraph (see above message subject). Seriously. Here's why.

    I opened *At Swim-Two-Birds* yesterday morning. The first thing I see is this bit of Greek right after the title page. It looks like verse to me, twelve syllables. Dactylic hexameter, right? Never mind the novel itself: it's weird and quirky, and maybe you have to be Irish and a little boozy to understand it. But the epigraph started looping through my head like a familiar tune that you can't recall the words to. I got out your little Liddell & Scott *Greek-English Lexicon* to work out a translation. You'd probably have done it in a snap, but, funny, you don't answer my emails.

    Most of the day I actually did what I've been dreading – forced myself to start on the bills and paperwork that have been accumulating since You Know What. Rewarded myself with breaks of translating those twelve syllables. And finally late last night I turned them into three respectable lines of blank verse. Here they are:

> For all things break asunder, fall away,
>
> Departing each from each and winding up
>
> Abandoned, out of joint, lost to one another. . . .

I know what you're thinking, Dan, and how you're going to say it: tilting your head to one side, tapping the side of your nose, you're going to say, leaning back in your desk chair, stretching out those long legs of yours – "Sounds like Yeats, Dee. 'The Second Coming.'" You're   right. That's exactly how I'm feeling, Dan, and probably why it came out that way. From my toes to my eyeballs I feel like I'm falling apart, and not just me but everything about me, the gutters, the kitchen table, the world itself. Here I am, supposed to be reading a rollicking romp of a novel, intended to take my mind off my Situation, and I'm translating twelve syllables of ancient Greek that tell me what I know in my bones already.

Okay, so, Danny, which Greek playwright have we got here? What play? How should those twelve syllables be translated, and how does the blasted thing fit to a rollicking romp of a novel? How does anything fit without you? How do I make sense of anything?

Love.

P.S. How do I do anything without you? How do I make sense of anything? How do I go on?

P.P.S. Off to the Library. The way we used to go. Together.

Subject:	Canoodling: In the Library of Congress
Date:	7/24/2002 17:30.56 P.M. EDT
From:	dndyoung2@owl.com
To:	dndyoung1@owl.com

Dearest,

So I walked bravely over to the Library this morning, planned to sit in the Main Reading Room along with all the other old fogies. Barely got past the reference desk. Wondered if I should return all your stuff on our Study Shelf to the Return to Stacks Shelf, tell the librarian on duty that the prime user of Study Shelf 1434 is no longer. Managed to sign in. Put in call slips for a couple of things about Flann O'Brien, in hopes of solving the

Mystery of the Greek Epigraph. (Nearly typed "Greek Epitaph" in that last sentence.) Got a little shaky. Left after an hour.

Walking home I remembered how we used to sit side by side on that bench overlooking the Independence Avenue-2nd Street intersection. Remember how you whispered once that we should focus on one body part as it presents itself again and again? And couldn't stop giggling? The nose! The curves and folds of the human ear! I won't try this without you, lest I start laughing all alone in public on Capitol Hill, letting loose that screeching sound caught in my chest and have everybody — including the Capitol Police — take me for a madwoman.
Love.

Subject:	Re: Ἐξίσταται γὰρ πάντ'
Date:	7/25/2002 01:41:06 A.M. EDT
From:	dndyoung2@owl.com
To:	dndyoung1@owl.com

Dear Dan,

I forgot to mention: Halfway home this afternoon (yesterday, actually), I got another one of my Stunningly Brilliant Ideas. (You remember the last one, the Melville Moby-Day idea I hatched in January just before Papa died? Spending all that time in his room at the nursing home or in the chemo infusion room with you, planning the round-the-clock reading of *Moby-Dick* on August 1, 2007, to celebrate Herman Melville's birthday and the 150th anniversary of what you always called the Greatest American Novel? Remember planning the menu, the guest list, and the press releases? Remember?) Today's SBI: now that I've transliterated that pesky Greek epigraph into Roman lettering, I'll google it. *Existatai gar pant ap allelon dicha.* It looks odd, but it's worth a try. Maybe something will turn up. If it does, you'll be the first to know.
Love.

Subject: You Won't Believe This
Date: 7/25/2002 02:28:49 A.M. EDT
From: dndyoung2@owl.com
To: dndyoung1@owl.com

Got one hit. In the whole of cyberspace exactly one hit, a site called "Lally Has a Blog: The Obtuse and the Impenetrable." I don't know what a blog is or what to do when one finds oneself in one, but there I was, in one and eavesdropping on a conversation among a bunch of graduate philosophy students:

> Posted by Arthur L./ August 5, 2001 12:14 PM: Seriously, what do you think the main differences are between the analyticals and the continentals?
>
> Posted by yanotoo/ August 5, 2001 20:01 PM: "Existatai gar pant' ap' allelon dicha."
>
> Posted by Del Bourget/ August 5, 2001 20:16 PM: Accordions. Oompah bands. Alsace.

Weird, right? My first reaction was disappointment: No answer to my question. But then I saw this cute little gizmo off to the side:

Email Lally – ☺levans@qmail.com

Remember that kid we both taught years ago named Lally Evans – an artist, poet? Here I was, in the middle of the night, connected to her thanks to a line of Greek hexameter that says nothing in the world is connected to anything else whatsoever. What delicious irony!

I tried sending Lally this message:

Subject: Message from an Old English Teacher
Date: 7/25/2002 01:58:29 A.M. EDT
From: dndyoung2@owl.com
To: levans@qmail.com

Dear Ms. Evans:

Are you the same Lally Evans my late husband Dr. Daniel Young and I taught in the 1980's at Remington School in Washington DC? I'm trying to find the source of the Greek line, *Existatai gar pant' ap' allelon dicha,* and the only result of my late-night googling has been your blog. It would be enormous fun to connect with you, despite what the hexameter seems to me (with my weak Greek) to mean. Here's my stab at a translation:

> For all things break asunder, fall away,
> Departing each from each and winding up
> Abandoned, out of joint, to one another
> Lost. . . .

Either my translation is wrong or the fact that I am writing to you now affirms that the Greek original expresses a bogus sentiment. Reply, please.

Best regards after all these years, and yours hopefully,

Dorothea Young

Isn't this a hoot, Dan? I'm all atwitter. Now I open my email hoping for messages from dndyoung1@owl.com and levans@qmail.com.

Yours, my love,

Dee

Subject:	Re: You Won't Believe This
Date:	7/25/2002 16:38:51 P.M. EDT
From:	dndyoung2@owl.com
To:	dndyoung1@owl.com

Dearest Dan,

No reply from Lally. Or from you. Spent the day on survivor spouse paperwork. Awful. Sorry for myself. And damned angry at you. Feeling down, downer, downest.

Love, such love, ever,

Dee

Subject:	Stay on, Dearest
Date:	7/25/2002 21:27:15 P.M. EDT
From:	dndyoung2@owl.com
To:	dndyoung1@owl.com

Dan, dearest,

Pecked at dinner in front of the TV (more bad news). Then fooled around on-line again, reading everything around the edges of our OWL account homepage, all the links, rules governing email accounts, passwords, privacy. Ever wonder what happens when an email account's primary box holder is no longer, shall we say, available? Wise old www.owl.com doesn't tell what to do, how to handle You Know What. One sentence appealed to me, though:

The primary screen name cannot be deleted.

Apparently, once you exist on the internet, you always exist. Period. Deleting the Primary Screen Name probably causes something awful, too unspeakable for words. Everything would fall apart, disappear even. Cease to exist. ("Things fall apart because the sender has grown cold. More anarchy is loosed upon the world.") Like what you said is called a "blue screen of death," the "fatal exception" from which there is no recovery, the crash that makes lost files irretrievable, immediate operation and long-term function impossible. Sounds familiar.

You see where I'm going here, Dan.

Better keep the old Primary Screen Name and your mailbox up and running. So, as prophylactic protection against Chaos, you're going to keep that email address. No matter what.

Endurin' love, my love, in cyberspace.

Dee

Subject:	Still No Word
Date:	7/26/2002 00:13:53 A.M. EDT
From:	dndyoung2@owl.com
To:	dndyoung1@owl.com

Dearest Dan,

It's raining – hard. Can't sleep. Heart's pounding, mind's racing. Keep checking my email for messages that don't come. Feel the urge to go to the Library after breakfast if the rain stops.

Love.

Subject: [No Subject]
Date: 7/26/2002 19:30:27 P.M. EDT
From: dndyoung2@owl.com
To: dndyoung1@owl.com

Dear Dan,

Spent the day at the Library. Resolved to resurrect the old Bathsua Project where I left off last summer. Puttered with old notes, stuff on shelf 1434. Found the source of the Greek line. There it was, on page 2 of *The Flann O'Brien Reader*, which was on our shelf. No kidding: "O'Brien asked his boss in the civil service, John Garvin, for a Greek epigraph, and Garvin, who had read the manuscript, offered some Euripides, *Hercules Furens*: 'For all things go out and give place to one another.'"

That's it. Not at all like my version. So I spent the rest of the day with Euripides and *Hercules Furens*, or more properly as you would say, *ΗΡΑΚΛΗΣ ΜΑΙΝΟΜΕΝΟΣ*. It was with all the Loeb Classics on the second floor, Alcove 6 in the Main Reading Room. The line comes in a cheery speech early in the play before the agony sets in. Amphitryon, the father of Hercules/Herakles, is comforting his daughter-in-law Megara, saying her hero-husband hero will return and set all things right:

> Daughter, a fair wind course may yet befall
> From storms of present ills for thee and me.
> Yet he may come – my son, thy lord, may come. . . .
> Sooth, men's afflictions weary of their work,
> And tempest-blasts do not always keep their force;
> Nor prosperous to the end the prosperous are;
> For all things flee and yield each other place.

So there's the line. How cheerfully it rings in English. And yet I hear a note of muffled fear. Herakles does return from his twelve labors, but doesn't bring relief. Instead he wreaks havoc, in a fit of madness slaying his sons and wife before Amphitryon's eyes. Those ancient Greeks make modern life look positively tame.

Amphitryon's steadfast, cheating hope in that speech is no comfort. Despair doesn't give way to prosperity. Nobody comes along to set things right. There's no basis to trust in fair winds soothing storms or present ills. Just the opposite, in fact.

I'm battered back and forth, Dan, one minute wishing I could share Amphitryon's foolish hope in the first scene, the next knowing I share his terrible, terrible grief at the play's end. In the final scene he bends to listen for his son's breathing:

>Hush, peace:
>Can't his woes for just a moment cease
>And find in slumber's kind oblivion release?

Remember when we did that with Nate, Dan, bending to listen for his breathing even after it had stopped? Of course you do. Are you with him there, darling? Kiss him for me. Is there release there where you are, Dan, in slumber's kind oblivion?

I know that you and Zo love me best when I'm funny. A joke here, a pun there, a comic pose, a laugh, a strut. Make 'em laugh, make 'em laugh. But how will I ever get things perky, cheeky, chipper, flippant again?

Love,

Dee

P.S. I don't know what I'm saying, Dan.

P.P.S. Only time my heart wasn't racing from worry today or I wasn't in a fog of confusion was when I was in the Library.

P.P.P.S. About this email stuff: every time I call up the OWL account, I scroll down the user options for the joy of seeing your name. I wish I could sign in as if I were you, and get inside that private space with you. But OWL won't let me sign in as you. The password I thought was yours gets the loathsome *"invalid password, goodbye"* response. Did you change your password to spite me?

P.P.P.P.S. I'll ask Neddy about opening your mailbox.

P.P.P.P.P.S. Zoë said on the phone just now that we should discuss granting her powers of attorney so she can get a grip on the paperwork. She also said we should start looking at assisted living places. She doesn't think I should be living alone here on the Hill. I hear her thinking: *senile dementia.* I'm only 66 years old, damn it.

P.P.P.P.P.P.S. What in the world am I supposed to do, Dan? Tell me, darling, what to do with myself.

—ᴍᴍ— *Two* —ᴍᴍ—

Subject: Books and Gutters
Date: 8/01/2002 01:15:30 A.M. EDT
From: dndyoung2@owl.com
To: dndyoung1@owl.com

Dearest Danny,

I went to Jess Hall's Monday night for the book discussion. Felt like a fish out of water in that room full of young people who did their best to make me feel a part of things, even while they danced around what we had in common. You.

They all seemed wowed at my tech-savvy on the blog business and the out-of-the-blue near-connection with Euripides. Didn't mention Lally's name – they would have rolled their eyes and started reminiscing about her at Remington. Instead one of them said, "Write a short story about it, Ms. Y." They all nodded in agreement. Then a big silence fell over the room. Until somebody said it was time to start on *At Swim-Two-Birds*.

O'Brien's onto a brilliant new way to develop characters. They wander in and out of the frame of the whole novel and the novels-within-the-novel that the narrator of the frame story is writing. Does that make sense? Everyone in the book has a spot in two or three levels of the story: X is writing a book about Y, who is writing a book about Z. And X appears in Z's story, Z appears in X's story, and of course they both appear in Y's. The characters are totally recyclable. Saves the author time and trouble inventing new ones, and maybe there are already too many fictitious characters anyway. Just think how nice it would be if more authors did that: The literary landscape would be less crowded, and folks we're fond of wouldn't be dropped like hot potatoes once we close their books. You like Holden Caulfield? He won't be put out to pasture (in the rye, heheheh), or Anna Karenina flattened permanently on that railway trestle. Here they are again, this time together in a torrid romance, with Atticus Finch on hand to add a plot twist! What a brilliant idea, not just for characters in fiction. Right, darling?

The evening was a lot of fun, actually. I loved sitting back and listening while those kids-grown-up yammered about literature, talking as if books really matter. Which they do, of course.

Yesterday, though, there was a freak storm. Rained cats and dogs. I was ironing in the basement, when Zoë called to make sure I was okay. Out of nowhere we got into this huge crying fight.

"Mom," she said, "why don't you go to the Library regularly again? Pick up that Bathsua Whatsit Project you were working on before Daddy —" She couldn't say the word.

"Before Daddy died?" I finished her sentence for her. My voice had a mean edge to it. "Before nothing started to matter anymore?" I said.

"Oh, Mom," she said. "I hate when you're like this. What do you want me to do? What can I do?"

"There's nothing you can do. Nothing I can do. Nothing I want to do."

"Mother," she said, sounding all sensible and grown up. (Which of course she is. I can hear you say so.) "Mom, you've – we've – got to start to do, just *do*, whether we can or want to. Doing is all we've got."

I got so mad I almost hung up on her, and then the rain started pouring over that gutter and flooding in under the basement door. In gushes. Huge, inexorable gushes. And I started screaming at her, just screaming.

"Zoë, there's water, water coming in everywhere!" I screamed it over and over again and started crying.

And then she was crying, too. "Mama, I'll be right over, I'm leaving now."

She was crying and shouting at me, and I was crying so hard I could barely hear her.

"Unplug the iron," she gulped. "Go upstairs."

I gulped.

"Call Jack – "

Gulp.

" – from the kitchen and tell him to – "

Gulp.

" – find the wet vac and the extension cord – "

Gulp.

"– and meet me at your house as soon as he can. I'll be there in ten – "

Gulp. " – minutes, Mom. Hang up the phone now and do what I said."

The phone connection ended so abruptly that all I could do was stop crying and do what she said, as if I were a broken machine that suddenly started up on autopilot or something.

The whole business probably explains why I dreamt about gutters again last night. This time it was a nightmare. You were in it. So was Nate. We couldn't save him, no matter how hard we tried.

I'm afraid to go to sleep. How do I get messages from you?

Love,

D

Subject: Gutters and Other Matters
Date: 8/02/2002 07:27:36 A.M. EDT
From: dndyoung2@owl.com
To: dndyoung1@owl.com

Dan,

Zoë is maddeningly practical. After she and Jack got all the water out of the basement last night, she announced that she would stay overnight in her old bedroom and call a roofer in the morning to unclog the gook in the gutters and downspouts. She's taken the day off. "August – no patients," she said. Hah. And is going to spend the day here "getting things under control." She says we're going to air the house out today, tonight, and tomorrow. Jack's going to stay with me in the house overnight so I can leave all the windows open to prevent mildew. I heard her tell Jack she's afraid to leave me alone on the Hill with the windows all open. Even with the beefed-up Capitol Police presence after 9/11, she said that with the Congress on recess the neighborhood's too deserted for me to be safe. And Gracie "suddenly" called and "begged" me to take her shopping all day tomorrow as her early birthday present. They're ganging up on me. I'm on round-the-clock watch.

Love,

Dee

Subject: Truth in Fairy Tales?
Date: 8/04/2002 07:27:36 A.M. EDT
From: dndyoung2@owl.com
To: dndyoung1@owl.com

Dearest,

After dinner last night Zoë brought down the copy of the Hans Christian Andersen fairy tales from her old room. Said she had to find that story you used to read to her, "The Snow Queen," about the little boy whose heart has turned to ice. She was fit to be tied because she couldn't remember the word he was trying to piece together out of letter-shaped ice shards. All she could remember was that after the ice crystal pierces his eye and his heart gets frozen, he becomes a smarty-boots and is mean to his sister, who loves him, and then he disappears.

At first I couldn't recall the word either, but I remembered that in the end the sister finds him, her burning hot tears melt his heart, and the ice-letters magically rearrange themselves into that word, whatever it was.

Jack remembered the boy got new skates at the end of the story, but he couldn't recall the magic word either.

Burning tears, melting heart, ice letters turning into a magic word. The story won't leave my head. Zoë's ordered me back to the Library tomorrow.

Love,

Dee

Subject: Restarting the Bathsua Project
Date: 8/05/2002 06:45:53 A.M. EDT
From: dndyoung2@owl.com
To: dndyoung1@owl.com

Dear Dan,

Okay, I'll do what she says and go to the Library regularly. I'll sit in the Main Reading Room the way we used to, re-read Frances Teague's *Bathsua Makin, Woman of Learning*, tidy the seventeenth-century stuff still on shelf 1434 where I left them in February, and maybe get on with that biography of Mistress Makin I used to talk about doing.

Maybe no one will notice I'm shaking. Love.

Subject: Re: Restarting the Bathsua Project
Date: 8/05/2002 15:18:45 P.M. EDT
From: dndyoung2@owl.com
To: dndyoung1@owl.com

Dearest Dan:

They're installing Jersey barriers – hulking cement and metal contraptions – on 2nd Street between the Metro station and Independence Avenue, and at the drive leading up to the Library. Mostly I walk on the quiet streets on the Hill to avoid the post-9/11 security, but today I turned south onto 2nd Street to see the crepe myrtles alongside the Madison Building. I know how you used to love them at this time of year. They're beautiful, in full bloom, and the warm air reminded me of your arm over my shoulder. But the x-ray belt and walk-through at the door to the Jefferson Building gave the place that edgy feel of an airport, not a library.

Once inside, though, and past the tourists, the Main Reading Room was as calm, as stately as ever. For the first time in ages I enjoyed a look at the dome and the oculus. There at the very top is that pastel of a woman and child against a perfect sky, all soft blues and greens and pinks. It was so comforting I could have wept for joy.

An old scrap serving as a bookmark fell out of the Teague book when I took it off the shelf. I must have left it there ages ago, copied down from something else I was reading:

> I drag my table to the window
> and write to you –
> here in this beehive cell
> on this globe rocketing through space.
> > – Eugenio Montale's "News from Mount Amiata"
> > (trans. Robert Lowell)

I tried composing a few lines of my own in reply:

> What do you see through your window?
> As I am at this table
> reading in the peace of the morning
> in this venerable library,
> might I come for a moment into your mind?
> Might you also be in your beehive cell

looking through the window of your mind
toward mine?

It's a start. Love.

Subject:	Re: Re: Restarting the Bathsua Project
Date:	8/08/2002 20:05:54 P.M. EDT
From:	dndyoung2@owl.com
To:	dndyoung1@owl.com

Danny,

The good-luck penny in my pocket set off the Library security x-ray machine this morning. But there was the good omen of being the first reader, with that heady mixture of awe and audacity when you seem to have all that learning all to yourself.

As if by magic, the books I had requested yesterday had arrived. From all the books in that enormous collection someone found Barbara Lewalski's *Writing Women in Jacobean England* and Sara Mendelson and Patricia Crawford's *Women in Early Modern England 1550-1720* and put them on the shelf beside Teague's *Bathsua Makin*.

The prize, though, was a book about the influence of letter writing on the early modern novel, James How's *Epistolary Spaces: English Letter Writing from the Foundation of the Post Office to Richardson's Clarissa*. Did you ever think the invention of the P.O. gave birth to the English novel? Well, it did, dear heart. Listen up.

Cromwell established the P.O. in the 1650's to monitor plots, a last-ditch effort to stem the tide (note my rush of metaphors) of potentially seditious correspondence. Instead, says How, it became "a space of connection, providing permanent and seemingly unbreakable links between people and places." Wow. He then describes the psycho-sexual excitement (yes!) of imagining letters full of intimate, private material rubbing up against each other (!!) in the dark anonymity of the post office. This scintillating situation (note the alliteration, dearie) gave rise, says How, to the epistolary novel, especially if you toss in a faceless post office bureaucrat capable of reading those secret letters. If you buy How's argument, the snoopy postman becomes the novel reader, the voyeur looking lustfully over the writer's shoulder.

Imagine that! I glanced hungrily at the chapter headings and gobbled up How's introduction. Here are two more morsels for you to savor, darling (another comely string of metaphors, eh?), two of How's chapter epigraphs: "An odd thought strikes me: we shall receive no letters in the grave" (Samuel Johnson to James Boswell). Bah! Much better is Paul Auster's comment about his mailbox in *The Locked Room*: "It was my hiding place, the one spot in the world that was purely my own. And yet it linked me to the rest of the world. In its magic darkness was the power to make things happen."

I read all morning, Dan, and halfway through the afternoon. Zoë was right, but I won't tell her. Don't want her to get too smug.

But I wonder: Am I ready to stop the research for good and commit myself to writing the book about Bathsua? Or will I just bolt at the magnitude of the project? Research is so seductive. There's always one more buried treasure out there to exhume. And turning the research into a work of my own is so daunting! Can I give credible shape to all the pieces of someone else's life when my own is such a mess?

Any suggestions? Incantations I might try? Libations I might pour? Omens I might read? Maybe I'll procrastinate for a while by proofreading that digest about Bathsua I was working on back in September, after You Know What.

All my love,

Dee

Subject:	[No subject]
Date:	8/12/2002 00:34:12 A.M. EDT
From:	dndyoung2@owl.com
To:	dndyoung1@owl.com

Beloved,

Today would have been our forty-first anniversary. I love you.

Subject:	[No subject]
Date:	8/12/2002 07:25:12 A.M. EDT
From:	dndyoung2@owl.com
To:	dndyoung1@owl.com

Dear Dan,

Off to the Library. One advantage of spending the day there: I can avoid the stuff Zoë says I should start on at home. Like changing the account holders on bills and accounts, acknowledge condolence notes, go through your stuff. Can't do any of it.

By the way: *The Post* and *The Times* are irksome these days. Maybe I should cancel my subscriptions and just read fiction. Living *through* and *in* fiction might not be such a bad idea. The Real is so damned awful these days. I'm more than half-ready to give the Surreal a chance. It and the Unreal might just do the trick.

Love.

Subject:	[No Subject]
Date:	8/12/2002 16:12:25 P.M. EDT
From:	dndyoung2@owl.com
To:	dndyoung1@owl.com

Dearest Dan,

Peeped into the Rare Book Room and requested their first edition of Mrs. Makin's 1673 *Essay to Revive the Antient Education of Gentlewomen in Religion, Manners, Art and Tongues. With an Answer to the Objections against This Way of Education* [sic] for tomorrow morning. It may let me hear her voice. When she wrote it she was about ten years older than I am now, so she'd certainly seen a lot of life. Deaths, disasters, dislocations, and disappointments, just to name a few of the downers among the D's, Danny. But she kept plodding on. I wonder how.

Love.

Subject: That wonderful grandson of yours
Date: 8/14/2002 15:47:53 P.M. EDT
From: dndyoung2@owl.com
To: dndyoung1@owl.com

Dear Dan,

Bless his heart, Neddy came over this morning to help me with some computer stuff. He was very patient, showed me how to set up a better filing system and get the laptop to be less crotchety. Promised to teach me how to attach attachments to email messages.

"The key to a well-running PC," he said, "is defragmentation."

Pretty profound, eh? Wonder what he made of that dinner conversation the other night about the boy with the frozen heart. (Maybe he can help me, too, from going to pieces every couple of days?)

Anyway, he stayed for lunch. I asked him to teach me about blogs later this summer.

He looked at me funny, said he'd help me start one. "Do you need a website, too, Gram?" he asked.

"No," I said. "I heard about this blog business and wondered how they work."

"Sure, Gram," he said, "but Mom said you were working on this Bath-something Project. What's that about?"

Found myself explaining my fascination with this old seventeenth-century school teacher. Neddy didn't seem to find it too terribly odd that I was researching a classics teacher who lived and died in London ages ago and combined marriage and motherhood with teaching and writing at a time when women didn't do such things.

"Sounds good to me, Gram," he said. "She sounds a little like you and Grandpa combined, only —" and then he turned suddenly serious.

"What were you going to say, young man? Just blurt it out."

"Like you, only even older."

"Yes, Ned, three hundred and thirty-five years older." I tried to sound faux-stern but am pretty sure my eyes managed to twinkle as I looked at him over my glasses.

He smiled and blushed in that dear way of his. "I bet she'd like you, Gram," he said.

"And I bet she'd like you, too, Neddy."

"*Ned*, Gram. Remember?"

"Yes, of course. Ned. You're grown now, dear boy. How proud your Grandpa is . . . that you're taller than him and your mother now."

"I know, Gram." He sat up a little straighter, leaned in toward me. "I miss him, too."

"I know you do, Neddy."

"I wish we could talk to him. Sometimes I imagine I can. Does that sound crazy?"

"No, dear. Why, actually – " I stopped myself, almost told him. Instead I went back to the Bathsua business, tried to make the transition seem seamless. I think it worked. "In fact," I said, "this research and writing that I'm doing about my seventeenth-century teacher friend is a little like your imagining talking to Grandpa. You get engrossed in it and suddenly you feel as though the person is coming right back to you from the dead."

He gave me that quizzical look he inherited from his mother. And from you.

"Well, almost," I rushed to say. "But it's an awfully good feeling that maybe you can revive someone from the past. Someone who, you know, left a paper trail."

"I think I get it, Grandma." He smiled. "Go, girl," he said.

Can you imagine, that grandson of yours called me *girl?*

Love.

Subject:	So I've been thinking. . .
Date:	8/15/2002 00:43:22 P.M. EDT
From:	dndyoung2@owl.com
To:	dndyoung1@owl.com

Dearest Danny,

I'm done with the Bathsua essay, but I'm in no way satisfied with it. The record of her life just makes me want to understand what is unrecorded – the lived experience, the inner life – whatever you call the processes that helped her endure and even face down the challenges that the historical record conveys. I want to imagine her right beside me.

This terrible year since 9/11, this *annus horribilis* – wasn't it Dryden who called 1666 *annus horribilis*? How did people survive without losing their minds? Could Bathsua teach me a thing or two about that, like the loving sister in *The Snow Queen*, who'll touch me with her tears, and cause the words frozen in my head and the heart frozen in my breast to melt and make all things clear? (And maybe I'll get a new pair of skates, too?)

Love,

Dee

Subject:	Sorry I've been out of touch
Date:	8/22/2002 20:48:53 P.M. EDT
From:	dndyoung2@owl.com
To:	dndyoung1@owl.com

Dearest,

Came down with a terrible headache last Tuesday night, then spiked a fever. Zoë said I looked like the wrath of God, called me all skin and bones with bags under the bags under my eyes, and insisted I come stay with them. Don't worry. She said I was just exhausted. She left unsaid but made clear anyway that if she hadn't behaved heroically and nipped it (me) in the bud, things might have gotten much worse.

So I've been babied all week. Interrogated about my eating habits (eccentric) and sleep patterns (erratic). Zoë Young Mayer MD placed me under house arrest with her and Jack and Gracie and Ned in Tenleytown. (You encouraged that daughter of ours to go to medical school, and she turns on her own mother like that.) Put me on vitamins, nutritional supplements, and two little gray pills twice a day. ("At first they'll just help you to ease up a little." she said. "They'll start to kick in in a couple of weeks." They made me sleep like the – you guessed it. Now they're just making me mellow.) No walking far in the heat of the day, she said, no Metro trips home to the Hill. No late nights in front of the computer. Zo makes me eat three square meals a day, insists that Gracie make me elevenses and tea besides. I've grown positively fat and lazy. And bored. Zo wouldn't let me read for three days, then handed me an Agatha Christie mystery and said I'd have to be satisfied with it or nothing. Said if I wanted excitement I could play Go Fish or do a jigsaw puzzle with Gracie. They have me napping every afternoon and sleeping for eight straight hours a night besides. Jack announced that I would be allowed a nightly game of Scrabble as a special treat. Boy, am I bored.

They barely let me out of their sight. Someone's always with me except when I'm in the bathroom or sleeping. Surprising they didn't post a 'round-the-clock guard at the foot of my bed.

Hence my lapse in messages for a week.

I do feel better. Not myself, but better. A little flighty and vague at the same time, if that makes sense. Zo said that if I didn't come round she was going to make me see Dr. McNair. Can you imagine? We both taught Lizzy when she was a scrawny thirteen year old, and now she's Dr. Elizabeth McNair, MD/PhD. I promised I'd behave – eat better, keep taking the little gray pills – just one a day now – if they let me go home.

I won last night's Scrabble game. My reward's a trial release. The one stipulation is that I hire Ned as my houseboy until school starts. Today was our first day. He went with me to the Safeway, drove us both home in my car, offered to weed the garden or help go through your stuff, my choice. I chose the garden. Not ready to deal with your stuff. Maybe in November. Or January. Or never. So we made dinner together, ate together, watched some TV together. He's sitting in your chair in the study right now, canoodling on his guitar. His smelly sneakers are at the front door. It's quite lovely to have him around, smelly sneakers and all. He said his mother told him that if he'll go with me, door to door both ways, I can go to the Library for a bit tomorrow. "It's a deal," I said. He'll walk me to the entrance of the Jefferson Building, then leave me to my own devices until one, when we'll meet at the 3rd Street exit and walk home for lunch. Then he'll do whatever he wants to until returning here around dusk. He'll stay in Zo's old room. I'm on parole, but I like it.

Love,

Dee

Subject: !!!THIS YOU REALLY WON'T BELIEVE
Date: 8/23/2002 06:24:38 P.M. EDT
From: dndyoung2@owl.com
To: dndyoung1@owl.com

Darling,

What happened today defies all reason, even more than the Ἐξίσταται γὰρ business last month. (Why do these things happen to me?) Is it the little gray pills?

This morning Ned walked with me to the LoC entrance. After security I headed for the Rare Book Room to read one more time that 1673 first edition of Bathsua's *Essay on Reviving the Antient Education of Gentlewomen.*

I'm sitting there reading, and suddenly falls out from the back page this tiny scrap of faded old paper inviting a reader's response. It had all those wonderful imperfections of old handmade paper, Dan, varying thickness, those fuzzy edges that mean it was made from old rag. It wasn't a bit yellow or discolored, although the ink looked brown with age. The old-fashioned handwriting was a little atilt and scrabbly, definitely the work of an old woman's hand. Here, I've copied it for you:

29 May 1673

Dear Reader,

I cannot but wonder on your Reception of my little Booke. In ye modest Hope y^t it will not be dispis'd but might find some Approbation, I am

Your most humble Servaunt

Bathsua Makin

from my Lodging in Long Acre at ye upper end nr Drury Lane at Mrs Stokes next door to a goldsmith

Instead of thinking about the absolute absurdity of it, I penciled an answer. Here it is verbatim:

August 23, 2002

Dear Mrs. Makin,

How strange to find myself replying to your note of 29 May 1673, which by some miracle I found tucked away in this copy of your *Essay to Revive the Antient*

Education of Gentlewomen. Forgive the pencil handwriting and tiny scrap of paper. The Rare Book Librarian is watching. I shall tuck this little note into the fold of yours and return this afternoon to see if, by yet another miracle, you have replied.

Very sincerely yours,

Dorothea Vance Young

I tucked my note into the back of the little book. All while the Rare Book Librarian had her back turned. It's too absurd. Bathsua Makin's been dead for three and a quarter centuries, and I answer her note as if writing to her were the most normal thing in the world. My face was hot and my hands clammy, but I managed to gather up my notebook and pencils and ask the librarian to hold the *Essay* until I returned later to finish with it. She acted as if this were just an ordinary, inconsequential moment.

Went down to the Main Reading Room to catch my breath. All I could think to do was to pull something off our reader's shelf and pretend to study it. What if she writes back? I kept thinking, meanwhile feeling like a fool, like I was losing my mind.

The joke would have been on me, if what happened next hadn't happened. But it did.

Palms sweaty and heart pounding in my chest, I went back to the Rare Book Room an hour later and requested Makin's *Essay* again. In it was Bathsua's reply:

23 August 2002

Dear Mistress Young,

There is a tiny Niche beneathe ye Loeb Classics on ye seconde Floore of Alcove 6 in ye Main Reading Room. Look there tomorrow Morning. I am

Your humble Servaunt,

BRM

Spent the rest of the morning pretending to read the *Essay*, turning pages, all the while glancing up now and then toward the Rare Book

Librarian, who was perfectly oblivious, bustling between the charge counter, her desk at the center of the room, and the door to the stacks.

More than once the thought crossed my mind that the librarian was playing a silly trick on me, passing notes as if we were schoolgirls, preying on my gullibility, enjoying a private joke that maybe she tried now and then on people she took to be hobby-scholars like me. Maybe this is what librarians do for laughs: mess with the minds of readers just for the fun of it, to tell their librarian friends how many dabblers they had led down the garden path, duped into thinking they'd found a magic way to commune directly with the subjects of their study.

Should I confront that librarian? Get all high and mighty about a government employee playing tricks on average citizens? But then she'd see the note I'd written in response, and I'd feel like a fool all over again. She didn't look the practical joking type. And what would be the harm if I simply played along?

So I hid the two slips of paper in my notepad, then returned Makin's *Essay* for good before meeting Ned for lunch. Walking home I kept thinking about the craziness of what had happened, what I had done. How would I explain it to Zoë? "I was researching Bathsua's teaching methods, and she wrote me a note proposing to explain them to me directly"? She'd listen, hang up, and call Lizzy McNair and discuss the side effects of the little gray pills.

Maybe I shouldn't have told you this. I won't tell anyone else. I should have learned by now to keep my own counsel.

Tomorrow is Saturday. Won't go back to the Library until next week. Let matters sit.

Tell me I'm not losing my mind.

Subject:	Re: !!!THIS YOU REALLY WON'T BELIEVE
Date:	8/24/2002 02:28:49 A.M. EDT
From:	dndyoung2@owl.com
To:	dndyoung1@owl.com

Dearest,

Am going again to the Main Reading Room this morning. I'll have a look in that little niche in the open stacks on the second floor of Alcove Six. Reading some of the Greek and Latin authors wouldn't be a bad idea. They're what Bathsua read, and therefore part of her back story. So my reading them isn't procrastination, right? Still, I wish you'd help me think through how to start, Danny.

Love.

Subject: !!!Reply!!!
Date: 8/25/2002 15:12:27 P.M. EDT
From: dndyoung2@owl.com
To: dndyoung1@owl.com

Dear Dan,

Found the following tucked in the little crevice between Aeschylus and Euripides in Alcove 6, level two:

This 24th day of August, 2002

> [E]t timide verba intermissa retemptat.
> Then, timidly, she once again employs
> Her long-lost power of speech.
>   – Ovid. *Metamorphoses.* Book I.

My dear Mistress Young,

We seeme to have taken each other quite by Surprise. It has been so long since I penn'd yᵗ little message & tuck'd it inside my *Essay* yᵗ I nearly forgot it was there. Call it a silly old Womans Fancy. I had hop'd for a contemporary Reader's Response. When none came, I c'ld not resist hoping yᵗ some distant Reader might finde my Wordes & reply across yᵉ veile of Time & Death.

Silence hangs heavy & thick now for me, yᵉ Habits of yᵉ Penne long unpractic'd but fondly recall'd. Might we correspond?

With best regards to those whom you hold in your Heart.

I am youres most sincerely,

Bathsua Reginald Makin

Post Scriptum. This little Niche beneath yᵉ Loeb Classics might serve nicely for yᵉ Conduct of our Correspondence.

Post Post Scriptum. I like yᵉ olde-fashion'd Touch of using Epigraphs for our Correspondence. Please indulge my Fancy. Like you, I have a fine Library here upon which to drawe. What is it you are studying in yᵉ Library of Congress? (What an odd Name for a Library.)

Post Post Post Scriptum. How strange 'tis to write a Date in yᵉ new Millennium!

What do you make of it?

Love in puzzlement.

P.S. Yes, I'm still taking the gray pills, two at bedtime. I sleep soundly, wake refreshed. Feel fine all day, full of energy, full of life.

P.P.S. No, haven't told anyone else about this.

P.P.P.S. No, they don't frighten me, these letters from beyond the grave. In fact, I welcome them. Other things frighten me much, much more.

Subject:	If only. . .
Date:	8/26/2002 00:56:37 A.M. EDT
From:	dndyoung2@owl.com
To:	dndyoung1@owl.com

Dear Dan,

If only I could tell someone about you and our life together, about this past year of disease and death, with 9/11 and the anthrax scare, with the war news about Afghanistan and Osama bin Laden and Al Qaida, and now this crazy talk about war in Iraq. And the year of your headaches and vomiting, your lying curled on your side in bed, your muffled moaning in the night. About doctor visits and chemo and surgery and radiation that all failed. About Pa's death. Our last year together was a nightmare, Danny. If only I could wake up from it and you were here and we were together, like we were in that photo on my screensaver, only you'd be healthy and all we'd have to worry about was whether DC will get a baseball team, not if terrorists were going to bomb us to smithereens.

Maybe if I concentrate hard enough on Bathsua, and with her bridge the chasms of time and death, I can bridge them with you, too, my darling. Maybe she can teach me to be patient and brave, teach me how to walk a steady course in this crazy maze that's more filled with sadness than I know how to bear. I'd rather you did all of this, my darling, but I'm not hearing from you, and she's already written back, not one letter but two. And in ink, no less, not the fleeting insufficiency of pixels.

I've fiddled with my poem, the one modeled after Montale's. Wrote it for you, darling, but now it's for her.

When I was little I imagined books on my bookshelf murmuring to each other through their bindings after I had gone to bed. If only we could be like that – side by side, whispering. All night long.

Am I angry at you, Danny? Yes. Furious you're not the one writing me back. Or maybe I'm just going mad, darling?

Love.

P.S. Neddy showed me how to attach things I write to emails. Might send you copies of what I write to Bathsua. Might also transcribe her letters for you to read. Will keep us busy.

August 26, 2002

> I drag my table to the window and write to you – here in this beehive
> cell on this globe rocketing through space.
>   – Eugenio Montale. "News from Mount Amiata"
>   (trans. Robert Lowell)

Dear Mistress Makin,

The good-luck penny in my pocket set off the security alarm this morning as I entered the Library. I hoped it wasn't an omen. I wanted the day to seem quite normal, despite the fact that I was on my way to Alcove Six, second floor, to look for your letter. And there it was, where you promised. I hope this is not a hoax, or if it is you'll make it seem totally plausible.

I was the first reader here this morning. The feeling of awe and audacity that I had all this learning all to myself actually cooled me down from the hot embarrassment I feel about starting a correspondence with the subject of my research. It's just too absurd to believe that you, a woman of the seventeenth century, have, from the other side of the veil of time and death, as you say, replied to my little penciled note. Things like this do not happen in real life.

You ask what I am doing here in the Library of Congress, in the heart of my beautiful, troubled city, the capital of this nation that did not exist even as a dream in your day? I've been researching you, in hopes of writing your biography. But I'm changing my mind somewhat. Yes, I want to understand your accomplishments as a scholar, writer, and teacher, but the research isn't enough. How did you manage it all – that's what I'm wondering – being a professional and also a daughter, sister, wife, and mother living in desperate times? I find myself imagining you – excuse me if I ramble on – imagining you explaining to me how you managed to stay patient and brave through it all. I live in desparate times, too. Bad things have been happening all year. I need steadying. I need to sort out what has been going on, but I also need to figure out how to go on. If this makes sense.

The Montale poem in my epigraph above will, I hope, be a harbinger of what this correspondence might perhaps become. (I looked up "harbinger," by the way – it comes from the Middle English *herbergeour,* a messenger leading an army to shelter). The poem has prodded me to write a new poem of my own:

> Dear mother,
> dear sister I never had,
> what do you see through your window?
> As I am at this table
> reading in the peace of the morning
> in this venerable library,
> might I come for a moment into your mind?
> Might you also be in your beehive cell
> looking out of the window of your mind

toward mine?

Might each of us at this moment

be thinking of the other?

When I was a child I used to imagine the books on my bookshelf murmuring to each other through their bindings while I slept. Could we be like two such books, whispering what is and what is not written in them?

But I get ahead of myself. You will, I hope, be pleased to know that one excellent scholarly biography has been written about you by Professor Frances Teague who, you will be further pleased to learn, is a woman, a university professor, and a renowned scholar of feminist history and literature. Her work is entitled *Bathsua Makin, Woman of Learning*. I've put a copy on my Reader's Shelf. Number 1434.

Before my husband Daniel got sick, I tracked down as many of Professor Teague's primary and secondary sources as I could here at the Library. Then September 11 happened, and our world turned upside down. More on why and how later. Suffice to say, to keep my mind off how frightened and miserable I was, I wrote a digest of my research, complete with careful source citations. I've left a copy of it on my Reader's Shelf, too. Feel free to read it. The work on it was good and worthwhile at the time. It was necessary, but not sufficient. I long to know wonwhat lies behind the print record.

Yours truly,

Dorothea (Dee) Young

P.S. Why are you willing to write to me?

P.P.S. May I call you Bathsua?

28 August 2002

Τρὶς δέ μοι ἐκ χειρῶν σκιῇ ἔικελον ἢ καὶ ὀνείρῳἔπτατ'.
– Homer. *The Odyssey.* Book 11.

My dear Mistress Young,

I am flatter'd & surpris'd. Biographies are usually written of yᵉ Famous & yᵉ Great, are they not? I am neither.

To answer your Question: Time here hangs heavy. Now and then receiving a Note from you would be pleasaunt. So, too, would be writing to you, seeing my Hand move across ye Paper, ye Ink appearing as if by Magic upon ye blank Page. Y^t is reason enough, I trowe, for oure Correspondence.

Oure Letters might, perhaps, go beyond mere Pleasauntries. We might commit to Paper what it rarely, if ever, preserves. I doubt y^t I shall put aside ye Reticence of my Time & Place or y^t we shall understand one another, giv'n ye Differences of my Renderinge of ye Mother Tongue & yours. We may perhaps catch Glimpses of one another, but to see what ye other has seen, know what ye other has known, fear what we each have fear'd – these, I trowe, are impossible.

Remember Odysseus' Attempt to speak to his Mother in ye Underworld? I began this Letter with ye Bard's very Wordes. Y^t was ye Encounter of a Mother & Son, and yit he saide, "Three times she flitted out of my reach like a Shadow or a Dream." If y^t be so for Mother & Son, how can two Strangers ever make themselves known to each other?

And yet, what is ye Harm in trying?

You ask'd to call me by my Christian Name. To do such seemes most unnatural. So my Answer is No. Not yit. Perhaps in ye Future.

Let us give this Correspondence a try, & only if it please us.

My Hand is unpracticed, & Lassitude & Stubbornness settle in on one late in Life. I keep Secrets of my own, & not a few entrusted to me by others. But I shall answere your Letters now & then. Needless to say, for my sake there is no need to hurry.

With best Regards,

I am yours most sincerely,

Bathsua Reginald Makin

August 29, 2002

Her memory speaks more
Than what can be, or hath been said before:
It asks a volume. . . .
    – Bathsua Makin. "Elegy for Lady Elizabeth Hastings Langham."

Dear Mistress Makin,

I've often thought it was a miracle that books I hoped to read found their way to my shelf in this enormous library, the largest in the world. For the library staff this is an ordinary chore, but for me it's miraculous. This correspondence of ours strikes me as just part and parcel of the miraculousness of this Library. The miraculous is commonplace here while the ordinary world outside is thoroughly off-kilter.

Your letters offer the possibility of miraculous refreshment after my *annus terribilis*. This week I feel strangely rejuvenated, despite the stultifying heat of Washington in late August. I feel a rush of will and energy to begin something new and unthought of until now. I feel like the boy in the old fairy tale who suddenly feels his frozen heart melt, all the frozen words he has been unable to arrange suddenly finding their proper places and pouring forth from his mouth in song.

Last night, for example. Trying to understand why the study of Greek gave you and Dan such pleasure, I struggled my way through a lesson in a textbook he taught from. Doing the exercises, I felt that I was engaged in a wrestling match I knew I would lose but had to try anyway. Suddenly, miraculously, the translation fell into place:

> Τόν τε γὰρ οὐρανὸν εἶδε καὶ τὸν ἥλιον ὑπερ τοὺς λόφους
> ἀνίσχοντα καὶ τὰ δένδρα τῷ ἀνέμῳ κινούμενα· καὶ ἐτέρπετο
> θεώμενος· πάντα γὰρ αὐτῷ κάλλιστα δὴ ἐφαίνετο.
>
> He saw the sky and the sun rising over the hills and the
> trees moving in the breeze. He rejoiced in the seeing.
> Everything seemed very beautiful.

Things suddenly seem very beautiful: the oculus above this Reading Room, the hands of invisible librarians, my own hands writing.

Does this sound foolish?

Yours truly,

Dorothea

P.S. I appreciate your reticence about my calling you by your given name. Nothing prevents me, however, from signing with mine and inviting you to reply with same.

--⁓-- *Three* --⁓--

September the second.

> And for ther is so gret diversite
> In Englissh and in writyng of oure tonge,
> So prey I God that non myswrite the,
> Ne the mysmetre for defaute of tonge.
> And red wherso thow be, or elles songe,
> That thow be understonde, God I biseche!
>   – Geoffrey Chaucer. *Troilus and Criseyde.*

My Dear Madam –

To answer your last Question – I do not find your Reasoning foolish. Each Day offers ye Possibilitie of Miracles, I trowe, altho' I was slow to see this in mine own Lifetime. I propose we suspend our Disbeliefe & accept ye Miracle of Correspondence. Perhaps in time we shall know what has brought us together. But for ye nonce let us simply write to each other.

We must accept our many Differences. Certainly we shall misapprehend each other, & tempted tho' I be to seek Explanation for every Detail, I shall resist asking endless Questions. You, too, I hope, will pass over ye Idiosyncrasies of my Style & put aside, insofar as you are able, ye all too human Tendency to be discomfited by y^t with which one is unfamiliar.

As to your Question in a prior Letter, why do I chuse to correspond with you? It would amuse me to know what is said of me after so many passing Years. To know how one is remember'd is a fancy y^t we here entertain. And what is more, I am curious to know how lives are liv'd in Times remote from mine own. One can read of ye Past but not ye Future.

I do have two Questions for you at the Outset, however. What do you wish to know of me? And what should I know about you?

I eagerly await your Reply &, in amicable Anticipation of it, I am,

Most sincerely,

Your humble Servaunt,

Bathsua Reginald Makin

P.S. Today marks ye Anniversary of ye Great Fire. Not ye first Fire I witness'd in my City, but ye greatest in its Destruction & Fame. More of y^t later.

September 5, 2002

Dear Mistress Makin,

My thanks for your reply.

You ask to know about me and what I hope you will tell me.

As to the former, the short answer is that I am a widowed sixty-six-year-old American, a mother and grandmother. I was a teacher for many years, retiring several years ago to lead a more reflective life and to care for my aging father. Then my husband got sick and my father, too. My father died last winter, my husband a few months later, in mid-June. Now I am alone in a house filled with echoes and books.

As to what I wish to know, put very simply – or not simply at all: the secret heart truths, the inner life merely hinted at by the surviving print record.

For a long answer to both questions, look in our hiding place next week.

Sincerely yours,

Dorothea Young

Subject:	Answering Questions
Date:	9/07/2002 19:32:17 P.M. EDT
From:	dndyoung2@owl.com
To:	dndyoung1@owl.com

Dearest Dan,

As promised to Mistress Makin I've written an essay explaining the new direction I propse to take on the Bathsua project. I'll share it with you, too, my darling, as soon as Neddy teaches me how to attach a document to an email.

Am terrified of next Wednesday. Zoë says I should try going to the Library on my own now that Ned's back in school, although she too is alarmed about next week. Maybe if Monday's okay and Tuesday, too, by Wednesday I'll feel safe. I'll spend the morning in the Main Reading Room, jotting a few notes in the quiet company of books and book lovers. The library staff, security guards, and a few other silent readers already look familiar. It'll be a safe haven, I hope.

I'm doing okay. That's the trouble with these little gray pills. I'm doing okay. No downs. No ups. Just okay. Sleeping okay. No dreams. No late-night googling. No crazies. No exhilarations. Okay, though, is okay. Maybe okay is actually pretty good.

I love you, Danny. I miss you. I'm afraid of getting used to the ache of missing you. The way we both did with Nate.

Love,

Dee

9 September 2002

> *Πολλὰ ἔχων ὑμῖν γράφειν οὐκ ἐβουλήθην διὰ χάρτου καὶ μέλανος, ἀλλὰ ἐλπίζω γενέσθαι πρὸς ὑμᾶς καὶ στόμα πρὸς στόμα λαλῆσθαι ἵνα ἡ χαρὰ ἡμῶν πεπληρωμένη ἦ.*
>
> I have many things to write to you, but I would y^t I had not to use only Paper and Ink and might instead come to see you and talk with you Face to Face, so y^t our Joy might be complete.
>
> — Second Letter of John. verse 12.

Dear Mistress Young,

Thank you for your Note of 5 September and ye Promise of your Letter of Introduction. For your Loss mention'd in ye former, my sincerest Condolences. As to ye latter, in eager Anticipation of it I am,

Most sincerely

Your humble Servaunt,

Bathsua Reginald Makin

September 11, 2002

Dear Mistress Makin,

Today is a terrible anniversary, the completion of a year of fear and grief both personal and national. Somehow, having completed this *annus horribilis* I feel, inexplicably, both numb and brave, and strangely permitted to let go of hesitations and niceties.

The enclosed will, I hope, answer both of your questions. And it may, I fear, puzzle and anger you. Please excuse my errors and presumptions, my "myswriting" and "defautes of tonge," my blunders, slights, insensitivities, gaffes, errors of both commission and omission.

Come what may, I eagerly await your reply. Beside finding your letters in our little niche, might I not also hear you whispering to me in dreams?

Yours truly, and as truthfully as possible,

Dorothea Young

Enclosure: "Answers, Questions"

Answers, Questions

(For Bathsua Makin)

'Like' and 'like' and 'like' – but what is the thing that lies beneath the semblance of the thing?
– Virginia Woolf. *The Waves.*

So many details about me will sound foreign to you, so many questions about you will sound impertinent. I know what you are thinking: only miracles can bridge our differences. But let us believe in such miracles. I'll just rattle on, come what may.

I was born in 1936 just outside Boston, Massachusetts, where I did all my schooling. From my earliest childhood, I loved books and reading and wanted to be a teacher when I grew up. I majored in literature in college to fulfill that plan. In 1960 I landed a job teaching English at The Remington School, a private school in Washington, D.C., where I met Daniel Young, the Latin and Greek teacher. We married in 1961, remained in DC and taught at the same school until two years ago. For more than forty years we were best friends, colleagues, husband and wife. Dan gave me all I could ever ask for, and more. He died in June.

So I am widowed now, and retired after almost forty years of teaching. I am the mother of two. Zoë, our first child, is a physician. Her little brother Nathaniel died in infancy. Zoë has a lovely husband – as lovely, perhaps, as mine

– who appreciates the intelligence, practicality, energy, independence, loyalty, and generosity that I like to think Zoë learned in our household. We – I – have a grandson and granddaughter who please me no end. They live nearby, in a DC neighborhood called American University Park, ten stops away on the Metro from my house on Capitol Hill. I am the child of a shy, disciplined man whose one great adventure was serving in the United States Army during World War II, and of a beautiful, troubled woman whose laughter and song alternated with rage and despair throughout my life. My mother died ten years ago. My father died this past winter. I am the sister of a man five years younger than I, an engineer who lives in Vancouver. (Vancouver is in western Canada; the Metro is an urban underground public transportation system; World War II – how do I explain it? I'd better not stop to explain everything or I'll never finish!)

When we were first married, Dan and I bought a little row house on Capitol Hill where we lived comfortably and without extravagance for the whole of our marriage. We used to spend Thanksgivings and a couple of weeks every summer in a cabin Dan's parents owned on a pond in Maine. I still live in our house on Capitol Hill. We didn't get to Maine last Thanksgiving. Or this summer either.

I think I have enough savings for my old age.

Dan was the smartest, most curious, and most consistently cheerful human being I have ever known.

The Washington Post and *The New York Times* arrive on my doorstep every morning. Unlike Dan, I leave most of them unread. I've been thinking of canceling my subscriptions, but I know Dan would disapprove. Most of my news and views about politics come from National Public Radio's "Morning Edition" and "All Things Considered," which I listen to during breakfast and dinner, and "The News Hour," which I watch on public television after dinner.

I read a lot of literary fiction. I belong to two book clubs. I am a now-and-then poet. I dabble at gardening, piano playing, and, lately, the study of ancient Greek.

I am right-handed, a former cat owner and a meat eater, a wearer of half glasses for reading. I write with pencils, roller tip pens, and on a personal computer. I do not bite my fingernails. A cup of strong coffee every morning with breakfast and a glass of wine every night with dinner are my only chemical addictions, although lately I've been taking a little gray pill that I think may be addictive. I used to enjoy my own cooking, preferring savory over sweet, vegetables over fruits. I eat more protein and carbohydrates than I need, more cholesterol than is good for my arteries.

I am a bit overweight for my height, which is a bit below average. I wear no makeup, except some lipstick when I remember to put it on and some concealer to hide the dark circles under my eyes when I'm going to see Zoë. She fusses at me about my looks and sometimes lately about my health. Despite her advice, I don't color my hair, which has turned from dark brown to a salt-and-pepper mop that I wear in a short crop tucked as tidily as possible behind my ears. If I am unaware of the camera, I can look lively and good-humored. (Sometimes, as in the photo on my computer screensaver, I look alarmed. Or disheveled.)

But for Dan, I've never had a best friend.

I am not religious. Sometimes I wish I could pray. When Nate died, I abandoned the idea of a benevolent God. Now I envy people who believe that God is a positive force in the unrolling of human history. The efficacy of praying is easier for me to accept than the notion that a God hears and answers prayers. If that makes sense.

I took some time off from teaching when Zoë was born. I returned to Remington after Nate died, teaching parttime when Zoë was little, fulltime when she was older. Having her with us at Remington meant that we had one family schedule, one circle of friends, a common vocabulary. I taught high school students writing and literature in every genre – epics, plays, short stories, short poems, essays, and novels – everything, it seemed, from *The Odyssey* to *On the Road*. In end-of-year evaluations my students said I was fair, smart, playful with ideas. They said I loved learning, encouraged a spirit of inquiry, and respected individuals and their differences of opinion. My colleagues said they valued my honesty and my sense of humor.

I hope you can decipher my writing, Mistress Makin. What do you make of *Washington, D.C., Boston,* and *Maine; radio, television,* and *computer; cholesterol, genetically transmitted disease, carbohydrates, roller-tip pens,* and *lipstick?* Can you imagine women with university degrees? Or voting? I hear you asking: The novel a school subject? Diversity of opinion a prized value? Literary analysis? Playfulness and a sense of humor as pedagogical goals?

My side of our correspondence will sound as alien as if I were from another planet! How different are our worlds! Your century and mine! Electricity! Clothing! Communicating instantly across distances, traveling with ease from place to place, even across oceans and continents! The changes in medicine, the standing of women!

We have both lived in times of tumult far beyond our control. Surely my side of our correspondence will be grounded in the grand public issues of my place and time. I long to hear your views of the equivalent issues of your time and place. Living as you did on the periphery of the Stuart court and connected through your brother-in-law John Pell to the likes of John Milton, you surely bore witness to many of the most momentous events of your age. You have lived what I have only read of: civil war, the execution of King Charles, the death of his daughter – your pupil! – the suspension of monarchy, the Rump Parliament, the Long Parliament, the Cromwells and the Protectorate, the Restoration, the Great Plague, the Fire of London! The intellectual, political, religious and cultural foments, the radical changes involving science! Emigration to the New World! Comet sightings! If only I could hear your thoughts on any and all of these extraordinary developments!

There is much that we share, Mistress Makin. We have raised children, cared for aging parents, stood by spouses through sickness and health. We have mourned parents, husbands, babies and watched our love of siblings slip away from us. And always the cooking and cleaning; earning and saving and spending. And the teaching.

As teachers, we have been entrusted by others with the care of their children. We have loved being teachers who watch our students master and even surpass our skills. And we are, both of us, lovers of the order and mystery of language, endlessly compelled to work with and wonder at the words that both express and obscure our thoughts and intentions.

Most of what I know of you comes from black-blurred-to-gray words on paper. In the Library or at home at my desk, I often find myself looking up from the paper, trying to fix you in my mind's eye, looking inward for signs of you in memories of my own girlhood and womanhood. From what I have read about you, I can almost conjure up the movement of your hands, the slant of your eyebrow, the curve of your cheekbone, the occasions and shape of your smile, the vocabulary of character conveyed by the angles of your gaze.

But I want to know more. I want to see you face to face, side by side, with your parents, your sister, your husband, your children, your students. I want to hear your footfall quicken as you approach your classroom in the morning and your home in the afternoon and slow as you walk to visit your infant children in their graves and your father in Bedlam. I want to hear the sound of your laughter and tears, the songs you hummed as you soothed your babies and mourned for them, your voice talking with your husband and father. I want to see you standing at your lectern or beside your students in your classroom by day and seated by candlelight preparing your lessons at night.

If I try, I can almost see you eating at your kitchen table, reading in your chair beside the fire, looking up for signs of rain or scraps of sunshine in the little wedge of sky above your half-timbered house tightly fitted among others, looking out your door for welcome signs of your husband and children, looking down your narrow street for fearful signs of the ravages of war, the Fire, the Plague.

There is so much to wonder about: Your mother, of whom there is no record, is invisible: What is her story? Ithamaria, your sister, whose name survives only in a christening record and in letters by her husband: What secrets did you share? Henry Reginald, your father, whose professional life is documented in the diaries of his students: How did he come to teach you and prepare you to be his teaching assistant? Why did he end his life in Bedlam, and how did you bear it?

The boys nearly your age you taught in your father's classroom: how did you manage them? Richard Makin, whom you married when you both were twenty: was he there in that classroom? Was it there that you fell in love? Your first book, published when you were sixteen and presented by your father to King James: what made you undertake it? Was Richard present when King James referred satirically to educating girls: "To make women learned and foxes tame have the same effect: to make them more cunning"? Were you the anonymous learned maid presented at Court, about whom the King asked, "But can she spin?"

Might I convince you to tell me about your life with Richard? What were you like together in the quiet, ordinary times and in the difficult ones? I know that you bore eight children, that there were financial worries, and that Richard left you in the 1650's – I know he wasn't dead, because your brother-in-law John Pell wrote that Richard was "away." Why did he leave? Where did he go? How did you bear it?

What secret life did you share with your sister Ithamaria? What explains the mystery of the christening within weeks of each other of two of your infant daughters? Surely they were not birth sisters. And what were the bonds and rifts between you and Ithamaria's husband, John Pell? He wrote to Ithamaria insisting that she break off with you. Why?

Your children: You saw one die in infancy and another in early childhood. There were six more. I long to hear about your mothering of both the little ones and the ones who grew to adulthood. What was special about Henry, your youngest? I've read your letter to the Countess of Huntingdon saying that he was "lying heavily upon me" when he was in his teens, and John Pell's letter to you urging that you send your son out to the care of any man rather than remain "under your wing." What is the story behind these shreds, these rags of recorded fact?

And then there is your professional life: I have read your defense of education for young women, your advocacy of modern and practical studies for both boys and girls, your short biographies of educated women of antiquity, your consoling poems written to memorialize former students. I want to talk with you!

And how, I wonder, did you sustain such energy, wisdom, and good humor well into old age, when – in your seventies, widowed, very likely alone and self-supporting – you started a school for boys and girls together, teaching natural science, mathematics, grammar, rhetoric, and logic? Wise men praised your "encouragement of Learning and ye advancement of Science, whether in ye Adult or Juvenile" and called you "Literissima Mulier" – a most lettered woman. In your last surviving letter thanking an elderly doctor for his kind praise, you observed, "Prosperity and adversity in this life are ever tied and untied," and noted in Greek *Δεί γὰρ τον τέλειον ἄνδρα θεωρητικον ἐιναι τῶν ὄντῶν της πράκτικον τῶν δεόντων* – that doing what needs doing – in Latin *facienda facis*, in Hebrew עשׁה עשׂה – is the goal of "the practicall Philosopher." How did you preserve such calm wisdom to the very end?

I could go on and on. I have time – too much time, really – and so I write. It takes me out of myself. At all hours, day and night. I feel compelled to write, and to you in particular. I don't know why exactly.

September 30, 2002

> I could rather wish, that some quaint discourse might passe among us, a tale or fable related by some one, to urge the attention of all the rest. And so wearing out the warmth of the day, one prety Novell will draw on another, untill the Sun be lower declined, and the heates extremity more diminished, to solace ourselves in some other place, as to our minds shall seeme convenient. If therefore what I have sayde bee acceptable to you, let it appeare by your immediate answere.
> – Boccaccio. *Decameron*. The First Day. [John Florio trans. 1620.]

My dear Madam,

I am by turns confus'd & amus'd at what you have written, but throughout flatter'd by youre Attentions, overwhelm'd by Memories, & touch'd to ye Heart by youre Candour. I shall read youre last Letter many times over & stop at youre Reader's Shelf to study Professor Teague's Book & youre Digest. Regarding the Accuracy of ye Details in what you call'd "the terrifying permanence of print," I shall reserve Comment for later Stages in oure Correspondence.

A Confession is in order. I propos'd you undertake the prior Assignment in order y^t you demonstrate youre Capacities before I committed myselfe to this Correspondence. You have pass'd my Examination. Yes, let us write back & forth, oure Letters a precarious Bridge across ye Space & Time between us.

But now, my Dear, I propose y^t we refine oure Plan: Enough of mere Letters back & forth. Let us set before us as oure Model Boccaccio's *Decameron*. You have read it, surely? Firenze, y^t beautiful City of Flowers, was ravaged by ye Plague. Nothing could mask ye Stench of Infection & Death, nor hir'd Minstrels subdue ye Wails of Tribulation. An elegant little group of Gentlefolk betook themselves to a little Palazzo in ye Hills above ye Citie, where ye Sight of verdant Hills & Fields – &, perhaps, a larger View of Heav'n – might soothe their keen Distress. Y^e Palazzo was spacious & fair, its commodious Hall & Chambers adorn'd with gladsome Flowers, its cool Well & fine-stock'd Cellar well-suited to ye Tastes of Gentlefolk. In such a Setting did ye Lady Pampinea propose they pass ye Time untill ye Pestilence ran its course in ye Citie below. She invited her Companions to take turns telling Stories – Tales or Fables, Truth or Fiction – passing ye warm Hours of ye Day preparing them & ye cooler Hours of ye Evening telling them to each other. Y^e Gentlefolk agreed. Story-telling is a Balm as satisfying as ye Water from ye Palazzo's Well, as wholesome as ye Palazzo's well-swept Rooms garnish'd with Flowers, its Floors carpeted with Rushes.

Tales ever dispel ye noxious Odours of Distress & Death, indeed giving Friends a wider View of Heav'n.

Yours most sincerely, & eagerly,

Bathsua M.

P.S. I note y^t Professor Teague alter'd ye Spelling, Capitalization, & Orthography of Writings of my Daye to ye standards of yours. Do you wish me to do ye same?

--~~-- *Four* --~~--

Subject: Remember London?
Date: 10/06/2002 10:24:04 A.M. EDT
From: dndyoung2@owl.com
To: dndyoung1@owl.com

Dearest Dan,

It's a year since our trip to London. Remember how brave we felt, flying so soon after 9/11? How special we felt when people recognized we were from the States and smiled so sympathetically? How compelled we felt to retell where we were that terrible morning? How we clung to each other all through that trip? I picture us walking arm in arm, searching for traces of Bathsua in the hubbub of the City. I hoped our search for her would distract us from the fresh memories of 9/11 and our fears of what awaited us back home.

Remember how past, present, and future jostled for our attention? Life's a mishmash, I guess. Remember having espressos at Starbuck's a few doors down from Saint Andrew Undershaft at the corner of Saint Mary Axe Street? Bathsua probably rolled a hoop or teased a kitten there when she was a girl. Next to the mossy gray-stoned churchyard where her father's schoolroom must have been was a modern-day construction site. Asphalt was underfoot, but you said the packed earth of the 1600's certainly lay sleeping beneath it.

Remember visiting the Museum of London nearby? We stood in that darkened little maroon-velvet booth watching the miniature electrified diorama of the Great Fire of 1666. Remember? We watched and rewatched the little show, transfixed by the pretend early-September evening sunlight fading to darkness over tiny half-timbered buildings, a little lightbulb coming on, then flickering ominously in the bakery window on Pudding Lane. Artificial flames licked at the neighboring houses and shops. We smiled as an actor's recorded voice dismissed the event: "Pish! A woman might piss it out!" The little lighting effects and a cackle of recorded static simulated the spreading fire. We stood mesmerized by the little show conflagration. The distant past seems so quaint, so toy-like, in the face of the glass, concrete, and steel of the present. But I wonder: When the past and future meet at the crease-line of the present, don't they speak to each other, with us listening? Strangely, the little diorama evoked TV images of 9/11 and blurred nightmare memories of Papa's stories of World War II in Europe. That odd, dislocated feeling of memories rushing at each other from opposite sides of my life. You felt the same, I'm sure, although you didn't say so. Just shook your head as if you were thinking something serious.

And remember walking to Whitehall, past the entrance to the War Cabinet Rooms Museum, to the Banqueting House, past the window King Charles walked out of toward his beheading in 1649? In an hour of the present we moved from the terrors of the 1940's to those of the 1640's, through the shadows of last September toward the misery we faced at home.

That last morning in London before returning to the doctors' appointments and tests and treatments, walking across that glistening new stainless steel footbridge over the Thames, remember? The tide was low. Ahead of us was the Tate Modern. We crossed the river through a wind-shimmering panorama. Old Southwark Cathedral stood nearby and construction cranes, too. Future buildings and storied spires pierced that cloudless sky together. I couldn't hear your voice in the wind. You were pointing out landmarks. I was terrified. You linked your arm through mine, and my panic eased a little. "No matter what happens, Dee – " you said. And you stopped midsentence. I knew what you were thinking. I did then. I do now.

Love.

P.S. Strange, scary news: random drive-by shootings – murders! – going on in various places around the Beltway. More evidence that this *annus horribilis* isn't over and it's not just mine.

October 7, 2002

>...Time counted by anxious worried women
> Lying awake...
> Trying to unweave, unwind, unravel
> And piece together the past and the future,
> Between midnight and dawn. . . .
>   – T.S. Eliot. "The Dry Salvages"

Dear Mistress Makin,

Thank you for your reply. And thank you for your offer to adjust seventeenth-century writing norms to twenty-first century style. How accommodating you are! My answer: only if (or when) you choose to. I am in your debt for undertaking this correspondence; it would be rude of me to impose any conditions. And as to your proposal that we follow Boccaccio's model: what a fine idea! After years of asking students to spin out tales, I'm willing to do the same. The worst that could happen: our efforts will fall flat on their faces. But we have no one to save face with but each other. No worries about an audience – you are dead (presumably), and no one is looking over my shoulder expecting me to have something to show for my hours in the Library. We have no one to please but ourselves.

I'm planning a story for you about my childhood, centering on my mother. I have before me a little black-and-white photograph of my family at the Statue of Liberty in New York Harbor. My mother had cornered a passerby to snap the picture. In the background a gray sliver of Lower Manhattan separates a gray sky from equally gray water. My mother's face is half-obscured by her wind-borne scarf. My father is smiling his beautiful smile. My brother Josh is wearing a plaid wool hat and jacket. Seventeen and moody, I am huddled against the wind.

I wrote a moment ago that no one is reading over our shoulders. Not quite true, perhaps. I plan to send my husband Dan copies of what I write to you. He's dead, but I email him almost every day, twice or three times a day when I'm feeling especially lonely. Unlike you, he doesn't write back.

This story will take time to write. Look for it later in the month.

Sincerely yours,

Dorothea Young

P.S. Everyone except students calls me Dee. Please do, too.

47

Subject: Gardening and Grammar
Date: 10/11/2002 23:10:09 P.M. EDT
From: dndyoung2@owl.com
To: dndyoung1@owl.com

Dearest Dan,

I've been trying to work a little every day to put the garden to bed. The exercise and fresh air should feel good, especially at midday when the sun is warm. But the dire warnings about these drive-by shootings – they're calling it a sniper! – have me really rattled. So I'm more often trying to keep busy indoors and avoiding listening to the news. I'm doing a little Greek translating, in your honor. It's a helpful distraction. This afternoon I spent three hours in silence on nine lines of the *Odyssey*. It felt good.

Overall my mood is dreadful. The world's gone mad. With war news and sniper news everything I do seems so trivial, selfish, futile. I'm like Nero dancing and fiddling while Rome burns.

So I'm feeling sorry for myself and missing you pretty much all of the time. It's like I'm dragging an enormous, heavy suitcase through an endless, dimly lit tunnel, and the only bright spots are writing to you, struggling with Greek, working in the garden, corresponding with Bathsua. Zo and Jack and the kids try to help, but they're weirded out, too. Sorry I'm not more fun. Love.

Subject: Happy Birthday, Darling
Date: 10/12/2002 16:43:11 P.M. EDT
From: dndyoung2@owl.com
To: dndyoung1@owl.com

Dearest,

I've written you a birthday present. I hope you like it.
Love, always.

Attachment: "Unbidden Gifts"

Unbidden Gifts

Sun up: work
sundown: rest
dig well and drink of the water
dig field: eat of the grain
Imperial power is? and to us what is it?
—Ezra Pound. *Canto XLIX.*

My work gloves are nearly destroyed after the long summer. Neddy offered to help put the garden to bed, but I said no. I want to feel the work, so gloveless and careless of thorns, I pull wild morning glories off the back fence. The sun sinks beyond the mulberry tree; there's a mournful chill in the air. My thighs ache from stooping. But these physical discomforts are well suffered: No protection, no complaint.

Crumbling and freezing, crumbling and freezing, I mutter as I work here amid the wreck of tomato vines and skeletal pepper plants. The nights are cool and days shortening. There's bound to be a freeze soon. I salvage a basket of green tomatoes.

I abandon the clippers (remember their yellow handles?) for more bare-handed work with a shovel. There's comfort in the weight of digging, in the rhythmic lifting and dropping, shovelful after shovelful. I love the pain in my shoulders and arms, the new blisters on my hands. The wheelbarrow is full, a tangled mass of withered squash vines, hollowed-out and spotted tomatoes. I lurch the wheelbarrow toward the compost heap.

An ambulance siren screams its way along Independence Avenue. Over the last thirteen months I've become an expert on the sounds of sirens, their direction and frequency telling me how desperate to let myself be: numbly desperate that the wailing signals a new national emergency, flailingly desperate that it's one person's, one family's, distress. Heaving the wheelbarrow's contents onto the compost, I make a mental note: *one ambulance, one person.* I wince. *One person, whose heart must be pounding, pounding, pounding, staring numbly up at the ceiling of the ambulance, the gurney jerking with the rhythm of the rushing vehicle, the siren coursing overhead.* An ordinary, private misery on a Tuesday afternoon in October, not the roaring next cataclysm we've all been expecting since 9/11.

I straighten my back slightly, a little pain radiating reliably out from my shoulders. Two mockingbirds insist on something terribly important in the raggedy elm next door. *Listen to the birdsong,* I tell myself. *Do a little mental arithmetic to keep other thoughts at bay. Calculate the relative ratio of our garden to the city.* I steer the wheelbarrow back to its resting place against fence separating our yard from the alley. The garden is maybe twenty feet square. That's four hundred square feet. Each city block is a tenth of a mile on each side. *A tenth of a mile times a tenth of a mile,* I calculate. *One-hundredth of a square mile on the grid that was laid out as a ten-mile square, a hundred square miles. And there are eight houses on each side of the block.* The math problem is too difficult to do in my head, so I simplify it: *My little garden is a twenty-foot square,* I remember, *about the same size as my old classroom. Two four-hundred-square-foot safety zones.* The idea calms me for a moment. *Don't think about the sirens or the way the sky was, that heartbreakingly beautiful blue on that Tuesday morning in September. Don't think about the year just past. Think about the safety zones, the little Edens. Think toward spring.*

It's getting colder. Nothing more needs doing. I carry a basket of green tomatoes to the kitchen door. Find myself humming a musical line from *The Fantasticks,* the way I used to:

> *Try to remember the time in September,*
> *When life was yellow and oh so mellow. . .*

The sounds of crows and a car horn mingle in the dwindling sunshine.

Now I'm at the kitchen sink, watching my hands wash themselves. A glance up at the woodcut on the kitchen wall of a woman kneading bread reminds me of a story written my last semester at Remington, by a red-headed prodigy who, in addition to her regular schoolwork, taught herself Greek grammar the summer before her junior year. She wanted to read *The Symposium* and *The Odyssey* with Dan before she graduated. I remember making a mental note to resist the urge to steal an ingredient she used in that story. It told of a young writer discovering the life of Saint Elizabeth of Hungary, the patron saint of bakers. Really, the young writer thought, Elizabeth should be the patron saint of writers, too, who knead material into something startlingly different from what they started with.

I put the tomatoes on the kitchen counter beside my computer. I log onto the internet and type *patron saint* into the Google prompt box. Elizabeth of Hungary is indeed the patron saint of bakers. Francis de Sales and John the Apostle watch over writers, and Saint Fiacre guards gardeners and taxi drivers. Saint Barbara, imprisoned in a tower before her martyrdom, is the protector of towers, firefighters, and those trapped by fire. The archangel Michael watches over security guards and police officers, just as he stood watch at the entrance to Eden.

All my life I have been kept safe, well protected from the soul's pain, the chill of tears, from sharp distress. I have lived all my life in sanctuaries built for me by others – my home, my kitchen, my classroom, my garden, the embrace of loving arms, the peaceful streets of our neighborhood, our beautiful city, our fortune-blessed homeland. How do I thank those guardian angels for their kind protection?

I can almost hear the answers: Bake bread. Put up jam and relish. Teach Ned to drive. Do puzzles with Gracie. Wrestle with words. Work in the garden. Eat and drink, love your family, the living and the dead. Correspond with anyone who's willing to write back.

Subject: Happy Birthday, Darling, continued
Date: 10/12/2002 23:57:16 P.M. EDT
From: dndyoung2@owl.com
To: dndyoung1@owl.com

Dearest,

I had trouble with the Homeric verbs and word order, but I have them now, the nine lines in Book 11 where Odysseus reaches out to touch his mother in the Afterlife:

> So she spoke, and I, my heart still sorely troubled, longed to catch the spirit of my dead mother. Three times I rushed forward towards her, my soul urging me to catch hold of her; three times she flitted from my hands like a shadow, like a dream. My heart's sharp distress grew exceedingly, and I cried out, my words taking flight: 'Mother mine, why don't you wait for me? I long to catch hold of you, so that even here in Hades we both might throw our arms around each other. Haven't we had enough icy weeping?'

How beautiful are the bird images – ἐλέειν ("to catch hold"), ἔπτατ᾽ ("flit, dart, flutter") and πτερόεντα ("winged") – and the notion that words, too, have wings, darting away from us, startled, singing for their own sake, taking eager flight! I like thinking of you, Bathsua, and me that way, turned into songbirds, mockingbirds or house wrens maybe, calling to each other from neighboring trees, some of our words comforting messengers, others mere expressions of pleasure in making any sound at all.

As ever, with all my love.

October 14, 2002

> Τρὶς μὲν ἐφωρμήθην, ἐλέειν τέ με θυμὸς ἀνώγει,
> τρὶς δέ μοι ἐκ χειρῶν σκιῇ εἴκελον ἢ καὶ ὀνείρῳ ἔπτατ᾽.
> Thrice I called her Name, sprang toward her,
> Thrice she flitted from my Arms like yᵉ Shadow of a Dream.
> – Homer. *Odyssey*. Book 11.

My Dear New Friend,

I have been seeking, longing for yᵉ Touch of my Mother's Hands, yᵉ Sound of her Voice. Sometimes she seems to step toward me from Shadows of yᵉ Past and my Dreams. Sometimes I see someone who resembles her. The sight catches at my Heart and draws me back to her for an Instant. You know that Feeling, as fleeting for you there as 'tis for us here. Even here one rarely crosses Paths with those we knew.

Homer writes that Odysseus call'd forth his Mother's Shade by drinking from a Cup of wine-dark Blood. Or is it a Cup of blood-dark Wine? Neither form of Magick works. We can only summon yᵉ beloved Dead with scraps of Memory and Stories they us'd to tell.

My Mother was a great Tale Spinner. Her favorite Subjects were virtuous Women from Holy Scripture, yᵉ familiar and yᵉ obscure. She embellish'd Scripture's sparse tales of Women's Lives with her own Inventions, to impart to Ithamaria and me, I trowe, some moral Messages, or Secrets of her own otherwise unrecorded Life. Likely, too, she found Pleasure in Invention itself and us'd Scripture because 'twas at hand. Her Stories remain with me, their Secrets undecipher'd even to this Day, yit bearing Witness to her Wisdom. Like yᵉ unnam'd Woman of Valour in

Proverbs, she is more precious to me than Rubies.

I am finishing my first Story. Such Pleasure fills ye Writing of it: Once ye Spinning of a Tale from a Thread of Memory begins, what a surprising Fabric is woven!

Sincerely yours,

Bathsua

Subject: Up early, finishing my first story for Bathsua
Date: 10/20/2002 06:23:34 A.M. EDT
From: dndyoung2@owl.com
To: dndyoung1@owl.com

Dearest,

I feel like a high school kid with a first story due that's now going to be read by – or perhaps aloud to – others. I already have clammy hands and a knot in my stomach. You have your copy; Bathsua will get hers tomorrow.

On the home front: Ned takes his driver's test today. Am putting up green tomato chutney this week when not writing. The sniper business and the war news are disturbing my sleep. Bigtime. In the wee hours I turn on that Big Bad Voodoo Daddy cd you left in the stereo, crank up the volume, and dance in my nightgown, my bare feet slapping the floor in the darkness.

Yours, ever,

Dee

October 21, 2002

> The memory is sometimes so retentive, so serviceable, so obedient: at others,
> so bewildered and so weak; and at others again, so tyrannic, so beyond control!
> – Jane Austen. *Mansfield Park.*

Dear Mistress Makin,

Today is my mother's birthday. She has been dead for more than ten years, and I still try to fill the emptiness between us, to make sense of the watery guilt that seeps into the hollows of my heart whenever I think of her. Why that emptiness, that wreck of silence when I think about her? It is as if there's an empty room in me that's just that – empty. Where did the love go, and why? And there's anger and disappointment over the emptiness that's no one's fault, not hers, not mine. Is this a failure or a form of love?

My cursor is moving the word *love* across my laptop screen. I must have lingered on that last paragraph, and just started pushing it along, as if it were a dreadful burden.

Enough preparation. Here's my story about my mother.

Sincerely yours,

Dee

Enclosure: "Attachment"

Attachment

The mere habit of learning to love is the thing.
– Jane Austen. Northanger Abbey.

Have you wondered how you learned to love when you were a child? Your skin remembers your mother's comfort when you were an infant: the press of your mouth to her breast, the touch of her cheek on your cheek, her hand on yours. For your whole life there is the imprint of that first physical form of love. It comes especially when you lie curled and ready for sleep.

In my earliest memories I am lying awake, five or six years old, in the half-light of bedtime. The streetlight casts a gray pearliness on my bedroom wall. An occasional car's headlights make pale trapezoids shift eerily across the ceiling. I strain to listen, in those trailing strands of time before sleep comes, performing those little insomniac's rituals of hair twirling and folding and unfolding my hands, first under my cheekbone, then under my jaw bone, then under my pillow. I hear my parents in the living room downstairs, my father clearing his throat, my mother's voice rising in pitch and volume. My mother's voice is insistent, dramatic. That memory flickers into the rising and falling roar of airplanes taking off and landing at the Naval Air Station near our house in coastal Massachusetts where a narrow causeway attaches our peninsula to the marshy mainland.

I also remember lying in the grassy shade near the arborvitae in the back yard, my tongue examining the space where one front tooth had fallen out. It must have been the summer of 1941, just after I finished first grade, when most of my classmates were also suddenly toothless. I remember my mother working nearby, jabbing the sandy soil around the marigolds and wrenching crabgrass from the lawn. She had made me a tent of sheets hanging from the clothesline. I am pretending to have survived a terrible catastrophe. I must have caught a whiff of the news of the war in Europe, the hushed, scarcely mentioned back story of my early childhood that surfaced when my parents argued after they put me to bed. My father had decided, against my mother's wishes, to enlist in the army before the US went to war.

In the dreamy logic of childhood, my head filled with the drone of planes going out from the Naval Air Station and coming in over the water, I was sure that This Was It. With a six-year-old's wisdom, I knew the pilots weren't practicing for nothing. Alone under my make-believe backyard tent, I told myself the story *Everyone in My Family Is Dead but Me*. In one version I try to remember what my mother's face looks like. Lying in the grass with my eyes squeezed shut, my baby brother in the net-covered carriage in the shade of the arborvitae and my mother not ten feet away, I cannot picture her in my mind's eye. Nothing comes except shifting colors and shapes imprinted on the insides of my eyelids. Her voice rises clearly above the sound of the garden trowel scraping the soil and the buzz of summer insects, beneath the roar of airplanes: "You want to leave me? Go to the war and die?" And the sound of her tears.

Now, sixty years later and ten after my mother's death, I look at a black-and-white 1950's photograph of the four of us, my parents and my brother Josh and me, standing before the skyline of lower Manhattan, that persistent symbol of American energy. We had driven to New York from Massachusetts. The centerpiece of the trip was a visit to the Statue of Liberty. In the photo Papa is smiling broadly, handsomely, on the left; Josh is smiling, but less, his head tilted slightly toward mine. Between Josh and my mother, I am sulking at the stranger taking our picture. My mother looks like she is in a different photograph entirely. Her hair is uncovered, wild in the wind, and her eyes are squinting dark pools. A scarf billows up from her collar, its flying fabric obscuring her mouth. According to the conventions of family photography, she must be wearing a smile behind that unruly scarf. The family expressions descend in minor thirds from my father's broad, inadvertently flirtatious grin through my brother's half-smile and my ironic bunching of the cheek muscles to that glare in my mother's eyes, which hovers between rage and despair. Through childhood and adolescence, I was carefully self-protective, purposefully ignorant of the causes of her mood swings. Now, looking at that photograph, I struggle to understand and forgive them. What kind of love is that?

Mostly I remember my mother's incredible emotional range. I feel it vibrating behind me when I stand in my kitchen rolling out pie dough. The rolling pin was hers before it was mine, made by her father, my grandfather, a carpenter, who had tapered the ends of an oak dowel on his lathe, a gift for his only daughter. Its patina, the color and gloss of a golden pie crust, should comfort me, but it doesn't. I resist baking pies, I think, because, looking down at my own hands I see my mother's, her left thumb and index finger, pulling the dough fiercely outward from the pie pan, jamming the dough inward toward the center, shoving the pan around a few degrees as she turns it for the next fluting. She crams the pie into the oven, then wipes her hands disconsolately on her apron and her damp forehead with the back of her arm. She dials the phone, its earpiece cradled against her shoulder, slices an onion, tears rolling down her cheeks, and talks on the phone in Yiddish to her mother, as she did every day until my grandmother died.

In this memory I'm standing in the kitchen doorway, the screen door slapping shut behind me, my chest catching and heaving, having just run in across the back porch all the way from Nickerson's, the neighborhood variety store several long blocks away along the shore road. It's a Friday morning, probably a year after the war ended, which makes it the summer of 1946. Josh is napping in his carriage on the porch. My mother is wearing the sleeveless lettuce-green sundress she had just finished sewing, her arms damp with sweat. Despite the summer heat she's baking a pie, roasting a chicken, making potato kugel for Shabbos dinner. I stand in the doorway, torn between speaking and silence, terrified of the repercussions of both. My mother looks up, startled. The conversation with my grandmother hasn't properly run its emotional course.

"It's gone. My bike's gone." My gasping for breath is both real and imagined. "I parked it against the wall at Nickerson's and went in to look around, get a . . ." I am about to say that I had gone in to get a candy bar, but guilt for a silly extravagance silences me. My whistling breath eliminates the need to lie. "It's gone. So I ran home. I didn't know what else to do."

The shiny two-wheeler had taken me almost a year to learn to ride, my mother holding the back of the seat while I struggled to pedal along the road. She had clenched her jaw and forced herself to force me to keep trying. Finally, exasperated by her fear for me and my fear of falling, she had simply let go and watched as I careened down our block and fell, tears streaming, only to turn and see her standing there, arms akimbo and tears streaming, too, desperate, and small in the distance.

Now I see her untying her apron and smoothing it across the edge of the kitchen counter. Her lips are pursed. She lowers the temperature knob of the oven, propels me out of the kitchen, past the red Formica table and vinyl-covered chairs, out onto the porch. She unbrakes Josh's carriage, and we rush down to the shore road, then turn left. The beach – it is low tide – is on our right, then the tumble of granite rocks. In the distance the Naval Air Station is quiet now with the war over. I can't remember any words, only a floury smear of butter on the front of my mother's dress, her golden arm, her white sandals, toenails carefully manicured and painted in clear polish, the whir of the carriage wheels on the pavement. I remember the flap-flapping of my sneakers and the damp rubbing of my thighs against each other as I struggle to keep up. We move quickly along the road, into and out of patches of shadow and sunlight. An olive-drab military truck passes us on its way to the navy base. The driver wolf-whistles at my mother, who stares straight ahead, jaw tight, striding along ahead of me.

"What about the pie?" I ask, feeling clumsy and stupid and fat and guilty all at the same time. "It'll burn," I wheeze. "It's all my fault." Gulls wheel overhead near the low-tide edge of the water to our right, laughing, screaming at us.

I rub my tear-wet cheek with the back of my hand. We are at the variety store now. I point to the spot where I had parked the blue two-wheeler, now just a patch of shadow beside the cement steps leading into the store. My mother doesn't miss a stride and heads alongside the store to the alley behind. Josh is starting to stir. The seagulls still laugh at me. And there it is, my bike, tumbled among the trash cans. My mother flicks her tongue behind her teeth, making the familiar sound of relief and dismissiveness I often heard her make when my father left the room. How did she know the bike was there, with the trash, a place I never thought to look? Is she relieved that it is not lost or pleased to note that she had found it and I hadn't? She rights it and hands it to me, turns back to Josh in the baby carriage and heads for home.

Go ride and play; catch up with your friends. That's what I wished she had said that day. But memory tells me otherwise. What I remember is that she strode back along the shore road, and I followed, wheeling my bike, not riding it, appreciating in an odd, punishing way the thud of the bike's bulk against my leg.

My mother taught me that love is complicated. Eager that I do things for myself, she nevertheless did not seem sad that I depended so much on her. She insisted that I learn to swim, ride that bike and, later, drive a car when she couldn't do these things herself. Yet she did not look disappointed that I was terrified about putting my face in the water, falling off the bicycle, or driving alone when I first got my license.

I spent the rest of the day playing with Josh on the porch while Ma finished cooking, vacuuming, and pruning the arborvitae. Just before Papa came home and it was time to set the table for dinner, she and I played double solitaire at the dinette table. The bike wasn't mentioned.

—∼—

My mother died suddenly of a heart condition in December 1992. She had been frail for years, unable to travel but unwilling to tell me what exactly the doctors had told her of that heart condition. She probably had the lingering effects of childhood rheumatic fever common among ghetto children of her generation. But I think it wasn't medical, that Heart Condition of hers. On the way to her funeral Papa said that theirs had been a fifty-five-year-long unhappy marriage. I was horrified when he said it, but I know it was true. For my whole childhood, my whole family had been a little solar system centered on my mother. A few neighbors were, at best, remote galaxies. In the family narrative Papa was a plodder with no imagination, no sense of humor. My mother was the one who put color into the otherwise drab stinginess of our life by her alternating fierce tirades and frenzied cheerfulness. I wonder what kept her heart from exploding. During agonizing visits and strained phone conversations in her last years, my mother raged against my father's dogged silence. "See," she would say. "He just sits there; he won't talk to me; not a compliment or a nice word. He reads the newspaper, every page of it. Why won't he talk to me? And he left me, abandoned me, to go off to the War, and all these years. . . ." Then she would shift to my betrayal of her love: "And you, you left, too. Left me here alone with him." She would trail off.

At our mother's funeral Josh spoke of the laughter he remembered from his childhood. Then, before we said Kaddish, I recited Donne's "Death Be Not Proud" from memory.

October 24, 2002

> When thou feel'st no grief, as I no harmes,
> Yet love thy dead, who long lay in thine arms.
> — Ann Bradstreet. "Before ye Birth of One of Her Children."

My dear young Friend,

I was mov'd to weeping by "Attachment." So full of Heart's Pain. How difficult 'tis to comprehend others' Lives. Tho' we must, doing so may betray their Trust. Do you not agree?

In reading your "Attachment" I wonder at your Candour, which conveys your Faith in me as your Reader. Thank you for that Trust.

Yours truly,

Bathsua M.

Subject:	Some good news
Date:	10/24/2002 17:12:01 P.M. EDT
From:	dndyoung2@owl.com
To:	dndyoung1@owl.com

Danny – They caught the snipers. At least that craziness is over. Love.

October 25, 2002

May it be Thy will, My Lord, that no mishap be caused by what I do.
– Reb Nechuniah ben HaKanah. *Berachot* 28b.

Dear Bathsua,

My thanks for your tears and recognition of my trust in you as a friend and reader. Do I agree that we betray others' trust when we tell their stories? No. What else are our lives but different versions of the lives of others? To tell our own stories we must tell theirs. We must try to do no harm, of course, or to do as little harm as possible. But to stay silent would be a greater betrayal. Do not expect me to keep everyone else's secrets. Do you?

Faithfully yours,

Dee

Subject:	So what did you think? and another matter
Date:	10/27/2002 22:53:27 P.M. EDT
From:	dndyoung2@owl.com
To:	dndyoung1@owl.com

Dearest Dan,

Remember how I got all tied up in knots when a week passed and I hadn't returned a set of papers? The next day I'd fuss inside when a kid would ask – politely, of course – when I was going to give them back. I can imagine now how that kid felt. So, Teach, didja like "Attachment"?

Hey, Danny. I dreamt last night that we made love. And I woke up crying. So, Love, didja have that dream, too? Was it good for you, too? Love.

October 28, 2002

שְׁמַע בְּנִי, מוּסַר אָבִיךָ; וְאַל-תִּטֹּשׁ, תּוֹרַת אִמֶּךָ.
כִּי, לִוְיַת חֵן הֵם לְרֹאשֶׁךָ; וַעֲנָקִים, לְגַרְגְּרֹתֶךָ.

Hear, my child, the instruction of your father, and forsake not the teaching of thy mother; for they shall be as an ornament of grace unto thy head and chains about thy neck.
– Proverbs 1:8-9.

My dear Friend,

To answer your Question: Yes, I try to keep others' Secrets. Or hide them behind mine own Invention.

My first Story is enclos'd herewith. It being done & I reliev'd of the writing of it, I shall take my ease & natter on about this and that.

I rarely see anyone in ye Alcove 6 Balcony, except you on your weekly Visits. You do not notice me, but I glimpse you climbing carefully up ye narrow spiral Staircase, stopping as you enter ye Alcove, checking to see y^t you are alone. You always slip those folding half Glasses from their little silver Case as you approach ye final Range of Shelves, then adjust ye Lenses & bend down as if to scrutinize ye Books thereon. I like this little Charade & also your Habit of balancing that Packet of Foolscap atop those little green Books, then using your Body to hide from Sight ye fact y^t you are slipping Papers from or into ye Space below ye Shelf, rather than a Book from ye Shelf itself. Handily done. I like your absentminded Expression, your Lips purs'd as if you were deep in Thought.

By y^e by, I cannot help but admire ye comfortable Dress you Women eschew these Days, those easy-fitting long Breeches & loose Tunics. How much more practical than our long Skirts & snug Corsets. Your Shoes look sturdier & more sensible than ours, too, keeping your Feet warm & dry, I expect, on rainy Days like today. I wonder where I might find a pair. Nor would I mind a pair of those folding reading Glasses.

I observe from your Letters y^t your writing Apparatus allows you much greater Efficiency than our Inkpots & Quills. My Father & I devis'd a method of Speed Writing, call'd Radiography, a compress'd, encoded System (rather ingenious, I must say) for those needing to write quickly. The Library must have some Record of it. Unfortunately, Radiography's association with Espionage prov'd dangerous to our Family. To my Father, especially. More on this Matter later, perhaps.

Trying your modern writing equipm't would afford me much Pleasure, altho' I doubt I could accustom myself to it. And despite my Curiosity about Modernity, I do love ye look of Penmanship. I would especially enjoy seeing yours. Much of one's Character appears in ye way one shapes Letters & places Words upon ye page. Do you not agree? Much is told by Ink Blots & cross-Hatchings, Slants & Sputters, telltale Signs of Emotion. I wonder, does ye careful Sound of your Voice on Paper (so to speak) result from your Writing Machine or from your Character & Turn of Mind?

On another Topic altogether: Do you recall ye engraving with ye Inscription from ye first Chapter of Proverbs y^t Professors Crawford & Mendelson found for you in ye Harleian Archive? of ye Woman with downcast Gaze, with ye Birdcage on ye left, helping her Daughter with her Lessons? I've seen you staring at it in ye Reading Room. Let me tease you with a few Questions about it: Am I ye Mother helping her Child, urging her not to forget me? Or am I ye Child gazing off toward her Future? How might you understand ye caption – *Forsake not ye Law of thy Mother* – as ye child looks up and away from ye Lesson? And why did ye Artist stop at ye first half of ye Verse? Are we meant to complete ye second half for ourselves?

And ye invisible third Personage through whose Eyes ye two Figures are depicted: Who might this Observer be? Is he – or she – amus'd or befuddl'd to see a Woman of scant Education teaching a Maid to read?

And while we entertain Questions, my dear: Do you imagine y^t we here in ye World of ye Dead are fix'd at a particular Age of our living Selves, at ye time of our Death, say, or at an earlier, more robust Time? Am I Batty Reynolds, ye Child, or Bathsua Makin, ye old Woman? Or am I all & everyone, ye Child at her Mother's Side, ye young Teacher, ye new Wife, ye grieving Mother, et cetera, et cetera? Might I not be Multitudes?

Do you wish I would tell you directly about ye Past & ye World of ye Dead? Do you wish I would roll out ye Magic Carpet of my Past like a Rug Merchant showing his Wares? I cannot. Y^e past, like ye future & perhaps ye present too, is hidden from us all, forever.

Enough. Herewith find my first Story.

Yours, etc.

Bathsua

Enclos'd: "Far Above Rubies"

Far Above Rubies

צוֹפִיָּה, הִילְכוּת (הֲלִיכוֹת) בֵּיתָהּ;   וְלֶחֶם עַצְלוּת, לֹא תֹאכֵל.

She looks well to yᵉ ways of her Household, and eats not yᵉ Bread of
Idleness.
  – Proverbs 31:27.

It doth appear out of Sacred Writ that Women were employ'd in most
of yᵉ great Transactions that happened in yᵉ World. . . . Miriam seems
to be next to Moses and Aaron.
  – Bathsua Makin. *Essay on Reviving yᵗ Antient Education of Gentlewomen.*

"Let us try to make less Noise, Child. Your Father's working."

"Papa's always working. He said I could go with him to yᵉ City this
Morning. And now I have to wait and be quiet & sit still until he's ready."

"Yes, dearie, Papa's always working on something, studying & writing.
'Tis a good thing, too. And yes, you're to be quiet & still & patient. 'Tis
what's expected of little girls, Batty. Come, sit by me & we'll make up a
Story to pass yᵉ time. When we're done, Papa will surely be ready. He'll say,
'You've been such a good girl, Batty. Now 'tis time for our Adventure at
Westminster. Mama will have a quiet rest while Itha sleeps.' And then off
you'll go, yᵉ two to Court. You'll be Eyes & Ears for me, my Darling. Now
can I persuade you to sit here on what's left of my Lap? No? Then be a
good Lass, & help your Mama by putting a few things into the basket yᵗ
Papa will carry. Some bread & cheese & apples for you to eat as you walk
along together. There's a good Girl. And now while I sit here & try to be
quiet & content for both of us, I'll tell you a Story."

"Please, Mama."

"Remember Miriam, second only to her brothers, Moses & Aaron? She
was a little Lass once, just like you, observant & full of Energy & a good
Help to her Mama. And she grew up to be a great Leader, a Prophetess &
Musician! Just think of them, dearie, those Hebrew women & children who
accounted for more than half yᵉ Israelites. They needed Miriam, a special
one of their own, to rouse them to exchange yᵉ familiar Slavery in Egypt
for yᵉ unknowable Adventure of Freedom in yᵉ Wilderness that would take
them into yᵉ Promis'd Land. What a Wonder those Women must have been,
my Child!"

"Yes, Mama."

"Do you remember yᵉ name of Moses's mother, Batty?"

"No, Mama."

"No wonder. She's nearly nameless in Scripture. She's only nam'd twice, once in Exodus & again much later, in Numbers."

Tell me her Name, Mama."

"Jochebed. 'The Lord's Glory,' her Name means, yᵉ Mother of Moses, & Aaron & Miriam, too. 'Of all yᵉ Hebrew women, she must have been one to marvel at, don't you think, to have borne & rear'd Children yᵉ likes of those three? I cannot imagine her sitting in her chair, striving to be calm & quiet! Let's talk about Jochebed, Batty, & her good daughter Miriam, while we await your father."

"What will you do, Mama, while Papa & I are out walking?"

"I wish I could walk with you into Westminster as I us'd to, & see all yᵉ grand folks & their Hustle & Bustle. But Papa says I mustn't tire myself. So I'll sit here quietly & wait for you, my good big girl, my Eyes & Ears, & your busy, important father, to come home with Tales of yᵉ City."

"I hope we have an Adventure to tell you when we come home, Mama."

"You will, my dear. Even the Ordinary can be turn'd into a good Story. While we wait for Papa to come down from his study, I shall tell you a story about Jochebed. Do you remember yᵉ story of yᵉ Baby Moses, when his Mama put him in yᵉ little reed basket?"

"And put him down in yᵉ bullrushers?"

"Bulrushes, my Darling. Papyrus, it must have been. What yᵉ ancient Egyptians us'd for writing paper."

"Funny to think on, Mama. If yᵉ Egyptian Papas wrote on Papyrus, did their Mamas write on Mamyrus?"

"No, dear. Papyrus is yᵉ name Egyptians gave to yᵉ River Grass they made into Paper. I suppose 'tis where yᵉ word Paper comes from. And perhaps you're right, it's for yᵉ World yᵗ Papas live in, not Mamas. But let's keep our eye on Moses's Mama, Batty, on Jochebed, & on her daughter, Moses's sister, Miriam."

"All right, Mama."

"What did Miriam do when Jochebed put Baby Moses in yᵉ Basket among yᵉ bulrushes?"

"She waited by ye side of ye River. She kept an eye on her baby Brother in ye little Basket & waited until ye Princess, Pharaoh's daughter, came to ye riverbank & found ye Basket & took ye baby to be her own little boy & rais'd him in Pharaoh's palace & nam'd him Moses."

"Well told, dearie. But now let's imagine how those near-impossible things came to be. How Jochebed came to put her baby at ye very spot along ye river bank where ye Princess would find him, how she help'd ye Princess tend him, how in fact she sav'd him & readied him to be ye one to lead his People out of Slavery in Egypt & into ye Wilderness of Sinai, how she tended also to Aaron & Miriam, readying them to help ye Children of Israel become ye Household of ye Lord. Do you know that part of ye Tale?"

"No, Mama."

"Few people do. And do you know why?"

"No, Mama."

"Because few people bother to tell ye stories of ye silent Women who stand behind their busy Fathers & Husbands & their famous, able children."

"But you do. 'Tis what you're doing now, Mama."

"Yes, my child. Now Amram, from ye house of Levi, work'd very hard for Pharaoh, his master. And Jochebed, Amram's wife, also from ye house of Levi, was a Midwife & a wet-nurse in ye Palace."

"Like Mistress Goodkins, Mama?"

"Yes. Like Mistress Goodkins, who helps when ye Queen births ye royal babes. And help'd me, too, when you & Itha were born and, God willing, when ye new little one comes. Jochebed help'd ye fine Egyptian Ladies & poor Hebrew Women birth their babes, but only ye Egyptian babes did she nurse afterward, for ye Hebrew Women nurs'd their babes themselves. Jochebed attended ye Princess at ye birth of her first Child, Pharaoh's first Grandchild. But ye babe was stillborn, & there was much weeping in the Palace. Pharaoh was very sad & disappointed, & being Pharaoh he turned his sad feelings into anger & jealousy. ''Tis all the fault of t y^t Hebrew Midwife,' he said. And his Heart turn'd against all ye Hebrews from y^t day forward. He didn't just make them work, he — "

"I know, Mama. He made them suffer boils & frogs!"

No, dearie. Plagues came later, & they were visited by ye Lord on ye Egyptians, not by their Pharaoh on ye Hebrews."

"That's when Moses said, 'Let my People go'?"

"Yes, dear. But when Pharaoh's grandson died, he was so jealous of ye Hebrews & their babies y^t he order'd them to kill all their boy babies by throwing them into ye River."

"That's terrible, Mama."

"Yes, 'twas. Pharaoh made y^t Law just after Jochebed's third child was born, a goodly baby boy, who didn't cry or fuss at all, but stay'd quiet & calm for three whole Months."

"Not a difficult babe, like Itha & me, Mama?"

"He was a quiet babe. Some babies are quiet & some are not. But no babe is too difficult, my darling. This was just a quiet one who, like all Newborns, had such a look of Wisdom & Understanding on his little face y^t Jochebed was certain he was destin'd to do Good in this World. So despite Amram's insisting they obey Pharaoh's order, Jochebed decided to disobey."

"She was very brave, Mama."

"Yes, my child. She was indeed brave. And wise, too. She knew keenly ye Difference between Right & Wrong. She would not take ye babe's Life. Such was her Courage, Batty. It could have meant ye Deaths of herself & her Children, & even of her Husband. Even worse, it could have meant harsher punishment for all ye Hebrew Slaves. But despite her fears, she kept ye Babe tightly swaddl'd at home, & had Miriam & Aaron keep close watch over him while she & Amram were away at work."

"They were good helpers, Mama?"

"Yes. Every day, Jochebed left her children in their tiny house among ye Hebrew Slaves & walk'd to work at ye Palace, terrified lest Miriam & Aaron would forget what she had told them & ye babe would be discover'd. She imagin'd herself & Amram returning home to Desolation. *Pharaoh's Law says I must throw* y^e *child in* y^e *River, throw him in* y^e *River,* she thought to herself again & again, her thoughts matching her footfalls along ye path to ye Palace. As she walk'd along ye River's brink, she wonder'd what to do. Should she do what was safe or what was right? What was safe wasn't right, nor what was right at all safe.

"One morning, walking along ye Path, scarcely noticing dragonflies glinting among ye Papyrus reeds & ducks dipping down to feed in ye Water, suddenly she realiz'd, as if by a Miracle, that yᵉ Right & yᵉ Safe were both in her power. Yᵉ Solution was beautiful. And it fit perfectly with yᵉ Letter of Pharaoh's Law.

"Jochebed thought her way through yᵉ Solution, one step at a time. Yᵉ Princess, she knew, was a good young woman, kind & generous & yᵉ Apple of her Father's Eye. She knew, too, that yᵉ Princess was almost dying of Grief because of yᵉ Death of her own babe, & that Pharoah was at his wit's end to know what to do. Yᵉ Princess would be a good mother, loving & wise, brave & good. And beloved enough to melt her father's stubborn Pride. Yᵉ riverbank, Jochebed knew, was yᵉ only place where yᵉ Princess could forget some of her Sorrow, especially yᵉ spot where Papyrus grew, where dragonflies darted & ducks dipp'd their heads into yᵉ Water. And yᵉ River was Holy to yᵉ Egyptians, yᵉ source of Life, not of Death."

"But Pharaoh said to kill yᵉ Babe by throwing him into yᵉ River."

"Yes, my child. 'Drop yᵉ Hebrew babes into yᵉ Water,' Pharaoh had said. Jochebed came up with yᵉ perfect Idea. She had her son Aaron help her make a special basket in yᵉ shape of a little boat, an Ark, – "

"Like Noah's Ark, Mama?"

"Exactly. Yᵉ Hebrews who saw yᵉ little boy building it thought he was playing. In fact, he was helping his Mama."

"Just like I help you, Mama?"

"Yes, my Darling. And Jochebed show'd Aaron how to daub it all over with Pitch, to keep it afloat."

"And they put yᵉ Babe in yᵉ Ark?"

"Yes. Before dawn yᵉ next morning Aaron & Miriam help'd to put him in yᵉ little Ark-basket, & Jochebed & Miriam took turns carrying it to yᵉ spot beside yᵉ River where yᵉ Princess always walk'd in yᵉ cool of yᵉ morning. Jochebed set yᵉ Basket among yᵉ Papyrus reeds where her bright-eyed little son might watch dragonflies darting in yᵉ sunlight & listen to ducks going *kerplop* in yᵉ water. She knew her goodly baby would chuckle with delight at yᵉ Miracle of Life all about him. And that yᵉ Princess would hear yᵉ infant's laughter & be mov'd by this Miracle from yᵉ Life-giving River."

"That's beautiful, Mama."

"Yes, 'tis, & Miriam, yᵉ little lass, was part of it. Jochebed said to Miriam, her daughter, 'Be my eyes & ears, my child. Tell me everything yᵗ happens.'"

"As I will tell you what I see & hear today when I walk with Papa?"

"Yes, Batty."

"And Miriam did as her Mama said?"

"Yes, & more. She did as she was told, & she us'd her Imagination. Just as you do, my darling. When yᵉ Princess saw yᵉ babe, she look'd at him closely, watch'd him smiling & glancing about him with those bright eyes, heard his sweet baby sounds. Just then Miriam stepp'd out as if by Accident along yᵉ path. She too regarded yᵉ boy & smil'd. 'What a pretty babe, your Majesty!' she said, proud of yᵉ way she made her voice sound surpris'd. 'Yes,' the Princess replied. 'He must be a Hebrew babe,' she added. 'That is possible, your Highness,' said Miriam. 'But Hebrew or not, 'tis a goodly babe, one any mother would be proud to love. And call her own.' Yᵉ Princess regarded yᵉ girl closely. 'May I help you carry him, your Majesty?' Miriam ask'd. Yᵉ Princess agreed. And Miriam lifted yᵉ child from among yᵉ reeds & placed him in yᵉ arms of yᵉ Princess, who pitied him & at that moment began to love him. 'But how will I feed him?' she ask'd. 'My Mama is a Midwife & a wet-nurse in your Palace, Your Majesty. Perhaps she can think of what to do.' And yᵉ two, yᵉ Princess & Miriam, walk'd companionably along yᵉ path to yᵉ Palace, where they came upon Jochebed. And Pharaoh's daughter said to her, 'Take this child & nurse him for me. I will pay you wages.'

"So Jochebed nurs'd yᵉ child every day at yᵉ Palace. And Pharaoh, who lov'd his daughter, saw her growing strong again, even beginning to smile. Gazing from his window, Pharaoh was surpris'd to see a goodly little boy playing in yᵉ women's courtyard of yᵉ palace. He smil'd at yᵉ Restoration of his daughter's spirits & ask'd nothing about how it had happen'd.

"So yᵉ boy grew. Jochebed shar'd him with Pharaoh's daughter, who took him as her son & nam'd him Moses, for she said, 'I drew him from yᵉ Water.' Are you ready for your Adventure with Papa now, my child?"

"Yes, Mama."

And they both look'd up. They did not know how long Papa had been watching, nor how long he had cast his sweet smile in their direction.

Subject: Musing
Date: 10/29/2002 01:27:52 A.M. EST
From: dndyoung2@owl.com
To: dndyoung1@owl.com

Dearest,

I look forward to Bathsua's letters with such excitement! I think I understand why I'm writing to her – for the same reason I write to you. But why does she reply, not you?

I can hear your answers: Maybe "she" is just someone at the Library, one of the desk clerks who glances up now and then as I read in seat 275 or climb the spiral staircase in Alcove 6. Or a librarian, maybe, or that tall ascetic-looking shelving clerk I see in the Reading Room, moving a book cart from the Circulation Office to the Reader's Shelves and back again. Or maybe it's another reader, the bearded man who sat to my right the other day, the one with the long face and aquiline nose, or the woman to my left, with the strong veins on her hands, the heavy garnet and silver ring on the middle finger of her right hand. Or do you suppose "she" could even be "me"? Who's taking all that trouble to turn those modern *the*'s to *y*'s, to apostrophize those past-tense verbs, to follow seventeenth-century noun-capitalization conventions?

Am I going mad, Dan? I feel – what do I feel? – I feel hollowed out and heavy at the same time. In the dark and squinting against the light at the same time. When I read Bathsua's letters and write to her, I feel like I'm coming out into the light. Otherwise I'm dark inside and falling into more darkness. So I write and write, and read and re-read, to stay in the light.

If Bathsua Makin's *really* writing to me from the dead, well, the reason why is obvious, isn't it? To come back to life, to be validated by the living. If she's someone right here or if she's me, well, it's pretty much the same thing, really, isn't it?

I write your name, Dan, and you're alive, at least for an instant. It's all about defying the Void. Zoë calls me every other day to make sure I haven't fallen into it. Look at all those people with cell phones pressed to their heads talking and listening, leaving messages on answering machines. The "In Search Of" ads in the back pages of magazines, the book club, the search for Lally Evans – they're all the same, Dan, aren't they? To feel invisible bonds tugging at us, helping us believe we can withstand that overwhelming cosmic loneliness, this *vita terribilis*.

I said a while ago that this stage of grieving feels like I'm dragging a heavy suitcase down a long, dark corridor. What if the suitcase is really empty, and it only *feels* heavy? And the corridor really leads nowhere at all, except in a circle, and it's not long, it's just that my steps are so slow? Or that it's not dark at all, but my eyes, dazzled by some impossibly bright light, are shut or burned into blindness? Am I going mad, Dan? Is that what this stage of grieving is about?

Your Dee

P.S. What do you make of Bathsua's alluding so coyly to Whitman? "Might we not each, then, be multitudes?" she asked. You noticed that, too, didn't you?

P.P.S. And Bathsua's voice, Dan, whose is it? Have you heard it before?

⚊ *Five* ⚊

Subject: Good morning, darling
Date: 11/1/2002 7:32:42 A.M. EST
From: dndyoung2@owl.com
To: dndyoung1@owl.com

Darling,

Another Halloween, Thanksgiving soon. Everything done for the first time without you is an agony. If I stop doing the old, familiar things and only do what I've never done before, will the misery go away? But if I don't do what's old and familiar, won't I stop being me? Won't I forget you?

Zoë invited me on a trip to Paris next month, just the two of us. I'm afraid to go. I can't imagine Thanksgiving or Paris without you.

Somebody in the MYOPIA Book Club proposed we read *Anna Karenina* over the winter, but I'm even afraid of reading books I read with you near me. The past colors everything. I'll be reading along and remember how I read it the last time, nestled, nested beside you in bed or toes touching on opposite ends of the sofa. I'm afraid tears will come the way they did all those years ago when you read me the horse racing chapter.

This is terrible. Does it mean I can't read the books we loved? How do I give up Paris? And springtime? Should I move out of this house with you in it everywhere? And give up waking up in the morning?

Love,

D

Subject: Better now
Date: 11/2/2002 3:37:48 A.M. EST
From: dndyoung2@owl.com
To: dndyoung1@owl.com

Darling,

The book club decided to read Paul Auster's *New York Trilogy* instead. Your copy is on the shelf behind your desk. We didn't read it together, so maybe I'll be okay. Unless you wrote notes in the margins. We'll have Thanksgiving dinner at Zo and Jack's. Agreed to go with her to Paris over New Years. I'll keep the house, do my best to wake up every morning. But I've switched my place at the breakfast table and have breakfast *after* I get dressed, not before.

Love.

November 4, 2002

> If our last decade or two of collapsing assumptions has been a period
> of unusual discomfort, it is reassuring to know that the human species
> has lived through worse before.
>   – Barbara Tuchman. *A Distant Mirror.*

Dear Mistress Makin,

Your last letter and story were bright spots in a dark week. Reading "Far Above Rubies" several times reassured me that women are strong and resourceful. And I loved the story-within-the-story's bright sunshine and the intimate conversation of mothers and daughters. Thank you.

You're interested in my folding glasses and modern clothes, yet you write with those old-fashioned conventions, the "y^e's" and such. In exchange for your writing in modern style, I'd be happy to buy you the glasses and a pair of trousers, but for now I'll live in my world, you in yours. Let's leave it at that.

Warm regards,

Dee

Guy Fawkes Day 2002

> He wept the flames of what he loved so well,
> And what so well had merited his love.
> — John Dryden. *Annus Mirabilis.*

My dear Friend,

This letter, I hope, finds you in good Health & better Spirits. I am gratified y^t you found comfort in my last story. No need, of course, to leave anything but Letters & Stories on our shelf. I mention'd my interest in your clothes & glasses merely in jest, my dear.

This day commemorates ye fail'd 1605 Plot to explode ye Houses of Parliament. Night Fires reddening ye Sky to ye Colour of Blood are ye stuff of my Nightmares. In ye story I am composing, I shall tell of such a Sky. It did not drip real blood, but y^t is my recurring Nightmare.

Your obedient servant,

Bathsua Reginald Makin

November 6, 2002

> We enter upon a stage which we did not design, and we find ourselves
> part of an action that was not of our making.
> — Alasdair MacIntyre. *After Virtue: A Study of Moral Theory.*

Dear Mistress Makin,

Good to hear from you. I am working on another story in memory of my mother. Concentrating is difficult because of daily terrorism alerts and war-readiness bulletins. Thankfully, the snipers who terrorized the metro area last month (don't ask – just have a look at the back issues of the *Washington* Post) have been arrested and taken into custody pending trial. I try to ignore the news, but it inevitably intrudes. How did – do – you remain calm in the face of night terrors?

Gratefully yours,

Dee

November 7, 2002

September 2, 1666. The Lord's Day. Poor people staying in their houses as long as till ye very fire touched them, & then running into boats, or clambering from one pair of stairs by ye water-side to another. And among other things, ye poor pigeons, I perceive, were loth to leave their houses, but hovered about ye windows & balconys, till they burned their wings, & fell down. . . . We were in great trouble & disturbance at this fire, not knowing what to think of it. However, we had an extraordinary good dinner, & as merry as at this time we could be.

September 4. This night Mrs. Turner (who, poor woman, was removing her goods all this day into ye garden, & knows not how to dispose of them) & her husband supped with my wife & me at night, in ye office, upon a shoulder of mutton from ye cook's, without any napkin, or any thing, in a sad manner, but were merry. Walking into ye garden, saw how horribly ye sky looks, all on a fire in ye night. It was enough to put us out of our wits; indeed, it was extremely dreadfull, for it looks just as if it was at us, & ye whole heaven on fire. I after supper walked in ye dark down to Tower-street, & there saw it all on fire, at y^t Trinity House on y^t side, & ye Dolphin Tavern on this side, which was very near us, ye fire with extraordinary vehemence.

7th. Up by five o'clock; and, blessed be God! find all well; and by water to Pane's Wharfe. Walked thence, and saw all ye towne burned, a miserable sight of Paul's church, with all ye roofs fallen, and ye body of ye quire fallen into St. Fayth's; Paul's school also, Ludgate, and Fleet-street. My father's house, and ye church, and a good part of ye Temple ye like.

— *Samuel Pepys's Diary.*

My dear,

How to remain calm in ye Face of Terror? Consider my contemporary Samuel Pepys's Example on ye nights of ye Great Fire. While no Philosopher, he offer'd wise Counsel for times of Trouble & Grief: Bear witness to ye Suffering & Courage of others, admit the possibility of ye Lord's Hand in all things, enjoy your dinner, & be as merry as you can be. And remember: John Dryden, ye great Poet of my century call'd y^t time *Annus Mirabilis,* a Year of Wonders, not *Annus Horribilis,* a Year of Horrors. Keep your eye on ye Wonders.

As ever, faithfully yours,

Bathsua M.

Subject: Bathsua's helping
Date: 11/7/2002 23:42:12 PM EST
From: dndyoung2@owl.com
To: dndyoung1@owl.com

Dearest Dan,

Remember how, on winter afternoons, I used to sit in that pool of sunshine in my classroom after my last class, hoping the light would ease my winter blues? Seasonal Affective Disorder, they call it, *sad* for short. How clever. I seem to have found a new pool of sunshine, darling. Bathsua's letters. She writes back, even if you don't.

Love.

November 15, 2002

> She lives in you and in me, and in many other women who are not here tonight, for they are washing up the dishes and putting the children to bed.
> – Virginia Woolf. *A Room of One's Own.*

Dear Mistress Makin,

Your advice and Sam Pepys's help chase away the gloom. Thank you. So do sunshine and exercise. Today I also have another mood brightener – putting final touches on the enclosed story for you. I walked for a bit this morning in the bright, brisk sunshine and now, in blue jeans and tennis shoes, a faded turtleneck and my husband's old sweater, am at his desk finishing this second story about my mother.

I've written in the first person again, but understand, please, that the "I" in the story isn't really me. Almost but not quite. "Lee" tells this story. My Zoë is the story's Livvie. The reason for my mother's grief and anger lies hidden behind the fictional "Uncle Rob." You could say I'm mixing lies, obfuscations, and truth. That's what fiction writers do. Writing lifts a veil, a weighted, freighted veil, from my eyes.

Dee

Enclosure: "Inconsolable"

Inconsolable

My mother was a part-time *lamed-vovnik*. Aren't we all?
My mother was someone who was born and gave birth and died.
– S.L. Wisenberg. "Sheets."

"Can I have Grandma's pearls? I know they're fake, but I'd like to. . ."

I watch Livvie lift my mother's triple-stranded choker of artificial pearls from the tangle of costume jewelry on the kitchen table. Last week, the day of the funeral, my father gave me all Mom's jewelry, the fake pearls and base-metal pins encrusted with bits of glass and pasteware, as well as the platinum-and-diamond heart pendant and opal necklace, the pear-shaped diamond ring, all tidily sorted in little compartments of an old cardboard candy box that still smelled of my mother's dresser drawers. Later, packing for the flight home from Providence to DC, I dumped the lot into a plastic bag, threw the box into the trash, and stuffed the bag into my suitcase. All but the diamond ring, which I put on my own finger, turning the stone inward and squeezing my hand into a fist so I felt the tear-shaped stone's point imprint itself on my palm. Feel a little pain, Lee, I said to myself. Everyday, feel a little of it.

"Of course, Livvie." Often when she was little I glimpsed my daughter going through my jewelry. Dreamily holding a necklace to her throat and mildly gazing into the mirror, she looked like a young woman in a Vermeer painting. Now, in her last semester of high school, Livvie has put aside her own small cache of necklaces and earrings, preferring instead fray-cuffed jeans and her dad's old plaid shirts worn over faded tees.

"Of course," I repeat. "They're all yours if you want them." One day I will remove from my hand Mom's ring with its tear-shaped diamond and sell it for thirty-six dollars, לו, *lamed vov* in Hebrew numerology, to the man Livvie chooses to marry. To conduct the sale in a multiple of eighteen, חי, *chai,* is to give life, the ultimate Jewish Ur-gift. Sell it, not give it, so the formal little transaction will redeem the ring from Mom's sadness and anger, so that this meaning of לו, double חי, double life, will cancel out the other meaning of it, the mad-saintliness that I fear could pass through me to my daughter.

Livvie smiles at me, oblivious to the weight of my memory.

—⁓—

I lay reading on the glider swing on the tree-shaded back porch of my parents' house. It was a lazy, sun-dappled June afternoon. I had just finished junior-year college examinations and felt both guilt and entitlement for lolling about, reading novels for a few days before starting my summer job in the factory where my father worked. The job was beneath me, I believed. My classmates all had internships in Washington or office or lab jobs. Or they were traveling in Europe at their parents' expense. What a waste of my fine education, I grumped, working for minimum wage all summer. It was horribly depressing. At least reading fiction was an escape.

In the kitchen Mom was humming a tremolo soprano line of harmonic-minor improvisation. Sounds of running water and opening and closing cupboard doors meant that, as usual, she was spending the entire day making dinner, interrupting each stage of preparation to tidy the counter and wash, dry, and put away every utensil she used in the process. I imagined her profile, those beautiful, chiseled features facing the kitchen window and the blooming hydrangeas beyond. She had planted them herself, to hedge in some peace of mind against her sadness.

What a relief, I thought, from how it had been all winter and spring, when Mom had phoned me in the dorm every day after breakfast, crying about the *insanity*, the *horror* of her baby brother's approaching – *impending*, as she put it – marriage. In October my Uncle Rob had met and fallen hard for a beautiful, incomprehensibly competent blond. He proposed in December, then called home to announce that he and Clare were getting married in the spring. Through Mom's gasping tears at eight o'clock every morning from January through March, I listened to *what a terrible mistake Robby was making*: Her brilliant, handsome baby brother was marrying for love – *for love! what is love but an illusion? Wasn't he deserting her just as her own mother had left her high and dry by dying last summer?* Couldn't he see *the insanity! the horror! the unbearable waste!* of it all? My college friends sidled past my room as I sat there, silent, listening to my mother scream and weep about the *horrible mistake* Robby was making. *He's throwing his life away, letting lust trump reason!* I was mortified, certain everyone could hear the screaming through the telephone line. The phone receiver painfully pressed against my ear, I tried to capture in my skull the sound of the ranting so none of it seeped into the hallway.

I tried murmuring something comforting to her – "Clare's so smart, so capable," I heard myself saying. "She's so beautiful and resourceful."

I knew Mom didn't care. She was too convinced by the overwhelming evidence of her own inner narrative, too full of her own grief, to see anything but *the insanity! the horror!* of what Uncle Rob was doing.

"What does he know about love?"

"He's old enough and smart enough to make up his mind on this, Mom. They'll be fine. Uncle Rob will be fine. You'll see." I mouthed the words.

"What does he know about life? What does he know about her? Throwing everything — everything! — away for her! Marrying her! Marrying!" She spit the words into the telephone. They impacted my skull, painful bursts of static, little insulting ions of contagious hatred.

Somehow we got through the wedding. I returned to campus for spring classes and got a part-time job in the college library. Having to be at work early each morning before classes, I could avoid most of my mother's phone calls.

My favorite class that semester was the Milton Seminar. Professor Dean's white curls, moist blue eyes, and doughy softness belied how demanding she was. She had foresworn marriage, the rumor had it, choosing instead to care for her aging parents until they died, at nearly a hundred, both of them, leaving her, now in her seventies, alone. I couldn't put out of my mind her little introduction to our study of *Paradise Lost.* "This is the tale of our grand parents," she had said, paraphrasing Milton. "As with our own parents, we begin by loving them wholeheartedly. Then, suddenly, they seem to be stripped of what we had loved them for, and we despise them wholeheartedly." She took a deep breath and looked significantly over her glasses at us seated around the seminar table, her eyes a little more watery than usual. "Then one day," she continued, "suddenly our eyesight changes. We see them in a new light. We understand them, also wholeheartedly. We feel for them. Pitying them, we love them for what we now know they have endured, perhaps in loving us. And that is the subject of Milton's *Paradise Lost.* Open to page one."

I turned from the sounds of Mom's humming and fussing in the kitchen to the book I had set aside for this week in June, the gift Uncle Rob gave me before his wedding. The new translation of André Schwarz-Bart's *Le dernier des Justes, The Last of the Just,* was an odd bridesmaid's gift, but typical of my bookish uncle. In the sweet early-summer sunshine, I cracked the binding and started to read.

Suddenly I was chilled to the bone. The Holocaust – along with cancer, war, and the end of love – was a topic my parents had carefully avoided when I was a kid. Such things were best never mentioned, lest they rise up and waken our nightmare demons, come alive to torture and kill us.

One paragraph caught me up short. It answered a question I had never dared to ask:

> According to tradition, the world reposes upon thirty-six Just Men, the *Lamed-Vov*, indistinguishable from simple mortals; often they are unaware of their station. But if just one of them were lacking, the sufferings of mankind would poison even the souls of the newborn, and humanity would suffocate with a single cry. For the Lamed-Vov are the hearts of the world multiplied, and into them, as into one receptacle, pour all our grief. . . . When one of the Just rises to Heaven, a Hasidic story goes, he is so frozen that God must warm him for a thousand years between His fingers before his soul can open itself to Paradise. Some remain forever inconsolable at human woe, so that even God Himself cannot warm them.

There lazing on the screened porch, for the first time I understood my mother's harmonic-minor humming, that tear-burdened raised seventh degree of the minor scale. Suddenly I grasped the cause of the unquenchable sadness when she sang, even when she laughed, the melancholy of her gaze out the window at the blue, blue hydrangeas, the press of her palms against the edge of the kitchen sink. Here it was, the intensely private explanation of the secret never spoken aloud or in private: My mother, so strong and beautiful, whose melodies were the soundtrack of my childhood, who loved me so exclusively and possessively – she was one of the Thirty-Six! I had just learned the word *Weltschmerz* in a modern philosophy course, and here I was with my very own *lamed-vovnik* who, indistinguishable from mere mortals and unaware of her station, bore the world's pain that would otherwise agonize the souls even of the newborn! Without Mom's sadness, humanity in general – and I in particular – would suffocate with a single cry! She was the receptacle into which poured all the grief of those who, like me, could laugh and sing in major keys, like Uncle Rob could fall in love, without the fierce ownership of the world's everlasting pain! On the porch reading Schwarz-Bart I suddenly saw myself passing through the stages Professor Dean had spoken of, stepping across the magic threshold to adulthood.

Later that summer, although at first she tried to hide it, Mom told me she was taking valium and librium, *to calm the nerves, make life less of a miserable burden.* She stopped railing against the *injustice of it all,* stopped crying at *having sacrificed every possibility for happiness for the sake of others.* Instead she slept through the August afternoons, the house quiet, the air soft, a breeze ruffling the starched curtains.

Sleep was a relief at first. Later, after I returned to college for senior year, Mom told me she decided to go off the drugs. The little tablets numbed her, she said, putting her into fogs that lifted only to leave her as grief-stricken, or more so, than before. Better to live the *Weltschmerz,* although she didn't know the word for it.

─⚹─

Driving to the airport after my mother's funeral, I told Livvie my *lamed-vovnik* theory. "What I remember most of all about your Grandma," I said to her, staring at the highway ahead of us, "was the sound of weeping within her laughter." Livvie gave me a quick glance. Then her profile was silhouetted against the moving image of tidal marshlands and low hillocks of scrub pines beyond the passenger-side window. I recognized that I didn't feel grief at Mom's death, unless grief was only an emptiness. Looking toward Livvie, seeing her tender profile, pale and beautiful in its emotional impressionability, I caught myself. Oh, God, no, I thought. Am I a conduit through which passes the soul of a *lamed vovnik* from one generation to the next?

─⚹─

A week has passed since Mom's funeral. We've finished sitting *Shiva,* the traditional week of Jewish mourning. Livvie has finally gone out with her friends. The house is quiet. I am alone with my journal. There are things I have to write down so I won't forget:

Oh, my Mother, how must it have felt to have Love and Pain, Beauty and Anger so exquisitely intertwined? I see the mad-saintly in you. When I play the piano, even Chopin, I cannot for the life of me get the *Weltschmerz* into the musical line. Why do I wear this hard little shell, this carapace, around my heart? Is it your gift to me, Mom? Why were you transfixed by the world's pain, while I, thin on feeling, emotionally like weak broth, muddle along through life's minutiae, spared of it? Or will I eventually become like you, or worse, not? In your rages, you used what I now know is the ultimate, universal lamed vovnik's Ur-cry to the young. Your beautiful, strong hands frozen in a gesture of despair, your once-beautiful face contorted in suffering, you poured out your grief against an unjust world: *"How can you – how dare you – turn your back on me? How can you do this to me, after all I have borne for you?"*

November 21, 2002

Dear Dorothea,

Though we do not see each other face to face, we do, even in our Silences between Letters, see into each other's Hearts. Sometimes Silence is profounder than Speech.

Your humble Servant,

Bathsua M.

November 21, 2002

Dear Bathsua,

Thank you. I agree: we imagine each other's responses without the burden of explaining them. When I was teaching, writing comments on every student's paper became a heavy burden of responsibility. How could I strike just the right balance of approval and suggestion for improvement? It's a relief just to read and consider, without the obligation of responding.

Thank you for calling me Dorothea.

Yours sincerely,

Dee

Subject: Thanksgiving Day
Date: 11/28/2002 11:51:27 A.M. EST
From: dndyoung2@owl.com
To: dndyoung1@owl.com

Dearest,

Just heard something on the radio about President Lincoln's official proclamation of Thanksgiving, so I googled it. It sounds like Samuel Pepys's advice that Bathsua sent me. Even in dark days, we have to celebrate the "blessings of fruitful fields and healthful skies, . . . bounties which are so constantly enjoyed that we are prone to forget the source from which they come." I picture you, Sam, Bathsua, and Abe all gathered at a table in friendly conversation, on a first-name basis, sharing a holiday meal together. Is that what you're doing today?

I'm on my way in a minute to Zoë and Jack's. So glad we decided to postpone the trip to Paris for a month and to stay here in DC instead of going to the cabin in Maine. I don't think I was ready for either.

The children are in charge of the preparations, with Zoë and me just consulting. Adorable. Just got off the phone with Jack. He says he wants me to go for a walk with him on the Capitol Crescent Trail while Zoë and the children consult. A walk with Jack means a talk with Jack without Zo. I know what it's going to be about: He's got ideas about what to do with your things. Probably planning to do the sorting while Zo and I are in Paris. Can't decide if I'm grateful or angry. Either way, I have to admit I have much to be thankful for: Love above all. Angry though I am at Whoever it is Who has taken you from me, I am grateful to that mysterious Power Who has given me this dear family and this correspondence with you.

Love,

Your Dee

PS. I found your copy of Cavafy poems last night. Remember these lines from "Waiting for the Barbarians"? They pretty much sum up my present state of mind:

> Why this sudden restlessness, this confusion?
> (How serious people's faces have become.)
> Why are the streets and squares emptying so rapidly,
> Everyone going home so lost in thought?

Want me to track down the original Greek for you at the Library, so you can have the fun of working out the translation for yourself?

November 30, 2002
Dear Dorothea,

I know you will not find this Letter & its accompanying Story until next week, when you return to ye Library after your Holiday. Suffice to say in advance of your reading "In My Mind's Eye: Y^e Sky," I am most attach'd to it. I am glad we agreed not to comment on each other's work. 'Tis simpler for both our Writing & our Reading.

Your humble servant & friend,

Bathsua M.

Enclos'd: "In My Mind's Eye: Y^e Sky"

In My Mind's Eye: Y^e Sky

'Tis all in pieces, all coherence gone.
— John Donne. "An Anatomy of ye World. Y^e First Anniversary."

September ye 20th.
Dear Kitty,

Papa tuck'd us in bed. I've been sky watching while Itha sleeps. 'Tis all aglow over Saint Botolph's & Bedlam, alongside Bishopsgate. A glowing sky perchance bodes ill. I'm afraid of another bad dream. Mama says I'm silly. She says bad dreams aren't Heav'n-sent, & only silly billies believe ye Sky foretells ye Future. She says ye Sky holds wonderful Stories from antient Imaginings.

I cannot see Saint Botolph's Steeple from my window, nor hear ye Madmen moaning at Bedlam. I can imagine them in my mind. I hear birds cooing. Mama says they're mourning doves – not morning doves, doves of morning – but doves that moan like ye sad, mad folk in Bedlam. Maybe they moan because they've lost their little chicks to prowling cats. I've nam'd you Kitty, but not for a minute do I think you snatch little Nestlings. No, not you. You are my everlasting imaginary Friend. I tell you whatever comes into my mind, Stories I make up for myself & ones Mama tells. I'll tell you my Dreams if I remember them, & my Fears, too.

Soon yᵉ Sky will be inky black.

Most sincerely yours,

Bathsua R.

September yᵉ 21ˢᵗ.

Dear Kitty,

When yᵉ Sky gets too dark I shall stop writing. Then I'll look for Star Families. Papa pointed some out to Itha & me last week when we walk'd out beyond Saint Botolph's & Bedlam. We left Mama at home with Baby. Papa pointed out seven stars in Ursa Major, yᵉ Big Bear. He drew imaginary lines between them. I think they look more like their other name, yᵉ Big Dipper. Names are odd things.

Up in Ursa Major is a blur of Starlight. Papa call'd it a Comet. I can see its bright little Head – Papa call'd it its Comma – & its smudgy Tail. Papa said it's an *Ephemeron*. He show'd me how to write yᵉ word in Greek. I'm tracing yᵉ Letters in my palm now. Papa said I should, to practice spelling it in Greek: *το ἐφήμερον*. He said 'tis something with a very short Life. "An Ephemeron doesn't last," he said. "It comes all of a sudden, then disappears in a few days or weeks. But yᵉ Stars," he said, "last forever."

Your friend,

Bathsua R.

September yᵉ 23ʳᵈ.

Dear Kitty,

Last night Papa took us walking again to look at yᵉ Comet. He knelt down. Itha & I stood together in yᵉ snug space between his knees. Itha scratch'd & mumbl'd. I love being with Papa, looking skyward & list'ning to his soft nighttime Voice. He talk'd to us both, but only I listen'd. Ita's eyes kept closing. "Just another minute, my Dears," he said, "before we go back to your Mama." He patted my shoulder. "Stars seem to move all together across yᵉ Sky night after night," he said in his Teacher Voice, yᵉ one he uses in his Classroom, where I listen sometimes. "But 'tis we here on Earth who move. Yᵉ Stars seem to stay together in little Families, but really they're far apart from one another. Y^e Comet comes & goes among them, all alone."

Stars stay together in little Families, Papa said. Like our family: Mama & Papa, Itha & me. Now Baby makes us five. She's not christen'd yet. Mama says 'tis bad luck to say Baby's name aloud 'til 'tis set at her Christening. I heard Mama & Papa whispering, & I know what they will call her. But I mustn't set it down in Writing. So I shan't tell you, Kitty, even though I want to. If I speak Words, they come & go, like ye Comet does. But if I write them down, they're fix'd, like Stars. Where do Words go once they're spoken? Where does ye Comet go when we can no longer see it? Where do we go when we die? Yours most sincerely,

Bathsua R.

September ye 24th.

Dear Kitty,

When we look'd at ye Stars, Papa, & Itha & me, Mama stay'd home with Baby. Papa's Voice was low & soft, as if he were telling us Secrets. He pointed out Ursa Major again, his Hand right there beside my ear. He drew invisible lines again from Star to Star with his pointer finger. "Now you'll always make out Ursa Major, Batty," he said. "Look for ye big Water Dipper, even when 'tis in a different place in ye Sky than 'tis tonight. But ye smidge of Light, the Comet, will last only a few more Days or Weeks & then disappear." Yours most sincerely,

Bathsua R.

September ye 25th.

Dear Kitty,

We went Sky-Watching again last night. Papa held my hand when we rush'd past Bedlam. Moaning came from ye open windows. "Some call daft those who try to understand ye mysteries of ye sky, Batty," Papa said. "Y^e wise ones are those who look at Moon & Stars with special Eye Pieces & make careful Reckonings of ye Positions of Ephemera like this Comet, night by night. One day we'll understand them, their comings & goings, what they're made of. Those who believe ye Sky foretells Disaster here on Earth are daft, I think." There was a chill in Papa's voice. He carried Itha. Her hair was flung out across his shoulder like ye thready Tail of ye Comet. "Stars, ye Moon, & y^e

Ephemera too, they're just Matter & Light far, far away. They're unaware of our little comings & goings. Others will prove them so, I'm certain."

I wanted Papa to keep talking in his secret-y Voice, but we had reach'd our door. Mama's Shadow was dark against ye bright Hearthlight. She was stooping, one hand press'd to her back. When she heard us at ye door she straighten'd & smil'd. Papa push'd me softly in toward her, but she turn'd away again toward ye Cradle beside ye hearth. I couldn't see her face. Papa carried Itha up to our attic room. I follow'd.

'Tis nearly dark now. Itha is sleeping while I write & look out our window. She has curl'd herself into a little ball, then suddenly flings her arms & legs away from her center.

Since Papa explain'd ye Comet & showed us Ursa Major, I've hoped for cloudless nights. I hurry to bed instead of dawdling after supper or gawking at Moll, ye harelipp'd neighbour girl. Papa ask'd her to help tidy up while Mama's busy with Baby. I love looking out my window at ye night Sky & tracing ye shape of Ursa Major. I see ye smudge of Light, τό ἐφήμερον.

Your friend forever,

Batty

September ye 26th.

Dear Kitty,

Y^e sky is full of Clouds & Rain today. There'll be no stars tonight. Moll's been minding Itha all day long. I don't need minding. I'll gladly sit in ye doorway to Papa's Schoolroom & listen to ye boys doing lessons. Papa leaves ye door open a crack for me, even with ye draughty wind. I like to hear their voices. Papa hushes them when they all talk at once. His voice is loud & stern, not how it sounds when he teaches me.

Moll is plaiting Itha's hair. She keeps glancing at ye stairs & tilts her head to hear if Mama's calling. Mama & Baby haven't come down to ye kitchen today. Y^e Sky is dark. Y^e linden tree between our house & ye Church is shaking its leaves. Y^e new mouser, Kit, is nowhere to be seen. The songbird in ye cage beside ye kitchen door must think it evening. Its little head is tuck'd under its wing.

I will practice declining τό ἐφήμερον ye way Papa's teaching ye boys. I like how ye word looks on ye chalkboard Papa gave me. 'Tis like ye ones ye schoolboys use, only smaller. Papa says ἐφήμερον's like any other second declension neuter Noun, perfect for grammar practice.

Your friend,
Batty

September yᵉ 27ᵗʰ.
Dear Kitty,

Rain again. Papa says we mustn't postpone yᵉ Christening. Baby isn't well. Mama's kept to her room again today. I hear her singing. Her Voice is low & sad. She rocks in her chair to keep time. Yᵉ floorboards squeak.

I've just put seven raisins on yᵉ table in yᵉ shape of Ursa Major. I'll use a wee feather for yᵉ Comet, τό ἐφήμερον. When Moll finishes helping Mama, I'll teach her what Papa taught me about yᵉ Comet & Stars.

Your friend,
Bathsua R.

September yᵉ 28ᵗʰ.
Dear Kitty,

There was a big Storm late yesterday, with Rain & Wind & Thunder. Afterward 'twas dark, but clear. Papa took me out to stargaze, just yᵉ two of us. Itha stay'd home with Moll.

"Yᵉ Comet has mov'd a bit," Papa said, "relative to the Stars. Tonight let's look for yᵉ Star that never moves." He pointed alongside Ursa Major toward a bright, blue-white Star. Papa call'd it Polaris. That means it marks true North. Then he show'd me yᵉ giant upside-down W he call'd Cassiopeia, yᵉ Lady in yᵉ chair, beyond it. Polaris is constant, he said, never moving in yᵉ Sky like other Stars do. It guides Sailors & Travellers on their journeys. "Yᵉ other Stars seem to wheel around it," Papa said. A Star," he said, "is a Sun like our Sun. But 'tis so far away it looks to our eyes like a pure point of Light." I don't understand.

Polaris has three names. Even with three names it's only one star. 'Tis yᵉ Pole Star in English, *Stella Polaris* in Latin, and *Alpha Ursae Minoris* in what Papa calls macaronic Greek-Latin. Ursa Minor is yᵉ Little Cub beside yᵉ Mama Bear. Then Papa show'd me Arcturus, a bright golden Star on yᵉ other side of Ursa Major from yᵉ Pole Star. "Arcturus means Bear Watcher," Papa said. "It stands guard over Ursa Major and Ursa Minor."

I remember Papa's words exactly & how he said them. "Yᵉ Comet's ephemeral, Batty. It will go just as mysteriously as it came." He smooth'd my hair. "But Arcturus, ye Bear Watcher, & Ursa Major & Ursa Minor, & Polaris, they are always & forever." His Voice caught, like a sleeve on tree bark. "And Polaris, Batty, will guide your coming & going, now & always. Let's walk home, my child, to your sisters & your mother." We turn'd & walk'd, Papa & I, Arcturus & Polaris right behind us. I felt them there behind my head, steady & unflinching, one golden bright, ye other a sharp point of blue-white Light. Itha was asleep when I climb'd into bed. Mama & Papa talk'd in ye room next to ours, Papa mostly. Mama's voice was softer. She spoke only now and then.

Your friend forever,

Bathsua R.

P.S. Moll says Comets foretell bad things, especially when there's Thunder, Wind, & Lightning. Despite what Papa says, I'm afraid I'll have bad Dreams.

September ye 29th.

Dear Kitty,

Papa says Moll is wrong. He says ye Future isn't written in ye Stars. Old Stories are. One reason to learn Latin, he says, is to read ye old Stories. At bedtime tonight he told us ye Story of Ursa Major & Ursa Minor. Callisto was a beautiful Nymph. Zeus, King of ye Gods, fell in love with her. She had his baby, Arcas. But Hera, Zeus's wife & Queen of ye Gods, heard about Callisto & Arcas. She was very jealous & angry. Hera turn'd Callisto into a Bear & sent her away into ye Wilderness. When Arcas was grown, he became a Huntsman. One day he happen'd upon Callisto. She was still a bear. He didn't know she was his Mother, & he kill'd her. Zeus was very sorry. He took pity on them, Mother & Son, & placed them in ye Sky as two Constellations, where they live forever, side by side.

Y^e story is terrible & beautiful, & I love it. I can tell it over & over to myself when I look at ye Stars. If Itha didn't fall asleep ye minute her head hits the pillow, she might like it, too.

Mama us'd to tell us Stories when she put us to bed. Now I tell them to myself.

Your friend,

Bathsua R.

30th September, ye Lord's Day.

Dear Kitty,

Papa's taking Itha & me to Church today. We must pray hard for Mama & Baby. Stormy weather, with Wind & Thunder & spits of Rain. Maybe Moll is right, that Wind & Weather & Stars know ye Will of God. If they do, perhaps I should pray to them, too?

Yours truly,

Bathsua R.

October ye 1st.

Dear Kitty,

Itha's catterwalling. Our songbird's dead. I left ye cage door open when I fed her. Our mouser Kit kill'd her. He left her on ye floor beside Mama's chair. Papa's cross because our commotion disturb'd his class. Moll's rushing up & down to Mama's room with basins & towels. She's muttering under her breath.

Your friend,

Batty

October ye 2nd.

Dear Kitty,

Mama is still upstairs, moaning & rocking in her chair. Papa took Baby to Saint Andrews this morning. I watch'd him go.

When Papa came home he gave Baby to Moll. "Her name is Anna now," he said. "Take her up to her mother." His voice sounded strange again, like a sleeve rubbing on tree bark. He turn'd to Itha & me & knelt down beside us. He press'd us so hard I could scarcely breathe.

I'll probably have my Nightmare tonight. In it ye Comet turns to Blood & pours down red from Ursa Major & Polaris & Ursa Minor. Then ye whole Sky glows red, & it pours down onto Bishopsgate & Saint Mary Axe Street. When ye Blood starts to touch Saint Andrew's Steeple, I always wake up.

Your friend,

Bathsua R.

October ye 3rd.

Dear Kitty,

Mama's weeping & rocking upstairs. Papa was with her, then he clos'd her door & came downstairs. Baby Anna is dead, he said. Now he's gone to Saint Andrews to see about her Burying. I wish you were real, Kitty.

B. R.

October ye 5th.

Dear Kitty,

There's a full Moon tonight. I watch'd it for a long time above ye rooftops. Itha's curl'd up against my back, snoring. Now & again she squirms & lets out a little mewing sound, then sighs & settles against me. Often I mind her pushing against me. I don't mind so much tonight.

Mama came down from her room this morning when Papa took Anna to Saint Andrews. Mama sat in her chair under ye empty bird cage.

"Run, Batty. Get your Lesson Book," she said.

I could barely hear her. "Get your Lesson Book, Batty," she said again. Her words gladden'd me. But it was a strange kind of Gladness that wasn't glad through and through. I cannot explain. I went to my corner beside Papa's Classroom & found my Book.

"Come here, chick," she said. I stood close by her.

Itha was teasing Kit with a bit of string. Mama put one hand on my Book, ye other on my shoulder. "Read to me. Show me how you read." She look'd down at ye Book in my hands, & I read to her. When I glanced out ye open door, I saw Papa standing in ye Churchyard in ye Rector's arms. I never saw Papa weep before. We are four little Points again, I thought, Mama & Papa & Itha & me. Like ye four Stars on ye Big Dipper, but without ye Handle. Baby Anna has gone somewhere else. She was our very own ἐφήμερον & now she's gone from us. I can make neither head nor tail of what I was thinking. Papa walk'd toward us, his head downcast at first. But he look'd up & saw us, Itha with Kit & Mama & me with my Lesson Book. He gave a funny close look as he enter'd.

Your friend,

Batty R.

October ye 14th.

Dear Kitty,

I look'd for ye Comet last night. I look'd all about, in Ursa Major, near Arcturus & in Ursa Minor & Cassiopeia, too. I squeez'd my eyes shut, so tight they stung hot & wet. I thought I saw a faint Smudge on Cassiopeia's lap. But 'twas only a fancy.

I ask'd Mama for a Story at bedtime. I ask'd for ye story of Cassiopeia, ye Lady in ye chair. She smil'd a little & said, "Perhaps tomorrow."
Your friend forever,
Bathsua R.

October ye 15th.
Dear Kitty,

No Stories last night or tonight. Mama's ill. No Stars. Y^e Sky is murky.
As ever,
B.R.

October ye 21st, 1607.
Dear Kitty,

A stony grey Sky. Mama has died, Papa said. But Mama had promis'd us Cassiopeia's story, I said, & now there's no time for it. By & by, he said.
Faithfully yours,
Bathsua R.

All Hallows Day.
Dear Kitty,

Moll said yesterday that Spirits would walk abroad last night. I had ye bleeding Star Nightmare again & woke screaming. Papa held me & rock'd me 'til it stopp'd. In Church today I pray'd for all ye Souls departed from us. Mama & Baby Anna especially.

At bedtime Papa told us ye Story of Cassiopeia. About her Beauty & Pride in her Daughter, & ye Gods' Punishment for Pride. Poseidon put them in ye Sky, Cassiopeia in an Ivory Throne & her daughter nearby but just below, so she could gaze down on her Daughter forever in ye night Sky. Papa said Poseidon forgave them & that's why they're in ye Sky together.

Even with such a bedtime Story I am afraid to close my eyes.
Your faithful friend,
Batty R.

November 4th.

Dear Kitty,

Last night I told Papa I'm afraid to fall asleep, lest I have my bad Dream again. He brought Mama's chair & put it near our bed. He said he'd read by candlelight there instead of downstairs. That way, he said, we could share ye Light as long as I needed it. Itha doesn't mind.

Yours faithfully,

Bathsua R.

November 6th.

Dear Kitty,

A red glowing Sky last night. Papa said it was Bonfires celebrating ye fail'd Plot against ye King & Parliament. Papa's reading near our bed. His candle glows on his book. He said I could write for a bit & then he'll read to us from ye book he's studying. It's call'd *Metamorphoses*, & 'tis about all things changing, he said. "'Tis in Latin, Batty," he said, "You won't understand, but ye sound of ye words will comfort you. They'll wash over you like clear white Starlight." That's exactly what he said.

Maybe I'll dream of Mama & Baby Anna tonight.

Your sleepy friend,

Bathsua Reginald

P.S. No bad Dreams for two nights straight.

Subject:	Am I betraying your trust?
Date:	11/30/2002 11:16:52 P.M. EST
From:	dndyoung2@owl.com
To:	dndyoung1@owl.com

Darling,

Last month Bathsua asked if I didn't think it was a betrayal of trust to use other people's secret stories to tell my own. I said no. Should I have your permission to tell our story in order to tell my own? I don't think so. But if telling you that I'm telling Bathsua the secrets we never spoke about will get a rise out of you sufficient to have you email me in reply, maybe it's worth it. Is that sentence grammatically complex enough for you, darling? Love.

— *Six* —

December 2, 2002

> To reconstruct is to collaborate with time gone by.
> – Marguerite Yourcenar. *Memoirs of Hadrian.*

Dear Bathsua,

How moving is your retelling of those momentous weeks of your childhood! Such depth of feeling! Sticklers for the "truth" might say that no seven year old could have written that way. Sticklers for the truth be damned!

Affectionately,

Dee

December 3, 2002

> And gladly wolde he lern and gladly teche.
> – Geoffrey Chaucer. General Prologue. *The Canterbury Tales.*

Dear Friend,

We said we wouldn't comment on each others' Stories, & yet you did, & with such Vehemence, against, of all people, Seekers of Truth. Why, I wonder. No need to answer.

I propose a new Direction. Perhaps it will calm you. Remember yᵉ early days of Teaching? Remember those days when you were new to your Classroom & new, too, to Love? I do. I work'd hard to concentrate on my Lessons, & yet, despite serious Intent, my Heart, otherwise occupied, interven'd. Let us carry ourselves back to those days, leaving moody thoughts behind. Let us free our Minds of Care & return to distant, happy Days.

Yours,

Bathsua

Post Scriptum. I shall try writing in your modern mode. 'Twill require some Discipline to write *y*'s as *the*'s, but I shall try.

Subject: Odds and Ends
Date: 12/4/2002 7:11:34 AM EST
From: dndyoung2@owl.com
To: dndyoung1@owl.com

Danny, dear,

I want to tell Bathsua what happened after Nate died. All of it. I won't wait for your permission. I'm used to your silence. In fact, the silences of our marriage are on my mind these days. We didn't talk about a lot of things. In fact, I'm saying more to you in these emails than I ever used to say aloud. Perhaps more to Bathsua, too?

Love,

Dee

December 4, 2002

Dear Bathsua,

Thank you for your suggestion. These days my mood is dark, and anger is close to the surface. I will write again when I am nicer to know.

Fondly,

Dee

December 7, 2002

> Suddenly the smell of a particular flower provides transport to a garden from one's childhood. . . . Memory is awakened, the world made whole, if only for a moment. But in that moment some sort of healing takes place, or so gardeners have believed for centuries.
> – Emily Herring Wilson. *Two Gardeners: A Friendship in Letters.*

Dear Bathsua,

I stopped by my old school yesterday to visit a former colleague and cast myself back into memories of the days when I first started teaching. It was my first trip back to Remington since Dan died. Being there felt odd – walking past my old classroom and Dan's, seeing the desks rearranged and occupied by students I didn't recognize. The sunlight peeping in through the windows was the same, though. An old morning symptom even returned – writhing stomach – plus a new one – a tightening sensation behind my eye sockets. I had to go outdoors for a gulp of fresh air.

I'm back in my study. The view of the garden out the window above Dan's desk – mine now – takes me back to those earlier, better times than did yesterday's visit to Remington. Stripped down to its essentials, the garden tells me things I've never spoken about. Even to Dan.

In the far corner is a Northern Spruce, its bluey-gray needles in tight, disciplined spikes. To the right is a White Pine, one soft-needled branch yielding meekly to the weight of a sparrow alighting on it. Dan and I planted the spruce and pine as tiny seedlings in the autumn of 1968. Zoë thinks we planted them to honor her sixth birthday. Dan thought they were our seventh wedding anniversary presents to each other. For me, planting them was our second memorial service for Nate. And symbolized a sea-change in our marriage.

Nate, our beautiful blond baby boy, died on December 27, 1967. Things fell apart, I guess you'd say, although Dan and I pretended they hadn't, for five-year-old Zoë's sake. We went through the motions of family life when school started up again after winter break. Every day Dan and Zoë drove off to school together. I took something right after they left, went back to bed and slept until noon. Then I got up and went to the market to buy ingredients for exactly one elaborate, time-consuming recipe that would take all afternoon to prepare. Dan and Zoë came home to the aromas of *canard à l'orange* or *boeuf bourgignonne*. I'd be in the midst of sewing a dress for Zoë, following a complicated pattern with smocking at the bodice, or knitting an elaborate fair-isle-patterned sweater with five, eight, ten bobbins of various colors bouncing at the back. I would help Zoë try them on, careful not to poke her with pins or knitting needles. At dinner there was small talk – *how was your day? what did you learn today? what did you teach?* In the wide seams in the conversation Dan and I looked at each other and saw only the mirror of each other's grief. We stopped making love. I lay in our bed as if it were my grave – limbs straight, cover up over my eyes, while Dan read until one or two. I'd waken to the light on, the newspaper strewn across his chest, the television blaring. We woke, in a stupor, and started each day again, no better wadded to the grieving.

By spring '68 we were afraid to talk of what was coming. The DC riots in April after Martin Luther King, Jr.'s assassination sealed the pact of the inevitable. I was offered a teaching job at the summer camp in Maine you used to go to as a kid. They let Zoë come along as a junior-junior camper. Dan got a fellowship to go to Prague to study the opening up of democracy there. (The Prague Spring, they called it.) The idea was to see how Dan and I would do apart. If it worked, he'd stay in Europe, and I'd take his teaching slot at Remington.

You know already it didn't work. Thank God. But how it didn't makes a story I'm ready to tell. The sight of those evergreens in the yard takes me back, as if you willed them to, to a time in the Maine woods that pulled me up out of that grave time, back into the light of our marriage.

Maybe the words to tell this story, long suppressed, will lift themselves suddenly onto the page, like a flock of birds nearly in unison rising silently from a field, not quite of their own mysterious volition, at some unknowable shared signal that causes the individuals to rise up all at once, whirl about, and head off together in a single direction, their wings beating the air in time as if to an invisible leader. I wonder what story you will write about those early days of teaching and loving. I imagine the two of us writing in a silent harmony, like two books beside one another on a shelf, bindings touching, or like two monks in a silent order, occasionally looking up and across the scriptorium, across slowly moving dust motes, which are energized, perhaps, by the movement of their pens.

Yours in trust,

Dee

December 10, 2002

> As plants in gardens excel those that grow wild, . . . so men by liberal education are much better'd.
> —Bathsua Makin. *An Essay to Revive y' Antient Education of Gentlewomen.*

My dear Dorothea,

The death of a child – I know it all too well. We have much in common. While there is much for us to share in this bitter subject, just now I prefer to look back on sunnier times.

Hence the story I am writing. In preparation, I've unearth'd a few old books from our library shelves. I have here on my desk an old copy of Doctor Lyly's *Grammar*, a volume of *Plato's Republic*, and a dusty copy of the Odes of Horace. To help me tell a story about my early days in my first classroom I need those old book friends.

Imagine looking out across another garden, the little churchyard that to this day lies behind Saint Andrew Undershaft along Saint Mary Axe Street. 'Tis late autumn 1616. I am sixteen years old, newly teaching in my father's schoolroom. Papa has just taken my little book, *Musa Virginea*, to present to King James, in hopes of persuading him to educate his daughters alongside his sons. Meanwhile all London is agog at the visitation of strange, wonderful travelers from the New World. That day, as if under some mysterious guardianship, I fell in love.

Yours most sincerely,

Bathsua

Enclosed: "Across a Distant Garden"

Across a Distant Garden

> Parmi necessario, otre a le altre circuspezioni, per mantenere et augmentare il grido di questi scoprimenti, il fare che con l'effetto stesso sia veduta et riconosciuta la verità da più persone che sia possibile. [It appears to me necessary to have ye truth seen and recognized, by means of ye effect itself, by as many people as possible.]
> – Galileo Galilei, *Letter 19 March 1610 to Grand Duke Cosimo II Medici.*

The Schoolmistress

There's that first-former, young Jemmie Meakin, high in Papa's apple tree. There's scarce enough light to see by. The school bell's not yet rung. Jemmie must have left home without breakfast again, so he's up in the pippin tree reaching to pluck an apple. He probably hopes that no one peering out the schoolroom window will notice him in this fog. But that shock of red hair is like a signal flare, unmistakable. Resourceful lad he is, and full of energy so early on a gray December morning.

Jemmie's come to school full of spunk and hunger. Has he also brought his sound common sense and uncanny memory for all the foolishness I offer that bright head of his?

When opening prayers are done, I'm to hear verbatim repetitions of yesterday's lesson from each of the first-formers. When 'tis Jemmie's turn he'll look through me with those, laughing Meakin eyes. After we have done the catechism I'll pose revision questions, trying to sound as stern as Papa did when he drill'd the lesson yesterday. *How many letters are there?* I shall ask, my stare aiming straight into those eleven-year-old eyes. *In English four and twenty, in Latin three and twenty*, I'll hear them say in reply in their slurry morning voices. – *What letter is there in English that is not in Latin?* I'll continue. – *That letter is W.* – *And how are the letters divided?* – *Into vowels and consonants. And what constitutes a vowel?*

Jemmie's lips will parrot the answers, but his mind will know how patently false and foolish are the recitations I require of him. Twenty-four letters in the English alphabet? What purpose is serv'd by counting letters, when their work and pleasure are to form words, conjure up sounds and sights, invent ideas? In the 1540's Doctor Lyly may have counted four-and-twenty English letters when he wrote his *Short Introduction to Grammar,* but any fool knows there are six-and-twenty now. And Jemmie Meakin is no fool.

Jemmie knows that a *J*, not an *I*, is the first letter of his name. He knows that hunger in his belly is spell'd with a *u*, not a *v*, despite what Doctor Lyly says and what I am expected to drone and drill into his head. I know there are better lessons to teach and better ways to teach them than this outdated, fusty book and this beastly ruler. Papa says I must use Doctor Lyly's *Grammar* and the tap of the ruler because the parents expect them. I know that Papa himself harbours doubts that he cannot admit aloud, and other ideas, too, that are even more seditious.

For here am I, a sixteen-year-old maid teaching in Papa's schoolroom because I'm fit to, while the lads, especially the older ones, snigger when they think I'm not looking. I see how Simonds D'Ewes and the others of his set regard me. And I see, too, the looks Jemmie's elder brother Richard sends my way from under those long eyelashes of his. But supervise the little lads I shall, because I know I am able.

Every well-made London boy must master good Latin prose, Papa says, *in order to make something of himself. The work of the world depends on Latin.* So I am told. *Lingua latina gives the mind strenuous exercise in an exquisite system of order, pattern, and logic.* So Papa says. I, too, love the mental exercise obtain'd as I read those muscular little syllables in Papa's books, the energy that vibrates when the forms jump from tense to tense, declension to declension. And the poems and stories – how they thrill me! Why not teach the lasses, too, not just the lads? But in this my first year I shall keep such ideas to myself.

The time isn't ripe for new ideas. Perhaps one day, and elsewhere. Here in my little world behind Saint Andrew Undershaft, I dream of worlds to come.

There are other worlds indeed. I've heard tales of visitors come to London from the New World across the Ocean, not just Englishmen returning, but red Indians, too, who are native to that place call'd Virginia. The woman in their company is the first of her kind to be converted to Christianity, to marry an Englishman, to bear an English child, to learn to speak our tongue. What a wonder our England must seem to her! And what a wonder – *mirabile dictu!* – to have liv'd in that strange New World from which she comes! Would that I could know her!

Such can never be, I know. Yet I know for a certainty that the world's a-changing. New ideas are born each day, and old ones falling away. One day students will be urged to ask questions, not merely memorize. Teachers will use other methods than rote and rule. Not only those pupils whose parents can afford it will be educated. Subjects will be taught that we have never dreamt of. And schools will be fill'd with as many girls as boys. These dreams will be truths come to pass, not just these fancies of an odd daughter of a quaint schoolmaster.

But to the business at hand and the likes of Jemmie Meakin. The lad must be examin'd this morning on the set nouns of the first and second declensions, this afternoon on the set present-tense verbs of first, second, and third conjugations. Papa expects this of me. So 'tis to be *haec via, hic servus, hoc signum. The road, the slave, the sign.* And *porto, doceo, pono. I carry, I show, I bear.* What can the quick mind of a lively boy do with such material? *The slave carries the sign. The road bears the slave. The sign shows the way.* Nonsense. All that is expected of Jemmie is that he commit such drivel to rote memory, with no mind to meaning, no engagement of his fancy.

What if I offer'd him other nouns and verbs to fit ye paradigms and tweak his conscience besides? *Hic puer, hæc magistra, hoc pomum. The boy, the schoolmistress, the apple. Optō, videō, carpō. I desire, I see, I steal.* Surely the lad will see lessons beyond the paradigm. How I long for mine own classroom to test these theories in practice!

The verger is sounding the morning bell. 'Tis time for me to put away my daydreams and line the boys up for morning prayers.

—៳—

The First Former

If I inch along this branch and reach a bit, I can – yes! – get one more little pippin to make three. One for breakfast, one for dinner, and one to trade for a slice of bread. They'll quell this hunger in my belly. I'll ask Master Reginald if I can sweep the courtyard at noontime each day this week as penance for yesterday's tardiness. Perhaps he'll offer some dinner porridge tomorrow and the next day. An apple here, a slice of bread and a bowl of porridge there – my belly rules my head. Hunger is stronger than those endless Latin verbs.

I shan't ask Mistress Bathsua about the sweeping or the porridge. She's too busy trying to be stern. Master Reginald's softhearted enough to yield a little. I shall swallow my pride to have fruit and bread and porridge to eat.

Mama says schooling will help me make my way in the world. I don't know what Latin's got to do with it. Mama also says I'm fitter than Richard for schooling, even though I'm younger. I've only been at it since Michaelmas and already I've advanced a bench. When we do our lessons after supper, I finish well before Richard. Granted he's ahead of me, but what he struggles over now will be easy for me in a year or two. When I do my recitations Mistress Bathsua tries to stare me down, but I surprise her by how easily I remember, how fixedly these odd bits take root in my head. I hear Master Reginald once and the words and their patterns seem to fall into my brain and stay there as if they always had been. Would that the food in my belly were the same. That I need to work for.

Would that the lessons were more filling than these singsong sounds I gobble up. Silly old Latin: *via, viæ, viæ, viam, viā; poetæ, poetārum, poetīs, poetās, poetīs.* But why always *via* and *poeta*? I might use *via* now and then, I suppose, being a city boy. But what do the likes of me, an apple-stealing son of a midwife-washerwoman and a deceas'd court servant – *filius servī mortuī* – care for poets?

Why can't we do grammar lessons with words that mean something, so long as they fit the pattern we're to commit to memory? Why not use real nouns in *declinatio prima* and *declinatio secunda* – *Magistra Bathsua*, for example, and *Magister Reginaldus*? *Magistra Bathsua Filia Magistrī Reginaldī est.* It hasn't been taught us first formers, but it works. *Nominativo*: *Magistra Bathsua, filia Magistrī Reginaldī, pulchra est. Genitivo: Oculī Magistræ Bathsuæ, filiæ Magistrī Reginaldī, bellissimī sunt. Dativo: I want to tell, Opto something Magistræ Bathsuæ, filiæ Magistrī Reginaldī, a secret – secretum. Accusativo: Meus frater Magistram Bathsuam, filiam pulchram Magistrī Reginaldī, amat.*

And what good does Latin do for an empty belly? I'd rather be out of doors everyday, following Richard about when he leaves the schoolroom at eleven to earn a few pence to bring home to Mama. He's able to cadge something to eat along the way. He gets to use his wits, stopping at one shop or another to do an errand here and there or a bit of hammering or whitewashing or lifting or carrying, all in exchange for something to eat and some coins to take home. And he gets to run about and see all kinds of folk on the street, hear news that's pass'd about everywhere. Just last Thursday Richard didn't return at all for afternoon lessons. He saw that Indian princess Poca-something walking along The Strand, he said, all brown and red as this pippin, in the company of ordinary Englishmen from Virginia and her own people, too. One of them, Richard said, had a face painted red, his hair all bunch'd in a lock atop his head, wearing fur and leather ornamented with shells. Richard said the princess was tall and carried herself proudly, for she's the daughter of a king in her own country. What a sight! I miss'd it, coop'd up in that danky little schoolroom, all cramp'd on that hard bench, sitting still for hours on end, learning bits of Latin.

The only thing that keeps Richard coming back to Master Reginald's schoolroom is the sight of Mistress Bathsua's fine eyes and figure. *Meus frater oculōs bellissimōs Magistræ Bathsuæ, filiæ Magistrī Reginaldī, amat.* He'd be out and about all day otherwise.

Richard said that the same afternoon he saw the Indian princess he'd been carrying quires of paper into Master Griffin's print shop. He nearly ran into Master Reginald coming out with a bulky parcel. Richard would have offer'd to carry it for him, he said, but he was afraid his schoolmaster would chide him for being absent. Instead he slipp'd into a shadowy doorway to escape the notice of Master Reginald, whose head is too full of Latin and Greek to light on any sandy-hair'd sixteen year old truant from school. I wonder what was in Master Reginald's parcel.

I hear Master Reginald's footfall coming from his rooms to the classroom. His pippins are safe in my pocket. The verger is on his way to the belfry to ring the morning bells. I can feel Mistress Bathsua's eyes – the fine eyes that Richard fancies – *sentiō in mē oculōs bellissimōs Magistræ Bathsuæ* – as I creep down from this apple tree.

—⚮—

The Schoolmaster

Almost time for morning prayer. Just a minute to review the lesson for the sixth form. Batty will line the lads up once the morning bell is toll'd. 'Tis a relief to have her help.

'Tis a bit dark yet. My eyes give me trouble. Arm's length is barely enough for me to see clearly. A few boys are up to reading this passage from *The Republic*. Oh, these aging eyes. I've heard rumours that special glass pieces may be crafted to improve one's vision. The Jews on Threadneedle Street are peddling some they've got from Holland. I must look into this.

Yes, here's the passage we'll work on this week, line by line. "Πρῶτον μεν φύεται ἕκαστος οὐ πανυ ὅμοιος ἑκάστῳ, first of all, we are not all alike; ἀλλὰ διαφέρων τὴν φύσιν, ἄλλος ἐπ᾽ ἄλλου ἔργου πρᾶξιν, there are differences among us that suit us to different occupations."

First the strict parsing and construing, word by word. But then we will consider the meaning. Different skills of hands and body, Socrates says, fit men to different occupations – farming, shoemaking, soldiering and the like. How abruptly the Great Schoolmaster shifts from workmen's to citizens' skills! I wonder which boy will arrive at this notion first. Simonds D'Ewes will parse and construe the grammar perfectly, but he won't grasp the meaning beneath it. His mind's sound, but small. He thinks 'tis only translation I'm after.

That elder Meakin lad will struggle with the grammar. If he studied his lessons more assiduously and miss'd fewer classes, he could parse as well as D'Ewes. But he'll understand Socrates' meaning well before he cracks the grammar: "The one who's φιλόσοφος δὴ καὶ θυμοειδὴς, in love with wisdom and passionate of soul, ταχὺς καὶ ἰσχυρὸς quick and courageous, not merely skill'd, he's the one destin'd to be μέλλων καλὸς κ'ἀγαθὸς ἔσεσθαι φύλαξ πόλεως, a good, true watcher, a guardian of the state." The others will regard yᵉ lesson as merely a translation exercise. But Meakin will grasp the meaning, see its importance.

Yet I fear Simonds D'Ewes, not Richard Meakin, is destin'd to be φύλαξ πόλεως, even tho' he is hardly φιλόσοφος δὴ καὶ θυμοειδὴς, ταχὺς καὶ ἰσχυρὸς. And Richard, whom I saw out the corner of my eye on The Strand last week carrying paper into Griffin's shop when I was fetching Batty's book, Richard will become a common labourer, or if he's lucky, a man in service to someone grand. D'Ewes, with his comfortable household, pasty complexion, and smarmy manners, is "one of the philosopher's well-bred hounds, τῶν γενναίων κυνῶν, perfectly gentle to their familiars and those they recognize, πρὸς τοὺς συνήθεις τε καὶ γνωρίμους ὡς οἷόν τε πραοτάτους εἶναι." So says Socrates. Richard, with his rough hands and fusty jacket, has the high spirits and strength of character for a role in statecraft that will never be his.

In the ideal state, money and breeding should make no difference. But in the real world they're all that matter. I saw Richard Meakin's young brother Jemmie yesterday morning in that apple tree and again just now, just as I saw Richard earning a few pence at Griffin's last week when he might have been in my schoolroom. The Meakins of this world live by their wit and grit and spirit. They scrimp and scrape to go to school, and in the end their hopes are dash'd, their ambitions disappointed. Meanwhile money and connexions buy places for the mediocre D'Eweses at Oxford and Cambridge, at the Inns of Court and in the Court and Parliament. Grinding a little Latin and Greek into a boy's head to make him a serviceable citizen misses the disappointing truth: Everything depends on station.

Here I am so high and mighty, theorizing about such matters. Am I any different from the dough-faced swots and sycophants who profit from cash and station? Why did I have Batty write *Musa Virginea*, if not for cash and station? Making her use her brilliancy to write smarmy compliments to the King and Queen and their brood of ordinary children and hangers on, as if they took any pleasure in the life of the mind? All the King glibly said when he was handed Batty's book was, "But can she spin?" He pass'd her book off with a crook'd finger to one of his gold-braided ciphers with whom he shar'd that contemptuous glance, that little piping laugh. What did I do but smile and bow and cringe? All I thought was of oiling my household's feeble connexion to the Court, in the hope that Batty's book and a few names dropp'd might earn us a tutoring appointment for a courtier's pasty-faced child. Or a royal pupil or two.

I humour myself believing that stipends from teaching the slow children of the rich let me keep the Meakins of this world in my schoolroom without charging their parents full fees. And feed them half-rotten pippins from the apple tree the little one is climbing down from this minute. I fill them with hopes they'll never realize.

These schoolboys think that my nose in my book and my daughter as my assistant mean I'm half-dotty and daft. Let 'em think it. It keeps 'em from surmising the dangerous thoughts filling my head.

Perhaps I should sail to America with Captain Rolfe and his Indian princess. A new world has room for an old schoolmaster with a head full of seditious ideas.

—⚏—

The Sixth Former

Jemmie's in the apple tree and Master Reginald pretends not to notice. Mistress Bathsua is peering out the schoolroom window at my impish brother.

Not one of them knows I am watching them. Who, I wonder, watches me?

Jemmie's plucking apples because there's not enough at home to eat. He's just like the picture in the first-form grammar book, of lads in the branches of a great tree. 'Tis meant to be yᵉ Tree of Knowledge and its fruit, Truth, that boys, hungry for knowledge, eagerly pluck. Quick-witted Jemmie may see the fruit as an emblem, but mainly for him 'tis something to fill his belly. He sees it, he wants it, he picks it. *Pomum videt, optat carpitque.*

Jemmie's plucking Forbidden Fruit from yᵉ Tree of yᵉ Knowledge of Good and Evil. And Master Reginald tempts lads like us to want to know more, to have more, when 'tis in our scope to want but not to have. The likes of us are destin'd only to be servants and day labourers with hungry bellies. Surely 'twould be better for us to be content with our lot and not seek more.

Master Reginald urges us on and also teaches us our limits. Why else would he have press'd upon me Horace's lines about knowing one's place?

Vivitur parvo bene, cui paternum
Splendet in mensa tenui salinum
Nec levis somnos timor aut cupido
Sordidus aufert.
He who lives small lives well,
Polishing for his table
His father's little salt cellar.
No fear or greed disturbs
His night's rest.

Master Reginald thinks I don't prepare my lessons. How surpris'd he'd be to know how many lines of Horace I have committed to memory, how often I translate them from Latin into English and back again, as if to taste them. He'd approve of my knowing backward and forward

Multa petentibus
Desunt multa: benest, cui deus obtulit
Parca quod satis est manu.
Many things wanted
Are many things lack'd.
It is good to be satisfied
With the little
One has in hand.

He'd be displeas'd that I despise these limits and take upon myself to know other lines.

Quis multa gracilis te puer in rosa
Perfusus liquidis urget odoribus
  Grato, Pyrrha, sub antro?
    Cui flavam religas comam,
Simplex munditiis?
What refin'd youth, sprinkl'd with perfume,
Urges himself upon you, Pyrrha,
Among the blooming roses,

In your pleasant grotto?
For whom have you arranged
Your shining hair
So elegantly
And so simply?

Fusty old Horace gives me fine words for longings that would mightily surprise everyone.

Standing here, peering at Master Reginald's little orchard, I look beyond Jemmie and the apple tree and his hunger and my family's station. All I see is Bathsua Reginald, my brother's schoolmistress, raising her hand to tuck that little lock of hair behind her ear. As God is my witness, to see that hand, that shining hair, that gesture explains why I come here. I long to do it myself, to touch that hand, that lock, that ear with my own. *Videō, optō, tangere desiderō.*

Master Reginald has others in mind as suitors for his daughter, wealthier young men who will go farther than I can ever hope. Fellows like Simonds D'Ewes. Or even grander ones. Why else would he have gone to Mister Griffin's print shop in The Strand to have that little book of hers printed – *Musa Virginea!* the very title! – if not to position her to catch the eye of promising young men who are refin'd, perfum'd?

If only I could catch her eye and hold her gaze with mine.

That afternoon in The Strand I avoided Master Reginald's glance, but not the Indian princess's. Walking with her retinue, that odd band of Englishmen and Americans, Princess Pocahontas – Mistress Rebecca Rolfe – look'd at me from under her dusky eyelashes. Would that I might exchange that glance for Mistress Bathsua's!

How does that verse from Horace go? Ah, yes:

O Regina, sublimi flagello
Tange Chloen semel arrogantem.
O Venus, queen of love,
With one sublime stroke of your lash
Touch haughty Chloe
Once, just once.

Princess of a New World, daughter of royal Powhatan, ruler of golden lands so far from home, whose uplifted lash gives me hope – touch my haughty teacher, teach her to love the likes of me!

—ᨆ—

The morning bell rings. Master Reginald enters his classroom. Jemmie Meakin comes down from the tree. Bathsua Reginald lines the boys up for morning prayer. Richard Meakin looks toward her with eyes full of longing.

Goddess of the old world, Goddess of the new: Hear his prayer.

Yes. She looks his way.

Subject:	In Haste
Date:	12/12/2002 07:32:36 A.M. EST
From:	dndyoung2@owl.com
To:	dndyoung1@owl.com

Dearest,

Just a quick note before I dash to the Library – must thank B for her latest story. Whoever coined the phrase "as silent as the grave" missed the boat as far as she's concerned. She is boiling over with stories to tell and has set the bar high for me, which is good. The story I just got from her is like "Rashomon," one little scene told four different ways. My story is chopped liver by comparison.

Just read Michael Ondaatje's *Anil's Ghost*. The premise is that the dead don't want to be voiceless. They can talk and want to. They want us to sit with them and listen.

Love,

D

December 12, 2002

> There was something comforting about going over and over
> each other's memories until they seemed like their own.
> – Anne Tyler. *The Amateur Marriage.*

Dear Bathsua,

Many thanks. Your letter and "Across a Distant Garden" steadied me. And I need steadying. My trip to Paris with my daughter is two weeks away, and already I have that off-kilter feeling that comes whenever I travel. Frankly, I'm not myself when I'm away from home. Just thinking of leaving makes me feel all aslant.

Since 9/11, I find travel especially dispiriting. All I can think of is that another shoe bomber will be sitting next to me on the flight. To calm my nerves I'll knit furiously while Zoë reads. It's illegal to carry metal knitting needles onboard airplanes now, so I bought a bamboo pair yesterday. This must sound crazy to you.

About "Across a Distant Garden": How you and Richard must have loved each other! And still do, I'm certain. Please say Love persists, even beyond death. I know about its shape-shifting over the course of a long marriage; if it persists after death how puzzling it must be, full of every moment, present and past, and future, too, without the softening blur of forgetting.

And what about the nature of time and the expression of it there where you are? Do verb tenses work as they do here? Or is time of a completely different nature for you and therefore expressed in some special form of a grand meta-tense? (How befuddled I was by the aorist when I studied Greek, having to distinguish between complete and incomplete actions. The aorist must be child's play, compared to the sequence of tenses in the Afterlife!)

And how do you manage there with everyone around you – and so many of you! – coming from so many different times, speaking such a Babel of languages, behaving in such contradictory ways? Someday when storytelling gets stale will you explain these things to me?

Now to the story I'm working on. It's set in the summer of 1968. I wasn't myself after Nate died. I was thirty-two and went off to teach at that camp in Maine. Dan and I were planning divorce without saying the word. We spoke in code instead: the DC riots meant we *had* to get Zoë out of DC for the summer, the Millers were *desperate* to have me teach at their camp, we were *thrilled* that Dan could accept the study grant to go to Prague. All of which masked the truth: We would have a trial separation before the Real Thing. It took that summer in the Maine woods to show me what the Real Thing really was – Love, pure and simple. Recognizing that truth underlies my story.

Summer 1968 was drop-dead beautiful, ironically so compared to the personal and political debacles. Our baby was dead; our marriage was falling apart; the Vietnam war, the riots, and the political assassinations were miseries. I tried taking prescription drugs, blaming Dan, and putting a fence around myself in a little classroom in Maine. And failed, of course. Thankfully.

That much is true. But memory plays funny tricks. Sometimes you have to make up stuff to tell the truth. I can't for the life of me remember the names of the kids I taught that summer, nor what I taught or what actually happened – if anything – on the little rise overlooking the pond. I remember feeling suspended over a quiet landscape and otherwise rocking, tossed completely off my moorings. I remember feeling queasy all the time. I'm using that "Lee" character again. Maybe I should change Dan, too, into Stan or something, but I'd rather leave Dan Dan. It's better that way. Zoë, sweet Zoë, bunked with the little Wrens that summer, and I saw her twice each day. But I'm leaving her out. Nor will I mention Nate and the grief. But they're all there anyway. You'll hear them behind the words.

Listen to me, explaining instead of writing. Why can't I stop thinking about writing and just do it, dip into the dream-clarity of the feelings instead of fussing over them? One thought, though, where the words perfectly match the feelings: how comforting it is to have you to confide in.

Yours in gratitude,

Dee

Subject:	To Paris, flying
Date:	12/26/2002 02:12:43 A.M. EST
From:	dndyoung2@owl.com
To:	dndyoung1@owl.com

Dearest,

Zoë and I leave this afternoon. Neddy's driving us to Dulles. Why do I need to fly to Paris when I can get there in my head or time-travel to all sorts of places just by reading B's letters and stories, writing to you, or just writing? But Zoë's adamant about this trip, wouldn't take no for an answer. In the face of her determination, I'm putty.

I get that sinking feeling in my stomach when I think about flying. That shoebomber business last winter, remember? I can't get the photo of his dirty sneaker with its scruffy tongue and laces, out of my head.

But Paris. Remember? Love, always.

December 26, 2002

> I felt unanchored and strange. Everything I saw in those early days as
> I took my surroundings in . . . made that feeling more acute. I felt that
> my presence in that old valley was part of something like an upheaval.
> – V.S. Naipaul. *The Enigma of Arrival.*

Dear Bathsua,

Here is my story about that summer in Maine. I won't be back to the Library until mid-January, so I shall wish you a happy New Year early. I'm hoping for a year of peace, but that seems unlikely. Maybe you can work miracles?

Warm regards,

Dee

Enclosure: "Starting Fresh"

Starting Fresh

> Familiar and unfamiliar swam and blended into a strangeness of dreaming...
> A wash of confused feeling went over her like wind across sweating skin.
> – Wallace Stegner. *Angle of Repose.*

The classroom was a cabin in the woods, about ten feet square, under pitch pines. The path to it was strewn with ochre-colored pine needles, and the half-hewn log that was the front step to the little porch could just as easily have served as firewood. The distance from the porch to the classroom could be taken in an easy stride, the entrance a rough-cut lumber threshold and lintel with no door. From waist height to the low ceiling, the wall opposite the entrance was fitted with a green chalkboard; below the chalk tray were raw pine boards, the various browns of the knotholes and the woolly texture of the wood grain satisfying contrasts to the smooth green of the chalk board above. On the two side walls windows opened entirely to the out-of-doors – no screens, no glass panes, no shutters, the deep eaves barely shading the room on sultry days and keeping the rain out on dismal ones.

Before the Camp Wanomee season started in late spring, Doris and Ben Miller, the owner-operators woke up the place, hiring the same crew of locals year after year to do repairs, replace roof shingles here and there and steps or thresholds that had rotted out, sweep away pine needles and residue of chipmunks who had found winter shelter. They would leave the wrens and robins nesting in the eaves. Just before the arrival of the counselors and teachers in late June, the nestlings would hatch and the last work of readying Wanomee – opening shutters, removing doors, trucking in last year's bedding and supplies from Lewiston and some new stuff from Portland – would carry on under the watchful eyes of the Millers and the nesting birds. Before the campers arrived on June 30, the parents would begin teaching the nestlings to fly.

It was the first morning in July. Everything about the classroom cabin was green or brown, Lee noticed, colors that naively blurred what was manmade into what was natural. Green pitch pines and green roof shingles overhead, brown pine needles and brown floorboards underfoot; brown threshold and lintel, green chalkboard. At the center of the cabin was a rough table made of a full sheet of plywood on sawhorse legs, surrounded by nine folding chairs.

Bird song seeped in through open windows along with the smell of Maine woods – not a smell, really, but the absence of one, just air cleaned to a fare-thee-well, Lee thought, by the essences that pines give out in New England air. Low early-morning shafts of sunlight slanted through the pines, the air so pure that its molecules seemed visible in the perfect stillness. Fresh sticks of chalk and an eraser rested on the chalk tray, a dictionary on the table. A hand-crank pencil sharpener clung to the wall alongside the entrance. Beyond the cabin adolescent boys' and girls' muffled voices shifted from the dining hall toward the sleeping lodges. That was all.

From home Lee had brought anthologies of poetry and short stories and a grammar and usage manual. Doris had assured her there would be eight copies of the short story anthology for the eight rising sophomores she had hired Lee to teach remedial language arts to for the six weeks of the summer of '68, plus a box of ditto masters, a working Gestettner copying machine, and lots of paper. Ben had taken Lee aside and assured her that all she would need were her good judgment, imagination, and enthusiasm for high school kids. "That's all it takes to teach kids at Wanomee," he said after Doris offered her the job in mid-April. "Especially when you're in our Maine woods. Away from all that city air."

So here she was, all and nothing in readiness. Standing alone in this little classroom, alert to the insistent pulsing sensation in her chest and temples, the sweaty feel of her palms, the twist in her gut, Lee heard herself breathing. The bravado of adolescents' voices drew closer, gradually drowning out the sounds of her own breathing. A fresh start, she thought.

Lee was relieved to be here. Winter and spring had been a long, gray stretch of despair. Despite the eager coverage of the Prague Spring that she and Dan had followed closely, the news had been almost unrelievedly depressing since December. The Tet Offensive, the escalating war in Vietnam, frustration with the Johnson administration's handling of it, a rapidly building anti-war movement on campuses all over America: it had all been grimly unsettling. Two assassinations, Martin Luther King, Jr.'s, in April and Robert Kennedy's just three weeks before she'd driven up to Wanomee, had bookended the riots at home in DC. Lee was cloaked in depression longer than she'd ever been before. Nothing was right or would be again, she had felt, what with war and death wherever her thoughts turned.

Lee knew it was right to escape to Wanomee for the summer. "I went to the woods to live deliberately," she remembered from a long-ago reading of Thoreau. I don't so much want to live deliberately, she thought. Just simply. Quietly. Away from protest marches, riots and war, away from Life's dismal aftershocks and death. Maybe the woods will teach me how to live, what to do. What in particular to do about Dan. Perhaps while they're at it, the woods can teach me how to start over.

After Dan left for Prague in June she tried to write long, breezy letters full of amusing, ironic detail, to keep him abreast of gossip and to match the frequency and tone of his correspondence. Where they were going she didn't know. Sometimes her efforts at flippancy in those letters took a dark, disconcerting turn. She tore up more drafts than she sent, of one in particular that she had written just before classes were about to begin.

The letter had scared her. She sent it anyway, wondering what Dan would make of her fierce words about war and the ironic blessing of a parent's losing a son before he could be sent off to fight in one. Before, her writing had been crisp, newsy, neutral. She pictured Dan reading that last letter, imagined him stopping and re-reading it, re-reading it three or four times more, wondering about her sanity. Straightforward, sweet Dan and the shattering of his idea of calm, reserved Lee.

Yes, she thought, standing in this classroom, a summer in Maine will be a relief, a respite from thoughts hanging in the air like a pestilence, clinging to her skin. Just this cabin in the woods, like Thoreau at Walden Pond. Just eight robust, uncomplicated teenagers, a few short stories, a few poems, she thought. Dan will reply with cheerful aerogrammes about the Prague Spring and Communism with a Human Face before he returns in mid-August. I'll send him handwritten notes about sunlight, birdsong, and quirky American teenagers. Until he comes back to DC, she vowed, there'll be no more sardonic gloom or ghoulish irony to startle or confuse him, just the easy verbal sparkle of their old relationship. And might be again.

The sounds of voices and footsteps swishing through pine needles drew Lee back to the present moment. She recognized the first three girls – bronzed, their hair tied back in nearly identical honey-gold ponytails – from the welcome session the night before. They were almost indistinguishable, she thought, with easily interchangeable names that sounded more like surnames than given names. Was the tall one Whitney, the one with mascara Bailey? Or Madison? They all had braces, perfect skin, and firm little breasts that preceded them under pastel Izod tee shirts. They arranged themselves to her left.

Close behind came a wad of boys, variously sized, pimply, with bigger teeth than their faces could contain. One was agonizingly skinny, the next agonizingly short, and the third with a ghost of a mustache, a pale, thick neck, embarrassing boy breasts and a stomach that trembled under the dark green Camp Wanomee jersey. No names came to mind for the trio. Lee checked her class list. Philip, Jacob, Adam, and Stuart. Lee felt a rush of pity for each of these three now scraping their chairs out from the table. Compared to the Whitney-Bailey-Madison phalanx, they were an embarrassment of clichés.

The two sets of three sat on opposite sides of the table, avoiding looking across at the other, one set out of thinly disguised superiority, the other out of scarcely suppressed longing. Even before they had taken their seats, Lee found herself making silent connections between herself and the fifteen year olds before her. She knew she shouldn't take sides. She'd always felt gawky and stumbling with the Bailey-Whitney-Madisons of the world, longing to be like them, yet fearing their power. Boys like these three, whatever combination of the Philip-Adam-Stuart-Jacob set was at the table, seemed destined to be her lot in life. Dan in tenth grade would have been the tiny one, she thought. Which might a son of theirs have grown up to be?

"Hello, folks." Lee's throat stuck in a tight knot. She surprised herself with that antiquated noun of address. *Folks?* What else to call them? Boys and girls? Kids? Guys? No, her instinct was about right: not condescending, not cute, not trying to invade their social space. *Folks* set just a little age distance between her and them.

"Let's wait a minute for the other two." She cleared her throat and glanced up at the doorway, one damp palm flat on the stack of books on the table in front of her, the forefinger of the other hand sliding a stray strand of hair behind her ear. "Why don't you try to give yourselves a little – uh – personal space that will suit you for class this morning, and – uh – we'll do introductions when everybody's here." She felt herself groping to fill the chasm of silence and awkwardness that had surfaced on the table. "Ah, here they are."

The last two arrived. By the process of elimination Lee knew the girl had to be Amy. She was pale and, with eyes downcast, clutched a green three-ring binder to her chest as if it were armor. A tinge of red lingered in her cheeks, a film of perspiration dusted her upper lip.

What had embarrassed her on the way, Lee wondered.

And then the reason was clear. Lee felt a matching rush of heat rise to her cheeks and, despite the cool of the morning, a sudden wetness in her armpits. She prayed no one noticed.

The eighth fifteen year old crossed the threshold, backlit in morning light. "I'm Adam, madam," he said to Lee, his gaze direct under a thick fringe of kohl-black lashes. The stance, the gaze, the satiric twist of the palindrome were a challenge and an assignation.

—∞—

A mid-July heat wave has settled in over northern New England. The weather had earlier been seasonable – cool mornings, bright noondays and afternoons, cool evenings – but this week the air is sultry, stale. After breakfast the heat already congealed in the little classroom. "Let's start off this morning with another little free write, just to get the *juices flowing*, so to speak, before we *take a stab* at the story you read last night." Lee puts a little tweak in her voice at the two hackneyed metaphors.

"My juices are already flowing, Lee, in this heat." Jacob's doughy face is damp. There are sweaty spots on his tee shirt.

Whitney smiles and rolls her eyes. Earlier she might have tossed him a withering glance, but the heat and humidity make even that little movement too much of an effort. Like the others she clicks a sheet of foolscap from her notebook.

"Let's try this prompt." Lee rifles through her copy of the short story collection until she finds the spot she marked the night before. "You'll probably recognize it from 'The Other Two,' last night's story by Edith Wharton."

There is a good-natured, collective groan.

"I didn't hear that, folks. As usual, you'll start by writing the prompt. Then let yourselves go with it." She pushes a damp strand of hair behind her ear. "Don't worry about what Mrs. Wharton meant by it, why she used it. Separate it from the story. Don't let the author control the flow of your writing. Just let yourselves *run* with it."

The directions evoke another groan. They have heard them before, every morning, in fact, but the idea of running in this morning's heat strikes them as a sorry joke.

"Okay," Lee continues, unperturbed. "Here it is. 'Oh, how stupid of me.' That's it. That's the prompt. Copy that down, please. 'Oh, how stupid of me.' Then just see where it takes you."

Pens begin scratching damply across paper.

Feigning disinterest, Lee walks around the classroom, looking out the window, occasionally glancing at each student across the table or from behind. She has chosen this difficult Wharton short story because she loves it, especially its tight-lipped treatment of strong emotions loosened by a grotesquely awkward situation. The story's themes of embarrassment and suppressed sexual tension seem especially apt for these academically challenged fifteen year olds at a co-ed summer camp. The diction is a stretch, she thinks, and the gilded-age setting alien to mid-twentieth-century adolescents, but she decided to use the story anyway. It's worth a try, she thinks, if only to distract myself.

Lee likes watching students as they do free-writes, imagining that in ten minutes of concentration she can see through their guarded surfaces to the mental operations that writing always loosens. Philip squeezes his pen until his knuckles are white, she notices, as if he's trying to force ideas out with the ink. With her left incisor Bailey bites her lower lip, oblivious to the pain on her perfect little cupid's bow of a mouth. Jacob prints in miniscule letters, as if believing the worth of his ideas is inversely proportional to his physical bulk.

From across the table Lee notices that Adam has written the prompt, nothing more. She prides herself on being able to read adolescent handwriting, even upside down, even misspelled and gawky. *Oh how stupid of me*, he has written, then leaned back in his chair until only its back legs support it. She can feel his gaze squarely fixed on her while the others write.

A fly buzzes in through the window.

Lee keeps her eyes on the papers on the table and continues her steady pace around the room. When she stands behind Adam, however, she finds herself staring at the way his hair curls slightly along the back of his head before turning to down on the nape of his neck. She continues walking in a slow circle, forcing herself to shift her gaze to Amy's page, to concentrate on the way it has filled up with evenly slanting, poised handwriting, and to Stuart's, now covered with cramped smudges.

Eventually she reaches the spot behind Adam's chair. She sees that his page too has begun to fill up: *So lets start of ths mornng with anouther little free rihgt, just to get the juces flouwing, so to spk, befor we take a stab at that story that you read last nigt. Lets try ths propt – start by writting it down and then let yurselvs go with it. Praps youl reconize it from someweare in Edth Wartons story, The Other Two, Dont worry about what she ment by it, why she usd it, jus seperate it from the story, don let her control the flow of your writtig. Jus see were it takes you.* He has written every word she said moments before, verbatim, even catching the words she tweaked with a little extra volume.

Lee ambles around the room, trying to keep her pace unperturbed, casual. Amy and Whitney have both started on second pages. A wren makes soft chit-chitting sounds in the tree outside the window. Madison is looking out the entryway. The others are forging ahead.

Lee composes herself by the time she reaches Adam again, looking over his shoulder at what he has written on the page of foolscap. After two blank lines, the writing continues:

> *Oh, how stupid of me?*
> *So lets start*
> *ths mornng*
> *free*
> *rihgt?*
> *get the juces flouwing?*
> *take a stab*
> *~~fast~~ tonigt?*
> *Lets try*
> *propt*
> *start*
> *Let yurself go?*
> *Praps youl reconize it from somewere*
> *dont worry about what is ment*
> *or why*
> *don control the flow*
> *Jus see were ~~it~~ I*
> *take you*

She feels a tumbling sensation somewhere between her heart and her stomach. Is she imagining it or has he turned her chaste, teacherly words into a seduction poem? Dyslexic he might be, and not quite sixteen, yet he has taken her words and is seducing her with them, here in this once-safe little cabin in the woods, in the presence of seven other apparently oblivious fifteen year olds. Birdsong outside the window is suddenly deafening.

She reaches the opposite side of the room. "Okay, folks," she hears herself saying, her voice low. She hopes the pauses between her words mask her breathlessness. "Let's take a ten-minute break. Then we'll reconvene and have a look at Mrs. Wharton's story."

There is a stir in the breezeless room. Chairs scrape against the rough-pine floor. She feels Adam's eyes, rimmed by those kohl-black lashes, rise toward hers.

—∞—

Head down, Lee strides hotly through the pine grove to her sleeping lodge, the one she shares with the swimming counselor and six twelve year olds. No one's here, thank God, she thinks. She rifles through papers on her makeshift desk until she finds the folder of Dan's letters. "Here, here I am, here's where I've been, where I'm going," she finds herself muttering, breathless. "Let me read one of these for a second or two before I go back."

"Dear Lee," it starts simply. The aerogramme is typed carefully, the way all Dan's letters are, and neatly organized in paragraphs, the page filled with perfectly formed, typed sentences, until the handwritten little "Thinking of you. Love, Dan," almost an afterthought in blue ink, slips in at the bottom. She reads the first two paragraphs, trying to catch the cool, steadying sound of his mind at work.

> Thank you for your last letter. I enjoyed hearing about your latest activities at Wanomee and your anthropological study of The American Adolescent. You're like Margaret Mead in *Coming of Age in Samoa*. Or Jane Goodall studying the life cycle of gorillas in Central Africa. They'd both be jealous of your assiduous description of habits and habitats.

> But seriously, the signs of freedom from the old-style Communism here in Prague continue to be promising. I wish I could write about it the way you write about your campers. Even more, I wish you were here to observe what's going on. All sorts of new publications are circulating. I wish I could read Czech. Everyone is giddy about the new Constitution. But there's also a fear in the air that all this freedom will make the Russians nervous enough to do something ruthless and stupid.

She skips to the end, hoping for a sign of intimacy, not the disembodied abstraction she thought she was growing used to.

Despite the excitement of being present at the creation
of a whole new political order here, I can't wait to get
home. I know how hard things have been for you, what
with everything that's happened. You were wise to get
away. This time apart has made me more eager to be
home than I can describe in words. I really look forward
to being back in DC, being with you, doing all the
familiar things we used to do, making a new start. I've
firmed up my travel plans. I fly to New York on August
tenth. Will you drive up and meet me? We could have a
weekend together there maybe, and then drive home to
DC? I really look forward to seeing you.

Fingering the blue aerogramme paper, Lee feels some of the energy of
the last few moments in the cabin between the lines of Dan's fresh, crisp
prose. She folds the letter carefully along its tidy, ready creases, returns it
to the folder, then settles the folder in among her teaching papers. Moving
toward the screen door, she hopes for a bit of a breeze, straightening
her shoulders and shaking them a little, as if to slip out of unseen traces.
Crossing the threshold into the bright air, she feels ready for "The Other
Two" and for seven of her students. In a minute, she thinks, maybe I'll be
ready for the eighth.

The rest of the morning's class is a disappointment. Not a disaster,
but a disappointment, dry and perfunctory. The discussion remains in what
Mrs. Wharton's story calls "the temperate zone," an unemotional skirting
of the heart of the matter. They underline all the references to awkward
embarrassment. Stuart counts eight times that the three men, Waythorn
and his wife's prior husbands, say "I'm sorry" to each other; Madison adds
that expressions like "I must apologize," "I hope you'll excuse me," and "I
beg your pardon, sir" bring the total to eleven. Whitney and Philip scour the
text for gestures that match Waythorn's embarrassment in the presence of
his predecessors. He is "pacing the room nervously," they note, "checking
himself," "nervously pulling off his gloves," "wincing," "stammering."

Jacob asks them to turn to the site of their morning prompt. "Look at
it," he says. They listen, staring down at their books as he reads aloud.

She set down the coffeepot, and reaching for the decanter

of cognac, measured off a liqueur glass and poured it
into his cup. Waythorn uttered a sudden exclamation.
"What's the matter?" she said, startled. "Nothing; only –
I don't take cognac in my coffee."
"What's cognac?" Bailey asks. Whitney jabs her with an elbow.
"Oh, how stupid of me," she cried. Their eyes met, and
she blushed a sudden agonized red.

—w—

The prior evening's thunderstorm has cleared the air of the heat and
humidity. Beyond Wanomee Pond the pine-covered hills stand in sharp
relief against the bright blue afternoon sky. Fair-weather clouds scud
overhead, shape shifting as they move eastward from the White Mountains
toward the Atlantic. Looking at the water, the hills, the sky, Lee feels some
of yesterday's confusion slip away, the way the rain and wind and flashes
of lightning cleared the air last night. Boys dive from the raft, the water
sparkling into shards as they break the surface. Girls sunbathe in little
clusters along the beach. Walking along the path from the cabins to the
pond, Lee sees the tight lineup of Whitney, Bailey, and Madison. She notes
with a little inward smile that Amy is with them, a bit off to the side, but
with them nonetheless.

Just beyond the musky scent of suntan lotion, Lee settles herself on
the rise behind the beach, where the sand meets the first scattering of pine
needles. She arranges herself on her towel so that her head is in the filtering
shadow of a scrub pine while her torso and legs are fully in the sunlight.
She sits at first, then lies back, still hearing the thumping beat of a song on
a transistor radio, the splashes of bodies leaping into the water.

Lee closes her eyes and watches patterns of color play on the insides
of her eyelids, shifting among red and magenta and deep purple. She
imagines young bodies glistening, the boys' backs wet, their hair dripping,
the girls' skin a smooth golden sheen, their hair in fine flying strands in
the warm wind.The sounds of splashing water slide to the back of her
consciousness. There is the distant drumbeat and the warmth of the sun
and then a pleasant feeling of release in her shoulders and pelvis. . . .

She feels someone watching her. She smiles at the thought. Is it Adam?
No. It is Dan, her Dan. She feels beautiful in his eyes, desirable, desiring. . .

Opening her eyes, Lee adjusts her vision from the mad, shifting, imagined colors through the filter of pine needles to the cloud-visited sky overhead, the pure-white cumulus shapes and the bright, clear blue beyond. After the swirling colors of the dream, the clouds are hard-edged. There, up and to her left overhead is a cloud suddenly transformed into – what? Lee smiles inwardly, reminded of Dan's gentle voice, the careful shape-shifting of his thinking from one paragraph in his letter to the next, his delicacy in wondering what will happen when they see each other again in August. Everything about him is restrained, no slipping and sliding into awkward feeling below the restraint, no madly shifting, exposed emotions, no embarrassment to either of them. Just clear, decorous paragraphs on sky-blue aerogramme paper, and everything that matters unsullied by words. With Dan even the bad will be good, Lee thinks. Even in the terror and despair there will be safety. She takes a deep breath, acknowledging a train of thought from which there will be no going back, and no reason to.

She closes her eyes. There is someone truly above her head, a shifting of the light, perhaps. She opens her eyes.

Adam is standing there, blocking her view of the sky above. He has come through the grove of pines behind her head, from the cabins, not from the pond. "About yesterday, Lee. I was only trying to make you smile." His voice trails off.

She rises to a half-sitting position. Looking at his face, she sees his eyes are turned elsewhere.

He hesitates. "You don't smile enough. You seem so serious, you know. Sad even." He shifts from one foot to the other, then sits down beside her. "I only wanted to make you smile." There is another pause. "I didn't mean to embarrass you. I can tell you're trying to decide something. Something important. I just wanted to make you smile while you do the deciding. I didn't mean to embarrass you, or anything."

They both face the beach and the pond and the pine-strewn hills beyond.

She smiles. "I know." She plays with a clump of pine needles, feeling their sharp points, their pliability, their slight stickiness. "You wouldn't happen to remember the last bit in that Edith Wharton story, would you?"

He nods. "I can't spell, but I notice stuff. Alice is pouring tea for all three of her husbands, first the two visitors and then poor old embarrassed Waythorn.

She hands him the last cup. And he smiles."

"He laughs, actually."

"I know," he says, dusting off his hands and rising to stand. "I wanted to see if you did."

Suddenly Adam sweeps forward and lifts Lee off the ground into a standing position. She finds her hands on his bare shoulders, his hands at her bare waist.

He drops his hands to his sides. "The mail's in. I just helped Mr. Miller with the sorting. You've got another one of those little blue airmail thingums with the foreign stamps on it. I thought you'd like to know."

Lee feels her face warm, her lips curve upward.

"Good – you're smiling now," he says.

Lee turns toward the main house. Behind her Adam is running toward the beach, toward the sound of the radio, the splashing water, the others. She gathers her towel and heads away from the pond toward the main house and the mail. I'm ready to start over, she thinks. I'm ready for the rest of it.

Subject:	I love you
Date:	12/26/2002 14:47:06 PM EST
From:	dndyoung2@owl.com
To:	dndyoung1@owl.com

Darling,

About to dash off. Taking Margaret Atwood's *Blind Assassin* to read on the plane. (MYOPIA book for February.) Happy New Year. I love you. I love you. I love you. I love you. I love you. I love you. I love you. I love you. I love you. I love you.

Dee

—⁓— *Seven* —⁓—

Subject: Home, safe
Date: 1/3/2003 20:37:32 PM EST
From: dndyoung2@owl.com
To: dndyoung1@owl.com

Darling,

Home at last. Exhausted and happy (happy!) to be home. Will write tomorrow.
Love.

Subject: I love you
Date: 1/4/2003 05:17:41 AM EST
From: dndyoung2@owl.com
To: dndyoung1@owl.com

Darling,

It was a lovely, bittersweet trip. Zoë did her damnedest to keep me "in the moment" (her words). She left me alone just one afternoon at my choice of a "safe" spot (i.e., not emotionally freighted). I chose the Musée d'Orsay, the Impressionist Galleries, and spent a glorious three hours in just two rooms, looking at those dear haystacks, rooftops, water lilies, and bridges over the Seine. There was the usual stream of viewers – tourists, businessmen, elderly couples and friends, art students, lovers. I sat and looked and looked, then started a sestina. When it's done I'll send it to you.

Zoë and I walked and walked, arm in arm, in thin Paris winter sunlight. It was lovely. We didn't talk much, just walked and stopped now and then for coffee and your favorite – tarte tatin. Then walked some more, lost along those avenues that all look the same and perfectly Parisian.

I finished *Blind Assassin*. I think you would have liked it for all the classical stuff, but I found it odd and eerie. Underlined this to share with you:

For whom am I writing this? For myself? I think not. . . .
For some stranger, in the future, after I'm dead? I have
no such ambition, or no such hope. Perhaps I write for
no one. Perhaps for the same person children are writing
for, when they scrawl their names in the snow.

Remember the time we stayed in that hotel in the Latin Quarter, in
that delapidated room overlooking the intersection of two avenues whose
names I cannot remember? The head of the bed felt like it was right
over the intersection and rickety. Remember? The wallpaper was yellow,
a faux-damask horror, and the furniture relics from right after the war.
Remember? We had taken the train from the airport with those grumpy
morning commuters who looked even grumpier when they saw our
suitcases cramping the aisle. And the hotel concierge grudgingly let us have
our room early, acting as if he were doing us an exceptional favor, and we
showered and went straight to bed at eleven in the morning. Remember?
And we made love, laughing at ourselves, two old fogies, making love on a
rickety bed in the middle of the morning in a cheap hotel with our heads
above the traffic? And fell asleep to the sounds of noonday, horns and
motorcycles and all, and woke up to the sounds of bullhorns and a protest
march of students and North African workers? And we laughed and felt
like bohemian, clandestine lovers? Wasn't it all wonderful, that rickety bed,
that traffic, those bullhorns and placards? And that mad, mad love? I love
you. I'll shower now and go to bed. And pretend.
Love.

January 10, 2003

> Domus sua cuique tutissimum refugium.
> Home is one's safest refuge.
> – Latin epigram.

Dear Dee,

Welcome home. I trust this letter finds you well and refresh'd after
your journey. Please tell me about Paris. I can only imagine it.

I've been hard at work on another story about teaching. This time, however, as they do every January, my memories rush at me from midlife, from those dark days in 1649, when our first King Charles walk'd through the window of the Banqueting Hall to his execution. As you know, I taught his second daughter, the Princess Elizabeth, even flattering myself that I cultivated in her my own love of ancient texts. Sleeping and waking (yes, we sleep here), I have brooded on that rabbinic prayer you cited in October: *May it be Thy will, My Lord, that my teaching cause no mishap*. I fear my teaching caus'd incalculable harm. Guilty fears – nightmares even – crowd my mind.

Forgive my tainting welcome greetings with anxious musings. I hope writing this story in verse and in the discipline of Sophoclean tragedy will offer a refuge from my nightmares.

In trust of your friendship,

Bathsua

January 16, 2003

> And she remembered how the shadow on the wall
> was a greater delight to her than the thing itself.
> – Vita Sackville-West. *All Passion Spent*.

Dear Bathsua,

Thank you for your welcome home. How can I describe how beautiful Paris is in winter? I wish I could show you the light refracting off the wineglasses at the little restaurant around the corner from our hotel. Or the flaky pastry on the *gateau des rois*, or the puddles in the sidewalk along the Rue du Vaugirard. Or the pleasure I enjoyed one afternoon in the Impressionist Galleries at the Musée d'Orsay, watching how steadily the sunlight caressed the Monets and Caillebottes, how dramatically the clouds raced across the sky over Montmartre. The windows on the north side of the gallery framed the panorama of the Right Bank. An elderly couple, arm in arm, turned toward the view, then toward me. "C'est beau, Sacre Coeur, n'est-ce pas, tout en face?" the man said. How beautiful it was! Sacre Coeur was suddenly awash in light. I started writing a sestina then and there. I'll send it to you when it's done. It won't tell you much; just the feeling of a sunny January afternoon in Paris.

I am eager to read your "Sophoclean tragedy." I'm writing another teacher story, too, but not with such an august forebear.

Yours in trust,

Dee

January 21, 2003

אֲשֶׁר בָּנֵינוּ, כִּנְטִעִים-- מְגֻדָּלִים בִּנְעוּרֵיהֶם: בְּנוֹתֵינוּ כְזָוִיֹּת-- מְחֻטָּבוֹת, תַּבְנִית הֵיכָל.

That our sons may be as plants grown up in their youth, our daughters as cornerstones, polished after the similitude of a palace.
– Psalm CXLIV.12.

Dear Dee,

The Princess Royal, Elizabeth, second daughter of our martyr'd King, was the jewel, the polish'd cornerstone of my teaching, as dear to me as my own children. I last saw her in life when she was a mere child, but often in dreams I have seen her since. Indeed, those imagin'd visitations, as real-seeming now as the hours we spent on her lessons, give me both pleasure and pain. To this day I see her pouring over the books I gave her from my father's library. I see her russet curls, her high pale forehead, that determin'd, round little Stuart chin resting in that soft white hand, its nails bitten to the quick. I see her, thin lips press'd firmly together, working through the Greek texts I lay before her, her gaze, even in those sad days, more direct than those of her brothers James, Duke of York, and Henry, the last time I saw them all together in the nursery at Saint James's Palace.

We translated Sophocles that winter and spring, the Princess Elizabeth and I, in the nursery, while the Princes look'd on. Sometimes I fancy it was my lesson that prompted her to urge the Duke of York to slip away into the Palace Garden during the after-dinner game of hide-and-seek one evening in April 1648. Disguis'd in maid's clothes, he was spirited away in the gathering darkness, bundl'd onto a skiff in the river in the early morning light, taken to a ship at Gravesend and then to freedom in Holland. I had given the Princess a few lines from the Prologue of *Electra* to translate. The Old Man, Orestes's tutor, ὁ παιδαγωγός, urges his royal pupil to embark courageously on a dangerous plan, to slip into the palace of Clytemnestra and Aegisthus and avenge Agamemnon's murder. My lesson perchance inspir'd the Princess to suggest the Duke's escape and caus'd that which follow'd. Assigning *Electra* for her study, was I not like that Old Man, urging my unsuspecting Pupil into danger that I was safe from myself?

"Νῦν οὖν Ὀρεστα – so now Orestes," the tutor whispers into his pupil's ear, "τί χρὴ δρᾶν ἐν ταχει βουλευτέον ὡς ἡμὶν – we must lay our plan in haste, for already – ἤδη λαμπρὸν ἠλίου – the sun's bright light – σέλας ἑῷα κινεῖ φθέγματ' ὀρνίθων σαφῆ – wakens the birds to sing their clear melody, and – μέλαινά τ' ἄστρων ἐκλέλοιπεν εὐφρόνη – the dark starry night is nearly spent." That whispering voice is conspiratorial, is it not?

The Daughter of a doom'd King and victim of her father's statecraft, the Princess Elizabeth liv'd a mere fifteen years, the last full of suffering. Her life was not unlike those of the daughters of the royal Agamemnon – Iphigenia, sacrificed to propitiate the gods, and Electra, defender against terrible odds of her father's memory. Quick with her lessons under my tutelage, the recogniton of her plight, I fear. I made her tragic ἀγων, her precocious ἀναγνώρισις. I witness'd surrounding her an imbecile chorus and its requir'd κόμμος, lamentation and wailing and beating of breast. A mere slip of a girl held in house arrest in one palace after another, surrounded by frighten'd guardians and servants, those ragtag supernumeraries and onlookers, she was ill cloth'd, ill fed, and ultimately sick to dying of Pneumonia at fifteen. And I the tutor – a witness or an abettor? A Sophoclean tragedy indeed, complete with masks and stationary odes, chanted strophes and antistrophes, all to the dreary, reedy piping of the αὐλός.

In her own hand my beloved Princess – fourteen years old – wrote of her last visit with her father, our King, the night before he was led through the window of the Banqueting Hall at Saint James's to his Execution before a gawking crowd. "What the King said to me," the Princess wrote, "y⁹ 9 and 20th of January 1649, being the last time I had y⁹ happiness to see him. He told me he was glad I was come. He wish'd me not to grieve and torment myself for him." Others present reported the King said, "Sweetheart, you'll forget this." "No," she replied. "I shall never forget it while I live." Pouring forth an abundance of tears, she promis'd to record the particulars.

Perhaps her tears were her κάθαρσις, her cleansing relief from pity for her father's plight, from fear that the same fate would befall her and her little round-cheek'd younger brother, Prince Henry, whose trembling hand she held in her own as they left their father, the King. But I misrepresent Aristotle's words. Catharsis, restorative Pity and Fear, comes not to yᵉ πρωταγωνιστής, the principal Personage of the Tragedy, but to those who observe, the Audience and, perhaps, the Author. So, in pride and in penance, I pour out to you my story. Forgive my ὕβρις in daring such a task. But what punishment can the gods mete out to one already dead?

Your (humble) servant,

Bathsua

Enclos'd: "My Lady Elizabeth, My Prize Pupil"

My Lady Elizabeth, My Prize Pupil

> Invention, Nature's child, fled stepdame Study's blows. . . .
> Thus, great with child to speak, and helpless in my throes,
> Biting my truant pen, beating myself for spite:
> "Fool," said my Muse to me, "look in thy heart, and write."
>   – Sir Philip Sidney. "Astrophil and Stella."

A Play in the Style of a Sophoclean Tragedy

DRAMATIS PERSONAE.

PRINCESS ELIZABETH, second Daughter of the deceas'd CHARLES I

DOROTHY SIDNEY, COUNTESS OF LEICESTER, presently Guardian to PRINCESS ELIZABETH and PRINCE HENRY at Penshurst Place

CAPTAIN ANTHONY MILDMAY, Governor of Carisbrooke Castle, newly appointed Guardian to PRINCESS ELIZABETH and PRINCE HENRY

OLD WOMAN, former Tutor to PRINCESS ELIZABETH

CHORUS OF SERVANTS

SCENE. Garden at Penshurst Place, Kent, a sun-bright late summer morning in 1650, larks singing, dew bedazzling blossoms that line pebbleston'd walks.

[THE OLD WOMAN ENTERS WITH DOROTHY SIDNEY, COUNTESS OF LEICESTER.]

OLD WOMAN. My heartfelt thanks, dear Lady, for summ'ning me
    To teach once more this fatherless royal child.

COUNTESS. All thanks now ow'd are mine, dear Mistress Tutor,
    For you have left behind your own dear ones
    To teach anew this hapless orphan child
    And give her semblance of the life she knew.

OLD WOMAN. My Lady is too kind. My coming here's
    A gift I would bestow most freely,
    For old affection's sake. And what is more,
    Your family has inspir'd the likes of mine
    To honour learning and to give to those
    In desperate need whatever they do lack.

COUNTESS. You are most welcome. And our plan is sound:
    We Sidneys do believe that words and books –
    Which we have surfeit of – are wholesome balms.
    The Earl, my brother, took the care in town
    Of these two royal babes, and brought them here
    To Penshurst at the urging of his King,
    The martyr'd Charles, his Liege. He vow'd to take
    The Princess and the Prince in seemly time
    To Holland, where their sister, Princess Mary,
    Together with the gracious Prince of Orange,
    Has open'd safe and loving arms to them.
    But 'til the stony Parliament agree
    To their remove, we Sidneys will provide
    A home and succour for this tragic Pair,
    Prince and Princess, too-young grieving heirs
    Of our murder'd King. But what news
    Of London do you bring today?

OLD WOMAN. In town
    Rumours swirl the Royal two are dead –
    Died of grief, or poison – or transported
    To America or placed in service,
    The Princess to a seamstress apprentic`ed

And to a lowly cobbler her brother Prince.

COUNTESS. These rumours in the main are false, and yet
    A grain of Truth they bear. Indeed 'tis true
    The Princess is quite ill, near sick to death,
    And transported out of London has she been,
    And scantily provided for by those
    Who should have taken greater care.

OLD WOMAN. What, ill?
    Again? Or still? How so? My precious child!

COUNTESS. 'Tis a fact. The Doctor at Saint James's,
    Sir Theodore, did send us written word
    At the time the Princess first arriv'd.
    Here are his very words about her health:
        [Reads:]

"The Princess Elizabeth was aforetime sad & somewhat liable to complaints of spleen. She suffer'd some from scurvy. From ye death of her Father she fell into a great sorrow, whereby all ye other ailments from which she suffer'd were thus in creas'd. Her pulse is rapid. She is pale, emaciated, wan, & frail. Her digestion has   virtually ceas'd to function."

OLD WOMAN. Alas, O tragic child!

COUNTESS. Sir Theodore prescrib'd some pills and salves,
    And hopes the country air may do her good.

OLD WOMAN. Alas, my brilliant, love-starv'd, star-cross'd child!

COUNTESS. Perhaps some quiet study, Mistress Tutor,
    The parsing of Greek verbs or Latin nouns
    Might soothe her mind, and these, in harmony
    With the gentle air of Penshurst, calm
    Her heart, revive her long-lost appetite,
    Renew her sweet and gentle smile, restore
    Some colour to those pale, pale cheeks and brow.

OLD WOMAN. I've brought my books and pencils, fond recall
    Of golden studious hours that we spent

Together. Let us now begin at once
A restoration of her health and strength.
Nature, sun, familiar friends, and study
Thus may help achieve what doctor's physick
Cannot bring about. My hope is this:
Your sunny, blooming garden will become
Both schoolroom and infirmary. By your leave,
Study will provide a healing balm
For all her ills. We'll open up our books,
The two of us, and like Orestes' tutor,
I will provide "a fair beginning
That I trust will place within our grasp
Sure victory, and mastery in all we do."

COUNTESS. As Scripture teaches, "Study to be quiet."
Let's now unpack your books, a certain cure.

[EXEUNT OLD WOMAN AND COUNTESS. ENTER PRINCESS ELIZABETH, MEANLY CLAD.]

ELIZABETH. Methinks I do recall some tear-fill'd lines
My dear old tutor had me memorize
From Sophocles' *Electra: [chanting].* "O pure sunlight,
And thou air, Earth's canopy, how oft
Have strains of my lament been sent your way?
I've often told you of the wild blows dealt
Against this bleeding breast when dark night falls.
How oft I do beweep my hapless sire!
Alas, my father died a death so cruel!
I'll never cease from dirge and sore lament
While I do look upon the trembling rays of stars,
Or on this light of day."

[ENTERS CHORUS OF SERVANTS.]

CHORUS ALL. Ah, Lady, Princess, sit you down and rest.

Take refuge here, we pray, in this mild grove.
We place this cooling cloth upon your brow,
And rub your wrists and ankles to restore
Some soothing peace and calming sleep, to ease
Your troubl'd thoughts and oft-disturbèd health.

ELIZABETH. The Countess, Lady Sidney, has sent you here,
To soothe her houseguest, offer balm and care.
You are most kind, solicitous, each one,
But I must walk me up and down, and weep.
Distracted I may seem, and full of woe:
'Tis my fate to keen and not to cease
From mourning my dear father, our dead King.
My brothers keep succession's hopes alive,
My sister binds our fate to Holland's crown,
My mother pleads our cause in France's court,
And I am left to mourn for all their sakes.

CHORUS ALL. Dear Princess, take our counsel, please, take heed:
Put aside your weeping and your grief.
Attend instead to Nature and this place –
Its groves and gardens, butterflies and birds.
Put off ideas of politics and kin:
To Nature turn your thoughts. This day we urge:
Seek sunlight, birdsong, wholesome gentle air.
Let Penshurst's summer pleasures cleanse your mind.

ELIZABETH. Dear friends, I see you strive to ease my woe.
You're well-intention'd – that escapes me not –
And true it is this garden offers sights
And sounds to calm a mind as griev'd as mine.
I know full well the truth of what you say,
But mourning for our King I shan't leave off.
Leave me to weep and sigh my father's fate.

CHORUS ALL. We came to offer succour for your woe,
But find, dear Princess, that our simple means
Are powerless to staunch your royal tears.

ELIZABETH. I thank you from my heart. Your help is kind.

CHORUS I. We leave you to your thoughts. But stay – we see
 The Countess coming now, a stranger with her
 Dress'd in antique black. Who can she be?

ELIZABETH. Her form's familiar, or do these weeping eyes
 Deceive me? Yes, I recognize her gait:
 She is my teacher!

*[EXEUNT CHORUS. ENTER COUNTESS AND OLD WOMAN CARRYING BOOKS. A
SERVANT FOLLOWS, WITH A DESK, TWO CHAIRS, AND A TRAY OF SAVOURIES.]*

ELIZABETH. Teacher! Magistra!

OLD WOMAN. 'Tis I, my Lady, pupil mine.
 I've come to check your lessons, fill your head
 Again with grammar – Latin, Greek, and more –
 Rhetoric and verse, some Ovid, Sophocles –
 We'll while away the days with books and pens.
 You'll see, my little Scholar, Princess Bess,
 How good it is to study, learn, recall
 The steadying lessons of the ancient past.
 Your loving guardian, Lady Sidney here,
 Has summon'd me to Penshurst, here to set
 A classroom in her garden.

ELIZABETH. A thousand thanks,
 Dear Lady Dorothy. I see you've brought
 My teacher and my books.

COUNTESS. My child, perhaps
 The care of this grave woman can suffice
 To lift the pall of sadness that you wear.
 I leave you in the best of hands, I see.
 I take my leave of both of you just now.

[EXEUNT COUNTESS AND SERVANT.]

ELIZABETH. You'll find that I've forgotten all I knew
 Except some verses close to my condition.

OLD WOMAN. Do not upbraid yourself, my child. Your mind
>   Was ever richly stor'd with goodly Latin
>   And with Greek. Some gentle urging soon
>   Will help the learning flow directly back
>   Like healing water, bright and sparkling stream.

ELIZABETH. I hope, dear Tutor, that your words are true.
>   For my part, though, what only come to mind
>   Are lines of poor Electra's sad lament:
>   "Without ceasing, like some nightingale
>   I'll wail and cry aloud to all
>   The load of grief that weighs me down."

OLD WOMAN. Perhaps we'll start reviewing grammar rules:
>   Steadfast paradigms, conjugations, stems,
>   Synopses of the present and the future tense,
>   Aorist, subjunctive, passive –

ELIZABETH. But I cannot cease from saying yet again
>   The words of bold Electra: "O Erinyes,
>   Furious, dreadful daughters of the gods,
>   Come help me to avenge my murder'd sire!"

OLD WOMAN. Hush, sweet child. Let's start with Ovid first,
>   And read some tales of love and summer sun.

ELIZABETH. Dear Tutor, antique Ovid did speak true:
>   All things change, and nothing stays the same:
>   I once was keen to study Greek with you,
>   To learn the tenses, syntax, lists of words.
>   But this no longer satisfies my heart.

OLD WOMAN. What would you study, Princess, by your leave,
>   To calm your grief, restore your wasted health?

ELIZABETH. I fear you will be angry at my choice:
>   I would the House of Atreus recall
>   And its vengeful, blood-scorch'd denouement.
>   The more the tale is fierce and rough, the more
>   I'd it prefer: Electra and Orestes

Spilling blood for blood – their mother's blood!
Clytemnestra's and her lover's, too,
Aegisthus's – for the blood-spill of their Sire,
Mycenae's Agamemnon, King who years before
Had slain their sister – blood on blood on blood! –
The weaker I become, the wilder now my rage!
The Furies seek Orestes! Look with horror!

OLD WOMAN. Alas!

[ENTER CHORUS, SILENTLY.]

ELIZABETH. [chanting]   *ὅτε ὁι παγχάλκων ἀνταία γενύων ὡρμάθη πλαγά.*
When the straight swift blow was dealt him
With the blade of bronze!

OLD WOMAN. Alas!

ELIZABETH. *[chanting]* *φέρε,*
πῶς ἐπὶ τοῖς φθιμένοις ἀμελεῖν καλόν·
ἐν τίνι τοῦτ' ἔβλαστ' ἀνθρώπων;
Was ever born in mortal such grave sin?"

OLD WOMAN. I still can match you, Sophocles's
word for word:
[chanting] "Take heart, my daughter, please take heart:
θάρσει μοι, θάρσει, τέκνον·
Still in heaven is Zeus, who governs all –
ἔτι μέγας οὐρανῷ
Ζεύς, ὃς ἐφορᾷ πάντα καὶ κρατύνει –
Leave thy bitter quarrel to him, my child –
ᾧ τον ὑπερλγῆ χόλον νέμουσα
μήθ' οἷς ἐχθαίρεις ὑπεράχθεο μήτ' ἐπιλάθου –
Forget not thy foes, but refrain
From excess wrath against them."

ELIZABETH. Though strong, my wrath does not exceed its bounds;
My bitter feud is not just mine alone.
You've made me read and think and feel
Through books – clear windows on the sadness of the world.

OLD WOMAN. My child, be still, take heed.

> The servants now are watching us. Take care.
> Perhaps my hasty coming stirs your mind
> To this unwise commotion. Now I see
> The Countess sends her women to attend you.
> Look, they come. Put on a mask of calm.

[EXEUNT ELIZABETH AND OLD WOMAN.]

CHORUS. What words did they exchange? What language speak?

CHORUS 1. We've tried to keep her calm, the royal child,

> With healing balms and simple remedies;
> We've rubb'd her temples, always set her chair
> In flower'd bowers, home to doves and larks.
> And now a rage erupts upon her! Mark!

CHORUS 2. They roar'd, as if in tongues. That dame I fear.

> She's all in black, and bearing books: she's robb'd
> Our royal guest of peace! And look! The sky!
> The simple peace of Penshurst now gives way
> To louring cloud and rushing, raging storm!

CHORUS 1. Let's go to them and see what, for our part,

> We can provide to soothe the maid, what tasks
> We can perform to calm her once again.
> Some soup, perhaps, or cooling fruit, or tea?
> Perhaps the music master's here –

CHORUS 2. Be still!

> Until that woman came we lived in peace!
> And now – she roar'd! The Princess roar'd, 'tis true!
> That woman all in black's a witch! Her books,
> Her chants, her eyes, her bearing – all bespeak
> Of witchcraft. Sweet was Penshurst, haven bless'd
> By heaven! Now this day we fear there's come
> Some mischief, malice – call it what you will.

CHORUS 1. She's but a teacher, so our mistress said.

> She taught the Princess Latin, that is all.

Her books are children's schoolbooks, nothing more,
How can you say such mischief could live here?

CHORUS 2.　　There's more than mischief, by our faith, we fear:
For boys the classroom's meant, and not for girls.
For girls to study ancient tongues, to speak
In unfamiliar words, 'tis all against
The law of nature, modesty, and right.
We swear, there's trouble here, and evil, too!
We cannot let it grow, infect the child!

CHORUS. We must report the mischief we have seen
To our mistress Lady. To her we must
Of what our eyes have seen give sharp report.
The storm's now past. Pray look, she comes, accompanied,
With a stranger, nobly dress'd. He seems
A military man. He bears a certain
Fierce authority.

*[EXEUNT CHORUS. ENTER COUNTESS AND CAPTAIN ANTHONY MILDMAY.
THEY WALK ABOUT IN CLOSE DISCOURSE.]*

COUNTESS. The storm has pass'd.
Welcome, Captain Mildmay, to our home.
You are our welcome guest at Penshurst, sir.
What brings you from the Isle of Wight today,
From rugged Carisbrooke, where you kept guard
And held our martyr'd King?

MILDMAY. Our politics aside.
I come from Wight to fetch the sorry maid
Orphan'd now these eighteen weary months,
Her father dead, whom we detain'd some time
At Hampton Court, our watchful custody
Sore tried there when he did escape.
The Princess here did play no little part
In that escape – complain'd, she did, of noise
From guards outside the chamber of her sire,

At which complaint her father did protest,
And tender feeling for the lass did cause
My colleagues to reduce the guard. And so
The king escap'd.

COUNTESS. I heard it spoken of.
The Princess even here sleeps fitfully
And wakes from troubl'd dreams near every night.
'Tis one of many ills she suffers from.

MILDMAY. Your Princess oft is wont to aid escapes
Of royal kin. May I remind you that
The Duke of York, her brother, fled the town
By her advice? They play'd at hide-and-seek,
And from her chamber he did steal away
In maiden's dress, to Gravesend, then by ship
To Holland. She's a crafty one, that maid.

COUNTESS. Her mind is active, but her health is weak.
You say you've come to fetch her? 'Tis not wise.
She is not well, I trowe. And indeed,
We've summon'd her old teacher in the hope
That old pursuits may do a bit of good.
She was a brilliant scholar as a child:
Perhaps some studies can distract her mind
From morbid thoughts that now infect her health.
We fear she's sadly changing for the worse.
Her situation's grave.

MILDMAY. So have I heard.

[ENTER CHORUS. THEY STAND AT A DISTANCE, LISTENING.]

MILDMAY. My brother Henry, Councilor of State,
Receives reports each day of lurid plans
Afoot, of insurrections tending toward
Disturbance of the fragile public peace.

CHORUS *[whispering]*. Reports each day of lurid plans!
Disturbance of the peace!

MILDMAY. There are designs against the Commonwealth,
Malignancies *[the CHORUS advances]* and evils that do pose
Contagious threats against the common good.

CHORUS *[whispering]*. Do you hear? Malignancy and evil!
Designs against the common good!
Contagion!

COUNTESS. But how does this concern my Lady Princess?

CHORUS *[whispering]*. The Lady Princess!

MILDMAY. I come to do the will of Parliament,
To move the Princess soon to Carisbrooke.
'Tis said the late King's brat who here resides
May be made use of by the rebel side.
'Tis best for both their safety and the State's
To spirit her away beyond the sea.

CHORUS *[whispering]*. Rebel spirits!

COUNTESS. 'Tis decided, then? I fear you act
In too much haste to set the matter right.
The Princess is not well. At but fifteen
She should be more robust and full of signs
Of womanhood. And yet each passing day
She seems to grow more pale, more wan, more frail.
I will show you. Come along with me.

[EXEUNT COUNTESS AND MILDMAY.]

CHORUS. What we have just now heard and also seen
Brings chills of terror to our veins. We know
'Tis summer by this sun and these bright blooms,
But in our hearts are icy dread and fear!
The Captain tells of lurid plots afoot
Against the State. The Princess rages on
And speaks in tongues in company of a witch.
Our lady Countess now must hear us tell
What dangers we suspect. Come, let's make haste.

[EXEUNT CHORUS. ENTER ELIZABETH AND OLD WOMAN.]

ELIZABETH. I am calmer now. Your counsel's wise and just.

OLD WOMAN. Your quarrel with the world cannot be won
    By beating at your breast or raging on
    Against the Lord. Alone, a girl, and ill,
    You cannot win against your father's foes.
    Far better to be calm and still.

ELIZABETH. I know, dear teacher, that you speak the truth.
    I must restore my health, and like Electra
    Find myself some champion.

[ENTER COUNTESS AND MILDMAY, LISTENING.]

OLD WOMAN. Your own Orestes
    Has already come. Your brother Charles
    To Scotland now has safely sail'd from France.

ELIZABETH. Can it be true? Dear teacher, do not lie
    To give false hope to such a one as I.

OLD WOMAN. Indeed 'tis true. Your champion has arriv'd.
    And now return your gaze to quiet books,
    I beg you. Study here with me, my child.

[ENTER CHORUS, LISTENING.]

ELIZABETH. And if my memory serves me now aright,
    Your own wise counsel echoes Sophocles:
    Orestes warns Electra with these words:
    "Keep silence for a while. 'Tis better
    To be silent, lest someone within
    Happen to be listening."

OLD WOMAN. Your memory is sound, dear child.
    Here are the very words:
    "ἀλλὰ συγ' ἔχουσα πρόσμενε.
    σιγᾶν ἄμεινον, μὴ τις ἔνδοθεν κλύῃ."

CHORUS. Listen to them! Hear: they speak in tongues!
    Muttering what next to do to undermine

Our Lord! That woman steals her wits!
Devilish things infect this sacred home!

MILDMAY. Listen to them! Hear: they speak and plot.
Muttering of espionage, what next to do
To undermine the state! That woman lures
The girl to her dark purpose, rebellion.
Perverse proceedings taint this once-safe home!

OLD WOMAN. What ho! What have we here? What claims,
What accusations, baseless, causeless charges
Make you this day against this hapless child,
My pupil, mild and frail, this sad Princess?

ELIZABETH. Mercy! My teacher's come to teach me Greek.
What nonsense claims are level'd 'gainst us here?

COUNTESS. Have you betray'd my hospitality?

MILDMAY. Have you betray'd the Commonwealth?

CHORUS. Do you betray decorum's rules for girls?
Choose modest silence, wise simplicity:
Leave whate'er is hard to comprehend
To men and boys. You maids: seek not to know
What is not yours to know.

ELIZABETH. Never!

COUNTESS. She faints. Help her to the house.

OLD WOMAN. My Princess, my prize pupil!

MILDMAY. Bear her to the carriage. We leave for Carisbrooke.

[EXEUNT ELIZABETH (BY FORCE), MILDMAY AND THE COUNTESS FOLLOWING.]

CHORUS. Seize the witch. She is the cause of this.

[EXEUNT OLD WOMAN (BY FORCE) AND SEVERAL MEMBERS OF THE CHORUS.]

EXODOS.

CHORUS 1 [chanting]. O parents, watch your daughters and take care,
Stay close, guardians! Protect your maids,

And keep them safe from every sort of harm.
Stop their ears; protect their modest minds;
New learning's dangerous to them. Resist
Strange lessons. Teach them how to sew and dance,
To sing and paint and knit. But keep them safe
From all books in foreign tongues. The likes
Of Sophocles and Plato bring ideas
That tempt maids' minds to think beyond their scope.
Hide from them the learning of their brothers.

CHORUS 2 *[chanting]*.   Desist, O teachers, tutors, from all sorts
Of application of the past to present times.
Keep learning simple and ideas eschew
That breed rebellion in the restless young,
Lest tender minds be hotbeds of dissent.
Keep classrooms safe from curiosity,
Lest learnèd minds set men – and women – free.

CHORUS (all). Desist, O daughters, ever asking why.
Resist, O women: do not to seek to know.
Remain in meekness, silence, ignorance,
Lest curiosity make anger grow.
Know your place, and know your sphere
Demands no more than simple, patient calm,
And steadfast sweetness, humble, passive grace.

END

January 24, 2003

> Right now, this is the place where I'm alive. How could there be any other
> place? Be here now. The language of this is sufficient. I am here now.
> – Eva Hoffman. *Lost in Translation.*

Dear Bathsua,

That desperate, tragic ending! That final speech insisting that women's lives are best lived in silence! What must be your insupportable grief in your pupil's death!

The news here is driving me crazy. Not a day goes by but the President and his advisors issue two kinds of statements: we're bravely preparing for war, but be fearful and watch out for terrorists in our midst. I think the warnings are meant to terrify is into blind acquiescence. Be resolute! Be craven! Military personnel are leaving the country for war stations halfway around the world, but go about your business as usual, live normal lives! Let's prove to our enemies that we are a fearless people! Stock your pantries with emergency supplies of food and water, and seal off the tiny crevices of your homes with duct tape to protect yourselves from the seepage of gaseous emanations from weapons of mass destruction! Plan an escape route from the city! Stay in touch with your loved ones!

All I have to counter the news is the distraction of our correspondence and my own foolish habits. I will not seal my kitchen windows with duct tape or plan my escape route from the city. I will not squirrel away food and water or look over my shoulder for would-be terrorists. Instead I write to you and turn my CD player up to full blast and dance wildly, ecstatically even, in my pajamas, to records of old swing-dance music. You should see me, arms flailing in time to the music, hips wagging, bare feet flapping on the floor. The more I am told to be bellicose and fearful, the wilder is my solitary dancing. The madder the news, the saner I feel, dancing until I lose my breath. Then I shower, put back on my prim teacher clothes, and sit down to write. The words come fast and furious. The loud music, the dancing, the writing! I have never felt so alive, so productive. And so mad.

I promise a story about student prodigies soon. I will never match the beauty and terror of "My Lady Elizabeth, My Prize Pupil."

With warm affection,

Dee

Subject: Have a look at Bathsua's latest work
Date: 1/26/2003 17:07:49 PM EST
From: dndyoung2@owl.com
To: dndyoung1@owl.com

Darling,

What do you think of the ironic chant of Bathsua's chorus that daughters – women generally – should be kept in their place, ignorant, uneducated? Obviously she doesn't believe it for a minute. Who do you think she is, Dan, this penpal of mine?

Love, D

Attachment: Bathsua's "My Lady Elizabeth, My Prize Pupil"

January 31, 2003

> 'Tis all in pieces, all coherence gone;
> All just supply and all relation.
> Prince, subject, father, son, are things forgot,
> For every man alone thinks he hath got
> To be a Phoenix, and that then can be
> None of that kind of which he is but he.
> — John Donne. "An Anatomy of the World. The First Anniversary."

Dear Dee,

I had my nightmare again last night. Weeping dry tears, I see a man, Prince, King, father, son, walking outward through a window, turning the light about him all to flaming shards of glass. I try to sweep the fragments into a tidy pile, but fail. Then suddenly I am in my classroom, no longer sweeping but teaching a lesson about the manufacture of glass and its near-magic properties of enlarging what is distant and turning it over, head to toe, toe to head. Children – my dead babies! – tumble all about, bawling, scratching. I stand at my lectern, before a folio volume of lesson notes that have suddenly gone all invisible, just craz'd indentations on the open page. I seize a pencil – has it been invented yet? – and rub its side roughly across the paper. Runic, incomprehensible letters rise white out of the graying paper. The screech of words emerging from their invisibility is intolerable. I wake before I can decipher anything.

Bathsua

Eight

Subject: Nightmares, Dreams
Date: 2/01/2003 23:56:04 PM EST
From: dndyoung2@owl.com
To: dndyoung1@owl.com

Darling,

Where do dreams and nightmares come from? And what are they, really? Bathsua has written to me about hers. For weeks now I've been starting my days with fretful, anxious feelings loosened, I suspect, by my dreams, unremembered upon waking, unresolved, as far as I can tell, by what I do during the day, and still unsettling me at bedtime. Now's a good example. Can't fall asleep. Wishing I could program my dream before I turn out the light, like choosing a video, slipping it into the VCR and setting it to play later. Tonight I want to dream about you and me making love in Paris. Or being teenagers at Remington, you and me, performing Benedick and Beatrice in the spring production. Would such dreams be too much too ask? I love you.

February 2, 2003

> On certain streets various eccentric or vulnerable people will pause, pleading for attention. There will be anomalies and contradictions just as there will be irresolutions and ambiguities. But there will also be moments of revelation, when the city will be seen to harbour the secrets of the human world. Then it is wise to bow down to the immensity.
> – Peter Ackroyd. *London: The Biography.*

Dear Bathsua,

I remember telling Zoë when she woke up, hysterical, from a nightmare,

"Go back to sleep, sweetheart. It was only a dream. It isn't real." But isn't that just an anodyne, what mothers say to calm their children and urge them back to sleep?

Nightmares and dreams – such truth tellers! And on the subject of dreams – they say reading is a kind of dreaming. So is writing. (And if they are both forms of dreaming, what are other forms of nightmares? Not reading? Not writing?)

I have finally finished our latest assignment. I hope it will distract you from dark thoughts. Writing it has given me great pleasure.

Yours, faithfully,

Dee

Enclosure: "Mysterium Tremendum et Fascinans"

Mysterium Tremendum et Fascinans

> Es raro que los libros estén firmados. No existe el concepto del plagio: se la establecido que todas las obras son obra de un solo autor, que es intemporal y es anónimo. [Books are rarely signed, nor does the concept of plagiarism exist: It has been established that all books are the work of a single author who is timeless and anonymous.]
> – Jorge Luis Borges. "Tlön, Uqbar, Orbis Tertius."

I love looking at human hands at work. I know every curve and wrinkle of my own, the crisscrossing veins, the bunched-up skin on the knuckles, the nubby fingernails. Perhaps this fascination with the mysterious, expressive powers of the human hand is shared by all artists, for whom life would be incomplete without hand and mind in holy partnership.

All those years of teaching high school English, I imagined being a writer someday, probably because the feel of a pen balanced on the groove just above the nail on the middle finger of my right hand seemed like the world's most perfect equipoise. What slowed me down grading my students' essays and stories was probably the secret pleasure of watching my hand write comments in the margins. Sometimes I'd plant a smart-looking *punct* or *gr* beside a line of text or be satisfied with a crisp little command about usage or grammar: *Watch subject-verb agreement! Take care with pronouns!* I also looked for opportunities to write longer, perkier remarks: *Avoid "padverbs"* like "very" and "really"! To intensify a verb, find a better one! Sometimes the comment became a private rumination about literature, logic, or the human condition that I shared like a private joke, with a student: Use the "literary present" when writing about fiction. I'd pause, the tip of my pen vibrating a quarter-inch off the page, then add a slightly plaintive please, and continue: Yes, use the past to write about historical figures, but write about literary characters as if they are still alive. Then, unable to resist: In a sense, they are, forever whatever age they are on the page. The margin filled, I'd place an ellipsis, draw an arrow, write a tiny p.t.o., fold the corner to claim more writing space, and continue: Literary characters, unlike the rest of us, never age, never die, so long as the book they're in exists. Aren't they lucky?!

I loved those little writing moments. Toward the end of my thirty-odd years of teaching they became the saving grace of grading papers. My favorite comments nattered on for another four or five lines of tiny, tidy handwriting: An argument in the negative is never as logically compelling as an argument in the positive. If I say, for example, "My birthday is not today," I haven't told you my birth date. To convince your reader, use affirmative proof. Sometimes I'd continue, hoping irrationally that the student would enjoy a little exegesis contrasting false optimism and logical positivism: I don't ask you to be a Pollyanna who says only what's nice! I want you to make your argument convincing by avoiding the fallacy of "negative proof."

Ironically, the best papers stole from me the pleasure of watching my hand eke out in the margins those micro-essays about style and logic. On the those I had to settle for a nearly wordless Wow! or Yes! or merely a ! to show my admiration for the thought or expression. Then I'd imagine the look of that student's hand – in the old days – holding a pencil and moving it across the page, or lately both hands poised or dancing over the keys of a QWERTY keyboard.

Now and then I worried that a wonderful paper had been written by someone other than the student whose name appeared at the top, a writer wise, fluent and, well, old, or at least older than I. My suspicions of plagiarism were nearly always groundless.

I've kept copies of the best writing I received, most of these dateless, some for all purposes now authorless, in an old box labeled "Super Papers." I've been looking through it as I write this essay.

Here's a passage from "The Manuscript" by Alex _____:
I sit cross-legged staring at the sun, populating this desert
with memories, the sand before me suddenly, as if by
magic, awash with snow and ice, with people suffering in
the slums of Calcutta, with the sounds of flutes and the
rustling of wind in bamboo. I have found the one holy
place, the guru, the Ganges. I have found the teaching.

How did a seventeen year old write those lines? I'd have been
enormously proud to have written them myself, had I been as gifted as this
boy who imagining being the translator of "a most intriguing manuscript,
a purportedly autobiographical account by one Shayk Ahmed al Jirud, an
eighteenth-century spiritual leader of a small Sufi sect in the Thar region
of Pakistan." At the end of "The Manuscript" – which, by the way, had no
grammar or punctuation errors – all I could write was limp praise fortified
by the story's own imagery:

A bold, important story. The passage about the mirage in the desert sun,
phrases like "the arching rainbow of burning bright water droplets" and
"the remembered weight of the snow" are stunning examples of dream
logic. May I have a copy, please, for my "Super-Paper Box"?

Despite the wisdom and erudition of "The Manuscript," I was pretty
confident then – and still am now – that a mere adolescent had written and
not plagiarized it. The story's Sufi Shayk Ahmed al Jirud prays to Allah like
a good Muslim, but he also worships Shiva, seeks a guru, and prays at the
banks of the Ganges. Alex had somehow hit upon a hybrid of Hinduism
and Sufism and, while filling his story with details that provided the color
and texture I had asked for, managed to envision the coming together of
two fiercely competing religions. I still feel more than a little jealous of
Alex's idealistic vision of a bridge across a seemingly impossible chasm.

Reading "The Manuscript" again today, I recall Alex's hands all these
years later: Bony and white, almost the color of paper, with knobby
knuckles and cuticles picked down to lurid pinkish slivers. I imagine the
fingers flexing until his hands are tight, nervous claws, quivering tensely
and then releasing to jab at the keys of his keyboard. The boy Alex must
have been – like me now – obsessed with enigmas of dreams shared by
two people, the going in and out of alternate realities, of sleeping and

wakefulness, remembering and writing.

Another of Alex's stories is further down in my Super-Paper Box, this one called "Mirror of Worlds," about a FedEx deliveryman named Rafael, whose dreams and reality morph in and out of those of the pin-stripe-suited man to whom he delivers a package. Imagine how I felt all those years ago, the paper on my desk and my pen poised over it, writing *Yes!* and *!* again and again down the margin:

> Rafael pulled up at his first stop of the day, his mind reeling suddenly. It was an architectural wonder – sixty-odd stories of translucent smoked glass. Peering through one of the panels he saw the shadow of his image superimposed on a dim version of an office in front of him. Secretaries sat typing in the murky world beyond the window.

And a page or so later:

> The man recognized him. Why would anyone behind the glass of this monolith know who he was? The suit grinned. His eyes were unmistakably from Rafael's dream, but the figure was young, Rafael's age. His manner was as slick as his gel-solid hair.

Here was a boy imagining doppelgangers and making me doing the same, then and now, decades later. Did he twenty years ago imagine what I am writing now? Is Alex, now a man, still dreaming of doubles, reflections, and worlds mirroring one another?

Near the top of the Super-Paper Box was a short story called "Inescapable Maze" by Ashley _____, another pale, enigmatic young writer whom I taught just before retiring. She too was prodigiously gifted, an idiosyncratically broad reader who had started her story with a passage from "Tlön, Uqbar, Orbis Tertius," Jorge Luis Borges's story about discovering an article on the linguistics of an imaginary continent in a non-existent encyclopedia of his own creating.

Ashley's story and its epigraph were so engaging that I went to the library to read the Borges story, even copying a few beautiful bits onto scraps of paper I pinned to the bulletin board beside my desk. I see them now, overlapping with art postcards depicting writers whose eyes tilt pensively downward toward their hands poised above pieces of paper.

Here's how Borges's "Tlön, Uqbar, Orbis Tertius" begins: "I owe the discovery of Uqbar to the conjunction of a mirror and an encyclopedia." Later, midway through it reads: "While we sleep here, we are awake somewhere else, so that every man is in fact two men."

Had Alex read this before writing "Mirror of Worlds" and "The Manuscript" as Ashley had before writing "Inescapable Maze"? Or do ideas and images like these just happen into the minds of certain kids the way they come into the minds of writers like Borges?

I remember that both Alex and Ashley were almost transparent in the classroom, students who didn't call attention to themselves and said little, who in fact avoided spoken language, gesture, and posture that might suggest what they were thinking. Don't get me wrong – they were in the same seats day after day at the seminar table, always polite and attentive. They took notes, did every exercise and journal entry I requested, and, like all the others, read aloud from the published stories I presented to illustrate various techniques and strategies. But these two were inscrutable, deflecting my attention from themselves to their classmates or turning it back on me as if they themselves were mirrors.

What was going on in their heads? Ashley and Alex seemed to come to life in their writing, as if they survived on a diet of ink and paper. What miracles of observation and recollection, of connection and association, made possible the stories they wrote in response to my assignments? I have no way to explain the mystery of their invention. Their stories often dwelt on the numinous on the one hand and, on the other, the slipperiness of language. Always their grammar, spelling, and punctuation were uncannily flawless. But their hands! Their hands called to mind distressed animals, small, agonized creatures: a crab missing one claw or a moth with a wing singed and tattered as it ricochets off a hot light bulb.

And then there was Jenny _____, whom I taught some time after Alex and before Ashley. I scarcely remember her physical presence in the classroom, but in my mind's eye I see her after school crouched by her locker outside my classroom, her bird-like legs folded beneath her, books and notebooks spread before her, kneading and rubbing her hands together, swaying slightly back and forth.

Those hands! Her fingers were pencil-thin, the nails bitten to the quick, the skin dry, almost papery, inflamed to a raw itching red in the crotches where each finger met the hand itself. She held her pencil as if it were another finger. When she first enrolled at Remington the others mostly avoided her, averting their eyes when they saw her, then adjusting themselves to her silent, swaying reveries that seemed like trances or voiceless prayers. In time, as her poems and stories began appearing in the school literary magazine and won prizes year after year at the English Department awards assemblies, her peers came to hold her in awe, the athletes learning to quiet their exuberant clunking about in her presence as they gathered up hockey sticks and tennis rackets, the actresses subduing their hystrionics as they rehearsed for each other.

Jenny's stories left me breathless, even more than Alex's had the year or so before, even more than Ashley's would a few years later, bringing together the details of ordinary life with a desperate love of language and a passionate fury over its limitations. There was also an aching longing for human touch and communication. It seemed to have been wrung from her.

Recalling Jenny's stories, I wonder about the silent screams of silk worms as they wring from their bodies glistening filaments that are eventually woven into fabric by people unaware of whatever pain produced them. Listen to this frail-strong child-woman's voice in "Cannot":

> This ink! These words, these dusty impediments to feeling! Is there any other way to express it? Must it always be through this dirty filter? Are these words the only way?

A page later, groping for substitutes for language to express feeling, she chose immediate, sense experiences that come at her as she goes about daily chores:

> The rumble of a grocery cart: its sigh. An infant's flute-like cry. I stop at the lobster tank. The brown creatures claw in despair at the glass walls. I press my hand against the tank; the lobsters jerk away.

For an instant, this synesthetic matching seems to work, although Jenny acknowledges it probably sounds absurd:

> The avocados: when you were sad. The watermelon: for your laughter. The yellow grapes: your displeasure. I

shake my head. No, no – not displeasure.

Expressing emotions through association with objects flickers on and off, an unreliable as solace for the failure of words:

> The trees, the sun, the moon, bookshelves, coffee. The
> cold air of dank mornings. Wind. The spots of pink I
> see when I close my eyes. I could have shown you so
> many other things. After all this, after the gift of dead
> words, what can I offer to make you understand?

Once again I look at my carefully penned notes in the margins of Jenny's story, the *Yes!*, the *Wow!* and the *I hear you!* in ink not faded exactly, just drier looking than I remember it. I flip to the last page for my final comment:

> *I believe in Chekhov's principle, "If you want your reader to weep,*
> *write coldly." I think you sometimes go a bit overboard, the style*
> *becoming somewhat overblown. Because I prefer restraint and*
> *understatement, I offer this not as a criticism but as a suggestion.*
> *Your "argument" (yes, a story can have an argument) in this*
> *stunning prose poem is very sound: language is a frail vessel to bear*
> *the weight of our feelings. But it is the best we have to offer. We*
> *have to keep trying to get the words right.*

In another story, "On the Art of Keeping Dead Moments," Jenny writes about the gnawing fear of forgetfulness:

> She stares at her mother's hands gripping the steering
> wheel. Knuckles like baby skulls, she says to herself, and
> looks down at her own fists clutching a stack of piano
> books, then at her wan reflection in the car window. She
> watches her face dissolve into the greenness of the trees
> outside, hears the echo in her head of the music she had
> played in her lesson ring loud, then soft, then empty, just
> as a bell's reverberations finally melt away into open air.
> She realizes how afraid she is that this moment will bleed
> away like the sound in her head of the music her fingers
> had played. She finds herself saying aloud, "Don't forget,
> don't forget the knuckles like skulls, the green river of
> trees, the echoes of music in your head; don't forget – "

Again I suspect that the mystery of these students' creative capacities is explained by Borges. They must have written in the same mental space as he did when he proposed his alternate of language and poetics:

> There are no nouns in the conjectural *Ursprache* of Tlön. . . .
> Nouns are formed by stringing together adjectives. One does
> not say "moon"; one says "aerial-bright above dark-round," or
> "soft-amberish-celestial," or any other string. . . . This world's
> literature is filled with ideal objects called forth and dissolved
> in an instant, as the poetry requires. . . . There are objects
> composed of two terms, one visual and the other auditory:
> the color of the rising sun and the distant caw of a bird. There
> are things composed of many: the sun and water against the
> swimmer's breast, the vague shimmering pink one sees when
> one's eyes are closed, the sensation of being swept along by
> a river and also by Morpheus. . . . There are famous poems
> composed of a single enormous word.

Just as I picture Jenny mid-sway, eyes alighting on that Borges passage, I imagine Ashley reading it, too, in the gathering darkness after school, one hand nestled in the hard-soft place where her jaw meets her neck, the other folded calmly on the book before her in a corner of the school library, waiting for her ride home.

In her story "Inescapable Maze," the one with the Borges epigraph, her last high school paper before she went on to Princeton to study classics, Ashley wrote about being a young writer with a frowsy old muse at her disposal:

> I closed my eyes, leaned back, spread my fingers apart,
> invoked my Muse. She's a touchy old gal, Ginger, none
> too fond of getting up before ten in the morning, who
> appears with a bang, boa around her neck and cigarette
> wedged between her lips.

Pen clutched in her hand, the narrator gets to work. Ginger looks over her shoulder:

> "You know what your problem is?" Ginger's head was so close
> to mine I could smell last night's liquor on her breath. "You're
> too sane." I stared at her. Suddenly her image dissolved into
> drops of color, like a watery rainbow, the sign of a promise
> God made with his fingers crossed. Then she was gone. I

strolled to the window, clasped my hands together.

Suddenly everything seems miraculously clear, full of promise:
The city scrawled itself across my field of vision. I saw the
two coffee shops across the street, both alike in dignity, their
employees decked out in competing colors, ready to back
the slightest quarrel. The neighborhood cop wandered by,
guarding the citizens not against ordinary thugs but against
roving bands of pigeons who looked back at him with keen,
greedy eyes. The world suddenly made impeccable sense.

Rejecting the has-been Muse of the conformist past, she embraces
Borges's logic, the logic of the illogical:

Almost immediately, reality caved in at more than one
point. The truth is, it wanted to cave in.

The narrator shuts the window, pulls her chair to her desk, picks up her pen.
The writing begins.

Subject: Kaddish Guilt
Date: 2/05/2003 06:17:17 AM EST
From: dndyoung2@owl.com
To: dndyoung1@owl.com

Darling,

Woke up this morning is a sweat. First emotion of the day: guilt. First thought to
explain: I didn't say Kaddish for Papa. Or for my mother. Or for you. Or for Nate.
Help.

Subject: Re: Kaddish Guilt
Date: 2/05/2003 20:40:16 PM EST
From: dndyoung2@owl.com
To: dndyoung1@owl.com

Darling,

So the anniversary of Papa's death passed without my taking note of it.
Or did I, while sleeping last night? Okay, I didn't say Kaddish for him. Or for

you. Or for my mother or Nate. Chalk it up to my defiance against religious tradition all these years. Yeah, I knew the rules about saying Kaddish. But chose not to follow them. And now all of a sudden I'm feeling guilty for that omission? When Nate died, I believed my anger justified my not praying. When Mom died, it was – I don't know what to call it. When Papa died, I was so, so tired. And your illness left me no time to feel. And when you died, it was hollowness and despair and no habit of prayer. Now I wonder if my sleeping brain has been telling me something. Better think about Kaddish.

Love.

February 6, 2003

> Lie you easy, dream you light,
> And sleep you fast for aye;
> And luckier may you find the night
> Than ever you found the day.
> — A.E. Housman *A Shropshire Lad* LIX.

Dear Bathsua,

I hope this note finds you well and less plagued by bad dreams. Less plagued than you were. Less plagued than I am. I wish I were sleeping better. War preparations are mounting; the terrorism alert level is up again, from yellow, elevated, to high, orange. Before dressing to go to the Library this morning (you won't understand this) I danced furiously for fifteen minutes in just my underwear, my wet hair whipping wildly about my face, to the sound of "You and Me and the Bottle Makes Three Tonight," played again and again, by a band called "Big Bad Voodoo Daddy." A *danse macabre*.

The winter sky is a bleak, stony gray. Along the sidewalk on my way to the Library I skirted unpleasant patches of slush, just melted from what must have been earlier a grimly dangerous obstacle course. I imagine you too avoiding such tainted puddles on your way from your rooms in Westminster to your classroom in Whitehall, or to market and back.

The weather forecast is ominous – a cold front approaching from the northwest is set to merge with a moist air mass arriving from the southeast. Perfect conditions for a sou'easter that will produce heavy snow. Blizzard news is added to bad dreams, war news, and terrorism alerts.

Zoë of course heard the panic in my voice when she called this morning. "Come stay with us, Mom," she said. "What if the power goes out? How will you get out if you need to? How will we get to you if you need help? You'll be better off with us than home alone."

"Then lend me Ned or Gracie," I said. "Better yet, both. I'd rather be trapped with them here than be a fifth wheel with you. They'll keep me company and shovel me out."

She agreed. I'm readying the spare bedrooms and grocery shopping for a house filled with young people. It will be like the old days.

Thinking ahead: might we write each other stories about those busy old days of mothering? I would like that. And you? If this blizzard is as dire as the weather reports say, I don't know when I'll be back to the Library. Your replies will have to wait until I return.

Warmly, in a cold month,

Dee

P.S. Here's a dark little joke I stumbled across in Margaret Atwood's *Negotiating with the Dead: A Writer on Writing*:

> The Devil comes to the writer and says, "I will make you the best writer of your generation. Never mind generation – of this century. No – this millennium! Not only the best, but the most famous, and also the richest. In addition to that, you will be very influential and your glory will endure forever. All you have to do is sell me your grandmother, your mother, your wife, your kids, your dog, and your soul." "Sure," says the writer. "Absolutely – give me the pen – where do I sign?" Then he hesitates. "Just a minute," he says. What's the catch?"

Subject:	Re: Re: Kaddish Guilt
Date:	2/08/2003 16:23:49 PM EST
From:	dndyoung2@owl.com
To:	dndyoung1@owl.com

Darling,

I've done my homework and some research. I feel better now. Ἐξίσταται γὰρ πάντ’ ἀπ’ ἀλλήλων δίχα. For all things change, making way for each other. Maybe I'll sleep better?

Love.

Attachment: Kaddish

Kaddish

> – Nothing could have been done. There is no use beating your head against the wall.
> – But I want to know why nothing could have been done. There is a use in beating my brain against the wall. What death really says is: *think*.
> – Leon Wieseltier. *Kaddish*.

My father died last winter, my mother a decade before that. Jewish tradition prescribes daily recitation of the Mourner's Kaddish for eleven months and a day after the death of a parent. I didn't follow that tradition. Now, however, I'm feeling guilty about that lapse, which wasn't because my father was a difficult man or that I harbored a bitter stew of anger and pity about my mother. Nor did I recite the Mourner's Kaddish after the deaths of my baby son or husband. At each loss I knew what the tradition expected and chose not to follow it, chalking that omission up to disaffection with organized religion, my belief that I was a secularist or a Deist or something. Or maybe it was anger. Theodicy. Now suddenly I'm feeling guilty and wondering what I've missed by not honoring this tradition.

What does a teacher do in the face of such bewilderment? Homework and research.

First the homework. I found an old prayerbook here at home that of course contained the Kaddish, and, surprised by recollecting long-ago lessons from religious school, sounded out the words of the ancient prayer. The text was in the handsome, blocky Hebrew alphabet, plus an italic Roman-type transliteration for those unable to decipher the original. There was no translation. Anyone needing to say Kaddish didn't need it. Remembering glimpses of others at funerals and bar and bat mitzvahs over the years, I stood and murmured the seventy-five guttural, breathy syllables that were both completely familiar and totally foreign.

Next came research at a local synagogue library, where I learned that the Kaddish was first composed and its traditions codified by Rabbi Akiva in the first century of the Common Era. In English it's called the Mourner's Kaddish. In Hebrew it's *Kaddish Yatom*, the Orphan's Kaddish. It is composed in a combination of Hebrew and Aramaic, the latter a Syrian dialect used as a lingua franca in the Near East throughout the periods of the writing of both the Hebrew and Christian Bibles.

The same form of the Kaddish is said after a spouse, sibling, or child dies, but then only for a month. For a parent, however, Kaddish is said for nearly a year. Perhaps the long mourning period for a parent arises from the fact that, at least biologically speaking, a parent is irreplaceable. We may choose a new spouse or have more children, but not so a parent. And perhaps the discipline of a long mourning period for a parent reminds us that, for as long as a parent lives, someone has the natural right to discipline us. At a parent's death, we have only the self and the tradition left to do it.

Surprisingly, the Kaddish prayer never names God nor asks God for anything. Indeed, it leaves open the possibility that mourners may be in states of both belief and active, persistent doubt. It seems to permit mourners to take as givens the inscrutability of first causes, of end-of-life suffering, and of love and loss.

While death, they say, is a fine and private thing, saying Kaddish is neither silent nor solitary. Known by the root of its second word, which means "holy" or "sanctified," the Kaddish contains a plethora of nearly synonymous verbs. Aloud, *yitgadal, v'yitkadash,* Kaddish reciters say, *yitbarakh v'yishtabakh v'yitpa'ar v'yitromam v'yitnasei v'yit-hadar v'yit'aleh v'yit-halal.* They speak of magnifying, making holy, blessing, praising, glorifying, raising, exalting, honoring, elevating, lauding, and extolling God's Name.

For traditional Jews the Kaddish obligation is to recite the prayer in the company of others, in a *minyan*, a gathering of at least ten Jewish adults. Some less observant Jews choose to say the *Kaddish Yatom* alone. I am told that it is recited in kitchens and gardens, porches, bedrooms, offices, hotel rooms and airplanes. One friend told me she said it on the top floor of the Musée d'Orsay, watching clouds race over Paris, and another waiting to serve jury duty. I've heard that it is said in Buenos Aires by Las Madres de la Plaza de Mayo, who march in memory of their lost children, *los desaparecidos.* The friend who told me this said it was the only time she cried while whispering the words.

It's the practice of many *minyanim* for each mourner to name the person being remembered, saying aloud the deceased's Hebrew name – in my father's case it would have been *Yisroel Moshe ben Yosef Yaakov v'Esther Reizl* – the intimate name given in infancy that includes both patronymic and matronymic. For a few seconds every day of the mourning period, the deceased is the beloved child of his or her parents.

The response to this public naming is, "May we remember these loved ones for a blessing. Amen." The key terms in that statement are *remember*, *love*, and *blessing*. And the verb form, too, is noteworthy, one that grammarians call the "conditional-future-hortatory." In the Kaddish nearly every verb is in that form, which we express in English through the helping verb "may." *Y'hei sh'mei raba m'varakh l'alam u-l'almei almaya.* May the Great Name be blessed always and forever. *Y'hei sh'lama raba min sh'maya v'chaim aleinu.* May a great peace from heaven and life be upon us. What tentative hopefulness this grammatical form expresses! It honors uncertainty: Future peace and life are longed-for possibilities, not guarantees.

Kaddish reciters take for granted the feeling of being completely off kilter. Yet being together within a *minyan* among others feeling similarly dislocated is itself a consolation. In English the word *consolation* has two parts, *con* meaning *together* and *sol* meaning *alone*. How apt – together in aloneness.

On certain holidays in the Jewish calendar and on the anniversaries of the deaths of loved ones, one is obligated to say Kaddish regularly. And when in the presence of other Mourners, one is always obligated to be mindful and respectful. There, too, go I, for are we not all in need of consolation, feeling gathered up together in our own aloneness?

Consolation is indeed at the heart of what may be the Kaddish's most mysteriously beautiful sentence: *B'rikh hu,* The Blessed One, *l'ela min kol birkhata v'shirata,* is above all blessings and hymns, *tushb'khata v'nekhemata,* above all praises and consolations, *da-amiran b'alma,* that are uttered in the world. There it is, the Aramaic word *nekhemata,* which is usually translated into English as "consolations." Blessings, hymns, and praises all extol The Holy One. But to what Great Mourner are *consolations* directed? Might God too need consoling? And how can God be consoled?

Perhaps the answer is in the Kaddish's last sentence: *Oseh shalom bim romav, hu ya'aseh shalom aleinu v'al kol Yisrael,* May the One who makes peace on high make peace upon us and upon all Israel. Twice we repeat the familiar Hebrew word *shalom,* peace.

V'imru amen. And let us say amen.

February 12, 2003

> I would like to hear your life as *you* heard it, coming at you, instead
> of hearing it as I do, a sober sound of expectations reduced, desires
> blunted, hopes deferred or abandoned, chances lost, defeats accepted,
> griefs borne. . . . I would like to hear it as it sounded while it was passing.
> — Wallace Stegner. *Angle of Repose.*

Dear Bathsua,

Snow is falling thick and fast. It's already above the third step at the front door. Gracie, Ned, and I are stuck as tight as ticks. After breakfast the three of us curled up in the den and read all morning. I'm re-reading Virginia Woolf's *Mrs. Dalloway.*

Dare we tackle a new assignment? Having two children in the house makes me long to remember the good days long ago when I was a young mother. But I well know that for both of us those were times of great losses as well as great joys. Dare we try to write about them?

Until I get back to the Library, for safekeeping I'll tuck my notes to you inside *Mrs. Dalloway.*

Yours,

Dee

Subject:	Snow
Date:	2/13/2003 13:03:57 PM EST
From:	dndyoung2@owl.com
To:	dndyoung1@owl.com

Darling,

Before ending early this morning, the snow had accumulated more than two feet. After breakfast the clouds started to break. Ned, Gracie, and I put on snowshoes and trudged along Constitution Avenue to look at the Capitol snuggled among great, pillowy drifts. The thick eddying whiteness softens all the hard edges of things. I felt my throat catch at the tenderness of it all. You should have been with us.

Love.

Subject:	Empty mailboxes
Date:	2/18/2003 13:03:57 PM EST
From:	dndyoung2@owl.com
To:	dndyoung1@owl.com

Darling,

> This was always a crucial moment of the day for me, and I found it
> impossible to approach it calmly. There was always the hope that good
> news would be sitting there – an unexpected check, an offer of work,
> a letter that would somehow change my life – and by now the habit of
> anticipation was so much a part of me that I could scarcely look at my
> mailbox without getting a rush.
>   – Paul Auster. *The Locked Room.*

Have gotten into the habit with Bathsua to start our letters with epigraphs. Why not open emails to you this way, too? This one from Auster is particularly apt, I think.

You haven't got much mail from me these days – with Ned and Gracie around I didn't have much time or inclination. They've gone back home now, and school has started up again. I miss them.

I finally went to the Library this morning. Nothing from Bathsua, which surprised me. The silent little cranny in Alcove 6 was empty. When will I hear from her? Or you?

Lonely. Love.

Subject:	Re: Re: Re: Kaddish
Date:	2/18/2003 PM EST
From:	dndyoung2@owl.com
To:	dndyoung1@owl.com

Darling,

> To go where? In that Dark – that – in that God? a radiance? A Lord in the
> Void? Like an eye in the black cloud in a dream? Adonoi at last, with you?
>   – Allen Ginsberg. "Kaddish."

As you may have guessed, I've started saying Kaddish. Quietly, at home, once a day – in the early-morning light or in the late afternoon dusk. In the kitchen, usually, looking out the window at the garden. I can recite it from memory now.

Also from memory, those days last winter when you were so sick from the chemo and I was visiting Papa at the oh-so-ironically-named Sunrise Gardens. Especially the day he pretty much gave up on the physical therapy, realizing he'd never walk straight-backed again. The day I saw that gray, shutting-down look, even though the nurses said his vital signs were all stable. The day they moved him to the fifth floor and the floor director scheduled the "Conversation." The meal trays he would leave practically untouched. The thermoses of home-made chicken soup I brought and he'd swallow two or three spoonfuls to humor me before waving his hand, closing his eyes, and turning to face the wall beside his bed. The time he turned toward me, looked me in the eye and asked, "Is this how it ends?" before closing his eyes and turning to face the wall again. The days when I left you at the hematology clinic and ran to sit beside him, reading to him while he just lay there, still, eyes closed, with that furrow of sadness, anger, worry, and disapproval above the bridge of his nose, and the veins on his neck where you can see the pulse throbbing to beat the band. What was he thinking? Was he chastising God for being *B'rikh hu,* The Blessed One, *l'ela min kol birkhata v'shirata,* above all blessings and hymns, *tushb'khata v'nekhemata,* above all praises and consolations, *da-amiran b'alma,* that are uttered in the world?

Subject: Writers' Block/Dreaming
Date: 2/20/2003 13:03:57 PM EST
From: dndyoung2@owl.com
To: dndyoung1@owl.com

Darling,

The words won't come. When I sit at my desk or the kitchen table, nothing comes. I look back at what I've written to you and Bathsua – it all seems futile, the attempts at humor, explanation, narration, description – all inept, inept, inept. Including the belated Kaddish recitations.

The only things that seem real are the grey lumps of dirty snow and rotten ice, the runup to a distant war, the clogging grief over dead babies, lovers, and leaders. I made a stupid joke to Bathsua about writing being a feeding off the dead. Words are cheap leeches, and I, once fancying myself a writer, now have no stomach for them.

I asked Bathsua to write about her children. She hasn't written all month. I sit here with idle hands, my dress and hair disheveled, the stove cold, no lights on, at a dust-covered desk. Have I offended the gods or the muses, or whoever rains down words? What am I to do?

Love, ashes.

February 21, 2003

Dear Bathsua,

Here in my usual place in the Main Reading Room. I feel a negative force field of your silence. We are real to one another, even in silence, I hope.

D

February 25, 2003

Σπονδαὶ δ᾽ ἐς τὸ πᾶν ἐκ μετοίκων
Παλλάδος ἀστοῖς. Ζεὺς ὁπανόπτας
οὕτω Μοῖρά τε συγκατέβα.
ὀλολύξατε νῦν ἐπί μολπαῖς.

Solemn peace shall there be,
Forever binding our people and those from afar.
God the all-seeing,
And Moira, the goddess of Fate,
Shall agree to it.
Now let voices warble in song.
 – Aeschylus. *The Eumenides.*

Dear Bathsua,

Still no word from you. I trudge to the Library every day to look in the space beneath the Loeb Classics. Nothing. I'm certain it's not because our hiding place has been discovered.

I have angered you. It must have been my thoughtless joke and my glib request to write about our children. Please forgive me.

As penance I am reading *The Orestaia* in Greek. It is slow, hard work. (I get the sense mainly from the English translation on the right sides of the pages.) This morning I came to the choral prayer in *The Eumenides*, which I have quoted above. Besides begging you for peace, I find that it also means a lot these days in another context: President Bush is preparing to take us to war in Iraq. May the gods hear the silent prayer for peace of one disheveled old woman sitting here in this Library.

How luscious is the sound of Aeschylus's verb ὀλολύξατε. Oh loluxateh.

Pace,

Dee

Subject:	Cleaning, grieving
Date:	2/26/2003 14:52:12 PM EST
From:	dndyoung2@owl.com
To:	dndyoung1@owl.com

Darling,

Finally got around to cleaning out the magazine rack beside your chair in the study. Came across a Shakespeare Theatre program from the winter 1999 season – remember? – for their production of "King John." Went to the book shelf, found the play script, started reading:

Grief fills the room up of my absent child,
Lies in his bed, walks up and down with me,
Puts on his pretty looks, repeats his words,
Remembers me of all his gracious parts,
Stuffs out his vacant garments with his form:
Then have I reason to be fond of grief?

Oh, Dan. Is it forty years since we lost him?

—⁓— *Nine* —⁓—

March 5, 2003

Have you ever seen a cornfield after the reaping? Laid flat to stubble,
and here and there, unaccountably, miraculously spared, a few stalks still
upright. Why those? There is no reason. Ovid's Medea, the Thyestes
of Varius (who was Virgil's friend and considered by some his equal),
the lost Aeschylus trilogy of the Trojan war -- all gathered to oblivion
in sheaves, along with hundreds of Greek and Roman authors known
only for fragments or their names alone. And here and there a cornstalk,
a thistle, a poppy, still standing, but as to purpose, signifying nothing.
        – Tom Stoppard. *Invention of Love*.

Dear Bathsua,

You've gone silent on me. The epigraph is a second peace offering.
That some artists and their works find lasting fame while others are lost
forever has surely puzzled you as it has me. So, too, that the memories of
so many fine and good people are lost forever, while others – no better, no
wiser – find lasting fame. (The metaphor of the surviving thistle and poppy
I know from reading Tolstoy. Probably it has been used by countless others
whose names are lost to me.)

I would love to discuss Stoppard's work with you. I saw his play "The
Invention of Love" a couple of years ago at a theater here in DC and read
the script during the week of our big snowstorm last month. The passage
above is preceded by another that I think you might appreciate. I have taken
the liberty of abridging it and changing one word. Despite those changes
and the original's one bit of enormous irreverence, I hope you, Stoppard,
and Tolstoy might approve:

> The real thing is only to shine some light, it doesn't
> matter where on what, it's the light itself, against the
> darkness, it's what left of God's purpose when you take

away God. . . . [Writing] is a small redress against the vast unreason.

Given the war talk I really need some light shining in the darkness. Please write.

Yours faithfully,

Dee

P.S. I changed Stoppard's "Scholarship" to my "Writing." Any thoughts?

March 7, 2003

> Many things, for aught I know, may exist, whereof neither I nor any other man hath or can have any idea or notion whatsoever.
> — George Berkeley. *Three Dialogues between Hylas and Philonous in Opposition to Sceptics and Atheists.*

Dear Bathsua,

A year or so ago I joined a cybergroup called SETI on Line, SETI being the acronym for "Searching for Extra-Terrestrial Intelligence." Scientists at the University of California at Berkeley started it. (How apt! Wasn't it Bishop Berkeley who famously asked, *"If a tree falls in the forest and no one hears it, does it make a sound?"*) Anyway, the SETI scientists were monitoring radio signals from remote Space, hoping one day to establish communication with intelligent extraterrestrials who might be somewhere out in the universe beyond our solar system. The scientists lacked computer power to process all the incoming radio signals, so they invited folks like me to give over to them the passive power of their screensavers when their computers were not in use. I know this sounds bizarre, but SETI on Line appeals to all sorts of reasonable people, scientists and engineers mainly, who believe that we here on Earth cannot be alone, the only sentient beings in the vast Cosmos. Why not listen for meaningful signals or send them out, even with no certainty they'll be received, understood, or replied to?

Why not, indeed? Maybe that's why people pray. Somewhere out there may be Someone Who cares for us and waits patiently to hear from us, Someone Who may one day respond.

Perhaps that's why I value our correspondence. I miss you, my dear, distant friend, my remote Listener upon whom I have come to depend as assurance of the unity of this thinly populated universe. Your silence reminds me of how I felt after my mother, father, husband, and baby son died. Empty.

Yours,

Dee

March 8, 2003

> It is useless to try to adjudicate a long-standing animosity by asking who started it or who is the most wrong. The only sufficient answer is to give up the animosity and try forgiveness, to try to love our enemies and to talk to them and (if we pray) to pray for them. If we can't do any of that, then we must begin again by trying to imagine our enemies' children who, like our children, are in mortal danger because of enmity that they did not cause.
>   – Wendell Berry. "A Citizen's Response to the National
>   Security Strategy of the United States of America."

Dear Bathsua,

A story in the midst of rising war news. I ran into my old teaching buddy Sophie at the grocery store. I haven't seen her since she got home from her trip to visit her son Sam, who is a newspaper reporter posted in Jerusalem. In the produce aisle surrounded by peppers, lettuce, and broccoli, she tells me this story about gas masks. I can't stop thinking about it. Nor can I stop writing to you, whether you reply or not. Here is a quick jotting:

In mid-December Sophie decides to fly to Israel to visit her son. And the day she decides she hears on the news George Bush saying, *Don't worry, everything will be all right, but maybe we should all get immunized for smallpox just in case there's some act of biological terrorism.* And somebody that same day tells her that Americans in Israel don't have gas masks like the Israelis do. So Sophie decides to buy a gas mask here in the States to take it in her luggage to protect Sam in Jerusalem from terrorists and Sadam Hussein's missles when war starts.

Where do you find gas masks for sale, Sophie wonders? So she googles "gas masks retail" and gets a gajillion hits. Israeli gas masks. Czech gas masks. Finnish. Russian. Military. Civilian. Her hands start to sweat, she tells me. Gotta find somebody who'll talk me through this. Finds one hit with a 703 phone number – local, she figures, no long-distance charges. So she dials, and the guy who answers says, *You got a few minutes? I'll give you Gas Masks 101*, and he lectures her for twenty minutes on the phone. Her ear starts to hurt, she says, from the phone pressed to it. *You don't want top of the line*, the guy says. *It's gotta look like what the Israelis have. You don't want to have something that the others are gonna grab. People do crazy stuff in an emergency, ya know?*

Sophie's a wreck now, she says, her hand squeezing the phone and sweating, her heart racing, taking notes meanwhile, like mad. The guy keeps talking. *You gotta get brand-new filters, not the old stuff, because the charcoal in 'em's got a shelflife of fifteen years, and the last time the Israelis needed them was, like, fifteen years ago.* And the guy says, *Ya gotta call Joe. At General American Security Products*, he says. *On Tamiami Trail in Florida. Here, I'll give ya the number.* She writes it all down, writing a mile a minute, thanks the Virginia guy, calls Joe in Florida. He answers, *G.A.S.P. Joe speakin'.* My God, she thinks, it's called *gasp. Whazzup?* Joe says. She tells him about visiting her son in Jerusalem. *Yeh, yeh*, Joe says. *We got gas masks. All kinds. What kind ya lookin' for?* Sophie can do all the accents. Telling me this story she starts sounding like she grew up in Brooklyn. *You spoke to Kyle in Virginia?* Joe says. *Okay. I'll send you what I gave my daughter in September. She made aliyah. Happy Hanukah, by the way.* How do you know I'm Jewish? Sophie asks. *Hey, who else but Jews are crazy enough to fly to Israel in the middle of a run-up to a war in the Middle East? I'll throw in an extra charcoal canister for good measure. And fedex 'em to you*, Joe says. *You'll have in a coupla days.* She runs downstairs to get her credit card, runs back, out of breath, and starts giving him her information.

Take it easy, Sophie, Joe says. *Everything's gonna be okay. Believe me. What's the address?* When she tells him, he says, *DC?* Yup. *Zipcode?* She tells him. *Whatcha been waitin' for?* What? *That's my best zipcode. I'm sending stuff there two, three times a week. Everybody there's already got my stuff. Your neighbors are way ahead of you, Sophie. Protective suits. Water filters. Protective shelters. Air scrubbers. You heard what Bush said the other day? I'll send you my catalog along with the mask. You might need for yourself.* Joe, Sophie says. It's my son I'm worried about. *I know, I know*, he says. *But you gotta look out for yourself. Ya know what they say on the plane about puttin' on the oxygen mask first before ya help the kid next to you?*

She's crying into the phone now and blows her nose, she tells me. *Gezundheit,* he says. But Joe, she says. *I know, I know,* he says again. *But everything's gonna be okay. Your son. My daughter. They'll be okay. And zey gezundt. Go and return in good health. You're a good mother, Sophie,'* he says. *I'm just sayin'.*

All this Sophie tells me in the produce aisle about her trip to visit Sam in Jerusalem.

Yours,

Dee

Subject: Protest March today with Neddy
Date: 3/08/2003 10:27:11 PM EST
From: dndyoung2@owl.com
To: dndyoung1@owl.com

Met Neddy after lunch at Metro Center and marched with him and thousands of others around the White House. I carried my cardboard sign reading "End This War Before It Begins" that I'd made after breakfast. It had a little American flag on top.

Funny, I was with Neddy and what seemed like millions of people, but I felt oddly alone, a part of a group and yet apart from it. We walked round and round the White House, chanting old antiwar songs like "All We Are Saying Is Give Peace a Chance." The crowd kept growing. The police steered us in wider and wider circles around the White House until, polite to a fault, they moved us onto the Ellipse and as far south as Constitution Avenue. The whole time I felt like a tiny cell in a giant organism. I bobbed my little sign up and down in rhythm to the chants and weakly added to the singing and shouting.

At about four o'clock, when our part of the crowd was on the Treasury side of Executive Drive, we all joined hands in a huge continuous chain. The police were polite, even deferential, maybe because so many of us looked like their gray-haired mothers, grandmothers, and teachers. They told us to keep moving and stay separated; that's what our permit allowed. When our part of the chain reached Pennsylvania Avenue, the police steered us up Fifteenth, toward H, away from the front of the White House.

Ned and I peeled off from the crowd. In the late afternoon shadows, we headed for home. He came home to the Hill with me, and helped make a festive little protest dinner. Told him about you and the antiwar marches of the Sixties. "You've gotta write this stuff down, Grandma," he said.

Zo and Jack and Gracie drove down and joined us for dessert, then took the dear boy home. He too misses you enormously, Dan. They all do. Love.

Subject:	Writing fast and furious
Date:	3/09/2003 9:37:49 AM EST
From:	dndyoung2@owl.com
To:	dndyoung1@owl.com

Danny darling --

Am resolved to write for an hour or so every morning for the rest of the month – or at least until the first day of spring. I've got this urgent need to put stuff on paper – or at least into pixels. Maybe it's the war. Or something happening in my head. Whatever it is, I've got to do it. Some stuff I'll leave for Bathsua, some I'll send to you, some I'll just leave here on my computer or in a desk drawer. I remember one of my teaching buddies used to say not even to lisft your pen, not stop to make corrections,just keep on gng. Going. And if the thought stream doesnt come to just type or write the same word againa dna gaion until it does. That's what I'm experimenting with now. I'm resisting the urge to stop and edit (maddening not to) but that will come later. The laptopprogeam is sent on auto'correct, so forgive the mistakes.

Thinking about the day of your diagnosis. And the drive along Rock Creek Parkway from school to the doctors office that morning. And the big black smoke plume we saw rising from the Pentagon into the blue, blue sky. And being inthe waiting room after the doctor told us what he had to and the nurse asking us whether we should get out fast be aus they had heard on the radio that a fourth plane was headed for either the White House or the Capitol. And we looked at her dazed. We were a few blocks from the White House and home was a few blocks from the Capitol. And we had just gotten word that you had maybe six months to live. So What did it matter whether we stayed or went home? and the doctor was right behind us coming out of his office and said, why don't you head up to Zoë's? she might need you with the kids and all? and I drove like crazy along Pennsylvania Avenue to M Street. Sirens were blaring. People were rushing on foot through the streets. You looked over at me, dully, wondering how I could drive like that, veering and stopping and starting all the way to Georgetown. I turned up 30th Street and stopped at the light at Q. It was quiet all of a sudden. I screeched to a stop at the light. There was a road construction crew standing on the sidewalk, the guys looking at us and scratching their heads in disbelief at what they had no idea was going on around them. And we screeched off again, up past Dumbarton Oaks, onto Wisconsin Avenue and past the Cathedral, up and up and up, away from downtown toward Zoë's.

Subject:	Re: Writing fast and furious
Date:	3/09/2003 10:38:12 AM EST
From:	dndyoung2@owl.com
To:	dndyoung1@owl.com

Danny darling –
Cannot resist the urge to edit. It's ingrained. And a safe kind of concentration. Thinking I should write to Josh. Apologize. Love.

Subject:	Re: Re: Writing fast and furious
Date:	3/10/2003 8:56:27 PM EST
From:	dndyoung2@owl.com
To:	dndyoung1@owl.com

Remembering how I couldn't tell Josh how tied up in knots I was at him when Papa was so sick. He'd send me those emails from California pontificating about how he'd handle the health crises differently and had big-time doc friends he'd like to involve in the case. But was too busy to come east to help with the care-giving or meet with the Georgetown docs Zoë had brought in. And yelled at me over the phone and made me feel like the village idiot when I couldn't remember the exact name and dosage of the med Papa was on. And then when he swooped in that weekend at the very end, he arrived at the hospital fifteen minutes before visiting hours ended and started second-guessing the care plan right there at Papa's bedside as if he couldn't hear what Josh was saying. Now I wish I'd started a huge, screaming argument in the parking lot in front of Zoë and Neddy and a bunch of strangers. That I'd told him to shut the fuck up and either fly out on the next plane or spend the next day just sitting with Papa – if he made it through the night – just holding his hand. Instead I just clenched my teeth and kept my mouth shut. I look back now and picture Josh at the funeral acting like he was the chief mourner. Then, too, I just kept quiet and seethed inside. Why couldn't I just tell him what I was feeling? Why do I always hold back and not let the feelings out? Is writing stuff like this a healthy cathartic now? Or am I just silently, privately picking away at old scabs the way I used to when I was a kid? I still have a few of the scars to prove it. I remember how for years I've felt hollowed out inside. Now I think the space inside me was filling up with silent anger. Until now I've felt incredibly small, like a hollow, tiny grain of something filling up with something unspeakably enormous. I don't want that hollowness to be filled any more with anger at Josh. Or anyone. What will let the anger out and maybe go away?

Oh, and this war stuff is making me crazy. Should write to Josh.

Love.

Subject:	Re: Re: Re: Writing fast and furious
Date:	3/11/2003 7:22:56:27 AM EST
From:	dndyoung2@owl.com
To:	dndyoung1@owl.com

Keep revisiting what Papa said to me, more than once. "Don't visit, Dee," he said. "Don't waste your time on an old fart like me." And how he asked me near the end – "Is this how it has to be?" And my dogged acceptance those awful weeks when you were sick from the chemo and told me, "Go, Dee, go sit with him," and I did as you said, and wondered guiltily why I hadn't felt the slightest bit the same way about my mother all those years before when she was so miserable and withdrawn. I've got a lot of darkness in me, Dan, that I think about when I'm alone and unbusy. And regrets.

And hollowness, negativity, negative space, too. They don't show so much
– or at least I thought they don't – when I'm in company or working. The
other day, though, when we were just sitting, the two of us, over coffee,
and I wasn't talking, Zoë asked me if I was angry about something, and I
answered, surprised and chagrined, "No. Why?" And she said, "Just a look
on your face. That's all." That darkness, those regrets, that anger that I
think I keep at bay most of the time – are they right out there in the open
all the time for everyone to see? And not just this year, this *annus horribilis.*
Is it just Zoë, because she's always been so tuned in to people's moods, or
has it been because we lost Nate and she watched us so closely? She's the
one who told me years ago that inside my head I'm a dispositional pessimist
and probably always have been, since my own childhood, not just since
Nate. Always expecting the worst. She's right. When I'm alone there are all
these negative thoughts. Wasn't losing Nate proof that the worst will always
happen? I walk down the stairs every morning and count them – careful,
don't trip, Dee, I'm telling myself without saying the words; careful in the
shower, Dee, don't slip and hit your head on the way down and bleed to
death; careful, Dee, don't choke on that vitamin pill. Even the best things
for me are always tinged with the inevitability of the worst. My day job is to
project a positivism that I don't feel inside. Nights are the worst. Could go
on and on, but I better not. Better stop.
Love.

Subject:	Re: Re: Re: Re: Writing fast and furious
Date:	3/12/2003 6:56:01AM EST
From:	dndyoung2@owl.com
To:	dndyoung1@owl.com

Wrote a short note to Josh. Apologized for letting the rift between us
grow to such proportions. Feel better.

So now, I think I should be honest with myself about the other rift, the
really big one – a silent chasm, really – that I caused and that you patched
over? My unspoken fury at you when Nate was diagnosed and suffered
and died? When we got the diagnosis, that chromosomal Ashkenazik death
sentence of Tay Sachs, I knew we shared the responsibility equally. We both

carried the gene, the doctor said. They didn't know from prenatal genetic testing back then, or at least we didn't go out of our way to know about it. Or I didn't. I was so busy denying things about my family, so busy keeping my mother out of my life, so busy pretending that I and you and our life together were all *sui generis*. The science told me it was nobody's fault, or the fault of both of us. But, boy, I sure blamed you and made you suffer. As if making you suffer would punish both of us.

 I can't write this.

 Dan, I am so so sorry. Did you ever forgive me? Will you now? Love.

Subject: Re: Re: Re: Re: Re: Writing fast and furious
Date: 3/13/2003 8:15:37 AM EST
From: dndyoung2@owl.com
To: dndyoung1@owl.com

Lots of stuff coming out in these daily rants, hunh? Relief from the way I feel about this crazy war and this president, who I could rant and rave about for hours. Instead I'm drilling down into the mothering and wifing and daughtering and sistering. Maybe because I can do something about them and not about this war, which I feel totally powerless about. This note is short. Am about to walk to the Library, write a note for Bathsua, read for a while. Need to clear myself out of my head, if that makes sense. Love.

March 13, 2003

> But how can I explain it to *you*?
> You will understand it less after I have explained it.
> All that I can hope to make you understand
> Is only events: not what has happened.
> – T.S. Eliot. "The Family Reunion."

Dear Bathsua,

 Any day now this war in Iraq could begin for real. Last Saturday afternoon my grandson and I marched against the war in a huge human stream around the White House. Thank goodness for the dear boy.

Yours, patiently,

Dee

Subject:	Re:Re: Re: Re: Re: Re: Writing fast and furious
Date:	3/14/2003 7:12:45 AM EST
From:	dndyoung2@owl.com
To:	dndyoung1@owl.com

Dearest –

Must be honest with myself. About how I closed up and drew away from you when Nate was-diagnosed-and-suffered-and-died. There. I said it.

Is that closed-up, drawn-away darkness my authentic I? I've often observed that, in the face of powerful emotional moments – grieving, loving – I feel hollow. Or turn the feeling into an idea. Has there ever been enough feeling in my way of feeling? Will I ever open myself to the full-bodied, full-throated, full-hearted richness at either end of the spectrum of joy and rage, love and sorrow? And everything in between?

P.S. I cannot avoid that weird long verb about Nate. Like the imaginary grammar Borges writes about in that "Tlön Uqbar" story. It's one verb of an enduring condition. (Is that the aorist?) There I go again.

Subject:	Re: Re: Re: Re: Re: Re: Re: Writing fast and furious
Date:	3/15/2003 7:42:01 AM EST
From:	dndyoung2@owl.com
To:	dndyoung1@owl.com

Dearest –

Okay, so today I'm not writing, just copying. But that's okay, too, right?

Pablo Neruda. Nobel Prize Speech 1971.
I have often maintained that the best poet is he who prepares our
daily bread: the nearest baker who does not imagine himself to be

a god. He does his majestic and unpretentious work of kneading
the dough, consigning it to the oven, baking it in golden colours
and handing us our daily bread as a duty of fellowship. And, if
the poet succeeds in achieving this simple consciousness, this too
will be transformed into an element in an immense activity, in
a simple or complicated structure which constitutes the building
of a community, the changing of the conditions which surround
mankind, the handing over of mankind's products: bread, truth,
wine, dreams. If the poet joins this never-completed struggle to
extend to the hands of each and all his part of his undertaking,
his effort and his tenderness to the daily work of all people, then
the poet must take part, the poet will take part, in the sweat, in
the bread, in the wine, in the whole dream of humanity. Only in
this indispensable way of being ordinary people shall we give back
to poetry the mighty breadth which has been pared away from it
little by little in every epoch, just as we ourselves have been whittled
down in every epoch.

Subject:	Re: Re: Re: Re: Re: Re: Re: Re: Writing fast and furious
Date:	3/16/2003 8:05:56 AM EST
From:	dndyoung2@owl.com
To:	dndyoung1@owl.com

Dearest –

Again, copying. Satisfying in its own way. Lines from Allen Ginsberg's
"Kaddish":

Strange now to think of you, gone . . .while I walk
on the sunny pavement . . .
I've been up all night, talking, talking, reading the Kaddish aloud,
listening to Ray Charles blues shout blind on the phonograph
the rhythm the rhythm – and your memory in my head
And how Death is that remedy all singers dream of, sing, remember. . .
. . .and my own imagination of a withered leaf – at dawn –
Dreaming back thru life, . . .
. . .No more to say, and nothing to weep for but the Beings

in the Dream, trapped in its disappearance,

sighing, screaming with it, buying and selling pieces of phantom,

worshipping each other,

worshipping the God included in it all – longing or inevitability? –

while it lasts, a Vision – anything more?

It leaps about me, as I go out and walk the street,

look back over my shoulder. . .

. . . you're not old now, that's left here with me –

Myself, anyhow, maybe as old as the universe –

and I guess that dies with us--enough to cancel all that comes –

What came is gone forever every time – . . .

. . .There, rest. No more suffering for you.

I know where you've gone, it's good.

No more flowers in the summer fields of New York,

no joy now, no more fear . . .

. . .Over and over – refrain – of the Hospitals – still haven't written

your history – leave it abstract – a few images run thru the mind. . .

. . . By my later burden – vow to illuminate mankind –

this is release of particulars.

Subject:	Re: Re: Re: Re: Re: Re: Re: Re: Re: Writing fast and furious
Date:	3/17/2003 8:34:21 AM EST
From:	dndyoung2@owl.com
To:	dndyoung1@owl.com

Dearest –

The copying's definitely no substitute for writing to you, for trying to reach you on paper the way we did that summer when you were in Prague, for speaking to you about all the ordinary things across the breakfast and dinner table, for communing wordlessly with you all those days and months and years, for imagining that we're together again. These all seem like a lifetime ago. They *are* a lifetime ago. Love.

Subject:	Re: Re: Re: Re: Re: Re: Re: Re: Re: Re: Writing fast and furious
Date:	3/18/2003 6:47:18 AM EST
From:	dndyoung2@owl.com
To:	dndyoung1@owl.com

Not doing so well. Lonely and so sad that Bathsua hasn't been writing back to me. Her silence is chilling. I can't complain to her lest she stop writing altogether. Nor can I find the right words to complain to her with. Wouldn't rage and "wrong words" be better than this silence?
Love.

Subject:	Re: Re: Re: Re: Re: Re: Re: Re: Re: Re: Writing fast and furious
Date:	3/19/2003 7:53:54 AM EST
From:	dndyoung2@owl.com
To:	dndyoung1@owl.com

I'm changing, Dan. Something's happening to me. Is it time or something else? Or maybe the hurting is changing? I want it to happen but I don't at the same time. Does this make sense?

March 20, 2003

> Now I sit at my open window, writing – for whom? Not for any friend or mistress. Scarcely for myself, even. I do not read today what I wrote yesterday; nor shall I read this tomorrow. I write simply so that my hand can move, my thoughts move of their own accord.
> – Hjalmar Söderberg. *Doctor Glas.*

Dear Bathsua,

I checked our hiding place this morning. All my leavings have disappeared; nothing's been left in return. Someone's taken what I've written. A tidying librarian? Or you? Are my letters discarded unread, or pored over without reply? I'll keep writing either way.

President Bush says we are at war and that it will end shortly. I doubt the latter.

Yours,
Dee

Subject: Re: Re: Re: Re: Re: Re: Re: Re: Re: Re: Writing fast and furious
Date: 3/21/2003 8:21:46 AM EST
From: dndyoung2@owl.com
To: dndyoung1@owl.com

Dearest –

First day of spring. Second day of war.

Love.

Subject: Shadows and Dreams
Date: 3/22/2003 22:53:06 PM EST
From: dndyoung2@owl.com
To: dndyoung1@owl.com

Dearest –

Amid my ashen mood two miracles:

First: a shadow on the dining room wall, cast by the sunlight through tree branches, that looked to be a stern profile, with deepset eyes, an aquiline nose. The visage shape-shifted into a benign face gazing straight at me. Mere shadows of light filtered, flittering, onto the dining room wall – or you?

Then: a poem, all at once:

> I dip down, my pen a net,
> And draw the words up like ready minnows
> Innocent I wish to capture them.
> No. They slip away like real minnows,
> Flitting away all together in one direction,
> As far from me as they can get
> Until they forget what sent them
> Swimming, shimmering, away.
> I draw up instead the memory
> Of a dream I had the other night:
> Two women stand together in three-quarter profile,
> Wearing old evening dresses,
> Antiques from some imagined clothes press,
> The fabric black fading into purplish-green,

The ruffles flattened.
The two lean toward one another, their mouths half open
As if about to whisper a special confidence
To one another. I strain to overhear
Their words.
They disappear, dissolve,
Swim away, sleep-baited.

Love.

~m~ *Ten* ~m~

April 1, 2003

וַתֹּאמֶר הָאִשָּׁה הָאַחַת, בִּי אֲדֹנִי, אֲנִי וְהָאִשָּׁה הַזֹּאת, יֹשְׁבֹת בְּבַיִת אֶחָד

And the one woman said, Oh my lord, I and this woman dwell in one house.
– 1 Kings 3.17.

Dear Dee,

Enough of this long silent spell. I have indeed been reading your letters. We both know the pleasure that derives from writing for its own sake, regardless of reception.

Remember that wry little Margaret Atwood jest you shar'd about trading others' souls to the Devil for the gift of writing? But never mind. 'Tis spring and, despite the war news, a time for new beginnings.

This morning wind-driven raindrops stream down my window pane, the droplets streaking toward and then away from each other, nearly joining for an instant, then sheering away and merging in the end, their separate identities lost into a greater whole?

You ask'd in February that I write about mothering my children. First I must write of being a sister to Ithamaria. Like those raindrops my thoughts about being a mother and sister run beside each other, streaking apart, joining for an instant, sheering away and merging in the end.

In childhood Ithamaria and I were like two berries on a single stem. Later as maids and young wives and mothers, then as old women, we shifted and changed in regard to one another, ever approaching and separating, approaching and separating until. . . . Ah, until –

In childhood Ithamaria and I shar'd one bed and our parents' love. Neither was divided equally. Itha occupied more of the bed, I more of the love. We shar'd the mourning of our mother and the care of our father, but those were not borne evenly either. Nonetheless, we shar'd a childhood, blooming womanhood, many years of marriage, much of the rearing of our children.

We shar'd much else besides, great and small. We had three children with the same names – my Mary, her Mary; my Bathsua, her Bathsua; my Johnny, her Johnny. When Richard and I were in dire straits and later, after he died, Itha divided her pin money with me, unbeknownst to her watchful husband. I imparted to her the little gossips of my schoolroom days and the news obtain'd in my comings and goings to Saint James's to tutor the Princess. She lov'd hearing me recount what I had overheard among the great and near-great. I shar'd with her reports of my small successes, she with me her small world of hearth and home.

Ithamaria is long forgotten by the living world. In life she stood in the shadows, mine and her husband's. You've seen her mention'd in Professor Teague's book. In her husband's entry in *The Dictionary of National Biography* she is a grudging aside: "John Pell, mathematician, cleric, agent in the Low Countries for Cromwell, inventor of the division sign ÷ , married Ithamaria, daughter of Henry Reginolles, an ambitious woman who died in the plague of 1666." She deserv'd better.

When we were small, our neighbors often mistook us for each other. Papa said our voices, our laughter, our childish prattle, were nearly one and the same. We sang in unison the melodies our mother taught us. But life set divisions between us, caus'd rifts that startl'd us into a hurtful silence we lack'd the will or power to break.

I am writing a story in my sister's honour.

Hopefully,

Bathsua

April 3, 2003

Dear Bathsua,

You've returned to me! My delight goes beyond words! Having discovered your voice – and mine! – over the months of our correspondence, I felt so lonely during those weeks of your silence. I was terrified you had abandoned me.

Fondly,

Dee

P.S. I've put Frances Teague's book back on ~~my~~ our readers' shelf.

April 10, 2003

וַתֹּאמֶר רָחֵל, נַפְתּוּלֵי אֱלֹהִים נִפְתַּלְתִּי עִם-אֲחֹתִי
And Rachel said, 'With mighty wrestlings I have wrestled with my sister. . . .'
– Genesis 30.8.

Dear Dee,

Thank you for leaving Professor Teague's book so conveniently on our shelf. I've had another look at it. She seems to admire me. I am flatter'd. Still, reading one's biography is like gazing at one's reflection in an old mirror: The truth is there, but oddly distorted.

Professor Teague reports the facts but offers few speculations. I like that. She lists, for example, that my daughter Bathsua was christen'd on 4 March 1628/9 at Saint Margaret's, Westminster, and Mary on 1 June 1629. As you know, in my day the new year began on Lady Day, 25 March. That, as you probably suspected, places the two christenings a scant eleven weeks apart, an oddity Professor Teague leaves unexplain'd. In my day babes were christen'd as soon as possible, often within a week or fortnight after birth. Such was the case with these two little ones, my little Bathsua and Mary. Why, you wonder, would two infant sisters be christen'd ten weeks apart? These two sweet babes – call them twins, if you like – are part of my sisterhood with Ithamaria and of the division between us.

You shan't hear from me the details of their conceiving or birthing, what promises were made, kept, or broken. No trail of ink attests to the truth – or falsehood – of the stories I shall now tell you to explain the birthing of these babes. Imagine what you will when you read my handful of bedtime stories, the sort mothers tell to lull their children to sleep.

Before Mama took sick and died, she rock'd in her chair and told us tales as the sky over Saint Mary Axe Street grew dark and quiet. I fancied she spoke only to me, while Itha lay insensate, her hair splay'd out on the pillow, tickling my face, her breathing deep and measur'd. I heard with my ears only, while the deep, dreaming part of Itha's mind listen'd to Mama spinning those tales, that dear lilting voice lulling us to sleep as we lay like two spoons nestl'd together.

Itha inherited Mama's story-telling gift. Years later, when we liv'd in

Westminster, our two growing broods intertwin'd in identical names and look-alike faces. Yet Itha prov'd the finer teller of tales of us two. When our husbands were away, we kept the children together in one or the other of our two sets of rooms in nearby houses, sharing the housewifery and childrearing, bickering good-naturedly as sisters are wont to do. Our little ones readied for sleep, we took turns telling them bedtime stories. As their breathing slow'd and their limbs tangl'd under the bedclothes, the stories unravel'd, mine always brisk and clipp'd, logical and straightforward, while Itha's, like Mama's, were richly detail'd, wondrous with mystery. Hearing my sister's husky, musical voice weaving a tale up and down, in and out, put me under the spell of the ancient bards, bewitching me to believe that I heard not only Mama's voice but also the mingl'd voices of generations of nameless story tellers since the beginning of time.

Now, these many years later, recalling Itha's stories, I remember her life tangl'd with mine. Stories are like that, testaments of their tellers and bound inextricably to their listeners. Listen.

Yours faithfully,

Bathsua

Enclosure: "Telling Tales"

Telling Tales

> As we see in water, though the wind cease, the waves give not over rolling for a long time after; so also in that motion made in the internal parts of a man, when he sees and dreams. For after the object is removed, or the eye shut, we still retain an image of the thing seen, though more obscure than when we see it. This is called imagination.
> – Thomas Hobbes. *Leviathan*. ch.2. "Of Imagination."

Settle down, my dearies. 'Tis time for a story to ease your way to the world of dreams.

Night the First

See this pretty handkerchief and its embroider'd posies in the corners? Ironing it today put me in mind of such handiwork I heard of long ago. Hush, my chickies, here is a story call'd "Clorinda's Strawberry Embroider'd Handkerchief."

Once upon a long, long time ago, in a land faraway, there liv'd an old widow'd queen who rul'd her country well for many years after the death of her dear husband. Her subjects rever'd her because she was truthful, wise, and good. The Queen had one child, the Princess Clorinda, who was as beautiful as her mother was truthful, as gentle as her mother was wise and good. They liv'd together in perfect harmony. Everyone in the realm prais'd and lov'd them as dearly as they had lov'd and prais'd the good King before them.

Now Princess Clorinda had green eyes, golden hair, and cheeks that turn'd a rosy red when she romp'd in the palace garden or swung on the palace swing. On warm days or when she had exercis'd especially vigorously, a little ruddy patch mysteriously appear'd in that sweet space between her eyebrows. When she rested or when a cool breeze blew, just as mysteriously as it had appear'd the little ruddy patch vanish'd into the colour of her smiling face. Once in a blue moon, as they say in that part of the world, if Princess Clorinda grew cross or stubborn or very, very sad, the little ruddy patch also appear'd. But her disposition was as sunny as the days in her mother's realm, and months often pass'd with nothing but the sun's warmth or vigorous exercise bringing the ruddy spot to Clorinda's face. And so life went on for the Queen and the Princess for year after happy year.

Some weeks before Clorinda's thirteenth birthday, the Queen undertook to embroider a pretty handkerchief with strawberries and leaves adorning the edges. 'Twas to be a present for Clorinda, the green leaves matching her eyes and the strawberries her rosy cheeks. While the Queen sat sewing, she watch'd her daughter enjoy the fine weather. Suddenly the old Queen felt an odd twinge in her side, which she dismiss'd as without consequence. But on the day before Clorinda's birthday the sky suddenly fill'd with ominous clouds. The wind had a sudden bite to it. The twinge in the Queen's side suddenly turn'd to a sharp, lingering ache. She consulted the Royal Physician. Sad to say, he was fearful. Tearfully, he told his beloved Queen that she suffer'd the same malady as her dear husband, and that she would, alas, soon die.

The Queen worried not for herself but for her beloved daughter and their realm. What would become of them? So she made special inquiries and arrangements. She summon'd the Royal Chancellor, who assur'd her of the peace and wellbeing of the realm. She directed the Royal Treasurer to open the royal treasury and bring a sapphire ring to her bedchamber. She order'd the Royal Councilor of State to review benevolent rulers in nearby kingdoms. She ask'd the Royal Prognosticator to divine the most auspicious dates for travel.

When the old Queen was satisfied with the reports of her royal advisors, she call'd Clorinda to her bedside and took her in her arms. "Do not fear, my beloved daughter," she said. "Just as your father provided for me, and his parents and grandparents for him, each generation for the next, I have made preparations for you to live a long, happy life after I am gone."

Clorinda, of course, grew very sad, sadder than she had ever been. The mysterious little mark on her forehead emerged in an instant and grew ruddier than it had ever been. Her mother kiss'd the flaming spot and smooth'd the golden hair. "Rest assur'd, my child," she said gently. "You have the love and loyalty of our people, who are safe in the care of our wise Chancellor. The Royal Treasurer assures me our treasury is secure. The Royal Councilor of State has help'd me choose which of our neighbour realms you should visit for a time. The Royal Prognosticator has set tomorrow as the right day for your journey."

Tears well'd in Clorinda's eyes.

Her mother touch'd a hushing finger to Clorinda's cheek. "Be brave and steady, my darling," she said. "Be as brave and steady as you are beautiful and gentle. Tomorrow you must go on a State Visit to the realm of our good neighbour, the young King Floristan." She gave her daughter a letter seal'd with the royal seal and address'd to the young King. Then she drew a small velvet sack from her reticule. "You will take this sapphire ring to him, my child, as a token of our realm's alliance with his." She placed the ring in its velvet sack in the trembling hand of her daughter. Clorinda's tears subsided, and the ruddy birthmark paled slowly under the spell of the Queen's calm words. "I entrust you, my beloved daughter, to the company of Orchis, the daughter of the Royal Prognosticator. She will be your maidservant and traveling companion."

The Queen summon'd Mistress Orchis, who, entering the Royal Bedchamber, directed a stiff little bow toward the Queen and the Princess. The Queen gave Orchis a map and a pat on the shoulder, then dismiss'd her and return'd to her confidences with Clorinda. She drew another package from her reticule and gestur'd the Princess to open it. "My child," said the Queen, "this handkerchief is embroider'd with special threads and needles. The green of the leaves is the colour of the hills of our beloved country.

The red of the strawberries is the colour of the depth of my love for you. Remember them both. You will return home, my beloved, when your mission as my ambassadress is complete. Take care on your journey, my child. In three days you and Mistress Orchis will arrive at King Floristan's palace. Keep this embroidery always with you, for it bears the magic of a mother's protection. Go safely, my beloved."

The exertions of the day were too much for the old Queen. That night she slipp'd into a deep sleep from which she did not waken.

Early the next morning, with the letter address'd to King Floristan, the sapphire ring in its little velvet sack, and the embroider'd handkerchief stor'd carefully in her satchel, Clorinda set forth. At her side was Orchis, who peer'd nearsightedly at the map given her by the old Queen.

While the two walk along, we must tell you about this Mistress Orchis, the Princess's maidservant and traveling companion. As the daughter of the Royal Prognosticator, she was, as you can imagine, privy to a few official prognostications and so fancied herself rather more important than she was. An angular young woman a few years older than Clorinda – and a good deal less pretty, may I add – with a beak of a nose and hair that was wont to poke out from her wimple this way and that, Orchis look'd nothing like her name. (Her father had given her the name in hopes that it would foretell her character. Alas, the Royal Prognosticator was better at predicting matters of state than matters of character.) Orchis was, in fact, as ambitious as Clorinda was beautiful, as scheming as Clorinda was gentle, as wily as Clorinda was beloved of her mother and her subjects.

Together the two walked on toward the realm of the young King Floristan, one girl beautiful and gentle, beloved and good, and the other wily and ambitious, scheming and self-important. On the first day they walk'd from the palace to the harbour. The weather was fine, so they made good progress, although Orchis murmur'd that her satchel was too heavy. On the morning of the second day they boarded a sturdy skiff that took them across the narrow strait separating home from the mainland. By noon of the second day they reach'd the forest at the edge of the realm of King Floristan. Over the course of the day Orchis's sour murmurs turn'd to a steady whine. "My satchel is heavier than yours," she grumbl'd. When evening cast shadows across their path, her look said, "Why are you the

Princess and I the maidservant?"

At nightfall the two stopp'd at a sheltering spot along the forest path to set up a little camp. "My feet hurt in these cheap, clunky boots," Orchis complain'd. "My back is tired from hauling this satchel. You should fetch the water for supper," she insisted. Her voice had shifted from a wheedling whine into an order, and her sidelong glance was positively threatening. Clorinda did not notice, or pretended not to. "Of course I shall fetch the water," she replied. "Rest while I am gone. When I return we will redistribute the contents of your satchel so that you will carry less tomorrow. I do not mind carrying more." And off she went toward the brook they had cross'd moments before.

After supper they redistributed the contents of their satchels and settl'd down for the night. An owl made a comforting *hoo-hooing* nearby. Sleep fell upon Clorinda like a blessing.

At sunrise, Clorinda rose for the journey's third day. She peep'd into her satchel as she had done each day before. Something was awry. The handkerchief her mother had given her was missing! She search'd again: No handkerchief and. . . . Oh, no! The letter to King Floristan was gone, and also the little velvet sack with the sapphire ring. Clorinda felt a flush and then a chill rush to her cheeks. She knew her ruddy birthmark flared forth more brightly than ever before.

"Lost your treasures, Princess?" Orchis's wheedling whine of yesterday was this morning's sinister snarl. Last night's threatening sidelong glance was today's menacing sneer. "I have them all," she said. "We'll see who's princess now. When we get to Floristan's palace, they'll take me for the princess and you the maidservant. Come along, 'Rinda," she said derisively and pull'd her and push'd her along the path. "Don't you dare tell a soul about this, or I'll do even worse to you than I've done already."

On the afternoon of the third day the two maidens arriv'd at the palace of King Floristan. Clorinda carried the heavy satchel and wore the clunky boots now caked with mud. Orchis was dress'd in royal finery. At her waist was a little reticule containing the letter to the King, the sapphire ring, and the embroider'd handkerchief.

To make a long story short, at the palace gate Orchis presented the letter to a waiting courtier who, scarcely noticing Clorinda, bow'd and escorted the maidens into the Royal Presence. King Floristan – young, handsome, with reddish hair and dimpl'd cheeks, not unlike your Uncle Richard's – received Orchis with full royal honour. She glanced archly at her serving maid. The King, however, regarded the downcast Clorinda, a lock of whose shining hair barely conceal'd the bright mark on her forehead.

"That is my maidservant, Your Majesty," Orchis said. "She has complain'd since we left home. Have your Under-Under Cook find some drudgery for her to do in the scullery." She gestured gracelessly, with a dismissive tilt of her pointy chin. A royal manservant bow'd to the King and the young woman he took to be the princess, then escorted the maiden with the ruddy birthmark toward the palace kitchen.

King Floristan watch'd the maiden as she bow'd discretely in his direction and follow'd the manservant from the hall. Something about her seem'd worthy of notice, but if you had ask'd him at that moment he could not have said what. Something about her carriage and the glow of her cheeks touch'd his heart. Only later would he understand why. Recalling himself to the moment, King Floristan glanced at the letter from the old Queen. He then look'd at the angular young woman before him. "Princess Clorinda – " he began.

The maiden was a trifle slow in returning his gaze, almost as if she had forgotten her name. "Princess," the King continued, "welcome. We shall have a festival meal tonight in your honour and introduce you to our subjects." He gestur'd to another royal attendant. "Summon my courtiers and ladies to celebrate the Princess's arrival." The attendant bow'd and departed. "One of my serving ladies will show you to your chamber and ready a bath for you." The serving lady bow'd. Orchis started toward the door before recalling herself. She bow'd a bit stiffly in the direction of the King.

The King return'd to matters of state. His Royal Chancellor observ'd that his master's concentration was not altogether what it had been before the two maidens had arriv'd.

Evening fell gently upon the palace. Courtiers and ladies fill'd the great hall, at one end of which musicians play'd softly. The table was set with beautiful goblets, tall candles, glistening china, splendid flowers. King Floristan escorted his guest to the table. She was dress'd in royal finery and looked about her with her beaky nose high in the air as the King held the chair beside his and waited while she folded herself into it. He noticed that she stretch'd her neck in pride and look'd scornfully at her mild-faced travelling companion, who stood quietly beside the kitchen door waiting for word of what was expected of her.

While attending to his dinner guest, Floristan could not resist glancing now and then toward her rosy-cheek'd maidservant. She look'd as if she'd never utter'd a complaint in her life. Floristan noticed that her white linen cap set off the gold of her hair and the rosy glow of her cheeks, that her simple green dress enhanced the green of her eyes and the grace of her figure. He saw, too, that the moment he glanced in her direction a curious bright mark appear'd in the pretty spot between her eyebrows. It looked a bit like a strawberry, he thought, as he took his place at the head of the table.

A few words now about this young King Floristan. Handsome, of course, as I said before, and wise beyond his years, he had ascended the throne at a young age upon the death of his elderly father. He pleas'd his subjects with his gentle strength and good judgment. Few knew, however, that he had been tutor'd in secret arts, the skill of reading runic writings from faraway lands and distant times, of understanding at a glance the composition of a dye, at a sniff the whiff of a potion, or at a taste the ingredients of a recipe. Quite a gift, may I say. What is more, he could read character from the gestures and demeanour of everyone he met.

At that moment in the royal dining room, just as savouries were being serv'd, something extraordinary began to unfold. The young woman seated at King Floristan's side open'd her reticule to present him with the royal sapphire ring. Out fell the embroider'd handkerchief that the old Queen had given just days before to her daughter Clorinda. The young King saw it fall. So did Clorinda, who let out a muffl'd gasp of happy recognition.

King Floristan instantly recogniz'd something. The embroider'd strawberries! He had seen just such a shape a moment before and earlier that afternoon! 'Twas the shape of the ruddy spot on the forehead of the golden-hair'd, mild-faced maiden standing at the kitchen door! The red of that embroidery he recogniz'd, too: 'twas a dye made of the blood of a loving mother! And the stitches he recogniz'd as well. They were a runic poem from the ancient days when the two neighbouring realms had been one! He reach'd down for the handkerchief and put it into his pocket for safekeeping, unnoticed by the young woman beside him.

"Here, my lord, is the jewel the Queen, my – mother told me to present to you," said Orchis to Floristan. "It comes with her good wishes for all you undertake."

"Thank you," said the young King gravely. He directed his gaze fully – some might say sternly – upon her face. "I am reminded this evening of a story that my beloved father told me many years ago on an evening such as this. He had learn'd it himself from an uncle and aunt, the rulers of a neighbouring country not unlike our own. May I tell it, Princess?"

"Why, of course," Orchis replied.

"Once upon a long, long time ago," he began, "in a country three months' journey from here, first by sea and then by land, there liv'd an old widow who ran her farm well for many years after the death of her dear husband the farmer." From the corner of his eye, he noticed the pretty maidservant listening attentively. "This farm woman – who was very old and trusting – had a servant, a lanky, stiff-neck'd young man, who took advantage of her honesty and simplicity and wheedl'd his way into the governance of the farm. In fact this young man managed to usurp the old farmer's place and steal control of the farm altogether. He made the old widow his servant, giving her the most menial chores in the barn and the field."

Floristan look'd again at the young woman at his side. At that moment she lifted the silver spoon beside her plate as if measuring its weight. "Just as I was expecting more of the tale," he continued, "Papa stopp'd and faced me directly – some might even say sternly. 'My son,' he ask'd, 'had you rul'd the province wherein this farm was situated, and had you receiv'd word of the state of affairs on the farm, what would you have done?'" King Floristan stopp'd. He regarded the angular young woman at his side. "What, my dear Princess, would you have done?"

Orchis put down the silver spoon. "Why, I would order that the young man be punish'd directly! I would have my servants grab him by the scruff of the neck and fling him out the door." Her voice rose. "Then I would have my sheriff beat him about the head and twist his nose – ." She seemed to enjoy the sound of her own voice. "Then I would order the sheriff to strip off his shirt and shoes, and cut his hair 'til he was bald on one side." She paus'd. "Then I would order the young man thrown into the well!" She let out a sound between a giggle and a hiccup.

King Floristan rose from his chair. "When I first set eyes on you," he said, "I suspected something was amiss. Something in your demeanour told me that you are not the daughter of my great uncle and aunt, the wise rulers of the neighbouring realm. And when you dropp'd this. . . ."

He drew the embroider'd handkerchief from his pocket.

Orchis's face grew suddenly pale. Her beaky nose took a sudden dip.

"When I glanced at its handiwork, I instantly read its secret messages. Immediately I knew the truth. Just as you would have punish'd the ill-natur'd lad in my story, I should punish you for trying to steal the place and identity of the maiden you were charged by your Queen, on her deathbed, to protect as you would a sister. Instead you betray'd her and tried to steal her birthright!" He turn'd to his courtiers. "What would you have me do?"

"Grab her by the scruff of her neck!" said the first courtier. The next added, "Fling her out of the house!" "Beat her about the head!" "Twist her nose!" "Strip her of her gown and shoes!" "Cut her hair 'til she's half bald!" "Throw her down the well!"

The young King turn'd to the real Princess, to Clorinda, who, standing like Rachel at the well, water jug in hand, look'd at him with brimming eyes, the rosy strawberry birthmark on her forehead shining like a diadem. "What would you have me do?" he repeated in a half whisper.

Her look told him everything.

"'Tis decided, then," said the young king, not taking his eyes from hers. He spoke to Orchis without looking at her. "You will go to the country, to a little farm I know, where there is a wise, just old widow. She will teach you how to love the truth and honour what is good." He smiled at Clorinda as he spoke to her companion. "She will teach you to become as gentle as you should be truthful and as mild-manner'd as you should be honourable. In exchange, you will live by the work of your hands and the sweat of your brow. If you learn to be good and wise and honourable, truthful, gentle, and well-manner'd, perhaps my Queen will permit you to return to our palace to live and work and thrive. And perhaps, once you are gentle, wise and just, honourable, truthful, and loving, you will be beautiful as well."

In three years' time Princess Clorinda and King Floristan were married. And they liv'd happily ever after, ruling their united realm in perfect harmony.

Eventually Orchis came to live with them. Yes, she was almost beautiful.

Night the Second

Time for another story, my chicks. Cuddle together and listen. Tonight's story is "Princess Isadora's Secret Treasure," about another princess in another kingdom altogether.

Once upon a time, in a faraway kingdom, there liv'd a widow'd king whom we shall call King Renaldo. He was learned and good, but entirely impractical, better with books than with the work of ruling a kingdom, and a little forgetful. His courtiers revered his sweetness and his generosity, but they half-smil'd when he forgot their names or important royal functions.

King Renaldo had two daughters. The elder, Barbara, was beautiful and brilliant. Her sister Isadora was neither. Court wags call'd her "sound" and "robust." Instead of long, shapely fingers like Barbara's, Isadora had firm, round hands that, had she not been a princess, would have been perfect for kneading the royal bread or weeding the palace garden. Instead of Barbara's high elegant forehead and fine sculpted cheekbones, Isadora had a shock of curly hair, round cheeks, and a plump little nose that, had she not been born to the blood royal, would have been perfect for supervising the aromas of the palace kitchen and the royal herb garden.

While Barbara preferr'd the State Rooms and Portrait Gallery, Isadora preferr'd the pantry, the out of doors, and the comings and goings of the servants. While Barbara admir'd the view from her chamber window of the formal gardens design'd by a young palace steward, Isadora enjoy'd peeping through the pantry window at the farm women bringing their wares every morning to the kitchen door at the rear of the palace. Barbara lov'd playing hostess to the scholars, explorers, and sportsmen who visited the King at the palace. On those occasions Isadora sat apart, tongue-tied, listening to the witty repartee that made her eyes swim and her ears roar.

So life went on at the palace year upon year. The princesses grew from winsome girls into eligible young ladies. Barbara's brilliance and beauty caught the eye of the sophisticated gentlemen at her father's court, but for reasons all her own she spurn'd their advances. Her heart was elsewhere. One day she surpris'd everyone by slipping off and marrying her father's steward, the young man who had design'd the formal palace garden. King Renaldo scratch'd his head at the love match. He would have kept Princess Barbara and her husband close by on the palace grounds, but the Princess and her new husband wanted to live on their own. So the King gave his new son-in-law stewardship of an estate far away in the countryside where Barbara and her husband went to live, in hopes of enjoying love happily ever after.

The courtiers and visitors to King Renaldo's palace noted the departure of the beautiful, accomplish'd Princess Barbara. With half-smiles they look'd askance – politely, of course – at the marriage of such a fine princess to a young man with such narrow prospects. What would happen to poor Barbara's elegant long hands, they murmur'd, when they met the rustic chores of a cottager's wife? The King's courtiers and visitors cluckingly spoke of "poor Barbara's plight."

Attention inevitably turn'd to Princess Isadora, the King's younger daughter, the one with the good heart, strong hands, and simple tastes. By now she was approaching the grand age of thirty, when most unmarried princesses remain unmarried for the rest of their lives. "What will become of her?" cluck'd the court wags. "She is so good, so sound, so – robust, but what will become of her?" Isadora, the princess who hid in the palace pantry to avoid the witty repartee of the King's guests, became the silent, tongue-tied hostess at his garden parties and state dinners.

Life at the palace went on thus for month upon month.

King Renaldo had by now grown old. His friends, too, were, in their dotage, no longer so eager to enjoy the royal hospitality. His visitors now were his old friends' sons who, passing through the kingdom en route to other destinations, paid courtesy calls on their fathers' behalf.

One such visitor was a young scholar returning home after receiving high honours at the University in a distant part of the kingdom. He arriv'd at the palace on the eve of Princess Isadora's thirtieth birthday, just in time for the party in her honour. The King insisted that the young scholar sit at Princess Isadora's right hand at the head table. Fresh from his success at the University, the young scholar regaled the Princess with stories of student life and his recent accomplishments and accolades. She listen'd quietly, appreciating his good looks and tales of the great world, and grateful to do nothing but listen to the sound of his mellifluous voice.

The fine wine and excellent cuisine at King Renaldo's table cast a warm glow over the evening. The young man noted Princess Isadora's compos'd features and her silent appreciation for all he said. In the soft candlelight she seem'd almost pretty – in a robust sort of way.

Delighting in the company of a sophisticated guest, the King invited the young scholar to stay for a time. He did so, and then he left, quite abruptly, with only a perfunctory farewell.

Several weeks after the young scholar's departure, Princess Isadora slipp'd into the King's study while her father doz'd over his reading. She look'd over his shoulder at the book and recogniz'd it immediately as the gift of the young man who had so hastily departed. He had promis'd her a copy of his *magnum opus*. She thought he had forgotten, but now she saw he had left it in her father's keeping.

"Father," Isadora whisper'd.

King Renaldo rous'd himself.

"Papa," Isadora said. "I have a favour to ask of you. It has been so long since I saw my sister Barbara, who lives the life of a poor cottager's wife, happily ever after, it seems, far away in the countryside at the other side of your kingdom." She lower'd herself carefully into a chair. "Can you spare me for a time, Papa? I long for some sisterly chatter."

King Renaldo fix'd his old, mild eyes upon his daughter. He noted that she look'd somewhat less robust than usual. "Why, of course, my dear," he said. "The country air will suit you. I shall order the palanquin. You may leave tomorrow. But first, my child, come here, and take two kisses from your dear old papa. Give Barbara one for me. Now off you go." He return'd his gaze to his book. Isadora rose quietly and went to her room to pack for her journey.

Early the next morning, before the servants began pottering about, while her father still slept and the palace was still quiet, with some effort Isadora carried her valise to the front door. She tiptoed to her father's study and, by the thin dawn light, found the book he had been reading, the gift left behind by the young scholar who had flatter'd her with attention three months before. She snatch'd it up, press'd it first to her lips, then to her breast, and tuck'd it under her cloak.

And off Princess Isadora went, a little wan, somewhat tired, dress'd in a billowy cloak with a little something tuck'd at her waist for safekeeping, to pay a six-month-long surprise visit to her sister Barbara, hoping that her visit would help her live happily ever after.

Night the Third

You've been so good today, good to each other, good to your two Mama-Aunties. So here is another bedtime story while you cuddle together like little nestlings. 'Tis a little fable, "Where Two Hedgerows Meet."

Once upon a time when the world was young, a tall oak grew where two hedgerows met at the corner of a wide field. The oak was elegantly leafy in that special way that distinguishes oaks from the other trees of the forest. The hedgerows form'd a dense, shady thicket, wonderfully overgrown with blackthorn and wildberries. The sunlit field nearby was fill'd with splendid wildflowers. All about, in the oak, hedgerows, and field, were delicious things to eat, seeds and berries, grubs and spiders, caterpillars and worms, and larvae and snails of every sort. 'Twas home to ever so many creatures, because the oak was so stunningly leafy, the thicket so densely shady, the field so grassy and sunny, and the whole corner so deliciously full of life.

In the highest branch of this fine oak two rooks were tidying last year's nest. They check'd the twig supports on the bottom, adding to last year's brown leaves a few of this year's green ones for the mattress in the middle, and more twigs for a fine roof on top. In springtime, when our story begins, Mama and Papa Rook were just finishing the construction, snatching twigs from the oak, snipping tender leaves from the hedgerows, readying everything for egg-laying season. Between bouts of nest building, Mama and Papa Rook soar'd companionably, wingtip to wingtip, over the oak tree, the hedges, and the neighbouring field.

In a slightly lower branch of the great oak a pair of Great Spotted Woodpeckers were also building a nest, enjoying its proximity to a wreck'd branch nearby. 'Twas springtime, as I said, and Mama and Papa Woodpecker, their white shoulder patches glinting in the sunlight, their red head feathers aglow, cried *chick chick* to each other as they fed on beetles and spiders that came at the price of *rat-a-tat-tatting*, the brain-rattling pecking and pounding of beak against bark that is the special work of woodpeckers. Gripping the bark with their sharp claws and using their stiff tail feathers for balance, they drill'd holes into the dead branch for future meals. Between bouts of nest building and bashing beak against bark, the two woodpeckers, the napes of Papa's neck rosy, of Mama's dun, frisk'd about, frolicking and making their sharp, *chick-chicking* cries.

Newly arriv'd in the hedgerow beneath the great oak after a long migratory flight from the south, a pair of nightingales chose a secret spot for their nest deep in a tangle of blackthorn. They kept their plain looks to themselves but shar'd with all the creatures in the oak, hedgerow, and field their famous song, a fast succession of high and low *hweet hweet hweets*. Between singing and nest building, their sturdy little brown broad-tail'd bodies fluttering about in the thicket, Mama and Papa Nightingale made their soft mellow mating music.

Tuck'd in a hidden corner of the field, near the shady hedgerows and the tall oak, was the ground nest of a pair of Meadow Pipits, their feathers a soft olive-brown streak'd with gray. Mama and Papa Pipit looked quite alike, and both sang their sweet, whistling call, an accelerating *tseep tseep tseep*, then a slowing *tsent tsent tsent* follow'd by a thrilling little trill so heartstoppingly beautiful that the woodpeckers and nightingales interrupted their *chick chicks, rat-a-tat-tats,* and *hweet hweet hweets* to listen. In the silences between outbursts of their song, Mama and Papa Pipit made merry in the corner of the field.

Now darting to a sunny perch in the oak, now to a shady one in the blackthorn thicket, was a pair of cuckoos, Mama and Papa, their feathers a dark blue-gray, with black and white barring on the breast. Papa Cuckoo sang his familiar *cuckoo*, while Mama Cuckoo harmoniz'd appreciatively with a bubbling *chuckle chuckle*, her bright eyes sparkling mischievously, as she look'd about. Amidst their darting and singing and looking about them at all their nest-building neighbours, Mama and Papa Cuckoo sported about in the sunlight and shadow.

And soon our drama begins.

New life is everywhere. Two young rook chicks cuddle in the round nest in the highest branch of the oak. Three white woodpecker eggs are cluster'd in their nest in a chamber of the oak. Four glossy, olive-brown nightingale eggs rest softly in a nest in the hedgerow. And five smooth, glossy meadow pipit eggs, white with heavy brown spotting, lie in the grassy nest at the sunstreak'd corner of the field where the hedgerows meet in the shade of the oak.

Mama and Papa Pipit are off for a moment, dining on insects in the hedgerow. Mama and Papa Cuckoo have no nest, so busy have they been with frolicking that they haven't bother'd to build anything at all. Mama Cuckoo, bright-eyed on a low branch of the oak, is singing her rich, bubbling *chuckle chuckle*. Then there is silence.

Mama cuckoo is suddenly still. Very still.

Her sleek wings and long tail bright in the morning light, Mama Cuckoo suddenly swoops down to the pipits' ground nest. She sits there for a long moment. The only sound is the humming of insects.

There are, you remember, five eggs in the pipits' ground nest. In an instant Mama Cuckoo nudges one small egg, white with brown spotting, until it slips over the side of the nest and falls to the grass below. Now there are four eggs in the pipit nest.

Mama Cuckoo sits pensively for another long moment in the pipit nest. Then lets out one low, soft *chuckle,* and flies back to her mate in the high branches of the oak. Once again five eggs rest in the pipit nest. They are all smooth and glossy, white with heavy brown spotting, But one is much larger than the others.

Mama and Papa Pipit return to their nest. Mama Pipit settles back onto the five eggs. Papa pipit resumes his heartbreakingly beautiful song, *tseep. . . tseep. . . tseep. . . tseeptseeptseep. . . tsentsentsent. . . tsent. . . tsent. . . tsent,* follow'd by a thrilling little trill.

In a week, in the nest at the top of the oak, the two rook chicks are growing nicely, their parents soaring companionably overhead. In the woodpecker nest in the chamber of the oak three nestlings are waiting, mouths ajar, for Mama and Papa to feed them grubs. In the nightingale nest Mama and Papa are delivering beakful after beakful of spiders to four open-mouth'd nestlings. And in the pipit nest four little nestlings and one enormous-mouth'd nestling are peeping loudly, waiting for Mama and Papa to return.

In the weeks that follow, at the edge of the tangl'd blackthorn in the hedgerow, Mama Cuckoo sits watching the pipits' ground nest. Mama and Papa Pipit are wearing themselves out serving up tidbits for their clutch, one of the nestlings, the especially ruddy one with the signs of white barring on its breast, rapidly growing larger and more demanding than the other four. Mama and Papa Pipit have scarcely a moment for their *tseep. . . tseep. . . tseep. . . tseeptseeptseeping,* their *tsentsentsent. . . tsent. . . tsent. . . tsenting.* Their thrilling little trills have all but disappear'd. They are too tired to make merry in the corner of the field.

Mama and Papa Rook are shrieking wild, approving *skree skrees* as their chicks make first attempts to fly. Mama and Papa Woodpecker are training their brood to practice their *rat-a-tat-tatting.* Mama and Papa Pipit are teaching their fledglings to fly.

At a distance Mama and Papa Cuckoo watch their orphan hatchling struggle to learn to be a cuckoo in a nest full of pipits. *Cuckoo,* says Papa

Cuckoo. Mama Cuckoo gives an ambiguous little *chuckle chuckle* at the doings in the pipit nest at the sunstreak'd spot where the hedgerows meet in the shade of the tall oak. One of the nestlings replies. *Cuckoo.*

Night the Fourth

How you wear me out at day's end, my little ones, with your nightly pleadings for another story! Here is "The Dull Twin and the Clever."

Once upon a time there was a king whom we shall call Henrico. King Henrico had two beautiful daughters, nearly identical twins, alike in nearly every detail, as alike as two berries on a stem, even down to the last half moons on the fingernails of their pretty hands. Let us call them Brenda and Alenda. They were born minutes apart. Princess Brenda was the elder but only by half a tiny moment.

The neighbouring kingdom was ruled by another king, whom we shall call King Maximilian. This king had two sons. The elder, Prince Ricardo, was a handsome, strapping fellow, but, alas, as dull as yesterday's porridge. The younger, Prince Giovanni, was small and skinny, not at all like his elder brother. Small though he was, Prince Giovanni was clever and full of ambition. He did not suffer fools easily.

The two kings, Henrico and Maximilian, were longtime friends. When their babies were born they form'd a pact that their children should marry when they came of age, the two pairs sorting themselves out however they chose.

When our story begins, Prince Ricardo had just turn'd one and twenty. To him, the elder, fell the choice of which twin to marry. But Ricardo was as dull as a bowl of yesterday's porridge. He could not tell Princess Brenda from Princess Ilenda, nor did he think to ask them questions to tell them apart. He scratch'd his big head with one burly hand and came to a decision. "B comes before I in the alphabet," he reason'd. "'Tis Princess Brenda whom I choose."

Brenda did not object. She found Ricardo handsome, in a rough sort of way. Theirs was a fine royal wedding, after which the two happy kings, Henrico and Maximilian, sent the new royal couple off on a honeymoon trip to last for a year and a day, the very day when Prince Giovanni would reach his age of maturity and his marriage to Princess Ilenda.

Alas, now our tale takes a dark turn. You wish Prince Ricardo and Princess Brenda were living happily ever after? You hope the same will befall Prince Giovanni and Princess Ilenda? Would that I could tell you such a story. Alas, happiness is not often ever after, even in the world of "once upon a time." Prepare yourselves, my dears, for sadness.

I forgot to mention that Princess Brenda had a mind of her own, a mind as sharp, I am afraid to say, as a thorn on a rose stem. Soon after she left with Prince Ricardo on their honeymoon journey, she realiz'd that her husband was as dull as yesterday's dish of porridge. And Prince Ricardo discover'd, despite the simplicity of his mind, that Princess Brenda was as prickly and disagreeable as a bed of nettles. Their honeymoon was a bitter affair for them both, each, alas, a disappointment to the other.

Remember that Prince Giovanni was intelligent and ambitious? Having observ'd Princess Brenda's wit at her wedding feast the year before, he assum'd his bride, Princess Ilenda, was as clever as her nearly identical twin sister Princess Brenda. When he and Ilenda were wed, he reason'd, their combin'd ambition and cleverness would put them head and shoulders above his sister-in-law and brother (who, you recall, was as dull as yesterday's porridge).

King Henrico and King Maximilian feted Prince Giovanni and Princess Ilenda on their wedding day and sent them off on a honeymoon for a year and a day, just like that of Prince Ricardo and Princess Brenda.

But sumptuous weddings are not always follow'd by happiness, and happiness does not go hand in hand with beauty or cleverness. Alackaday, my dear listeners! Our story takes another sad turn. On the first day of the honeymoon Prince Giovanni made the awful discovery that you, perhaps, suspected already. Princess Ilenda was as beautiful as her sister, down to the very half moons of her fingernails, but she was neither clever nor witty. In fact, she was as dull as – well, you know. And dull though she was, Princess Ilenda made a grim discovery of her own. She could read in her heart and in her husband's eyes a lifetime of sadness.

Neither wealth nor beauty, neither intelligence nor ambition guarantees success in the game of life. To this day our four royal personages pass their days wishing life were different.

Ah, my little ones, you are already asleep, dreaming, I hope, of what might have been.

Night the Fifth

Am I Scheherazade, teller of a thousand and one stories in a thousand and one nights? Not another bird fable, you say? No more about princes and princesses, kings and queens? Here we are on a rainy night in Westminster with a supper of good English soup and bread. Tonight you shall have from the mysterious Orient a story set in an oasis along the famous Silk Road. Have you never heard of the mysterious Orient, or of oases along the storied Silk Road? You've never imagin'd a sun-bak'd night rich with the smells of cardamom and coriander? 'Tis about time, my dear ones. Here is a story call'd "A Persian Miniature."

Once upon a time, in the days before Saladin and Iksander, in a distant country far beyond the headwaters of the mighty Euphrates, there liv'd a sultan – lonely, widow'd, and childless – named Amin. He made his home in a splendid oasis where soft desert winds redolent of cinnamon and orange blossoms blew through the cypress trees.

Our Sultan Amin is darkly, mysteriously handsome, with olive skin and a fine coal-black moustache. He wears an apricot-colour'd silk turban and a white linen caftan shot through with golden threads. On his feet are babouches, embroider'd silk slippers that turn up elegantly at the toes. Tuck'd in his belt is a short, sharp dagger of gleaming silver, studded with precious jewels. His splendid three-storied palace is encrusted with mosaics and surrounded by elaborate gardens, in which are set the smaller villas of his court favourites, loyal generals and captains in his army, which won all its wars long before our story begins.

Sultan Amin's country is at peace. He lives among friends, wears fine clothes, and dines on delicious meals. His palace contains every perfect detail – a steamy Turkish bath, a library full of beautiful illuminated manuscripts, a sumptuous roof garden fragrant with persimmon, and a jasmine bower fill'd with starry white blossoms. He has court musicians, two court poets – one writing in the epic mode, another in the lyric – and even a court perfumer.

In a word, Sultan Amin lacks nothing. Yet is he unhappy.

The smallest villa on the Sultan's grounds is nearest the palace. In it dwells Sultan Amin's orderly, Sub-Lieutenant Radaïs. Simple though this little villa is, 'tis beautiful, with white-wash'd walls and sea-blue shutters. A canary sings in its cage beside the one window overlooking the Sultan's garden.

At sunset, when the air grows cool, Sultan Amin paces the parapets of his roof garden and listens to the sweet, simple music of Sub-Lieutenant Radaïs's canary. As the moon rises and one, then two, then three, then a million stars bloom in the clear sky, Sultan Amin admires the simple peace of his orderly's little villa. He sees Sub-Lieutenant Radaïs himself, fram'd by the window with sea-blue shutters, puffing on his water pipe and leafing through a book by the light of a single candle. When Sultan Amin glances at the villa's rooftop, he sees his orderly's wife, Mistress Alida, and her handmaiden Sandra seated there, unnotic'd, or so they think, enjoying the fragrant breezes wafting from Sultan Amin's garden. After the day's heat, they have moved the canary's cage to the roof and are making ready for the night. Sandra is brushing her mistress's hair and humming to the waning song of the canary as her mistress winds balls of azure-blue cashmere yarn from a newly-dy'd skein in the basket at her feet. The scent of jasmine, the fragrant breeze in the cypresses, the soft humming and the inexorable appearance of stars in the black, black sky, all combine to cast a spell of peace over the desert, over the oasis and the garden, over the Sultan's palace and the little villa. . . .

Suddenly, without their knowing how it has happen'd, as if by magic, all four of our new friends, Sultan Amin and his Sub-Lieutenant Radaïs, Mistress Alida and her handmaiden Sandra, are in love. Sultan Amin suddenly finds himself smitten by Mistress Alida. The sight of her bare arms lit by the moon as she winds the azure yarn is irresistible to him. Sandra is suddenly enraptur'd by her mistress's husband, Sub-Lieutenant Radaïs: Rising from the blue-shutter'd window, the soft bubbling sound of his water pipe, combin'd with the scent of jasmine, is irresistible. Sub-Lieutenant Radaïs is suddenly in thrall to Sandra, his wife's handmaiden. The sound of her soft-humm'd accompaniment to the song of the sleepy canary floats down from the rooftop and winds around the chambers of his heart. Mistress Alida glimpses Sultan Amin's profile turn'd in her direction, fram'd by the starry sky. Her heart is full of love for him.

There they sit, as still as in a Persian miniature: Sultan Amin in his apricot-colour'd silk turban and white linen caftan shot through with golden threads, Mistress Alida with her hair over her shoulders and the azure blue ball of cashmere yarn in her hand, Sub-Lieutenant Radaïs with his water pipe and candle at the blue-shutter'd window, Sandra with her face tilted toward the gold-feather'd canary. There in that moonlit, faraway oasis, all in love, a love permanent, wondrous, and impossible, still'd forever under the starry sky, they go on living, not quite happily, but forever after.

April 14, 2003

Give us not to think so far away
As the uncertain harvest; keep us here
All simply in the springing of the year.
— Robert Frost. "A Prayer in Spring."

Dear Bathsua,

Your bedtime stories are beautiful. They hint at many things about you and your sister. I cannot decide which is my favorite. Perhaps they will melt the coldness between you and your sister as they have warmed my heart.

This morning in the Library I am searching *The Huntingdon Papers* for letters and poems you exchanged with Lucy Hastings. Next week I'll read behind the lines of your correspondence with your brother-in-law, now preserved in the *Pelliana*. Such rich, silent clues to your life! Later today I'll dig manure into my garden to prepare the earth for planting of "the tendre croppes."

What promise there is in April, and how muddled the world is! How dare I be happy? We are at war.

Warmly,

Dee

Subject: What if. . .?
Date: 4/20/2003 11:52:12 AM EDT
From: dndyoung2@owl.com
To: dndyoung1@owl.com

Darlin',

Bathsua has written her longest story yet for me. I don't know how she does it.

For my part, I'm plagued by war news and computer issues – little by little my beloved laptop is slowing down and having trouble starting up. Ned came over this morning to do some maintenance that he calls cleanup and defragmentation. I understand cleanup, but defragmentation sounds contrary to the natural state of things. (Remember *"Ἐξίσταται γὰρ πάντ' ἀπ' ἀλλήλων δίχα"*?) He said it'd be a good idea to pull files I'm not using off my hard drive and store them on some kind of external device. He makes it sound awfully easy, so I've sent him off to buy the external storage device and have a go at it. I'll make him lunch, and it'll be lovely to have him here with me – and a nice distraction from the war news. Love.

Subject: What if. . .? continued
Date: 4/20/2003 17:23:42 PM EDT
From: dndyoung2@owl.com
To: dndyoung1@owl.com

Darlin',

Ned asked what this giant *Bathsua Project* file and a whole bunch of subfiles and backups with similar titles are and can I get rid of 'em. No! I screamed. Nearly knocked him out of his sneakers. Won't tell him about the two mailboxes filled with pretty much the same stuff. Love.

April 21, 2003

> Just like a Bird when her Young are in Nest,
> Goes in, and out, and hops and takes no Rest:
> But when the Young are fledg'd, their heads out-peep,
> Lord! What a chirping does the Old one keep!
> – Margaret Cavendish, Duchess of Newcastle.
> "An Apology for Writing So Much upon This Book."

Dear Dorothea,

"How muddl'd the world is," you wrote in your last letter. (I saw you there in the Library, happy and sad at the same time, scratching your head about the meaning of so many things.)   Indeed, so much is all ajumble! This world's ever empty, ever full. Each day contains every day I ever liv'd, days full and empty, young and old, laughing and grieving. 'Tis hard to explain; I'll try another way: You have seen the birth and burial records of my first babies, little Anna and baby Richard. When they died, my husband tried comforting me by saying they would be waiting for me. They are indeed with me, one always and forever a sweet four year old, the other a tiny, needy week-old infant. But with me also are the grief of losing them that March day long ago, the noise and clutter of birth, the tiptoeing about of illness, the gaping silence when my Richard took them one day after the next to Saint Margaret's for burial. With me, too, are the crying and the laughing and the silence, and the squeak of my chair as I sat rocking back and forth. All at the same time. With me, too, are my other Anna and my second Richard, and the others, my Bathsua and Mary and Henry, all and always both tiny and grown and everything in between. Wonderful and terrible, 'tisn't it? In life Richard said that naming a new babe for one we lost would be a comfort. I replied that, if we would all be together one day in Heaven, as we were told, 'twould be a hopeless confusion having two Annas, two Richards, three and more if we added all the other generations as well. Richard smiled and did what he always did when I said something that amus'd him: he tuck'd that stray wisp of hair behind my ear. I can still feel it, his callous'd forefinger brushing my cheek, the rim of my ear, as it did when we were sixteen and fifty-six, and all the times between. Enough. You will see when your turn comes.

I see you there in the Library with two letters before you, John Pell's advising me how to dispose of my son, and mine thanking Lucy Hastings and noting how heavily that same son rests on my heart. What story lies behind those two letters, you wonder?

And why no word about any of the others? As you surely know, in life I left no other record of any of my other children. Not a word of my own daughters appears among the women mention'd in my *Essay to Revive the Antient Education of Gentlewomen*. Were my Annas, my Mary, my Bathsua no less worthy than Pythagoras's daughter Dama, or Cicero's Tullia?

I have a mind to commit to paper now what I never did in life. Of course Richard and I were not such parents as the wise Cicero and his wife Terentia, who together tutor'd Tullia to become her father's equal in eloquence. Nor, thank God, were my girls the likes of Hyppatia of Alexandria, Theon's daughter, who wrote so brilliantly of astronomy that, envied for her fame, she was cruelly slain. My daughters led unrecorded lives. They were good girls, sensible and sweet, and I lov'd them. That I left nothing about them in print for you to find is no measure of my love for them. Nor is it a special mark of affection for my sons that you have found scant mention of them. It was just the way of the world, nothing more.

I see you studying John Pell's April 1654 letter about the lads, searching behind the words for clues to the fates of my second Richard, my John and

Henry, and my feelings for them. "You hope to have one gone shortly," John Pell wrote, "and the next out of the nest before the end of this yeare." What did I feel, you wonder, when John continued: "Your youngest is too old to tarry under his Mother's wing; he will be better abroad with a Father, a Tutor, or a Master. For a hen with one chick, a little roome will suffice"?

How cross and sad that letter made me! For all his knowledge of algebra, how little my sister's husband knew of the mathematics of a mother's heart! The fundamental axioms of maternal arithmetic are these: Subtract a child and the sum of a mother's love can never be any the less. Nor does division exist in a mother's heart!

John Pell had one thing right: Babes leap the nest. They make their way without us, part of God's inscrutable plan to teach us sufferance and humility. We lose our children to illness, accident, or war. Sometimes anger, misunderstanding, or shame separates mother and child. Which is worse, these or death?

Some children stay with us, despite our wishes, despite the natural order. This much I will explain: My youngest, Henry, still tarried at home in 1667, twenty-five years old, under his poor old widow'd mother's wing. His neediness lay heavy upon me in that difficult time after the Fire and Plague. For better or worse, I kept Henry by me, a burden on my heart, but still my companion in old age, both a distraction and a comfort as I went about my teaching and writing, my only other distractions and comforts. Ah, I remember too much! Better to be silent.

As ever,

BRM

Subject:	Am writing again, thanks to defragmentation?
Date:	4/21/2003 12:27:03 PM EDT
From:	dndyoung2@owl.com
To:	dndyoung1@owl.com

Darling,

Thanked Ned again for de-fragmenting ("defragging," he called it) and doing whatever else he did. Told him it felt like spring cleaning. I think the computer's running a little better. Checked my mailbox and my big *Bathsua Project* files – everything looks pretty much the same.

Am feeling very productive. And oddly happy. Am writing a story for Bathsua on parenting. I think you'll like it. Have decided to include you – the *real* you – among otherwise fictional characters, to give me that wonderful frisson of your presence. Remember the stuff I told you ages ago about *At Swim-Two-Birds?* How good it feels to write you into a story! Still, I'm jealous that this fictional "Dora" woman, and her daughter "Livvy" get you all to themselves. Love.

April 24, 2003

> Y tal vez hay que se busca una cosa y se halla otra.
> [And sometimes you go looking for one thing and you find another.]
> – Miguel de Cervantes. *El Ingenioso Hidalgo Don Quijote de la Mancha.*

Dear Dorothea,

Even when the words began to flow like a stream releas'd from a bone-chilling freeze, I still felt a catching in my throat, as if tears were about to start. Truth to tell, those tears, this quaking in my throat, mark the love and loss of my own voice, the shaking fear that it will slip away from me again at any moment, leaving me in perpetual silence. So, my dear, now that my voice has been releas'd from frozen silence, here is an essay on the secret hoarding of a mother's heart. Our teacher Cicero might have nam'd such an essay *De Silentio.*

Yours in faith,

Bathsua

Enclos'd: "Keeping Mum"

Keeping Mum

> Curae leves loquuntur, ingentes stupent.
> [Light cares speak, huge ones benumb.]
> – Seneca. *Hippolytus.*

Language sustains life. Whose life would a mother more wish to sustain than her own child's? If an act as simple as putting pen to paper could extend a child's life one day more, what mother would not write and write and write? For the love of my beautiful lost children, all eight of them, I should have written early in the morning, late into the night, day upon day, pen and ink tracing from every possible angle the sweet curves of their cheeks, the curl of their hair at their temples and the napes of their necks. I should have put into words their smiles, the touch of their lashes against my lips when I kiss'd their clos'd eyes.

But I did not. Why my silence all those years about my children? I lov'd them, and language, too. *Philoglotta*, my father call'd me, lover of tongues. Yet I never wrote of my love for my own beloved children. I will voice it for them now by writing about silence. I will break my silence by writing about silence itself.

"Clos'd lips hurt no one. Speaking may." Thus Cicero paraphras'd Cato the Censor. Do we marshal silence to protect those we love – and ourselves? As the King's messenger takes care not to record the key to a cipher and send it in a letter, does not the troubl'd heart hide what is dear, lest those who mean us harm use our words against us? So I kept mum. When I did once break my silence, I paid dearly. Will you betray me, too?

Her Ladyship Lucy Hastings was excellently born and married into one of the noblest families in the realm. When first we met, she was already the Countess of Huntingdon and the mother of two children near the ages of two of my own. She knew I was a teacher. We met because of a shar'd a secret: Our parents – her mother, my father – had been committed to Bedlam.

"When these mournful days are over," Her Ladyship said, "and to soften the blows of these terrible times," – 'twas in the 1630's, in the dangerous days of the War – "will you come and teach my children?"

"Of course, my Lady," I said. "'Twould be an honour to do so."

So it was that in 1642, in the spring before my Henry, my youngest, was born, while I was tutoring the Princess Elizabeth at Whitehall, I taught Henry and Elizabeth Hastings as well.

Those were dreadful times, the war years. But I also enjoy'd good days – busy and fulfilling ones – when I pass'd through London's streets from home to the palace at Whitehall and then to noble households, giving lessons while my own little ones stay'd at home with women in the neighbourhood. My little Henry attended the lessons with me, for I carried him in my belly. The Countess of Huntingdon attended them, too, along with her tow-headed Henry and Elizabeth. She learn'd some Latin and Greek. We became friends. She ask'd that I call her Lucy, but I could not bring myself to do so.

Then my Henry was born, beautiful and perfect. With honey-gold curls he was a delight, the apple of Richard's eye. His infant cheeks dimpl'd deliciously as he woke from his sleep each morning, recognizing me anew as if he saw me every day for the first time this side of heaven.

Her Ladyship's Henry was already just such a beautiful boy, full of promise and possess'd of every advantage, heir to his father's venerable house, the family favourite. Richard and I named this our last babe for my father; I secretly hoped the lad would grow to be like Her Ladyship's lucky, beautiful boy as well. Within months of his christening, however, I knew something was terribly wrong. Her Ladyship was the only one to whom I entrusted this secret. My own fair-hair'd little Henry would come to inherit a portion of the tragedy of both his namesakes, Her Ladyship's Henry and my own Papa, Henry Reginald, who died mad in Bedlam.

The daily sweetness in Henry's dimpling morning smile fail'd to turn to recognition or speech. The women who minded him said he was odd, addl'd even. No surprise, they whisper'd, considering his mother's odd ways. But I ignor'd what I did not wish to overhear, busying myself with other people's children, too busy for my own. Every lesson with those who learn'd as effortlessly as they took breath was a secret reminder – or a blessed forgetfulness – of Henry's speechless, beautiful vacancy.

When he grew bigger, the rocking started, then the shrieking and babbling. My teaching paid to keep Henry under watch at home. His sweet infant insufficiency turn'd to mad rages. He kick'd and bit his caretakers. And me.

I heard what the local gossips said: "All that gadding about teaching those foreign tongues must have drain'd his tiny head." Were they right? Had my boy been addl'd from the womb? Did my attention to other people's children rob my own of his wits?

I kept the secret of my flaw'd child, my mad Henry. Taking him from home meant enduring the derision of strangers. Sending him to a mad-minder in some out-of-the-way hovel would betray the love for me I knew was lock'd behind his beautiful, hollow stare; putting him out on the street untended was too horrid to contemplate. So I hid him away at home, where he sat and rock'd, shriek'd and babbl'd, even as he grew bigger and stronger.

Only to Her Ladyship did I confide. And weep. She listen'd, said little, and watch'd her own children even more closely during the lessons. Sometimes she overpaid me.

Our Henry broke Richard's spirits. The sight of our boy swaying and staring at shifting shadows in the corner of the room where I kept him nearly drove Richard out of his mind. It drove him from our bed, from our home, from our marriage. He could not look into Henry's blue, hollow eyes, listen to his mad screeching, watch him snatch at my hands and arms, drawing blood where his nails scraped the skin, leaving purple welts where he squeez'd and twisted the flesh. Richard left me because I would not put away our beautiful, mad boy and because he was powerless to help him. Poor, poor Henry! Poor, poor Richard!

For a few hours a day I pretended away my boy's madness and the loneliness of my empty bed. Teaching healthy children distracted me from brooding continually about my damaged child, my failure as a mother and wife.

So did reading and translating. When I was not teaching or doing household tasks I reread what I had long before studied with my father, finding pleasure in Cicero's letters to Atticus. Late in the correspondence Cicero, that disciplin'd, stoical father daz'd with grief, tells Atticus that writing masks the lingering pain of the death of his beloved daughter Tullia. "I write all day long," he writes, "*Totos dies scribo. Non quo proficiam.* Not that I do myself any good by it," he admits. "But for the time being it distracts me. Not enough, of course. *Quid sed tantisper impedior – non equidem satis.*" Should I be grateful that some of the world's best writing grows from such suffering silence? What a price to pay.

Quiet study is not distraction enough. Nor does it pay the bills. When King Charles went to his death during that dreadful winter of 1649, Richard's livelihood disappear'd. So did my teaching stipends. The Council of State refus'd to pay what was due me for my tuition of the Princess at Whitehall before she and her brother Henry were taken away to Sion House after their father's execution. My

Henry was seven that spring. Richard and I had no money to pay the minders. I wince to remember how we sat, Richard and I, at the kitchen table, too worn to argue. He play'd with the crumbs on his plate, his eyes downcast. He could not put food on his family's table. His was the silence of defeat.

I remember'd Lucy Hastings, Countess of Huntingdon. Word came in June that terrible year that her handsome, accomplish'd son Henry, Lord Hastings, the apple of her eye, the heir to his father's title, at nineteen and fresh from University, full of the promise and vigour of a charm'd life, had contracted smallpox. On the eve of his wedding he died. His mother, her Ladyship, who had studied with me when I taught her children, my own Henry in my womb, must have been wild with grief.

Her Ladyship's pain was fierce and sudden; mine I liv'd with, dully, year upon year. So I broke my silence and wrote to her. Under the guise of a condolence letter I reminded her of my need. Richard look'd askance at my plan but did not stop me. Sad to say, I took advantage of her suffering, using the occasion of her grief to suggest a small sum of patronage to me, as her son's former teacher and mother of a child who lacked every quality I could extol in hers. I knew Her Ladyship would remember the irony that our two beautiful boys shar'd a name and that one, brilliant and possess'd of every advantage, was now dead, while the other, demented, liv'd on, a weary burden to his mother.

For the occasion I wrote a little verse elegy in Henry Hastings' memory. I compos'd it in Latin, to remind the Countess that I was her son's first teacher. Struggling through the dactyls, I distracted myself from thoughts of my own damaged boy. *En duplex aenigma*, I wrote, O double riddle! *Senex, juvenisq!* An old one and a young! To lose a young man on the threshold of life, when it is the old who should do the dying! That is what I wrote. Yet in my heart was the cruel irony that Her Ladyship had committed to the silent grave a son, a youth golden with every perfection, while I was committed to lifelong maintenance of an equally lov'd, equally beautiful boy, whose tragic imperfections were the secret of a distraught mother. *En duplex aenigma* indeed! The elegy's last lines elegy commemorate my unvoiced tears:

> *Carmine plus fari me, cum sim femina, digno*
> *Impediunt lachrymae: flere, silere, satis.*

Tears stifle: no more composing elegant verse.

I am a woman: To weep, to be silent, must suffice.

Grammar and scansion quieted my grief. Cicero would have been proud. Richard was not. The silence grew between us. He left, ostensibly in search of work.

The Countess's generosity tided me over. Few words describe those times. Weary weeks dragg'd on into silent years of eking out existence, tending my mad son. Work did not distract me. Familiar was the old tightening in my throat, the hot well of tears behind my eyes. My elder children could bear it no more. Like Richard, they left.

Over time sadness hardens into stoical silence, as the tortoise's shell gradually hardens into an impregnable carapace. Now and then I pok'd my head from my shell to hint of my need. In the late winter of 1654 I petition'd the Council of State for payment arrears for my tuition of the Princess. The petition fell on deaf ears. The embarrassment of begging was scarcely borne, yet I wrote to my brother-in-law, John Pell, that I was alone with twelve-year-old Henry, all the others having flown the nest. I hop'd John would send me a little something, for old times' sake. For a time he had cast a blind eye toward Ithamaria's giving us something for our maintenance. But he had grown weary of me and wanted no more part of my affairs. He replied, saying that Henry would do better with any man, his father, a tutor or a master, than stay under my wing. He must have known that nothing of the sort was possible: Richard was ill; the boy was unteachable; no master would take him as apprentice or servant. John's letter was insupportably grievous to me, yet I did not reply. What could I have said?

I kept my counsel for another decade. Richard was dead. There was the Plague. And the Fire. My boys were gone, and the girls, too. Only Henry remain'd, my huge man-child, babbling, rocking, wordless. So much lay in ruins, all hope lost. There was no more need for prideful silence, embarrass'd silence, self-protective silence. No more need for the secrecy.

Walking one day along the same streets, now deserted, the houses boarded up and decaying, that I had pass'd years before on my way from home to Whitehall and the fine homes of my former pupils, I remember'd the Countess of Huntingdon. We were both old now. Nearly twenty years had pass'd since Henry Hastings's death; Her Ladyship and her husband had another son, a new heir. Her grief for a dead son may have faded; mine had not. My Henry was a daily, ceaseless burden. What would happen to him when I died? I compos'd another letter to my old benefactor and friend: "My son lying very heavy upon me still," I wrote. "I have so much concernment to impart to you that I should be very glad to see you."

Her silence should not have surpris'd me. Yet it touch'd me sorely. At the time I suppos'd 'twas the formal silence of disappointment that one whom she had thought a friend was only a supplicant. Perhaps she fear'd opening an old wound or buying new trouble. To name an old sorrow gives it life anew. Better to be silent, pretend to forget.

Perhaps Her Ladyship meant her silence as a lesson to me, reminding me that silence is the stock-in-trade of women and the sometime habit of good teachers. My father oft observ'd that a teacher must sometimes grow still to let the lesson ripen in the silence of the pupil's mind. He had me commit to memory a line by Dante: *"La dimanda onesta si de' seguir con l'opera tacendo.* An honest question should be follow'd with the work done in silence." Pose the question, then wait. Even if the silence seems deafening.

Perhaps Her Ladyship sent a reply that never reach'd me. Perhaps her silence was only the inevitable fate of language itself: Words, so fragile, so ephemeral, can hardly be said to exist at all. Spoken, they disappear into the ether; written, they are lost, intercepted, destroy'd. she may have been trying to teach me, the teacher, the lover of language, that language is a fickle, untrustworthy friend. She may have wish'd me to learn that in the end all things leave us, fall away, disappear like chatter into silence.

Now that I have broken that silence to you, what will you do with its fragments?

Subject: Silences
Date: 4/25/2003 10:15:45 EST
From: dndyoung2@owl.com
To: dndyoung1@owl.com

Darling,

Bathsua, at least, writes to me. Ironically, about silence most recently. Okay, that old student whose blog I got into way back last summer didn't write back. Probably because she thought it was weird to write to an old teacher from high school, a time most of us would prefer to forget. But you? I half-hope my next story for Bathsua will raise a response from you.

In fact, writing it, writing both sides of our conversations, I almost hear your voice speaking to me. It's a lovely feeling. Love always.

April 28, 2003

Each bud a settlement of riches –
– Mary Oliver. "Goldfinches."

Dear Bathsua,

Working in my quiet garden, I thought all morning of your last letter and its melancholy enclosure about Lucy Hastings's silence. By now you must know of my sadness and disappointment – anger, even – in the face of such silence. We share this bone-chilling, existential loneliness, don't we? Like you, I know the complex feelings of writing and sending letters that are not reciprocated.

Enough of that. In a silent garden there is life and response everywhere, solace and nourishment for every sense. A flashing flock of finches rose and fled from the Swiss chard this morning. Violets volunteer bright blooms for admiration, and the lettuce rows offer up their thinnings for tonight's salad. I turned over great shovelfuls of earth for next week's planting, working in last year's leaf mould, adding cow manure. The odor at first was raucous and deep, dissipating as I turned the earth again and again, breaking it up into smaller and smaller clods, then sifting it with rotations of the pitchfork.

Homeland Security has lowered the terror alert level to the color of goldfinches and daffodils.

Tenderly,

Dee

Enclosed: "Landscape: Memory"

Landscape: Memory

The narrative of this shared memory is not simple.
– Rachel Hadas. "Frog Doctor."

The train, Manhattan-bound, lurches toward full speed after the station stop in Philadelphia. Nora looks up from her reading. The first rain since that awful Tuesday two weeks ago gives the rubbish-strewn landscape alongside the tracks a special luminosity. Something catches her eye for an instant before vanishing in the train's headlong rush north along the Amtrak corriNor: a pink tricycle teetering at the crest of the culvert, its front wheel turned at a crazy angle, silver and fuchsia streamers splaying out from the handlebars. What drama has left this child's plaything abandoned at the edge of the abyss, ready to take flight?

Nora remembers a tricycle just like this one, her daughter Livvy's, bought at a yard sale across from the neighborhood vegetable garden that she and Dan had started cultivating soon after Livvy's birth. When Livvy was five or so, she had pedaled that second-hand pink tricycle, and later a store-bought blue two-wheeler with training wheels, alongside Nora between home and the garden to help till the dark earth, then plant and pick peas and lettuce, peppers and beans, squash and tomatoes, the tilling, planting, and harvesting braiding through the years of child rearing.

The sweet memories make Nora smile, but a little transgressively, for they contrast so sharply to the desperate scenery that, rushing past her, has loosened them. Memory has been like that lately, she notices, full of ironic juxtapositions that life flings at her. Here she is, smiling at a memory and at the same time sad and anxious, en route to Manhattan for the first time since the terrorists' destruction of the Twin Towers, to help Livvy through the crisis that erupted in its wake.

"It's all wrong," Livvy said between gulps for air on the phone at two this morning. She sounded as though she were drowning. "I never should have come here, never should have started med school. I'm not cut out for this." She caught her breath. "What happened two weeks ago -- the planes, the bodies falling, flying. . ."

Her voice trailed off. "I can't study. Can't go to class. Can't sleep. My mind's racing, and I just lie awake here in the dark . . . . I don't. . . . I haven't been to class or labs since. . . . I can barely drag myself out of bed. And. . . ." Her voice was almost inaudible. "I don't know what to do. I feel like quitting. What should I do, Mom? It all seems so futile. . . . I. . . ."

Dan was on the phone in the kitchen. As with all middle-of-the-night parenting, Nora was sleep-dazed, incompetent, hoping the sound of Dan's breathing on the phone line meant that the steady workings of his mind were already composing a plan. When Livvy, at five, fell from her bed in the middle of the night, it was Dan who rushed to her, calmed her and assessed the pain, while Nora, slow to waken, even to the scream of their only child, had staggered to her feet and gathered what she could of her wits. Now Livvy, their smart, beautiful Livvy, who had been everybody's rescuer in middle school and high school, who seemed to do everything right and effortlessly in high school and college, was all grown up, a first-year at Mount Sinai Med School. And suddenly in trouble.

They talked on the phone every day since 9/11. But Nora heard something so different in their daughter's voice on the phone this morning that she decided to drop everything and head for Manhattan. She packed her bag before breakfast, made lesson plans for a substitute for the next week, and rushed from her last class to catch the train from Union Station.

Nora turns back to the page of Graham Greene's *The Power and the Glory* that she glanced up from a minute before. She isn't surprised, really, that the whiskey priest's introspection connects uncannily to her own:

> He was aware of an immense load of responsibility: it
> was indistinguishable from love. This, he thought, must
> be what all parents feel: ordinary men go through life
> like this, crossing their fingers, praying against pain,
> afraid. . . .

Nor that this explosion in her daughter's life started soon after 9/11, nor that yet another of her endless perimenopausal menstrual periods suddenly stopped today soon after Livvy's call.

The train lurches on toward Trenton. Nora closes her book, a forefinger holding her place on the lapsed priest's epiphany. She lets her head loll against the seat and her thoughts roam along a stream of loosely connected memories: last week she heard a sax player busking at the entrance of the Metro station at the spot where the outside air meets the tunnel air in a little whirlpool at the top of the escalator. Bits of paper swirled about along with the cool ribbon of an improvised jazz riff, a descending scale fragment that the sax player suddenly turned into a familiar melody – Try to remember the time in September when – .

Hearing songs from The Fantasticks immediately transports Nora back to those early days of mothering: Pushing the baby carriage along neighborhood sidewalks soon after Livvy's birth in mid-September, or, three years later, walking alongside Livvy on her tricycle, a little sack of vegetables dangling from the handlebars. Nora had amused her with songs from The Fantasticks on the way home:

> *Plant a radish, get a radish,*
> *Not a Brussels sprout —*

and

> *Try to remember the time in September,*
> *When skies were blue and oh so mellow — .*

Now, on her way toward Manhattan a quarter-century later, that September song freighted with entirely new meaning, Nora realizes how much has intervened in those years. Mothering a toddler gave way to raising a little girl, then a teenager and now a med student who arrived in Manhattan just in time to see the Twin Towers fall.

Nora catches herself. Go back to the safety of the Vegetable Song:

> *But with childeren,*
> *It's bewilderin' —*

She can't remember the next line. The other song intrudes, as it always does now, always will, she suspects, whenever she lets down her guard:

> *. . . The kind of September*
> *When love was an ember about to billow —*

The train slides on toward Newark. Keep your mind on the melody, Nora tells herself, to drown out the lyrics. If you work at it, you may stave off words that will lead, for sure, to catastrophic images. Maybe today you can get past the view of the Manhattan skyline across the Meadowlands, into the tunnel under the Hudson and all the way to Penn Station, without remembering that brilliant, blue-sky September morning.

Nora closes her eyes, hoping the train's steady rhythm will draw her into the half-trance she always feels in moving vehicles. It is too late. *That kind of September.* She tries to think of Livvy and that tricycle, but the words continue, uninvited. *When love was an ember.* She tries recalling the photo on her bureau of two-year-old Livvy on Dan's lap. *About to billow.* How close to the surface are images of September 11, now two weeks old. Will it always be this way?

How lucky she is, Nora thinks. No one she loved or knew died that day. She has been studying the daily Portraits in Grief memorial essays in *The Times*, looking for familiar names, reading the tender stories of ordinary lives, ordinary love, sons and daughters, husbands and wives and friends. There wasn't one person she knew.

The train is past Newark now, crossing the marshlands toward the Palisades, in full view of the Manhattan skyline. Saw grass rises from brackish ponds. The day's earlier mizzle has turned to fitful rain that dapples one pond and leaves the next smoothly, oilily black. It seems so random. A gull alights on the grassy margin, then slips into the water, effortlessly shifting from airborne grace to a fleeting standstill to another grace, waterborne. A road dead-ends into another pond. Nora notices a folding chair with a TV table beside it, facing the view of Manhattan that is now the saddest sight in the world.

The train hurtles into the dark tunnel. Nora puts her book into her backpack, her glasses carefully into their case, anticipating Penn Station, with all those ordinary people rushing about to reach their trains.

Nora wrenches her suitcase up the subway stairs at 115th Street onto Broadway and heads north toward Union Theological Seminary. The sun struggles to break through the clouds. Above the entrance the Seminary banner flaps bravely. Inside, the security guard looks up from his newspaper with a mild stare, notices the suitcase and points blandly to the right and a man's voice humming. Nora follows the gesture to the Residency Office and waits for a pause in the tune. "I'm Nora Gordon," she says to the young man at the desk. "I have a reservation."

"Yes, Miz Gordon. We're expecting you." The young man's voice conveys an effortless good will. "Nice to have you staying with us."

"I'll just register, drop my things in my room, if I could, and dash off to meet my daughter. She . . . " Nora catches herself from explaining.

"No problem. We saved you a room on the courtyard side. I think you'll be happy with it." The young man pulls an old-fashioned guest register from his desk and holds out a key. He smiles broadly. "Welcome to New York!" His round cheeks implode into matching dimples.

Nora smiles in return, feeling her already-full heart swell at the warmth of the old cliché. The ordinary moment is suddenly suffused with sacred generosity. Even the bored security guard and flapping banner have become emblems of rescue. Remember all of this, she says inwardly.

She signs the register and grasps the handle of her suitcase.

"Oh, there's one thing, Miz Gordon."

She has started toward the elevator, then stops.

"They're filming a 'Law and Order' episode here tonight, maybe tomorrow, too." The young man looks at his watch. "They're running the cables in an hour or so. For the tech trucks."

She stares in silent incomprehension.

"For the lights, the sound equipment. They film at night. It's that crime and trial show. You know, 'Crimes Ripped from the Headlines.'"

Nora feels a choking sensation at the back of her throat.

"So there might be some noise tonight, with the setting up and all. We've asked 'em to be quiet, but you never know. Don't worry. Someone from Union will be on duty in case anything bothers you." He gestures her on. "Don't worry," he repeats. "There's always somebody on security." His voice dissipates as she slips away. "Let us know if you need anything."

Nora heaves her suitcase onto the luggage stand by the window. Through the leaded glass panes overlooking the cloister she sees that the dogwoods have started turning shades of russet. Beyond are the seminary chapel's squat tower, dwarfed by that of Riverside Church, which blocks a sudden shaft of late-afternoon sunshine after a day of rain and heavy clouds. She notes the view hopefully: She promises herself to leave the window shade up to reveal the stonework tracery aglow in the day's freshest light.

She checks in the bathroom for a sign that her period, now so unwelcome and unexpected, has returned. It hasn't. She nods gratefully, then glances in the mirror at her graying hair that, in the filtered afternoon light, looks almost shot through with silver. Rushing to put on a little lipstick, she locks the door behind her and hurries down the stairs toward Broadway.

Nora sees Livvy's profile in the café before her daughter sees her. She looks exhausted, Nora thinks, and probably hasn't eaten properly in days. Her heart gives a little lurch at this disheveled version of her beautiful daughter, who always manages to look as if she has just stepped out of a designer sportswear catalogue. So unlike herself, Nora thinks.

Livvy looks up. "I should have met you at Penn Station," she blurts.

Nora smiles, touches her daughter's shoulder. "Don't be silly. I can find my way in Manhattan." She bends to kiss her daughter's cheek but catches the top of her head instead. Along with the tightening at the back of her throat she feels an echo of a twinge in her belly and a rise of sensation in her breasts. Or perhaps she only imagines them.

"You're here, Mom." Livvy fingers a packet of sugar. There is an uneaten muffin beside it. "I can't thank you enough for coming."

"We're together, sweet pea, that's what matters." Nora turns her whole gaze toward her daughter's eyes and reaches for her hand.

Livvy nods wordlessly.

"Let's stop at the Westside and get a few things for supper. I'll fix whatever you like. And then you should sleep. You look tired." Nora rushes on, as much for herself as for her daughter's benefit. "And have a little of that muffin, dearie." She goes to the counter and returns with two mugs of milky tea. "Drink up," she says.

Livvy does as she is told.

Nora suppresses any sign of surprise that this chin-forward, "Oh, Mother" daughter of hers puts up none of her usual resistance. Again she touches Livvy's forearm, leaves her hand there. "Hey, Liv, here's looking at you," she says, hoping the familiar line will draw a smile.

It does. Livvy forces a little quarter-smile and takes a long, slow drink of tea.

"Thanks, dearie." Nora reaches up and tucks a stray lock of hair behind Livvy's ear.

She notes that tingling sensation rising again in her breasts. It is as if her body can still, twenty-some years later, remember lactating. But how do I mother her now? she wonders.

"Dad called just before you got here. He wanted to know if you'd gotten in. We both worry about you, Mom." Livvy smiles again. "But that's just a ruse. We're really just making sure you're worrying about us." She pauses. "He sends his love. Said to remind you to charge your cell at night. And to call him." Livvy takes another sip of tea. Her voice seems stronger now. "Then he started reminiscing about the night I was born, Mom. He went on and on about forgetting where he had left the car in the hospital parking lot, he was so excited."

Her familiar low chuckle gladdens her mother's heart.

"For some reason, he needed to tell me that today."

The café is turning a silent shade of mauve in the early evening light. Nora lets herself catch a wave of memories and ride it to shore: Dan's face the day after they arrived home from the hospital when he got the phone call that his mother had died; her own gulping sense of incompetence when she looked at Livvy's birdlike little limbs, the frantic pulsing her infant chest above the unhealed umbilical cord just after Dan left for Ohio to help his father with the funeral. What was the Graham Greene sentence she read that afternoon? Something about being a parent and going through life afraid, fingers crossed. Looking over at Livvy, she remembers the quick alterations of exhilaration and exhaustion that are the natural conditions of new parents. What is the equivalent, she wonders, for parenting grown children in need?

They gather up their things. Lights are coming on along Broadway, beckoning neon shop signs, bright headlights and taillights. The sky is now a steely gray. Survivalist trees seem to hang onto life thanks to a miraculous intervention.

Mother and daughter walk arm in arm, their strides matching, in the current of pedestrians. Nora feels as if she was here and also watching herself here, among ordinary people going about the ordinary business of living that includes dramas like Livvy's. It is like that Breughel painting that Auden wrote about in the poem Nora just worked on with her sophomores: On a bluff above a sparkling bay farmers plow their fields, oblivious to the pale leg and tiny feathers just about to slip below the surface of the water. Icarus, plunging from his ecstatic, wax-winged flight, falls to his death while the others walk on, oblivious.

It is true for the sad, the sweet, and the sweet, Nora thinks, this uncanny juxtaposition of emotions. Here are the tragedies of the Twin Towers, the Pentagon, the field in Shanksville, and all those grieving families, and here she is with her daughter, walking arm in arm.

"I'd like to sleep with you tonight, Mom," Livvy says. "Not at my place. At Union, if you don't mind."

"Of course, darling," she replies.

At the Seminary they step carefully across orange electric cables snaking from generator trucks through the vestibule into the lobby. In their room, Livvy brushes her teeth and showers. Nora unpacks her suitcase and backpack and puts her laptop on the windowsill. Riverside Church's tower is lit brightly against the night sky.

Nora's cell rings. "Hi, Hon." It is Dan. "How's it going? How is she?"

"She seems okay, but I don't know much yet. Where are you, Dan, at work or home?" She doesn't listen for his answer, just races on, compelled to connect herself to him, not through present need but through their shared memories of the emotional logic of parenting. "Remember how crazy I was after she was born? How, when they had to put her under the sunlamp in the nursery to bring down the bilirubin level, I freaked out, thinking that neonatal jaundice was a terminal condition, and couldn't stop crying?" She doesn't bother to hide the catch in her throat.

"I remember, Nor. You weren't crazy, just wired, that's all, with the hospital-room faucet that wouldn't stop running and the maintenance man coming to fix it in the middle of the night." He chuckles. "Remember my throwing him out of the room?"

"Yup. And the night nurse —"

" — who tried to give you morphine, then realized she was in the wrong room? Oh, Nora, Honey. What a time it was."

"And you brought your wrenches to fix the plumbing?"

"And Liv got that awful rash on her face?"

"And the nurses kept styling her hair each time they brought her from the nursery —"

" — Sometimes a side part, sometimes a hook-shaped curl in the middle of her forehead —"

" — And in two seconds at the breast she looked like a wild thing, that black hair sticking straight out every which way?"

"Where are you, Dan, at home or at the office?" she asks again.

"No reason to rush home when you're not there. You know that."

She feels another clutching at her heart. "Oh, Dan."

"I know, there's always the cat for company." He laughs again.

She can hear him typing.

"Dan, you're talking to me or writing?" She feels her voice getting shrill.

"I'm trying to finish up stuff that can't wait 'til next week. And then I'm going to clear my desk so I can get out of here. I'll probably have to come in here first thing in the morning, but I'll be up there as soon as I can."

She can hear the radio behind the typing, behind his voice.

"You're there with her. That's what matters," he says. "Hey, Nor. Did you listen to 'All Things Considered' this afternoon?"

"Dan." She pretends to sound stern. "Where have I been all afternoon?"

"I know. But you would've loved this interview. On the new book about the tightrope walker who walked between the Twin Towers, back in the 'seventies. You know who I mean."

"I remember it happened. But I don't remember – "

"Yes, you do. You remember everything. Come on, Hon. What's his name? Philippe something. Well, this book sounds fantastic. I'll buy it for you tomorrow at the train station."

"Dan, it can wait." She smiles. There he is, her Dan, in love with stories and books. In love with her and their daughter, but also with listening to the radio at all hours of the day and night, while he works and reads and drives, while he sleeps. Even while they make love. Dan, whose idea of loving her is to do everything he can for her, from fixing the maddening drip of a hospital room faucet and tending a sick child in the middle of the night to buying books for her that she doesn't yet know she will love.

"Hey, Dan. It's late. Go home." Her heart is full. "Go home, go to bed."

"I love you."

"You're just sayin' that," she replies, as always, at the close of their phone conversations.

Livvy comes out of the bathroom in an aura of steam. "Was that Daddy?"

"Yes, sweet pea. He'll be up tomorrow. He sends his love."

In the bathroom Nora brushes her teeth and puts on pajamas. She checks, as she does every time in the bathroom, that her period hasn't started again. Back in the bedroom she glances at Livvy, whose hair is damply splayed across the pillow, her breathing low and rhythmical.

Nora reaches to close the window shade, then stops herself, remembering her plan for the morning. Something beyond the window catches her eye: The sky above the chapel has suddenly gone a dull black. Illumination of the church tower has ended for the night. Sliding under the covers on her side of the bed, she adjusts her reading glasses, opens *The Power and the Glory*.

How amazing, she thinks, life is. The book has fallen open to the page she read earlier in the day and forgot until this moment. The whiskey priest is lulled into an epiphany by the movement of the mule lurching along beneath him:

> His mind was full of a simplified mythology: Michael dressed in armour slew a dragon, and the angels fell through space like comets with beautiful streaming hair because they were jealous, so one of the fathers had said, of what God intended for men – the enormous privilege of life – this life.

Nora puts out the light.

She wakes with a start. Livvy is fast asleep beside her. For an instant Nora still rides the dream that awakened her. She was reading a story by one of those prodigious students she had every year or two. A sentence of the story had come to life in her dream, of its own volition: "The City had rented out gaps between skyscrapers to trapeze artists, who spread their nets between buildings and were now practicing near the thirtieth-story line." In the dream, the aerialist, practicing his impossible, faith-laden art in the vortex between two skyscrapers, was back-lit against a shimmering mauve and gold sky. His hair, caught in the play of wind, splayed out past his shoulders like silver streamers.

Dizzy, bedazzled by the dream-vision, Nora opens her eyes. There, horn at his lips, poised on the northernmost pinnacle of Riverside Church, caught in the early morning light, is a statue of the Archangel Gabriel.

In the bathroom, Nora is crestfallen at the sign of yet another period. Here am I, she thinks, menstruating still at nearly sixty, the mother of a grown daughter, with sympathetic uterine contractions and the tingling memory of milk letting down in my breasts, telltale signs of my childbearing history. Are memories just the tugging of invisible neurons? And are thoughts just flickering dream-visions carried like the bright-haired tightrope walker swaying in the abyss between two phantom skyscrapers, or like the archangel heralding grace?

Nora showers and dresses quickly, then peeks around the bathroom door. Livvy is just opening her eyes. Just remembering where she is, why.

"No need to rush out of bed, sweet pea. It's early. Get some more sleep."

Livvy closes her eyes, sighs, curls under the covers.

Again memories start to flow, uninvited, the here and now attached to other memories and dreams, connected by invisible wires. Nora remembers another story by another prodigy in her classroom, a story in which a young writer tracks down the life of Saint Elizabeth of Hungary, the patron saint of bakers. Who, Nora wonders, are the patron saints of trapeze artists and the parents of grown children?

As noiselessly as she can, she boots up her laptop. She waits as the screen organizes itself and the programs ready themselves for her commands. One hand poised over the keyboard, she reaches for her cell and punches in the home number.

"Hello?" Dan's voice at the other end is crackly with static.

"You're breaking up. I'll call you right back," Nora whispers. She slips from the room and goes downstairs to the seminary courtyard. The television crew is quitting after the night's filming. She dials home again.

"Hi, honey." Dan's voice is clearer now. "How'd you two sleep in one little bed?" He is eating while he talks. "How is she?"

"We slept like logs. At least I did. If Liv had moved, I'd have felt it." She chuckles. "The film crew worked all night, but we never heard a thing."

"Film crew?"

"This is New York, remember? We're on a TV crime show set. They're filming at the Seminary."

"Ah." Dan is unfazed. "So long as you and Liv are okay. I'm taking the same train you did yesterday. I'll be there by mid-afternoon." Silverware clanking on dishes and running water mingle with the sound of Dan's voice. "I'm rushing, Nor."

"So what else is new?"

Dan chuckles, just as she had. "I'll call you from the train." His voice grows soft, intimate. "Love you."

"Me, too."

Back in her room, with Livvy still asleep, Nora returns to her laptop and logs on to the internet. She looks over at her daughter sprawled now across the entire bed, her face resting calmly in the crook of her elbow, one fist balled up under her chin. Nora types *patron saint trapeze artists* into the search text box. No hits. She looks out the window, then types in *Archangel Gabriel*, and waits, eyes closed. In images that linger from her dreams, she remembers those suffering souls in the windows of the Twin Towers. Was the Archangel Gabriel there, too, invisible? Livvy stirs but remains in a sleep that contains no such questions. The look of her is more compelling than the list of hits. Nora feels the tug of her earliest moments of mothering, memories she hadn't reeled in in years.

"She can't be named," Dan had said, "until her eighth day, at least. They say the Angel of Death descends to look at newborns, to do them mischief. Better to wait until a baby's in the congregation to be named. That way we'll all look out for her together."

Nora remembers how mystified she'd been. Here was this rational, secular man giving voice to an ancient folk belief. To this day it puzzles her. She looks over at her daughter again.

Livvy is stretching, watching her mother with untroubled eyes. "What's up, Mom?"

"Oh, nothing. Just googling the Archangel Gabriel."

"Mom?"

"No, really. I've been thinking about the intervention of the divine in everyday life." Nora laughs at how sanctimonious she sounds. "The archangel Gabriel is outside the window, baby. I saw him yesterday and again this morning, silhouetted against the sky when I woke up."

"Mom?"

"It's a statue, Liv. I haven't gone all oobly. It's a statue on Riverside Church. Complete with trumpet. So I started thinking about archangels, guardian angels, last night and again this morning, and I googled him."

"Okay. So what did you find out?"

"When you were born, Daddy said you couldn't be named right away, we had to wait, because of, well, the Angel of Death. This morning I remembered that for some reason, and then I saw Gabriel, and thought, if your father said there's an Angel of Death that his baby girl needs protection from, shouldn't I look out for Guardian Angels to protect her? And in this modern world, where do you start but with Google?"

"You guys never cease to amaze me." Livvy stretches, smiling.

"That's what it's all about. Amazement. Amusement. In equal doses." Nora kneels before the tiny refrigerator she stocked with breakfast things the night before. "Fruit, dearie?"

"Not yet, Mom. Thanks." Livvy yawns. "I feel okay. Drained, but clean. At least cleaner than I felt yesterday." She pads to the bathroom. "What should we do today?"

"Do you have time to spend with your old mother?"

"I made an appointment with my advisor – she's our anatomy professor. She said she can see me at four if I come by her apartment at Riverside and 104th." Livvy says over the sound of running water, through the closed door. "How 'bout the Cloisters?"

"Perfect," Nora replied. "There's bound to be some stuff there about Gabriel. They've got all those *Annunciations*, don't they? I'm putting out yogurt and granola and strawberries. You've got to eat." She enjoys sounding decisive about the little things. "I'll run down to the cafeteria and get us each a cup of coffee and a bagel. Toasted?"

For the second time this morning Nora goes down the stairs to the lobby and out through the cloisters to the cafeteria. The TV crew is gone for the day, their cables rolled in neat circles in a corner near the doorway to the courtyard.

Unbidden, another memory, this one of swaddling their unnamed baby and whispering to her, comes flooding back. Hands deftly fold the white flannel square into a triangle and place the baby on it. *I'm going to whisper your name in your ear, sweet pea.* Now folding the bottom point of the triangle up to the baby's breastbone. *So you'll know it but that Angel of Death won't hear.* And folding the two other points, first one, then the other, around the infant's shoulders. *No, it's not Sweet Pea, not Lovey, although either would be a fine name. It's – .* Tucking in the corner to make a little bundle, a cocoon, the baby wrapped in it firmly. *I'll tell you, little one.* Bending down, lips to the tiny shell of an ear. The whisper went on, confident, confidential. *It's* – Only the open lips moved, silent, first puckering around an open O, then the tip of the tongue just barely touching the roof of the mouth, then the top front teeth touching the inside of the lower lip, then the mouth slightly ajar, everything moving as if to say aloud *Olivia*. Was it herself, Nora, doing the swaddling and whispering with Dan standing in the doorway watching, or was it Dan whispering and swaddling while she watched, silent, her shoulder against the doorframe?

After leaving Livvy on the bus, Nora steps off at the Seminary stop on Broadway at 121st Street. The earnest, soaking rain that started while they were at the Cloisters has subsided into streaks of sunshine and mist. She goes up to her room for a few minutes to herself while Livvy keeps her appointment with her advisor. Nora sits at the little desk and looks again at the art prints she purchased: Robert Campin's *Annunciation Triptych* and *Tapestry with the Annunciation, ca. 1410-1430*, both showing a beautiful, golden-haired Gabriel, trumpetless but with wide, elegant wings still in their in-flight position, approaching the modest Mary, who, eyes averted, shows no special surprise. She props the prints between the Graham Greene novel and the laptop and lies down on her bed for a few minutes before heading out across Broadway, through the Columbia campus, and then along Amsterdam, toward Livvy's building.

Livvy is at the doorstep, arms full. Just as Nora had suggested offhandedly as she'd left her daughter on the bus, Livvy has scooped up sheets and towels to take to the laundromat on Amsterdam. Nora passed it a moment earlier, noting more of those perfect epiphanies she has had since taking the train the day before: the façade of the Cathedral of Saint John the Divine cast a reflected glow of benevolent sunshine, even in the subsiding mist, through the plate-glass window opposite of Manny's Coin-Op Quick Wash 'n Dry, where, inside, just visible, a wizened man and an infant sound asleep in a stroller beside him wore the same expressions of calm, stoic sadness and wordless acceptance of the human condition. Nora felt her heart rise and then tumble as if from a great height when she glanced in their direction.

She notes also that the mist is clearing. Taking the last steps to Livvy's apartment building, she starts humming, inwardly at first, then her voice rises as a scrap of a distantly memorized, long-forgotten lyric returns: *Soon it's gonna rain, what are we gonna do?*

Funny, she thinks. I can remember that much but not the rest. And I'm crying. She dries her eyes with her sleeve just before glancing up to see Livvy.

"You know, sweet pea," Nora starts talking as if her daughter was at her side the whole time. "I read somewhere this old rabbinic story that says newborns know every word, every letter of Torah by heart. They know every word of every language, every emotion, every thought that any human being has ever had."

They turn and walk together to Manny's.

"Can you imagine?" Nora continues. "They know everything human beings are permitted to know. Of course they can't tell anyone. That's the wonder of it. God tells them they have to keep it all a secret. And you know what's just as wonderful? As they grow out of babyhood, they start forgetting everything. So for all our lives until we die, we are trying to recollect as much of what we've forgotten as we can. Learning is just remembering, my sweet, beloved child."

Livvy smiles. "'I'm not the only one in this pickle, thrown for a loop by what's happened.' My advisor's exact words. 'Just take it one day at a time.'" She yawns.

Dan arrives while Livvy is at the laundromat. Nora meets him at the door. "Look at you," he says, kissing her cheek, flinging his coat on the back of a chair. "How's the patient?"

It was Dan's line during every parenting emergency. When they heard that sickening thud in the night followed by the one scream, Dan leapt out of bed and arrived before Livvy had drawn breath for a second. When she sailed off the front steps on her tricycle and landed on the sidewalk, Dan came running, two steps at a time. He did the medical emergencies while Nora blanched at the first sign of blood. After all that menstruating, she thinks, smiling, I should have been able to stand the sight of blood.

The apartment door opens. Livvy is in her father's arms in a flash. "Daddy. You're here." She starts to cry for the first time in two weeks.

"Oh, baby," he says.

Nora remembers the rest of the lyric and sings it silently in her head, changing a pronoun here and there: *Then we'll let it rain, rain pell mell.* . . .

Livvy drops the clean laundry on her little sofa. "Hey, you two. Let's go to the Hungarian Pastry Shop for tea and strudel. I'll tell you some of the lame puns that come up in anatomy lab."

Nora exchanges a glance with Dan. Rescue, they say with their eyes, seems, not without several invisible scars, about to start.

Subject:	Okay
Date:	4/30/2003 7:48:31 AM EDT
From:	dndyoung2@owl.com
To:	dndyoung1@owl.com

Darling,

I woke up this morning saying to myself, "Okay, Dee, nothing's really okay, but you're gonna be okay." My house needs repairs. Okay. My computer's breaking down. Okay. I don't hear from you; of course I'm not going to hear from you. Okay. There's a war on and the country is a mess, but that'll be okay, too. Some things can be fixed. Some can't. Either way, it's okay. Love always.

Dee

～ Eleven ～

May 1, 2003

Her only gift was knowing people almost by instinct. . . . She had
the oddest sense of being herself invisible; unseen; unknown.
– Virginia Woolf. *Mrs. Dalloway.*

Dear Bathsua,

I'm in the Main Reading Room, happily anonymous. It's freeing to be
so unremarkable. And convenient for imagining the lives of others. The
merest surface detail – the tilt of a head, the touch of a hand to the temple,
the choice of pen or pencil – suggests a whole story. An unshaven guy in a
flannel shirt to my left has just crept, rumple-haired, into desk 321; a fresh-
faced, pony-tailed woman opposite me at 223 just glanced toward 321, who
pretended not to notice. There's a story here. And the woman with her back
to me in 167: her tidy chignon and the alignment of her head above her
spinal column offer an entire short story for me to unravel.

This power of observation and imagination seems new to me: Look at
that stoop-shouldered man across the aisle at 273, near the water fountain.
I see him most days I am here, nearly always in the same seat. Just now he
looked up over his half-glasses across the charge desk at the center of the
Reading Room, off toward Alcove 6, maybe even toward the balcony with
the Loeb Classics, toward our secret niche. He's resettling the wire frame of
his glasses against that little indentation above the bridge of the nose. He's
fingering his notepad and jiggling a pencil alongside it.

The sunlight coming in through the half-round window above Alcove
6 has lit up the lenses of 273's glasses. Which, I wonder, is his reader's
shelf? I recognize something sad and stalwart about him, his necktie and
white shirt, his cuffs roll-folded in that old-fashioned way of my father's

when he did the taxes at the dinette table in the 1950's.

What should I write about, Magistra, in the merry month of May?

In trust,

Dee

May 5, 2003

One man in his time plays many parts.
– William Shakespeare. *As You Like It.*

Dear Dorothea,

I, too, enjoy being in the Library. Don't look for me; you won't see me.

I am thinking about Shakespeare. What a writing master he is, not just a cultural diversion here, but a real teacher of the craft we aspire to. He advises that we write about subjects near at hand, especially those we would avoid. The challenge, of course, is to stretch the writing beyond one's own little circle of secret intimacies out to the wide circle of humanity.

Are you ready to write about your father? I am. Now that I have written about my son, so close to the bone, I think I am set to tackle anything.

Remember Lear's speech near the end of Act V, a sonnet nearly, spoken over the body of his beloved Cordelia? This old man, "jealous in honour, sudden, and quick in quarrel" is in "second childishness," a step away from death, "mere oblivion." In it he asks, "Have I caught thee?" Did you know, my dear, that Shakespeare also put that question in the mouth of another splendid old man, long past his prime? In *Merry Wives of Windsor*, Sir John Falstaff – – woos Mistress Ford with the same question:

Have I caught thee, my heav'nly jewel? Why, now let me
die, for I have liv'd long enough. This is the period of
my ambition. O this blessed hour!

Enough canoodling, as you put it. Go and write about what's close to the bone. Your heart will be in it. And so will mine. Old fathers. Let's do the same assignment at the same time.

Yours, faithfully,

BRM

P.S. Did you know that Shakespeare borrow'd that question from Sir Philip Sidney? "Have I caught my heav'nly jewel," asks Astrophil in the Second Song of *Astrophil and Stella*. Everything worthwhile, it seems, is borrow'd.

May 7, 2003

Come, let me write. And to what end?
– Sir Philip Sidney. Astrophil and Stella. Sonnet 34.

Dear Bathsua,

I am delighted by your Shakespeare lesson, Magistra! Thank you.

I shall follow your advice and write about my father. And Lear. I wish Papa had been more like Sir John Falstaff, but we work with what we have.

Yours,

Dee

P.S. I just looked at the Library's copy of *Astrophil and Stella*. Sonnet XXXIV has a little penciled bracket, apparently by a wayward reader – you? – around the following lines:

Come, let me write. "And to what end?" To ease
A burthen'd heart. "How can words ease, which are
The glasses of thy daily vexing care?"

Apropos, don't you think? You wanted me to find it, I expect.

Subject:	Re: Ἐξίσταται γὰρ πάντ' ἀπ' ἀλλήλων δίχα revisited
Date:	5/9/2003 13:43:27 PM EDT
From:	dndyoung2@owl.com
To:	dndyoung1@owl.com

Darling Dan,

Computer problems again. Ned says that my memory is almost full. That I am in danger of losing everything. Shades of "All things break asunder/ Fall away/ Departing each from each and winding up/ Abandoned, out of joint, to one another/ Lost." He says that to be safe I should "transfer stuff to memory sticks." Oh yes, memory does indeed stick. And that to avoid a crash I'd better back up. Boy, have I been doing that. But he's right: before you can go forward, you have to back up. That it's almost time to start fresh with a new computer and move on from the

OWL email account – "It's so old-school, Grandma," he said – to a new "provider" – one that's free and less balky. I love the terminology! Am almost ready. Love.

May 10, 2003

> He was a teacher, and it may be said that he had every right to teach because he spent all his time learning; and the things he learned were what he considered to be and called "the facts of life," which he learned not only out of necessity but because he wanted to.
> – Jack Kerouac. *On the Road.*

Dear Dee,

We are close. Closer than ever. Only the hardest is left.

In haste,

B

Subject:	Re: *Ἐξίσταται γὰρ πάντ' ἀπ' ἀλλήλων δίχα* revisited
Date:	5/12/2003 22:10:57 PM EDT
From:	dndyoung2@owl.com
To:	dndyoung1@owl.com

Dan, Darling,

I'm going to buy a new computer. And when school's out Ned's going to help me adjust to a new operating system and switch email accounts. Meantime, I'm tying up loose ends.

Love.

May 12, 2003

> This is the time when voyagers return
> With a mad longing for known customs and things,
> Where joy in an old pencil is not absurd.
> – May Sarton. "Return."

Dear Bathsua,

That modern epigraph in your last letter – by Kerouac no less – and about teaching! "Write from what you know," you say? You sound just like the writing teacher I was all those years at Remington. Write what's in the silences. Pay attention to the gestures, the silent hollows in your head, the emotional echoes of unremember'd dreams? What I said, you have said. Have I caught thee? As thou hast caught me?

A few loose ends need tying. Look for a letter in a week or two with another attachment.

Dee

May 21, 2003

O me, my heart, my rising heart!
— William Shakespeare. *King Lear*.

Dear Bathsua,

Here is an essay about my father. In my mind's eye he furrows his brow and purses his lips. I think immediately of Shakespeare's *King Lear*, the script of my role as the daughter of a life-saddened old man. To prepare for what may be our last assignment, I've just read the play for the umpteenth time. My first inclination is to write in the safe traces of a literary essay. But that would be like a chair in the hands of a lion tamer, keeping the feelings at bay. Just barely.

I've been fretting over something you wrote months ago: Another person's life, you said, isn't a writer's property to disclose. By what right, then, do I tell my father's secret story? Knowing that I am exposing him to a stranger's scrutiny would be so repugnant to him that he'd. . . . I don't even know what he would do. In his last years he told me he hated discussing his business affairs in Dan's hearing. I was horrified. But I understood. When age robs us of control over our own affairs, we guard even more closely the bits that we have left. By what right do I dare reveal his secrets? Is it cannibalistic to do so?

The writer's defense, I suppose, is that Truth is a nobler pursuit than Privacy. Fiction writers' tactics are cheap, but they work: Rearrange some details, add others, subtract something here and there, assign characters fictitious names, and *poof!* no more guilt! Folks won't sue you or hate you for the rest of their lives or yours, hang up the phone when you call, burn your letters, terrorize you in nightmares after they die. A writer friend told me she stopped dead in her tracks on a family memoir just before Passover. She couldn't face her father and sisters across the table. "Their stares!" she said. "Their angry eyes!" Yet here I am, recording the secrets of others. Shouldn't I guard those secrets on both sides of the grave?

But I digress. This assignment scares me. I'm afraid to look at my own "foolish, fond old man," to see that I "hast power to shake [his] manhood" when I insist he "should be ruled and led by some discretion that discerns [his] state better than [him]self." The words I write about him "sting his mind so venomously." I cry out, "O me, my heart, my rising heart"!

As ever, in trust,

Dee

Enclosure: "Living with Lear"

Living with Lear

Speak what we feel, not what we ought to say.
– William Shakespeare. *King Lear.*

The spring after my mother died, I began teaching *King Lear* to high school seniors. Witlessly, I insulated myself from the play's emotional power by pretending that it was only something to think about and take apart. I started by designing crossword puzzles, believing I could get away with vocabulary exercises for each scene of Act I.

The next fall my father came to live with Dan and me, in the little English-basement apartment in our house. Soon *King Lear* stormed my heart, transforming me into Lear's Fool, Cordelia, Goneril and Regan, all at once. Dan and my students took turns as the stage hands and audience, enabling the daily performances, and watching their inevitable denouement.

—⚍—

Fool. The man that makes his toe
What he his heart should make
Shall of a corn cry woe,
And turn his sleep to wake.

Sitting at the kitchen table in November I saw that my old *Lear* lesson plans made no sense. My father had been with us for two months. Our lives had been upended. The next time I teach the play, I decided, I'll have my smart teenagers look straight at the anguish of old age in their families – and me at the anguish of it in mine. We would all write letters to God about what was going on: Were their grandparents all fine – or was one of them growing fretful or difficult? Did they overhear any hushed conversations about to what to do with Grandma or Grandpa? Were there unpaid bills, incomprehensible Medicare and insurance claims, unbalanced checkbooks piling up in hopeless mounds, in drawers, on tables, on desktops? Were shrill phone calls grating across the late-night and early-morning silences?

But that plan terrified me. So instead of facing the debacle head on, I pulled out the old Act I crossword puzzles. The next morning I would have my students fit letters into tidy little squares. Meanwhile my father padded around the kitchen in slippered feet trying not to disturb my concentration.

I could feel my irritation mounting, my puzzles a gaping window onto my ragged, unvoiced rage at having my moody, petulant father living with us. The puzzle's crosshatched dark spaces underscored the inevitable fact: having Papa move in with us was a terrible idea. He started to make himself a cup of tea. He lit the back burner, then turned to fill the kettle and find the teabags. Then he padded off, forgetting what he had started to do. Remembering, he turned back, casting watery eyes in my direction. Had I noticed? I pretended I hadn't, instead writing in taut, anxious handwriting one question for the whole of Act I: *How do we know the old king is in decline?*

—☙—

Regan. Such unconstant starts are we like to have from him as this.

"What's your plan for tomorrow, Papa?" I asked, looking up from a stack of final exams.

I heard his huffed intake of breath. "I've got to go over to the Credit Union office at Walter Reed to roll over a CD that's maturing." He scuffed to the counter, put down his cup of tea made with two of yesterday's spent teabags.

"You can do it by mail."

There was another huff. "You know I don't trust the mail. I'll walk to the Metro, take it to Silver Spring, then catch the bus down Georgia Avenue."

I shivered despite the late-May warm spell. I pictured my father teetering on crowded Metro platforms, weaving across busy intersections through the rush of pedestrians – to say nothing of cars and trucks – approaching and passing him in both directions. It was no longer a question of if, but when, he would fall and I'd get the call to run to an emergency room.

I knew he took special pride in visiting Walter Reed Army Hospital not as a patient but on his own two feet, passing uniformed personnel, remembering military service half a century before. I pictured my father flashing his tattered photo ID to the MP on duty at the entrance, the young soldier smiling a little tenderly, a little patronizingly, at a sight he'd seen a hundred times before: the old soldier in baseball cap, sun glasses, and tennis shoes, with a cane instead of a swagger stick, easing out that cracked old military photo from his wallet with crabbed fingers.

Papa liked carrying a little briefcase, having a destination, mingling with the workaday world. What was more, he was terrified of losing what he valued most, his money, in the dark twin abysses of post offices and computers. He loved having bankers he knew by name, reminding me that he was on familiar terms with them, noting appointments with them on his calendar.

"It's a terrible idea, Papa. It'll take all day. You'll be exhausted."

"It's no problem," he insisted. "I'll take it easy walking to the Metro. I'll get a seat on the train. It's no trouble to transfer at –"

"No." I knew I sounded shrill even uttering just one word.

He scarcely missed a beat in the recitation. "– to transfer at Metro Center and take the Red Line to Silver Spring, then catch the G2 bus. It stops right in front of Walter Reed."

"Papa." I heard my voice rising. "You're not going by public transportation. You've got no business walking in the hot sun. The construction and traffic. . . ."

"But I can do it. I want to do it. I've always done it myself." Defeat was already undermining his querulous assertion of independence.

Why, I asked myself behind clenched teeth, are we having this argument again? Logic rose like bile. "We can do these things by wire transfer or – "

"Wire transfer?" he spat, his voice both furious and petulant. "Once – don't you remember? – Don't you remember the bank made a mistake? Besides – " I heard it before he said it. "Besides, a wire transfer costs ten dollars."

Sweat coated my armpits, anger the hollow spaces in my head. "Okay, you'll do it in person. But I'll drive you. My morning class is over at ten. I'll drive home and pick you up at eleven. I'll drive you door to door."

He huffed again, that irritating little puff of breath between his pouted lips that has echoed through my whole life.

My father was on the front steps, studying his watch, when I pulled up a few minutes later than I had promised. With his old blue plastic briefcase under one arm, he wore his baseball cap and dark glasses, a plaid shirt, chinos held up by red suspenders, sneakers. He had his cane but didn't use it to walk to the car. Seated and inside, he gripped the passenger door handle as if my driving were about to fling him onto the street.

"I'll leave you off at the officers' entrance," I said, pulling into the Walter Reed drive and approaching the MP for the ID check. I knew Papa liked that, the dignity of a special officers' entrance away from the hurly burly of enlisted men and their dependents. "Wait for me in the lobby, Pa."

"Okay, Dee."

"I'll park in the garage. Wait for me. I'll be right back."

Fat chance. I drove along crowded rows of parked cars, sweat trickling down my sides, along my thighs. I pictured Papa standing, legs apart in his characteristic at-ease stance that lent him a flicker of nostalgic self-respect. I felt the minutes mounting, the fatigue in his swollen legs mounting, the temperature mounting, my mood souring. I could read his thoughts: *What's taking her so long? I could have done this myself.* I swerved back onto Georgia Avenue and, traffic lurching alongside me, found a parking space on the street. The glaring sun and fume-choked air hit me like raking fingernails. I rushed along the long walkway to the MP, who waved me on. Maybe I wasn't the first daughter of a long-retired colonel he'd seen that day.

My father stood at the entrance just as I'd left him, just as I'd pictured him, swollen ankles above sneakers planted on the floor a foot apart, back nearly straight, gnarled hands at ease on the head of his cane, moist fawn's eyes gazing meekly straight ahead as if awaiting orders.

"Parking was tough," I muttered. "Where's the Credit Union office?"

"I don't remember. I waited for you like you said."

I don't think he heard me clear my throat or noticed my pursed lips, those habits of disgruntlement I had inherited from him.

We took the elevator to the sub-basement, then plodded through maze-like corridors. I looked at my watch. Noon. At twelve fifteen we reached the Credit Union office. The clerk was at lunch. My stomach growled.

The clerk returned a little after one. The computer was down. Papa looked at his watch disapprovingly. I felt like Goneril and Regan and didn't like it one bit. "Full of change his age is," I might have noted. My father's "long engraffed condition" of parsimony and disapproval had ground at me for years. He was, truly, an "idle old man that still would manage those authorities that he had given away." I felt like a fool, too, an angry one, watching him slowly scrutinize every entry on the deposit document the clerk filled in, kept in "idle and fond bondage in the oppression of aged tyranny." Surely Edmund was right: "Sons at perfect age and fathers declined, the father should be as ward to the son, and the son manage his revenue."

His business finally transacted, Papa was spent, hungry. Still he walked with a vestige of assurance that his CD was invested at four and a quarter per cent.

I was clench-jawed. "Never again," I muttered. "Never again will this be done on foot, in person, by you alone, the two of us together, or me alone."

Papa's sense of accomplishment seeped away, sucked down by fatigue, my unmasked anger, his unvoiced acknowledgment that he was indeed the shadow of his old self. In the car he saw it was nearly two thirty. Still he rallied, ready to puff himself up and sound important again. This time he played the generous host. "Can I treat you to a late lunch at Mario's?"

The thought of the rundown Italian café on Georgia Avenue made the bile rise again in my throat. "No thanks. Not today. You look tired." I managed to affix a little white lie to the truth. "And I have an important faculty meeting at three thirty." I couldn't spend the next hour with him, nor stay angry any longer. "Old fools are babes again," says Goneril, "and must be used with checks as flatteries." I'd checked his spirits, he mine, enough for a day. "I'll take a rain check."

"What about lunch? You have to eat, Dee."

"I'll drop you off at home. There's stuff in the fridge for you. I'll have something at the faculty meeting." I drove home, windows rolled up, radio and air conditioner both on full blast. Before driving back to school there was just enough time to splash water on my face, in hopes of washing away the grotesque Goneril mask that I'd worn since morning.

—꩜—

> *Lear.* 'Tis our fast intent
> To shake all cares and business from our age,
> Conferring them on younger strengths while we
> Unburdened crawl toward death. . .

Early the next October my father had a belly ache he couldn't ignore. It had been going on for a while, he said, but in his usual stoic way told me at the doctor's office, "I tried to ride it out." It turned out to be a gall bladder infection too far advanced to be treated laparoscopically. "If only you'd complained earlier," the doctor said.

So Papa went in for major surgery just as I was ending the Chaucer unit and starting to teach *King Lear* again. I sat through the surgery grading Chaucer essays on my lap in the waiting room, then made daily afternoon hospital visits after my first *Lear* classes. A week later, when he should have been discharged, Papa spiked a fever and was transferred from the surgical recovery ward to the ICU, intubated, placed on a respirator, intravenous feeding tubes, heart monitor, evacuation tubes, and kidney dialysis. I taught my morning classes, then rushed to the ICU at eleven to sit by my father's bed until twelve-thirty, returned to school a little before my afternoon class, then went back to the hospital for doctors' rounds late in the day. Zo and Jack stopped in when they could. Josh, long disinclined to get involved in our father's care, promised to fly in from Seattle.

On the third day of the ICU, I pulled Papa's health care Power of

Attorney from its file on my desk to reconsider whether we were violating his wishes not to sustain by heroic means a life that had become untenable. I took it with me to the hospital to consult with his primary-care physician. "Should we be doing all of *this*?" I asked him at the window of the ICU, nodding toward the bed where my father lay, his face a death mask surrounded by the white of the hospital linens, the snaking tangle of tubes.

"We're not *there* yet, Dee." The doctor looked up from Papa's chart. "I don't think we're quite there *yet*," he repeated, barely shifting the intonation from one word to the next. The nurse was busy checking evacuation tubes.

Every word, every phrase spoken was a missing piece of *King Lear*. My ambiguous little pronoun *this* and the doctor's vague *there* and *yet* let us avoid naming what we saw, a "fast intent to crawl toward death."

That November I gave up on *Lear* lesson plans. I turned over the classroom conversation to my students, in hopes that they might say aloud what I, trapped in the rush of events, had no time to think about – the murky darkness of old age and the accompanying end-of-life decisions that come into clear view to adult children in hospitals powered by the bulky, inexact engine of modern medicine. Only the young could speak of these matters with equipoise, with intellectual distance. A girl, beautiful, with a mouthful of braces and tousled hair, showed signs of understanding my situation. "Are you, okay, Mrs. Young? You look tired," she said. I nearly lost it then and there. The moat between professional and personal domains nearly gave way, tears on the verge of breaching the dam of self-control.

—⚹—

Lear. Tell me, . . .which of you shall we say doth love us most?

I once thought Lear's mad question comes out of the blue. A moment before, he said his goal was to avoid strife among his children. But now he sets a mother lode of strife in motion in a grotesque competition for love. Perhaps Lear can't remember what he just said. Or perhaps he's thinking of his own life's cross purposes: I say I love you, but do I really? And you seem to love me, but do you indeed? I think I trust you, but do you deserve my trust? You look like adults at this moment, but don't I always and forever see you as my dependent children?

How like Lear was my own father! How Lear-like were his stoicism, his detailed accounting of assets, his meticulously recorded ledger of budgets and forecasts by which he assured himself that his money would last. Like Lear, Papa was always hell-bent on keeping me at arm's length from the money matters. He maintained obsessive control, fueled by his desire to prevent more tension between Josh and me. Like Lear, Papa quantified love: "Your shares of my estate are equal," he told me after moving in with us after my mother died. "Still," he whispered conspiratorially, "I'd rather you knew about my finances than Josh." His voice trailed off, leaving unsaid whatever he felt. He knew I would give Zoë every penny of my half of his estate and that Josh would divide his half among his five children from three marriages. I had seen the impeccable pencil calculations on old-fashioned ledger sheets parceling out assets in two exactly equal shares that inevitably favored one child over the other by making one grandchild the beneficiary of one half of his estate and the other five mere one-tenth shares each.

The size of the estate wasn't enormous, but Papa treated it as if it were. It stood for a life spent saving, scrimping, hoarding even, based on the belief that meting out what we own – "our largest bounty" – is the expression of our love, as, unburdened, we crawl toward death.

Driving back and forth between school and hospital I understood the unspoken terror of my father's nervous calculations. Beneath all the plusses and minuses in his ledger was the existential nihilism of Lear's first conversation with Cordelia:

> *Lear.*   Speak.
> *Cordelia.*   Nothing, my lord.
> *Lear.*   Nothing?
> *Cordelia.*   Nothing.
> *Lear.*   Nothing will come of nothing.

—⧓—

> *Cordelia.* Unhappy that I am, I cannot heave
> My heart into my mouth. I love your Majesty
> According to my bond, no more nor less. . . .
> Good my lord, you have begot me, bred me,
> Loved me; I return those duties back
> As are right and fit.

"He's not eating," I told Dan after Papa was transferred to the post-ICU recovery unit.

Dan looked up over his glasses. "You're going to have to cook for him, Dee. Feed him. There's no other way to get him to eat." Dan threw his hands up in a familiar gesture of despair. "He's going to die if you don't do something." Dan wasn't ready to accept the inevitable of my father's drawn cheeks, closed eyes, and sallow coloring as he turned away from us to face the wall of his room.

That night after visiting hours I cooked chicken soup, baked old-fashioned *apfelkuchen*. Dan watched me ladle the soup, steaming, into pint-sized containers, then turn the dozen little apple cakes from the muffin pan onto a rack to cool. I gave him one to eat.

"You haven't made these old-timey things in years," Dan said.

I smiled and fitted lids onto the soup containers. "Men think food is love."

"Isn't it?" he said, climbing the stairs to bed.

I sat at the kitchen table reading until the soup was cool enough to go into the refrigerator, then turned out the lights and went upstairs. Eyes closed, Dan was propped up in our bed, snoring, the light still on, a book flopped open on his chest. I removed his glasses and turned out his light, kissed him on the forehead. When I reached to loosen the book from his fingers, he stirred, smiled and, sighing, shifted his position for sleep.

In making Lear a widower Shakespeare avoids portraying married life and concentrates instead on the father-daughter bond. Lear might have hoped – and my father, too – that his daughter would hold him "dearer than space or liberty" (Goneril's words), or be "alone felicitate in her father's love" (Regan's). But Cordelia knows better. A daughter's love for her father is supposed to differ from what she will feel for a man she chooses for herself. Cordelia leaves her father's court "with washed eyes," tearful perhaps, but cleansed, free of illusions. "I know you what you are," she says of her sisters. She might just as well have said this to her father, too.

I shed no tears that November. Instead, I followed Dan's advice and made chicken soup for my father, heated a portion to boiling every morning, poured it into a thermos, and took it with me to school and after my morning classes to the hospital. For the first week I fed him spoonfuls at lunchtime and again in the late afternoon. My students were writing their *King Lear* essays. After two weeks of the home-cooking therapy, Papa was feeding himself the soup and *apfelkuchen*. By the third week he agreed to eat from the hospital menu. He was discharged to a nursing home in mid-December. On the way there tears trickled down his cheeks. He kissed my hand when I settled him into the recliner in his little room. The kiss filled me with enormous sadness.

—ᴍ—

> *Edgar.* Give me thy hand! . . . Men must endure
> Their going hence, even as their coming hither;
> Ripeness is all. Come on.

My father stayed on in the nursing facility instead of coming home. He spent most of his days napping. His speech, when it came at all, was garbled, his memory scrambled. He dribbled his food when he ate. Aides transferred him from bed to recliner to wheelchair to toilet and back. He was showered once a week by two men. I paid the bills, balanced the checkbook, sorted Medicare and Blue Cross Blue Shield forms, did the taxes, sifted Pa's hoarded correspondence and financial records. I didn't have the heart to throw away the documents of a lifetime of thrift stored, antlike, lest he be overtaken by a season of forgetfulness. Lear's Fool says something about that habit of saving: "We'll set thee to school to an ant, to teach thee there's no laboring i' the winter."

—ᴍ—

> *Fool.* When we are born, we cry that we are come
> To this great stage of fools. This' a good block.

We are all poised on the verge of our own mortality. The abyss of death is right before our eyes, and, brought "to the very brim of it," as blind Gloucester says at the cliff at Dover, we shield our eyes to avoid looking in. But we cannot stop peeking over the edge. The view is terrifying.

In his last days I sat with my father for an hour or two every day, morning and afternoon. He seemed to be asleep, his lips snuffling softly as he breathed in and out, his head turned toward the wall. I read the newspaper aloud to him. Lear and Cordelia were never far from my thoughts:

> When thou dost ask me blessing, I'll kneel down,
> And ask of thee forgiveness. So we'll live

And pray and sing and tell old tales and laugh
At gilded butterflies, and hear poor rogues
Talk of court news; and we'll talk with them too --
Who loses and who wins, who's in, who's out --
And take upon's the mystery of things
As if we were God's spies. And we'll wear out
In a walled prison packs and sects of great ones
That ebb and flow by the moon.

A few days before he died, my father roused and asked me if we had time for lunch at Mario's.

This time I started with the truth. "Not today, Papa."

"Prithee, nuncle," says Lear's Fool. "Keep a schoolmaster that can teach thy fool to lie. I would fain learn to lie."

I tried to sound cheerful, but choked on my words. "How about a rain check?"

My father lifted one hand limply from the blanket. His eyes were open, wet.

"Okay, Papa. We'll do lunch today right after the bank." I lied. "Dan'll join us. I know he'd love to."

We were beyond the Lear-like fear that his heart was about to break into a thousand flaws, when he hated having me treat him like a child. I asked the doctor later what he thought was happening. "He doesn't want to look forward," he said. "He doesn't. . . ." His voice trailed off. Recognizing his own mortality, he could go no further, falling back on ambiguities for the terror that Lear faces, that we all face as we stare into the void that waits just beyond the brim of the cup of life.

May 24, 2003

> And all beit that he had therefore bene put up in Bedelem, afterward he beganne to come again to himselfe. Being thereupon set at liberty, and walkinge aboute abrode, his old fansies beganne to fall againe in his heade. Whereupon I beine advertised of these pageauntes and beinge sent unto and required to take some other order with him, caused him, as he came wanderinge by my doore, to be taken to the constables and bounden to a tree in the streete before the whole towne till he waxed weary. And it appeared well that hys remembraunce was goode inoughe, for he could then verye wel reherse his fautes himselfe, and speake and treate very well and promise afterward as well. And verylye God be thanked I heare none harme of him now.
>
> – Thomas More. "Apologie."

Dear Dorothea,

Henry Reginald, my beloved father, died in Bedlam. All his life his watchword was *mens sana*, the sane mind. He was a private, dignified man who quietly took care of his own affairs. How did he come to end his life in Bedlam amid the raving of poor mad folks?

After three score years and ten, "saith the Psalmist, all is trouble and sorrow." Doctor Burton reminds us in *The Anatomy of Melancholy* of the common experience of old men: "*Ex abrupto* they are overcome with melancholy in an instant: or they dote at last, *senex bis puer*, like an old man in his second boyhood, unable to manage their estates, full of ache, sorrow, and grief, children again, dizzards, carling as they sit, talking to themselves, angry, waspish, displeas'd with everything." But Bethlem Hospital, or Bedlam as we call'd it! I am asham'd, not of Papa but of myself and my family, who let – or made – it happen. I have often turn'd the events over in my mind, waken'd weeping at the memory of the sights and sounds and smells of that place, that terrible place, with my sweet, mild Papa there amongst the raving mad folk.

Honour thy Father and thy Mother saith the Fifth Commandment. Plato, too, reminds us: Γονέων δε ἀμελεῖν οὔτε θεὸς οὔτε ἄνθρωπος νοῦν ἔχων ξύμβουλός ποτε γένοιτ' ἂν οὐδεὶς οὐδενί – Neglect of one's parents neither God nor man ever recommended to anyone. Yet my father died in Bedlam. Why? Why was it permitted?

Perhaps a story will help me disburden myself that Papa was committed to Bedlam in Autumn 1634 and died there the following April. I do not know the whole of it. Who can ever know what is taken in secret to the grave?

I have chosen to tell this from neither my father's side nor mine. I shall tell it instead as it might have unfolded to someone outside the feeling of it. You will decide how the Blame – if any – should be parcell'd out.

In hopeful trust of your understanding,

Bathsua

Enclos'd: "Wit's End"

Wit's End

Ἐὰν δὲ τίς τινα νόσος ἢ γῆρας ἢ καὶ τρόπων χαλεπότης ἢ καὶ
ξύμπαντα ταῦτα ἔκφρονα περγάζηται διαφερόντως τῶν πολλῶν, . . .
οἰκοφθορῇ δὲ ὡς ὢν τῶν αὑτοῦ κύριος, ὁ δὲ υἱὸς πορῇ καὶ ὀκνῇ τὴν
τῆς παρανοίας γράφεσθαι δίκην. . . .

Suppose a man loses his mind due to illness, old age, difficult
circumstances, or all of the above. . . . What if this man considers
himself the master of his own affairs and yet is bringing ruin on his
household? Surely such a man's son must be at wit's end, not knowing
what to do, whether to register his father as a madman or not.
    – Plato. *Laws.* Book XI.

Standing at ease in his dark'ning gateway in the Bethlem Porter's
Lodge, Humphrey Withers observes everyone and everything coming
and going along Bishopsgate. The lengthening autumn shadows in the
asylum behind him settle down into a quiet early-October dusk. As asylum
Porter, Master Withers is accustom'd to the day's shifting sounds – the
basketman's footsteps crossing the hallway, pots clanging in the kitchen,
the chambermaid's broom swishing straw in the ward. Now and then he
hears a low moan, a snatch of raving, chains chinking on the floor above.
He takes less notice of the smells: In the foreground is the sweetish
odour of new straw and fresh goods deliver'd through the front gate by
a tradesman; below, from the kitchen come warm cooking aromas; more
distant but pervasive still is the rancour of urine-soak'd straw being taken
by a basketman through the yard toward Deep Ditch behind the West Gate.
Beneath them all is the deep scent of offal in the mad folks' cells.

The appointment as Porter to Bethlehem Royal Hospital was a boon
to Master Withers's purse. Family connexions enabl'd it. Thank God,
indeed, for family connexions! How else can one manage in difficult times?
And when are times not difficult? This snug Porter's Lodge accompanies
the appointment, steady governours' stipends add to his purse, and food
steadily crosses from the hospital kitchen into his wife Elizabeth's pantry.
Nearly every day a coin or two finds its way into his palm from tradesmen
doing business with the Hospital, and offerings from the mad folks' kin
who, to salve their consciences, put a little something in his ready hand.

Humphrey Withers is not a greedy man, but like everyone in the parish,
from Aldgate in the east to Moorgate in the west, he's not one to turn down

a bit of good luck. Lord knows, a turn of good luck is nothing to sneeze at: The slightest jolt – a fever, a sudden knock to the head, a misspoken jest about an aldermen, an odd alignment of the moon and stars or even speculation about it – and you could land on the street with only the shirt on your back. Or here in Bethlem.

Consider the latest admission, the threadbare old scholar with the rheumy eyes. Master Withers has seen him dawn and dusk for years, his nose in a book, walking from Saint Botolph's Bishopsgate toward Houndsditch and Saint Botolph's Aldgate at first light and returning thence at twilight. As often as not, he would stop to chat with someone or peep into a shop or here into Bethlem gateway. He may have grown a little dottier and more dishevel'd the last year or so, with those drooping stockings and ill-kempt collar, Humphrey thinks, but respectable enough for a grammar teacher at a charity boys' school in the Minories. One of his daughters kept house for him, but she married above their station the summer before last, and mov'd away, leaving her old father to fend for himself in the parish. But he's always seem'd sane enough in this not so sane world, Master Withers thinks.

Like a bit of lint in one's pocket, the old fellow has nested in the Porter's head. Oh, he mumbl'd aloud now and then, sometimes in English, but more often in tongues that no respectable Englishman could pronounce, let alone understand. A month or so ago Master Withers glimps'd the old fellow stopping a Jew peddler on Threadneedle Street to buy one of those odd new eye pieces that look like roll'd-up sheaves of paper. The very next morning – not that he was spying – the Porter saw the old fellow rambling about on the City Wall behind Bethlem in the pre-dawn darkness with the eye piece press'd to one of his rheumy eyes, staring up at the coin-bright disk of the moon or down into the shadowy garden of the Hospital. 'Twas rumour'd that the old fellow taught strangely – without caning, for example – and that he shar'd odd ideas with his pupils. Master Withers has heard – not that he's one to eavesdrop, mind you – that the old bird sympathizes with the Sabbatarians, expressing wonderment that The Lord's Day is celebrated on Sunday, the first day of the week, instead of Saturday, the seventh, when the Holy Bible insists that God Himself rested on the seventh day.

Yes, Master Withers thinks, glancing on this Friday afternoon into the darkening madhouse behind him, the old scholar always seem'd sane enough, compar'd to the rest of his melancholy crew. But in these dangerous times, here in the year of Our Lord 1634, one can never tell what little jolt can send a fellow over the edge at the urging of his household – or of the parish, the aldermen or even the Lord Mayor or the Privy Council, for that matter – into Bedlam.

This very morning the old man came for good, escorted in the dawn drizzle by a confident-looking chap of perhaps five-and-twenty, with the pale face and smooth hands of a scholar. The Porter had seen the young fellow – where was it? – a few days earlier. Ah, yes: he saw him, heard his voice even, with Richard Makin, whom he has known in the parish for years, coming and going, first as a boy, then a young man, and now in service at King Charles's court at Whitehall. Richard has the ruddy look of one who works for a living, unlike the pale fellow who brought the old schoolmaster this morning. For the week's care for the old man Master Pale Visage counted out five shillings as if loath to part with them. Must be kin, a nephew or a son-in-law. Contemplative, not raving or blubbering, the schoolmaster watch'd the transaction mildly, merely clutching under his arm his little bundle of possessions – the eye piece and a packet of books. His demeanor evok'd an unfamiliar warmth – was it call'd pity? – in the Porter's breast.

Master Withers snapp'd his fingers to catch the attention of Tom, the under-basketman.

"What shall we call this one, sir? Where do I take him?" Tom ask'd.

"Call him Henry." The schoolmaster's smooth, pale-fac'd companion put a blanket and a few utensils hurriedly into Tom's ready basket. "He'd prefer you call him Master Reginald, but plain Henry will do." He spoke as if the old scholar were invisible.

"Shall we be seeing you again at this time next week, sir?" The Porter ask'd the schoolmaster's pale companion. "Or will you be sending someone else along with the weekly upkeep and necessaries? Most of the folk here do best, sir, with a bit more than the mere basics. Something from home, perhaps?" The questions drifted into the morning drizzle unanswer'd.

The old schoolmaster, plain Henry, fix'd Tom the under-basketman with his mild, watery eyes and address'd him amiably. "And you, my lad, what shall I call you?"

"I'm Tom, sir."

"Can you read, Tom?"

"No, sir. I don't read, sir."

"We'll see to that, then, Tom." The schoolmaster turn'd to Master Pale Visage, who was studying a damp spot left by the dawn shower on his serge sleeve. "Bring me my primers, John, when you come next week. Slip them out without Batty seeing. You haven't told your sister-in-law, have you, where you've taken me? No, of course you haven't. You're a man of your word, John, a worthy son-in-law." His voice trail'd off into a strange string of musical syllables that rose and fell in a language neither Tom nor Humphrey understood.

Humphrey Withers saw comprehension rise in a blush on John's pale cheeks as he press'd into the Porter's hand an inscrib'd card:

> John Pell,
> MA. (Mathem.) Cantab.
> Saint Margaret's Parish, Westminster

Master Withers watch'd this John Pell, MA, (Mathem.) Cantab., turn and hurry along Bishopsgate toward Saint Botolph's. At the church door the fellow adjusted his shoulders against the rain and hasten'd smartly onto Cornhill toward Westminster.

"Be off with you now, Tom," Humphrey Withers said. "Put Master Reginald's things in the third bed along the west wall, lad. I'll bring him up directly once you've readied his place." The under-basketman went his way along the dim hallway.

The early morning drizzle stopp'd.

"Come along, my good fellow," Humphrey Withers found himself saying companionably to his new charge. "Have you had a bit of breakfast yet this morning, Master Reginald?"

The old schoolmaster shook his head. Dust motes in the Bethlem gateway shone in a sudden shaft of wan sunlight.

"Come then, sir, and we'll scratch up a bit of bread and porridge for you in the kitchen."

Something about the recollection surprises Humphrey Withers. Now, in the last rays of afternoon sunlight, he finds himself nodding sympathetically toward a band of ragtag parishioners hurrying from Saint Botolph's door along Bishopsgate. Each one clutches a sheaf of fresh papers. More poor folk from the neighbourhood, Humphrey Withers thinks, newly certified by Reverend Josiah Thorpe to be unencumb'r'd and loyal to Crown and Church, and therefore suitable for ship's passage to America.

Only yesterday, just after Thursday evensong, Reverend Thorpe had mention'd to Master Withers that he wish'd the old schoolmaster could join the steady flow of restless folk out of the parish, out of crowded London, bound for the New World. "Maybe on shipboard he'll turn his eye piece toward the heavens and see how reliably the starry firmament indeed revolves around us here on earth." The Porter had join'd the Rector on the steps of Saint Botolph's to watch the parish settle for the evening. Reverend Thorpe's nod toward the old schoolmaster reminded the Porter they had both spied him on the City Wall that morning, training his eye piece skyward.

"No more of his idle speculations on the church steps." Reverend Thorpe smooth'd his cassock across his ample stomach. "He's been trying to lure me to apostasy, that the Sun, not the Earth, is at the center of what the old fool call'd a Solar System! If the good Lord had wanted us to regard the moon and stars through a tube, he wouldn't have shap'd our eyeballs so." Reverend Thorpe smiled at his little jest. "The New World's a fine place for lunatic complainers who would have us doubt what we see, what we've been taught by our Holy Fathers!"

"Indeed, Reverend Thorpe, you must be right, sir," Master Withers had replied. He hadn't understood the rector's words, but he knew from his own observation that Master Reginald had an odd interest in moongazing. 'Twas amiss, too, to buy long eye pieces from street peddlers, especially Jew peddlers. Bethlem Royal Hospital, and America, too, were fit places for the dotty and the daft. "We've our fair share at Bedlam of folk with odd views, Your Worship." The Porter clear'd his throat officiously, then lower'd his voice confidentially. "Only last month we took in another who claims to have 'seen the Light.'" He tweak'd his words to show his disapproval of the wretched lunatic now in his care. "In a fine frenzy he claim'd to be the New

Isaiah."

"America's the place for some of them, Master Withers." Reverend Thorpe puff'd himself up importantly. "There's Bridewell, too, for blasphemers, whose ravings fly out 'gainst our Religion and King." He paus'd, pensive. "Then again, daft gentlefolk oughtn't be sent to either place for chastisement. So Sir George said when he told us to expect Lady Audley. 'Bridewell's no place to cure the distractions of your better class of lunatics,' Sir George said. 'Especially those with relations in high places.'" Reverend Thorpe look'd penetratingly at the Porter. "You recall – I remember seeing you standing in the Bedlam Gate as you often do, pretending to take a moment's ease, but eavesdropping on your betters, all the same." He enjoy'd making the Porter squirm. "Surely you recall Sir George's words."

The Porter cringes at the memory. 'Twas two years ago, almost to the day, that the Privy Council open'd its inquiry that brought Bethlem's "financial irregularities" to light. On the first Saturday in October, in the Year of Our Lord 1632, Sir George Whitmore, formerly Lord Mayor of London and now the President of the Boards of both Bridewell and Bethlem, had walk'd through the asylum gate and announced that the Master of the Hospital, Dr. Helkiah Crooke, had been remov'd from his post by the King's order. The Porter's own brother John Withers had prepar'd the report to the Privy Council laying on Dr. Crooke the blame for the disappearances of the penny loaves, weekly stones of beef, and pecks of oat flour that with alarming frequency fail'd to reach the table of the inmates.

The Porter's ears warm at the memory of it. Every month since, on first Saturdays, Sir George has inspected Bedlam's account books, examin'd the larder and peek'd into the cells, announced new policies, and overseen the admission of special patients. Sometimes the new hospital Master, Mr. Meverall, accompanies Sir George, and sometimes Reverend Thorpe, too, or an Alderman or other personage whose importance the Porter can only surmise. Saturday inspections are tense times.

Reverend Thorpe continu'd without a pause, ignoring the Porter's discomfort. "You recall Sir George's words, Master Withers. 'Expect the arrival here at Bethlem, sir,' Sir George announced, 'of Lady Eleanor

Audley, the widow of the late Attorney General for Ireland. She's now in Westminster Gate-House, ready for transfer to Bridewell, having been convicted of prophesying against the King. Bridewell's no place to check the mad ravings of our betters,' Sir George said, 'especially those with relations in high places. Something about Daniel's dreams in the lion's den, his prophecy against a king.' Why, Master Withers, she turn'd Holy Scripture into an harangue against good King Charles. 'They were dreadful words, sir, strong exceedingly.' Sir George stopp'd there, he did. I could have gone on for him, for I know the passage by heart. But I think it impertinent to lord it over my betters."

For the Porter's benefit and in a conspiratorial whisper, Reverend Thorpe recited a verse from Scripture: "I beheld till the thrones were cast down – ." Stopping suddenly, Reverend Thorpe look'd about at figures passing along Bishopsgate. After a hasty farewell he retir'd into his vicarage.

Humphrey Withers understood the Rector's haste and retreated to his own doorway. The Lady Eleanor, the mad prophetess, they call'd her, was indeed well-connected. Yet she had been imprison'd for preaching that Judgment Day would come if King Charles dared challenge Parliament and dismiss it. Lady Eleanor's noble family is favour'd at Court, so her mad enthusiasm was blam'd on an overheated brain and female distemper. And until she is pronounced "cur'd," she resides privately in the Master's House across the Bedlam gateway from the Porter's Lodge

The Porter suddenly again recalls the old schoolmaster whom he admitted this morning. Henry Reginald hardly seems the prophesying type, he thinks, nor a danger to the peace of the realm or parish. He will keep his nose in his books and his mouth mainly shut. Yet, the Porter acknowledges, the old man has some daft notions that set him apart, perhaps dangerously so, from the his neighbours. Still, he has a sweetness about him that the Porter has felt more than once. It seems contagious.

Why, the day before he chatted confidentially with Reverend Thorpe – Wednesday, it must have been – the Porter had seen Henry Reginald twice, in the morning walking toward the Minories and returning thence late that afternoon. Each time he was surrounded by schoolboys. In the dawn light they walk'd slowly, the old man laying a gentle hand now and then on the shoulder of a laggard. And in the late afternoon the lads had tumbl'd about and nuzzl'd him like puppies or sheep.

What was it that has given Humphrey Withers such a feeling of inexplicable sweetness? Try as he might, he cannot recall exactly. Nevertheless, details of the prior week return to him with stunning clarity.

'Twas Tuesday morning, for example. Returning from the draper's, Master Lansdale's shop, for the second time that week, Humphrey Withers had been overtaken on Threadneedle Street by Richard Makin and the man whom he now realizes is Reginald's other son-in-law, John Pell. The Porter had nodded absentmindedly at Makin, the Court dogsbody married to the prodigy lass who had taught school at Saint Andrew Undershaft when her father was schoolmaster there in King James's day. He hadn't recogniz'd the other fellow, but took notice because the two were so incongruous together and yet had discours'd so confidentially.

The Porter couldn't help but overhear them as they pass'd from Threadneedle onto Bishopsgate toward Bedlam gate. Richard Makin had spoken of "Father," and the other of "Henry," but Master Withers was certain they spoke of one and the same man. He did not rush ahead into the madhouse gate, but stopp'd at the corner to inspect the crumbling hospital wall where it abutted Saint Botolph's. He'd need to have a mason in for repairs, he remember'd thinking.

The bits and pieces of the story begin to fit together, as the stones of the Bethlem wall would, but for a fresh application of mortar. Hadn't the old schoolmaster this very morning said to the same pale-visaged fellow, "Don't tell your sister-in-law where you've taken me"? Hadn't he said, "You're a man of your word, John, a worthy son-in-law"? Why, Makin and Pell, Master Withers realizes, had been speaking of Henry Reginald. Makin is married to the parish prodigy, Master Reginald's elder daughter, and Pell, who had blush'd so conspicuously when the old man mumble-chanted in that foreign tongue this morning, is married to the younger daughter, the one who kept house for the schoolmaster, her father, until she married above her station.

Humphrey Withers flushes with satisfaction to connect the recollected snatches. It is as if, standing here remembering, he is watching the past happening anew. Memory, he thinks, can be a perfect record of the past, if only it can be decipher'd! He is full of a sudden joy, wordless and inexplicable, even as he silently attends to the flow of life before him on this ordinary October Friday afternoon before Bethlem Hospital. Tentatively at first, and then more confidently, he tests the quality of the inward magic thread of his memory, spinning it out, reeling in the conversation of John Pell and Richard Makin as they had walk'd near him.

They had been arguing.

"What's to be done with this foolish old man?" Pell had hiss'd into Makin's ear. "He ignores every warning."

"Nothing will come of this, John. You'll see," Makin's voice filter'd through the morning jostle of tailors, weavers and customers on Threadneedle. "It's nothing, nothing at all," he said. "Father's always had ideas of his own. He's always seemed a little crack'd at first to those who don't know him. The rumours have been around for years. They provoke laughter and head scratching and then are forgotten. Every parish has its resident eccentric. Henry's ours."

"Easy for you to say, Richard, to dismiss the old bird's rantings as nothing. You've nothing to lose at his expense." John Pell sourly faced his brother-in-law. "My case is different."

The contrast was not lost on Humphrey Withers – hissing words from the weaker man, mild ones from the stronger.

"How is that? How is your case different from mine?"

Pell cough'd. "My reputation's tinged by those with whom I associate. My standing. . . ."

Makin cut into the pause. "And I have no standing?"

"'Tisn't what I meant." Pell's pale cheek redden'd. "I'm starting out. You're settl'd, you have your place at Court. Your worth's known. I'm still making my way. I have to make connexions with the right people. You know, churchmen, men in the City, at the university, at Court. Having a ranting father-in-law with dangerous ideas jeopardizes my situation. I mean no insult to you, Richard, although you are, after all, merely – "

"I am merely what, John?" Makin's quiet voice rose in irritation.

Pell clear'd his throat. "I return to my first premise, Richard. I – we – must agree that Henry's present situation makes action on our part inevitable. Do you understand my syllogism?" High-sounding language, Pell's recourse, further redden'd his flush'd cheeks.

"Your what?" Makin drew himself up a little straighter.

"Never mind." Pell waved his hand dismissively. "My point stands. Fathers of boys at the school have complain'd to the headmaster. The rector at Saint Botolph's has heard rumours, too. These cannot be pretended away. There will be harges. Something must be done about him."

The conversation, like their footsteps, orbited ever closer to Bedlam, the center of the Porter's universe. He strain'd to hear.

"Even the Lord Mayor and Aldermen have got wind of him," Pell whisper'd, "sympathizing with Sabbatarians and Jews. Buying their goods is one thing, but listening to their talk is another." His voice dropp'd. 'Tis as good as dabbling in the occult. What's more, he's taken his private fancy about the ideas of Galileo into the classroom."

They had reached the corner where Saint Botolph's met the Bedlam wall. The Porter took an even more avid interest in crumbling mortar.

"He speaks with the wrong people in the parish. He pays calls at the back gate of Bethlem to mad prophets and doomsayers. He mumbles in Greek and Syriac in the street. I hear he's taken to singing in Hebrew." Pell's whisper had a rush'd intensity. "The schoolboys must have seen those scribblings in odd alphabets that he leaves lying about on his lectern. They surely speculate, the little smugglers, that he's a close companion of the dark side."

Humphrey Withers felt the hairs on the back of his neck rise.

"'Tis almost as if he's willing himself into Bridewell or Bethlem, Richard." Pell went silent, then spoke again, urgently. "I say we talk him into booking passage to America. There's a ships bound for Boston anchor'd in the Thames now. That would be less humiliating than having him committed by the parish – or worse."

Makin's brow furrow'd. "What about Bathsua and Ithamaria? Shouldn't we speak to them first? In fact, shouldn't we take him in with us?"

"His behaviour grows more precarious by the day. Don't you see it is dangerous?"

"Precarious, John? Dangerous? For whom? For Henry? Or for you?"

"Don't beg the question, Richard. We have a problem. You are avoiding it. I repeat: What's to be done with him? I'm at my wit's end about him. You are, too."

"Have you ask'd him what he wishes?"

"There you go again, asking instead of acting."

"But what does he say?"

"You know him as well as I do. He merely smiles, shakes his head, says nothing. Or says what you said a moment ago. I can hear that reedy voice of his: 'Tis nothing, nothing at all. Every parish has its resident eccentric. I'm this one's. It gives my neighbours something to gossip about, that's all.' Or he'll spout one of his aphorisms. You know. You studied with him when you were a lad. His head is full of little Greek and Latin gems."

Richard smiled. "I know. But remember, John, what Plato says." He faced his learned brother-in-law, drew from his memory a sentence long obscur'd by his busy, practical life, and spoke in a language so different from English that the Porter wonder'd how anyone could speak it at all. Full of odd, tumbling sounds, some from deep in the throat, others trilling on the tongue.

The Porter thought the words unnatural spoken by a man of Makin's station. He wonder'd what they meant – if they were a language at all.

Miraculously, as if Makin had heard the Porter's thoughts, he spoke in English as if for Master Withers's benefit alone, as if such words were the province of all men, not just the school'd ones. "*An old man's relatives shall keep him safe from harm, at home or in whatever way necessary, or be accountable to the State.*"

What a remarkable teacher Henry Reginald must have been, Humphrey Withers thinks, to have taught this working man so well that, after all these years, the words still remain'd in his mind, to be muster'd at a moment's notice! As remarkable is that, rewinding the filament of his memory, he can remember all that Richard Makin and John Pell said earlier that week.

"Don't try to make me feel guilty, Richard. I'm trying to be practical. 'Tis for your good as well as mine." Pell had only this bit of ammunition left. "You're just like the rest of this blasted family I've married into!" he hiss'd. His face suddenly lit up. "I learn'd my Greek as well as you did. Perhaps better. Plato also says that such a man's children can – no, *must!* – appeal to the State for help when an old man brings ruin and dishonour on his household. That's all I ask." Turning to walk away, Pell hurl'd one last barb. "Go home, Richard, to your learned wife. Do your homework under her tutelage. I'll act on my better judgment."

"You best take care, John," Makin said. "Plato and his Laws are on Henry's side. So are the gods." Makin had the last word, first in that tongue the Porter found so mysteriously appealing, then in English.

And another minor miracle occurs. The Bedlam Porter, who has never been to school, who has liv'd all his life in the English language, understands perfectly without translation what Richard Makin had utter'd: "*When the gods hear the pleading of a parent dishonour'd by his child, they will ignore that child's prayers. But when they hear prayers of a parent honour'd by his children, when such a parent asks the gods to bless such children, won't the gods listen and respond favourably? If they did otherwise, could they truly be call'd gods?*"

But even a miracle recall'd in awe must end. So the practical Porter, unus'd to experiencing miracles, let alone remembering them, stands, one shoulder leaning against Bethlem gate on an October Friday afternoon in the year of our Lord 1634.

Wait a moment. What did I hear about Henry Reginald and that school in Minories? thinks Humphrey Withers. Ah yes. He had gone to the draper's shop earlier in the week, on Monday, to settle Bethlem's accounts before ordering new blankets the next day. When Humphrey had enter'd the shop, Master Lansdale had just clos'd a sale with another customer.

The two men were gossiping as the customer gather'd up his goods. "Yes," he said. "Simon's a first-former. There was some difficulty at first. But it has blown over since I had my talk with the headmaster. No reason to keep silent about quality. Paying school fees is like buying yard goods. You are ow'd what you pay for. Do you not agree, Master Lansdale?"

"Indeed, sir." Tying up the bundle, the draper glanced toward Humphrey Withers in the doorway.

"Simon's a good lad. Always tells his mother and me about the day's lessons, you know." The customer was in a conversational mood. "Seems this schoolmaster is even more dithery than mine was in my day. Oppos'd to the rod, although I can't see why. Or he's too old and blind to see what these young scrappers are up to. The boys laugh behind his back and make all sorts of mischief, says Simon. But this caught my attention: 'Twas an odd story Simon told. Seems Master Reginald interrupted the grammar lesson and had the lads up and off their benches to do some play acting. Something about the Sun and Moon and Earth. Simon show'd the lesson to Susannah and me, first with the baby's cradle at the center and Susannah and me carrying balls of Susannah's yarn around and around the cradle and Simon marching along with us carrying the lantern. Laughing we all were, and the babe smiling to beat the band. And then Simon says, 'But Master Reginald says 'tis all wrong. "Earth and Man are not at the center of the universe," Master Reginald said.' And Simon put the lantern in the middle of the table and had us all, me and him and Susannah carrying the baby, all of us marching like fools around the lantern at the middle of the table. 'Master Reginald says the Sun's at the center, not the Earth or even the Baby Jesus. The Earth and other planets all move around the Sun. The Earth's just a speck of dust in an enormous universe in the mind of God.' Why, Susannah and I stopp'd laughing on the spot. The boy had taken it all in – he's quite a prodigy that way, don't you know." The customer paused. "But something's amiss."

The draper was all ears. "Your boy surely learn'd the lesson. What do you make of it?"

"I can't say, sir, but something's surely amiss. If you catch my drift, Master Lansdale. I spoke to the headmaster. He said he'd look into it. Said he'd heard the likes of it before, said – "

"Yes?"

"Mention'd you, Master Lansdale. Said you and the other Bedlam governors, sir – " Humphrey Withers was all ears.

" – Said you know what to do with folks who yammer on with crack'd ideas. Those were his exact words: 'The Bedlam governors know what to do with folks who – ' He mention'd an Italian name, sir. Galileo, I'm sure it was. Said the name soft-like, under his breath." The man whisper'd now. "Said the word 'heresy,' too, don't you know."

Master Lansdale shush'd his customer out the door. It was the Porter's turn for Bethlem's business. "Keep this mum, Master Withers," Lansdale said. "I'll tell Sir George myself."

With a sense of foreboding, Humphrey Withers pulls in the next memory, a mere image fram'd by a window at Saint Botolph's. Reverend Thorpe had been preaching last Sunday's sermon when the Porter slipp'd late into the pew beside Elizabeth, having just put morning affairs to rights at Bedlam. One of the mad folk had died in the night. The body had been remov'd, the bedding wash'd and air'd, the inmates calm'd.

"The One True Church," Reverend Thorpe said just as Humphrey Withers came through the door. "The Way. The One Way."

There was an approving hum. All heads faced the altar, nodding assent.

All but one. The Porter happen'd to glance out the window at that very moment and caught sight of a figure walking beside Saint Botolph's. Blinking at a shaft of morning sunlight he saw the only parishioner missing the weekly service: The old schoolmaster, Henry Reginald.

Still following his memories backward, the Porter feels the tug of a line of reasoning he has never follow'd before. He has never ask'd himself or his betters about the mad folk admitted to Bedlam, never wonder'd why they have been relegated to this reeking place already four centuries old, full of shivering, starving men and women who stare at him with sad, daz'd eyes. Something about the old schoolmaster now install'd in the newly vacated bed in the men's ward has made the Porter think beyond his chores, purse, and table: Henry Reginald is no madman, no danger to self or family, no arsonist or worse. He is no hideous, self-mutilating beggar, no howling wraith screaming out for divine wrath against wife or son, neighbour, priest, or King.

The Porter recalls the most recent official inspection, when Sir George and Mr. Meverall walk'd through the asylum gate last Saturday morning.

"A word, Master Withers?" Sir George spoke in his robustly professional way. "And how are our quaint charges?"

Humphrey had just ris'n from his breakfast porridge. Quaint indeed. "As well as ever, sir. As well as can be expected."

His answers, he realizes now, had a double ring to them.

"Everything is in good order?"

"Yes, sir, good order. Thirty lunatics, and we're indeed in good order, sir."

"Your new straw keeps the lunatics sweet smelling? And the number of mice is down? Are you in need of another cat? Or any other additional staff?"

"No, sir. I mean yes, sir, the new straw keeps the wards and the cells as sweet smelling as you could wish, sir, and the mousers are busy. They have matters well in hand, sir, so to speak." Humphrey appreciated his touch of humour. "And the weather's been warm and dry, so the folk take some recreation in the fresh air of the yard. A few of them read, sir, and some sew a bit and serve as helpers now and then along with the chambermaids and basket men. The activity helps occupy them and invigorates the blood, sir."

"But not so active as to overheat their brains?"

"Not so active as that, sir, or so it would appear to us who watch 'em."

"Mustn't be so warm as to impede their cure. There's a sedative power, don't you know, in cooling their overheated brains. Isn't that right, Mr. Meverall?"

"Indeed, Sir George."

"Are the sureties providing linens and paying their weekly securities?"

"Yes, sir, except for the paupers here at the parish's expense, you know. These we provide for, sir, as best we can."

"Indeed." Sir George glanced into the ward, his briefly rais'd gaze met by the glaz'd stare of an inmate.

In retrospect the Porter notes that Sir George could not have look'd into those eyes long enough to distinguish pain from sorrow, madness from insight, wonderment from hatred.

Sir George press'd on with questions, looking now into the yard beyond the ward.

A few root crops linger'd amid fallen leaves.

"Anyone fractious? No mischief between the men and women, I hope?"

"I should hope not, sir."

"No blasphemy?"

"Not to speak of, sir."

"No unreasonable sadness?"

The Porter's little downward-turning smile was lost on the two officials. "Indeed, sir. No unreasonable sadness." The pause between question and answer belied a wryly rhyming, silent retort. No unreasonable sadness, no unseasonable madness. Not here in Bedlam. Oh, no.

Sir George's questions came thick and fast. "And the accounts, Master Withers? All settl'd with the victualers and clothiers? Settl'd accounts with the draper? Order'd the night caps and blankets now that winter's coming on? See to it directly, Withers."

"Yes, sir."

"So, Withers, that will be all." With that Sir George went out the Bedlam gate and onto the open street before him.

The physician remain'd for another moment. "Any signs of contagion?"

"No, Mr. Meverall."

"Anyone in need of a bleeding or a poultice?"

No, sir." The Porter consider'd the man in the third bed along the west wall of the men's ward. Neither bleeding nor poultice would do him any good.

"Any need to call in the apothecary?"

"No, sir."

"Good, very good." Pause. "Good day to you, then." The physician went out into the Saturday morning sunshine.

The Porter's thoughts return to the present. It is still a late Friday afternoon in early October, although his mind has wander'd along a week's strand of memories. How different things seem now than they had a few moments before when, in the fading light, he came to stand here as the asylum quieted. What has come over him in these moments of reverie?

Candlelight is winking in windows along Bishopsgate. The sight of those points of light transports Humphrey Withers yet again, this time to the same time a week before.

Elizabeth had just return'd from her late afternoon Friday marketing. Putting her basket on the kitchen table, she began talking as soon as she clos'd the door behind her. "That old schoolmaster you've been watching, the one with the weepy eyes?" She remov'd her hat. "The one who comes by with books for the mad folk who can read? Who last week brought that basket of pippins for their table? 'A little fruit,' he said in his rasping voice, 'to sweeten their dinner and remind them of the season.' His voice trail'd off as he left, distracted-like, mumbling as he went? Remember how good the pippins were when I poach'd 'em up with a little wine and honey?"

The Porter remembers. The poach'd fruit had been curiously delicious, as had the handful of fresh pippins Humphrey slipp'd from the basket into his pocket to nibble now and then. The last fruits of the season, sweet and succulent. His mouth waters even at the memory of them.

"I see you remember, Humphrey. The fruit you recall, and the fellow who brought them? When I was doing my marketing, I saw him in the churchyard at Saint Andrew Undershaft, humming and filling his basket with pippins, droppings from that old tree in the corner of the churchyard. I paid him little mind, although he smiled pleasantly enough." Elizabeth bustl'd about the kitchen. "Strange to say, when I turn'd onto Leadenhall I still heard his humming. Perhaps the sound merely linger'd in my head, the way ditties do."

Humphrey only half attended to what his wife was saying.

She lit a candle against the gathering twilight, put supper dishes onto the table. "When I was on my way home just now, Humphrey, coming from the baker's, he was gone. But as I turned into that alley – I've heard it call'd Jews' Alley, but I'm certain it has no such name at all – you know, back behind Saint Mary Axe – I fancy I saw the old fellow again in the shadows."

Elizabeth's voice was soft in a pool of evening light. "I know 'twas him. He was humming that tune again that was still in my head. He slipp'd into a doorway at one of those tumbledown houses. My parcels were heavy, you know. Next time I do the marketing I wish you'd send young Tom along to help me, what with my back and the odd folk who are about at nightfall."

Humphrey Withers nodded.

Elizabeth's tale spun on as if there would be no end to it. "Why, in he went through a doorway. Put his basket of apples on the table there, alongside a pair of brass candlesticks and a braided loaf, golden and round, prettier, certainly, than the one I had in my bundle, that's the truth. I stopped to catch my breath – that crick in my side got me again – and I couldn't help but notice an odd sight through a crack in the shutters. A woman was in the room and a little mob of sniffly-looking children, and she – the woman, that is – planted a kiss on that fellow's sorry old forehead. The crick wasn't better so I stood another moment and – "

"Enough, Elizabeth," Humphrey Withers said. "'Tis quite a tale you tell, and important, I have no doubt. But can it wait? We have the folks' supper to serve and the hospital kitchen to tidy. Tomorrow Sir George and Mr. Metherall come for Inspection Day, or have you forgotten? We've work to do tonight. Save your tale for when we're done, my dear." Humphrey tried to sound professional and husbandly at once. "Now didn't I see a bit of cod in your bundle to add to the cook's stew for our supper?"

The Porter and his wife went about their chores companionably that Friday night. They took their ease together as they hadn't often of late. Master Withers dreamt that night of a round braided bread, of candles and a kiss. He slept deeply and woke Saturday morning especially refresh'd, his waking dream about pippins, eye pieces, and snatches of melody sung in a sweet harmony by the mad folk of Bedlam, under the mild, rheumy gaze of a reedy choirmaster in a threadbare coat.

The pleasure of that night's dreams comes to the Porter in a flash of recognition. Suddenly he feels improv'd, his soul sweeten'd. A veil lifts and reveals to the Porter an inward and outward vision. Standing in the dark, three stars newly visible in the Friday night sky above the parish of Saint Botolph's Bishopsgate in early October, in the Year of Our Lord 1634, Master Humphrey Withers of Bethlehem Royal Hospital experiences a full miracle: He is translated into the mind of one of his charges:

I'm so tired. How these puppy lads hang upon me! Each new generation of 'em calls to mind earlier ones. They're all intermingl'd now, so in my dream red-headed Jemmie Meakin, who went sailing off, bound for America years ago, walk'd into my classroom. He must be a grown man now, no longer a mere schoolboy. Lads who've grown into bearded, long-legged men spring up anew each day in my dream-classroom.

Remember little Michael Drayton? He's a courtier now and a poet, yet I daydream'd him today sitting alongside the new little lad Simon, who has just join'd the first form. Michael Drayton brought me a poem once – I wore out the copy but thankfully committed it to memory – how does it begin? Ah yes. 'My dearly loved friend,' he call'd me, how oft have we

In winter evenings (meaning to be free)
To some well-chosen place us'd to retire;
And there with moderate meat and wine and fire
Have pass'd the hours contentedly with chat,
Now talk of this, and then discours'd of that –

I'm so tired. 'Tis time to find some well-chosen place where the memories can flood around me without the interruption of the greedy present. Later in that poem Michael Drayton spoke of Kit Marlow's "fine madness." Now there's a plan.

But what to do about the children? My own and all these puppy boys? Can I do without them? And my books? What of my books? I've committed much of them to memory. They're so heavy to carry about.

Yes, "a fine madness." That's it. In a mad company, who would know if I got the words right or not? Think of the opportunities to talk of this, discourse of that. Some might listen, some might not. Just as it is now in my dream-classroom.

'Tis the very place to retire: There would be less than moderate meat, to be sure, and no wine, little fire. But I would be free. At last to speak of translunary things without the suspicious whispering. Only the laughter. I could bear the laughter. Indeed, I would enjoy the laughter. . . .

A fine madness, then. There's the key to open the gate and set me free. Aldgate, Billingsgate, Bishopsgate, Cripplegate, Moorgate. Where's the gate for the old, the bumbling, the useless, the man at the margin? Which gate for me? Aldgate, Billingsgate, Bishopsgate, Cripplegate, Moorgate? Not a one. It'll be the madhouse gate. Bedlam gate.

But how to get the key? Bathsua would surely disallow it. She'd insist on taking me in, settling me beside her fire, among the children, the books, the busy-ness. Richard would agree with her, sweet romantic schoolboy that he's been all these years.

I'm too tired to argue with them. I'll keep them out of it, instead depend on the others. Reverend Thorpe and the Porter and his observant wife: they've been watching me, the headmaster and William Lansdale, and the disgruntled parents of schoolboys. And John. He's afraid. I'll use his fears. Itha's so besotted with him that she won't resist. All those who've had suspicions about me, they'll each of 'em do what I need 'em to do. They've begun already. By week's end I'll be safely install'd. Such a fine madness.

In the comfortable autumn darkness stands Humphrey Withers. He has reel'd in all the threads of memory and understands.

Subject:	Plan B
Date:	5/26/2003 9:45:01 AM EDT
From:	dndyoung2@owl.com
To:	dndyoung1@owl.com

Darling,

Ned will download everything in my OWL email account onto memory sticks. I'll put them somewhere safe. Someday maybe I'll print them out. Maybe yes, maybe no. I don't have to decide right away. I'll close the OWL account at the end of June.

The Bathsua Project is almost done now. I'll put it away, too, for safekeeping. Maybe someday Ned or Gracie will find and read it.

I've hired Ned as my tech specialist. He'll help me select and buy the new computer next week, get me started with a new email setup, and design the blog I asked him about a while ago. I'm starting to think about a new writing project. So I've got a plan in motion, darling.

Love.

May 30, 2003

> Even if he does sit silently, it hardly means nothing's going on. Silence is just as likely to indicate the most profound ideas forming, the deepest energies being summoned. There may have been silence, but inside his head there'd been a whole universe. . . .
> – Kazuo Ishiguro. *The Unconsoled.*

Dear Bathsua,

Many thanks for your letter and "Wit's End." I appreciate your leaving them on my reader's shelf instead of our usual alcove niche. I've been carrying "Wit's End" around with me all week as if it were a specially wrapped present. I just read it again, my secret treasure.

Your father ended his life with bravery and dignity. That you treated it as a kind of detective story is a tribute to his intelligence. How much trouble you took to tell the tale in reverse time order! I think I understand why.

Before our correspondence ends, I want you to know how grateful I am for the very fact that you've written so steadily. Over the last eleven months you have become my one true and loyal friend, my careful reader, my writing tutor. Thank you.

While on the subject of gratitude: I'm grateful, too, that I have a mind that is pleased by ordinary Friday mornings like this one, by sunlight filtering through leaves onto this table, by that finch perched this minute on my bird feeder. I'm lucky, too, that I can coax and trick myself into trusting all sorts of worthwhile fictions and at the same time recognize when others lie. Like believing in you and at the same time knowing that when President Bush declared this war a "mission accomplished" he was lying.

What else am I grateful for? For the germination of the beans I planted last week. I pressed them into the ground, then covered them with a layer of soft soil. This morning I checked their progress. Maybe it was only my imagination, but I thought I saw the earth heave slightly above them, even heard them muttering, rustling, chuckling even, as their seed casings burst from the pressure of their profound energies.

Yours, truly,

Dee

P.S. Tomorrow is three centuries and three decades since you presented *The Essay to Revive the Antient Education of Gentlewomen* to your publisher.

— Twelve —

June 2, 2003

> Thy love is such I can no way repay;
> The heavens reward thee manifold, I pray.
> Then while we live, in love let's so persever
> That when we live no more we may live ever.
>   — Ann Bradstreet. "To My Dear and Loving Husband."

Dear Dorothea,

It is nearly time to bring our correspondence to a close. Only a little of the syllabus remains before we may call the course complete. To switch metaphors: As with a garden, our work together is ready to bear fruit. A bit more tilling, my dear, more telling.

Consider our husbands, for example. Your references to Dan, like mine to Richard, are (forgive the pun) embedded in everything we write. Dan and Richard are ever and always in the background, never the foreground – perhaps as we never foreground a limb, say, unless, God forbid, we harm or lose it.

I am composing a play about Richard. 'Tis set after the Regicide, when the two of us sat at our table and tallied our resources and debts – and found how short was our accounting. I'm nearly ready to share it with you. I am, as ever,

Yours faithfully,

Bathsua

Subject: Time to come clean
Date: 6/3/2003 06:23:40 A.M. EDT
From: dndyoung2@owl.com
To: dndyoung1@owl.com

Danny, darling,

So here's the truth: For eleven months I've pretended that Bathsua Makin has been writing to me – *me!* – from beyond the veil of death, that I – *I!* – was chosen to receive secrets of a life long lost. It was a lie, of course, an illusion. A self-delusion. I've kept this correspondence going, Dan, laying down each bit of this exchange, like bean after bean in that row I planted last week, to make the past enter the present, to break down this damned wall between the living and the dead that's been crushing in on me since you died. Does this make sense?

All that trouble telling Bathsua's last story, "Wit's End," in reverse time order! All those verb tense shifts, switching from present to simple past, present perfect and past perfect and back again! All that respelling of American *honor* to British *honour*, for goodness sake, that changing of past tense inflections unaffected by stress or consonant softening from *–ed* to *–'d!* You must know how exacting it was – and how satisfying – like those shifts in the early chapters from *the* and *that* to *y* and *y*. It was painstaking – but good pain that has given me relief from the bigger agonies of my otherwise dark, dark thoughts of this *annus horribilis*. This work to correspond with Bathsua has been an enormous gift I gave to myself. And now I'm nearly ready to be done, nearly ready to stop pretending that present and past can be merged or lived in simultaneously. Nearly ready to go on by myself. Just myself. Without her. Without you.

The school year is almost over. Two more assignments remain on the syllabus. Then I'll write one last lesson plan and tie up the loose ends of this course.

Love always, all ways,

Dee

June 5, 2003

> You have my
> attention: which is
> a tenderness, beyond
> what I may say. And I have
> your constancy to
> something beyond myself.
> The force
> of your commitment charges us – we live
> in the sweep of it, taking courage
> one from the other.
> — Denise Levertov. "The Marriage."

Dear Bathsua,

There's a line in a Tom Stoppard play, "The Real Thing": Henry, the central character, probably a stand-in for Stoppard himself, at some point, I can't remember when, says, "I don't know how to write love. I try, but it just comes out embarrassing." What's more, to write about my husband would be, as you say, like saying how I feel about my right hand. And, to be honest, I've been writing about Dan all along. You go ahead: Write now for both of us.

Ever,

D

June 10, 2003

Dear Dee,

I write as you say, for both of us and, I think in the tender spirit of the poem by Denise Levertov.

With deep affection,

Bathsua

Enclosure: "Table Talk"

Table Talk

בְּזֵעַת אַפֶּיךָ, תֹּאכַל לֶחֶם

In the sweat of thy face shalt thou eat bread.
– Genesis 3:19.

SCENE

A domestic interior. It is tidy, comfortable, simple. Soft June morning light – buttery-pale – bathes the room from a half-open window at stage right. At stage-center-rear is a slightly ajar interior door; there is a blanket-cover'd mass just barely visible through it. At stage left is an exterior door. Beside it are a bookcase and console table. The room's focal point is a plain wood dining table and three chairs. Simple, durable, serviceable. On the tables are small textiles in deep reds and blues. The room resembles a Vermeer painting and, depending on the director's concept, evokes one of those paintings directly or just hints at it. On a wall is a single painting or an an art print, tasteful but muted, and a windup clock whose pendulum swings throughout. In the bookcase are books and family memorabilia, all well-us'd and well-lov'd. A small jug of seasonal flowers and a candle (left from the evening before, snuff'd out) rest on the console table. Close at hand on the table are breakfast necessaries: a pitcher for hot or cold beverage, glasses or mugs, a fruit bowl, a wedge of cheese, a loaf of bread and a knife on a bread board. Now and then the actors, a man and woman, move about the room to get something or put it aside, but otherwise all the action occurs at or near the table. When the lights go up, the two are on stage. Birdsong fills the room along with the morning light. Only two chairs will be used by the actors. The third, placed between the other two, remains empty throughout the action. Someone else is at home beyond the interior doorway; the two actors allude by glance or gesture to this unseen person. This is the home of a married couple who have fit with each other and together in it for many years. As in every long marriage, however, accumulated, unspoken assumptions, secrets, worries, and grievances also fill the space. A well-used, old-fashion'd valise or carpet bag is downstage, close to the footlights. We see the action across it. One more detail: the couple has made love the night before, for the first time in a long time. This fact is not mention'd, but somehow the audience senses it.

CHARACTERS

RICHARD. Mid-fifties. He has work'd all his life with his wits and his hands, outdoors as much as in. He is lean, fit, full of energy, good-spirited, yet current worries burden him. He has always been a reader, but as an amateur, not an academic. He is comfortable in his body, but a little awkward this morning. Events and consequences beyond his control have lately caught up with him and make him uncomfortable. There are things he cannot say to his wife.

BATHSUA. Also mid-fifties. She and Richard have been married for over thirty years and have come to resemble each other. Their gestures match, and they finish each other's sentences. There is fatigue, endurance, and little softness about Bathsua: she has borne eight children, does her own housework, walks to and from work in all sorts of weather, and looks like the schoolteacher she is. Her hair is tamed rather than tidy; this morning, aware that it is more dishevel'd than usual, she fusses with it distractedly. Still in robe and slippers, she is late with this morning's activities, perhaps embarrass'd for having been in bed longer than usual. The audience senses that this room has lately been more hers than Richard's, that she is trying – not entirely successfully – to yield some authority over the space without giving up any.

HENRY. An adolescent whose uncoordinated movements and bestial sounds bespeak madness, dementia.

—⁓—

BATHSUA. [*Organizes the table for breakfast, pretending nothing's out of the ordinary, but knows everything is*] It's a pretty morning, Richard. I'm glad you're home at last.

RICHARD. So am I. It has been a long time. Too long, Batty, since we came downstairs in the morning, just the two of us, for breakfast.

BATHSUA. To a quiet morning kitchen, just the two of us. Yes. 'Tis suddenly quiet.

RICHARD. [*Looks about the room, fingers items that remind him of former times*] Little has changed, I see. Thank goodness. But it is quieter than before.

BATHSUA. Yes. when the girls left, each room grew quiet without all their bustle and clatter. And with the big boys gone as well. . . . Henry is quieter, too, now, and calmer than before. Surely you noticed that yesterday when you arriv'd. . . .

RICHARD. Yes. I noticed. He's more manageable, Batty. You've done wonders in my absence. My troubles attach'd themselves to him, I know. After I went away they rubb'd off the way. . . the way scabs finally fall off old wounds. Isn't it so?

BATHSUA. [*Tries to be careful*] Yes. Perhaps. He does pick up on the feelings around him, despite his other limits.

RICHARD. I'm glad he's better. And you, too, Batty, you're better, too?

BATHSUA. Let's not start, Richard.

RICHARD. [*Returns to the bookcase, thoughts of easier former times*] Still, 'tis almost like the old days. And last night? Remember?

BATHSUA. Of course I remember. 'Twas. . . almost like the old days. Almost. But nothing's quite the same. Nothing ever is. Or ever will be. How many years is it, Richard, since we were wed? Thirty-five? [*Muses*] Time only goes one way, doesn't it? Forward, not back, no matter how we wish it otherwise. [*Puts breakfast things on the table, setting three places, and hands Richard a previously open'd but re-folded letter without looking at it*] The nest is almost empty. Henry notwithstanding, I do rattle around here without all of you.

RICHARD. [*Opens the letter*]What's this?

BATHSUA. It came from John just after the boys mov'd out.

RICHARD. What does that self-righteous busybody brother-in-law have to say for himself? Where is he? Lecturing in Amsterdam? Consulting in Breda? Spying in Antwerp?

BATHSUA. He does get around, I'll allow him that.

RICHARD. [*Tries to contain his anger*] Oh, he gets around, all right. That much I can say for him. [*Between an accusation and a compliment, but more toward the former*] I have to hand it to him, he knows how to work matters in his own favour. I know you've always wish'd I had a little more of that skill in me, Batty.

BATHSUA. Let's not start, Richard.

RICHARD. But you do wish I were more like him. And so do I perhaps. John's always managed to be on the right side of things, even when the ground shifts beneath his feet. Adaptable, that John Pell. [*Muses*] How does Saint Paul put it? You know, Batty, in Corinthians?

BATHSUA. Isn't it a little early in the day for Scripture?

RICHARD. Come now. I'm rusty with the learning, but we both know you're not. How does it go? "*Omnibus omnium horarum homo.*" Is that it? A man for all things at all times.

BATHSUA. [*Smiles*] You're combining what Saint Paul wrote with that old grammar preceptum Papa taught us, Richard. [*Recites from memory while Richard takes an old book from the shelf*] Paul said, "I am made all things to all men, that I might by all means save them." The grammar preceptum was different: It was about Sir Thomas More, a man for all seasons: *Morus est vir omnium horarum.*

RICHARD. [*Laughs, thumbing the book until he finds the page*] Ah yes, the genitive of praise. But John Pell is no Sir Thomas More.

BATHSUA. [*Also laughs*] Certainly not.

RICHARD. Brother John's more like Saint Paul, then: [*Begins reciting from memory*] "To the weak became I as weak – "

BATHSUA. " – that I might gain the weak: – "

RICHARD. " – I have become all things to all men, that I might by any means save them."

BATHSUA. Yes: ἵνα πάντως τινὰς σώσω. [*Corrects Richard's translation*] That I might *by all means* save them.

RICHARD. John wrote to you out of the blue? I've never known him to be spontaneous about anything, let alone a letter to his "beloved" sister-in-law. Or did you write to him?

BATHSUA. I did give Ithamaria a note for John just after the boys left, but he must have sent this before I wrote him. In all likelihood, my note cross'd with his. You can tell – here, read it – that he hadn't yet learn'd that the boys had both taken lodgings elsewhere.

RICHARD. You felt the need to tell him of our situation. Again. And again he feels free to meddle in our affairs.

BATHSUA. Still, what John says has merit. I know you hate to give your brother-in-law the benefit of "I told you so."

RICHARD. [*Under his breath*] But you always do.

BATHSUA. Read it, Richard, before you pass judgment.

RICHARD. How can I not pass judgment, after all that's happen'd? John always bounces back, while I go under. And he always interferes with our lives, no matter what I want, no matter what you say to the contrary.

BATHSUA. Here we are again, Richard, right where we left off. The same old argument. . . . Just read the letter.

RICHARD. [*Reads*] *"Dear Sister: If your landlord will do the repairs on the house so you can stay in it, I think you're better off there month to month than moving and assuming a new contract for a whole year or more."* There he goes again, meddling in my affairs, giving advice where it's not wanted. Or did you write to him asking for help while I was . . .

BATHSUA [*Extremely busy with the breakfast things again; doesn't reply*]

RICHARD. Oh, darling. Not again. You ask'd him for money again. I wrote you I'd . . . [*Reads*] *"Your letters seem to say you hope to have one gone shortly: and the next you think will fly out of the nest before the end of this year."*

BATHSUA. I have to be practical, Richard. You know what my – our – situation is. [*Grows agitated despite her best intentions*] There's barely enough coming in from my pupils to keep the roof over our heads. The elder boys offer'd me pocket money, but they don't have much. They should keep what little they have, for they'll soon have other mouths to feed. I can't forever expect their aid when they scarcely have enough as it is. And the girls? What can I expect of them? What would you have me do, Richard? Who else can I ask beside Itha and John? Who? The Council? The wealthy parents of old pupils? I can think of nothing more to do, save pawning the clock or Father's books. [*The words tumble out. She has been waiting to explode.*]

RICHARD. So you wrote to John and ask'd for money. Again. And advice. Again. And he writes as if I'm dead. [*Reads*] "*For a hen with one chick, one little room will suffice.*" You make me out to be a husband who's abandon'd his brood, left you and the lad to the care of. . .

BATHSUA. You read into his words what isn't there. He is stating facts. Nothing more.

RICHARD.[*Reads again, interrupting, will not be sooth'd*] "*Before long, your friends will begin to tell you that your youngest is too old to tarry under his mother's wing.*" That's how he regards the boy? Like a lazy scoundrel, abandon'd, dependent on his mother? [*Reads again, his voice rising*] ". . .*that he will be better abroad with a father, a tutor or a master.*"

BATHSUA. Richard. . . .

RICHARD. How often will you remind me that I've been no help to you? John would have you send the lad abroad? In his eyes I'm as good as dead. I'm nothing but a journeyman, a day worker as easily dismiss'd as. . . [*Snaps his fingers*]. What else does Brother John have to say? [*Reads the rest of the letter, mockingly at first, in the end deflated*] "*Howsoever, the taking of a house, will not be so fit for you as lodgings, in your husband's absence. At his return he would have you free and not encumber'd with a lease, when he would remove to such a place as may be more convenient for him than the house in which he finds you.. . .*" Have you 'free and unencumber'd'? Whose words are those, Batty? What did you say to him? Why does he write so freely about my wants, my encumbrances? [*Having begun carefully, he now spits out words in anger. Damm'd up despair spills over. Meanwhile Bathsua fusses with the breakfast things, anxious lest the invisible person in the house hears them arguing.*] What did you tell him?

BATHSUA. I didn't tell him anything. Nothing at all about you. Just that the matter of the back tuition fees is still pending with the Counsel, that you. . . that we. . .

RICHARD. What? That I what? That we what? That I've been without work since the winter of '50? And it's four years now and still no prospects? That I've done day work, cadging errands here and there? That he spotted me at John Hodges's print shop, where I haven't work'd since I was sixteen? That I leave every morning and come back every night with nothing to show for the day but a few coppers and a dark mood? That I've taken up employment on Threadneedle at the Jew pawnbroker's? That I lodge in their midst to escape your disapproval? [*Holds something back*] Because I . . .

BATHSUA. No, I didn't tell him. I said nothing – *nothing* – not a thing about that. . . .

RICHARD. [*Suddenly calm*] I don't want to argue. I didn't come back yesterday to argue. Nor to add to your miseries. I came to patch things up, to say how sorry I am, how asham'd of myself I am. . . . To beg your forgiveness. To make you understand how asham'd of myself I am, Batty. How miserable I am without you. That I will never hurt you again, so help me, God, not a single hair on your head.

BATHSUA. I know this is difficult for you, Richard. . . . I've rehears'd this conversation over and over. Every time I come up short. I don't know what to say. All I can do is get through each day, go through the motions. Pretend it . . . never happen'd, I cannot. Turn back the clock? Impossible. What would you have me do? What would you have me say?

RICHARD. I can't reinvent myself to suit the times, to suit the need. I am who I am.

BATHSUA. I know.

RICHARD. I hitch'd my wagon to the wrong star. I remain'd loyal to the King, thinking that was how 'twas suppos'd to be. The ones I was loyal to, they lost. So did I. And I dragg'd you down along with me.

BATHSUA. No, Richard. Don't say that.

RICHARD. 'Tis the way of the world now. Loyalty means nothing. No one takes care of anyone but himself. Or herself.

BATHSUA. So what are we to do? How will we live? How will we put bread on the table? How am I to care for the lad?

RICHARD. I don't know, Batty. I made a ruin of things. That's all I know.

BATHSUA. Don't say that.

RICHARD. 'Tis true. I'm of no use to you.

BATHSUA. Don't say that.

RICHARD. You and Henry are better off without me.

BATHSUA. No, Richard –

RICHARD. 'Tis true. And John Pell is a better man than I, and more suited to advise you.

BATHSUA. Stop, Richard. The lad –.

RICHARD. And what of the lad? What if we did what John suggests: [*Reads*] ". . . *he will be better abroad with a father, a tutor or a master.*"

BATHSUA. I can't bear it.

RICHARD. [*Continues after a long silence*] Wait. How did Saint Paul put it? "That I might serve the strong I must gain the weak and be as weak."

BATHSUA. That's not what he said.

RICHARD. That I might serve the strong, I must take the weak and be as the weak.

BATHSUA. No, Richard. 'Tisn't what Scripture says. And you know it. "That I might serve the <u>weak</u>. . ." That's what it says.

RICHARD. I know. But how else can I save you from the circumstances I placed you in, if not by taking the burden from you and going away? And you will be free. . . .

BATHSUA. No, Richard.

RICHARD. I shall take on my head what is mine to bear, and leave you to. . . .

BATHSUA. No, Richard.

RICHARD. I will leave you to your excellences. To the work that gives you pleasure.

BATHSUA. I can't bear losing both of you.

RICHARD. Yes, you can. You will. You will learn to. Teach the sound ones, Batty. Leave the damaged one to me. [*The mass in the interior doorway moves*]

BATHSUA. And lose both of you at once?

RICHARD. And gain yourself.

BATHSUA. A heavy price for a small purchase.

RICHARD. No, my darling. A fair exchange. [*Takes up the old book again*] Remember the precepts your Papa taught us all those years ago when we were in school together, I in the classroom and you at the door? Here. I'll quiz you. "I married my teacher's daughter today, most sorely against my will."

BATHSUA. [*Smiles ruefully*] "*Præceptoris filia mihi invitissimo nupsit hodie.*"

RICHARD. "I will be your friend, full ready to do whate'er you ask."

BATHSUA. [*Crying*] "*Unde quo familiariter veteris amico paratissimus tibi ero.*"

RICHARD. [*Tries to coax laughter from her tears*] "Me thinketh her so rough and sore a housewife that I cared not and she were burn'd in hot coals."

BATHSUA. [*Cries and laughs at the same time*] "*Mihi adeo aspera et acerba viditur coniunx ut si ardentibus prunis cremaretur nihi penderem.*"

RICHARD. Yes, *mea cara*. And this: "Many a poor man's son by grace and virtue ascendeth to the heights."

[*The huddled figure at the inner doorway sways, moans. It is their mad son, Henry, who has listened and understood.*]

BATHSUA. "*Pauperum itidem filii gratia et virtute in summam dignitatem sepius evadunt.*" [*Embraces their son, who is calmed*]

RICHARD. Yes, God willing, the lad will prosper.

BATHSUA. My turn. [*Laughing through tears, takes the book from him*] "A man might as soon pick marrow from a hoe as squeeze three good Latin words from your forehead."

RICHARD. [*Also laughing and crying now, touches the hair at her temple*] "*Citius medullam a ligone expellas quam tria vocabula proba e fronte tua.*"

BATHSUA. "O the happiness of former times! But alas, this new misery!"

RICHARD. No laments, my darling. [*Releases Henry from her embrace*] Say this instead: "While these two lines are written, I am gone."

BATHSUA. "*Ubi hæ duæ lineæ exarentur, hinc abeo.*"

RICHARD. And this one: "Though it be bitter, take thy medicine with a good will. Soon it will work to thine ease."

BATHSUA. "*Hei antique felicitatis recordatio! Hei calamitoso huic tempori!*"

RICHARD. [*Gathers up the valise and goes to the exterior door with Henry*] No, my darling. Not those mournful words. "Though it be bitter, take thy medicine." Say it.

BATHSUA. [*Struggles to speak*] "*Licet amarum, cum equanimitate hoc antidotum accipito. Tandem – Quando – enim pariet tibi – mihi – nobis – commodum?* Though 'tis bitter, I must take this medicine. Soon – When – will it work to thine – mine – our – ease?"

RICHARD. [*Moves with Henry to the outer door stage right. There is a scramble of activity as they exit.*] *Vale, mea cara.*

BATHSUA. Godspeed, my beloved.

June 13, 2003

Dear Dee,

For old times' sake I cannot resist one more piece. Call it hubris, but what's the worst punishment a jealous god can visit on a once-living-now-deceas'd-and-fictitious correspondent?

Bathsua

Enclosure: "Transformations"

Transformations

Μέντορι ἐιδομένη ἠμὲν δέμας ἠδὲ καὶ αὐδήν.
The goddess still kept Mentor's build and voice.
– Homer. *Odyssey.* (final line.)

Down I swept and in an antique guise
Alit in a Library – a welcome spot.
A Reader look'd supris'd yet beckon'd me
With a gesture as if we'd met before,
And with her eyes alone she greeted me.
In the mote-fill'd silence I could read her thoughts:
"Dear Teacher – I entreat you – teach me
How to renew my life. And show me, please – "
No need to finish the request. She ask'd
So earnestly that swiftly I agreed
With just a nod, which she constru'd more bold –
And turn'd my assent to counsel from the grave.
I did not contradict – but stay'd and whisper'd low –
With grey eyes glinting, yet in borrow'd garb –
"I'll gladly tell you point by point my tale:
(Improvising now) – "My father was a teacher.
Like him" (the words just came to me as if
I knew them all along) " and I – like you –
Was – am – also a teacher – mother, wife,
And lover of books. Now here I've come

Coasting the wine-dark sea of memory –
Ready to offer what I have to teach
To you who wishes to hear me speak.
I've paid such calls before – regarded others –
But you of all seem eager – ready-will'd
To listen to my tales and memories.
And how I've come and whence and why – you ask?
You wish to know what wasn't written down –
What's hidden when the living die and take
Their secrets – great and humble – to the grave.
Of all of that – and more – I will speak now – "
Said I. But my assumèd form recall'd,
I chose to hold in check the greater gift –
Of what would come in time, how our encounter
Might change the course of how she'd lead her life.

    The Reader's hasty blush confirm'd my choice.
No need I saw for prophecy just now.
I kept it to myself instead – press'd her:
"Now Pupil – tell me who *you* have become."
The Reader then most cautiously replied –
"I'll strive to answer honestly. But know
I doubt myself and what I have to say."
"Trust me – " I said – clear-eyed – and settl'd
In the guise of one long dead. "Trust me –
And tell me – What has been your work?
Your life's details? Your family and friends?
Answer all my questions honestly:
What has been your life 'til now? Tell me.
What do you long for? Do not hesitate!"

    "You seem most curious – " the Reader said.
"And since you wish to know – " she took the tale up
Eagerly, as someone waiting long,
Starv'd to have an auditor, and cheer'd
 By my willing look, my steady gaze.
Until the Library's closing bell she spoke,

The evening shadows settling on us both.
Then I replied, still in outward form
Her Teacher ris'n from the past –
"For you I have some sage advice. Take heed –
Make ready for a journey of your own,
An inward and an outward odyssey.
Prepare yourself – and I shall be your Guide.
We'll make of it a double quest and learn
Who *I* was – who *you* are – exchange what's new
And what's long lost. Some secrets I shall share
But most – and best – are sure to come from you.
Stop reading only now and start to write –
Reach in and down and deep to find your way.
And search your memory – compose yourself
By putting words together – find yourself
Through them. You won't be my apprentice
Very long – for soon enough I know
The time will come you'll venture on your own.
The project rests with you. Take what I say
Into the very vessels of your heart."
      "Thank you, Teacher – " the Reader breath'd reply.
"I'll strive to do exactly what you say –
Become a pupil steer'd by a patient guide.
You've counsel'd me with wisdom. I won't forget."
I readied to depart. "Don't go – " she said. "Stay longer.
Although I see you're very keen to leave –
I beg you – stay. Sit by me for a while
Or wait at least for me to make some gift –
A keepsake of your visit, of the sort
A guest should give a host – or friend to friend."
I hurried to decline. "I must depart.
I must be on my way." My shape return'd
To its true form. In gathering shadows I became
Myself – the Gray-Eyed One. (My eyes' bright flashing
Near belied that fact.) "As for your gift –"
(My glinting voice inton'd) " – what you would give

In kindness – save for others. But think of me
When giving."
    And with these words I turn'd to leave,
Yet noted as I left the Reader seem'd
To change her form as well – and newly charged
With energy, her senses quicken'd, fill'd
With purpose. No longer passive Reader – now
Writer she'd become – prepar'd at last
Tto undertake the task at hand – like one
Inspir'd.
    As in that storied tale Telemachus
Told his homeland Ithaca farewell –
Set sail to Sparta – looking for his sire.
"I'm sailing off – " said he " – to sandy Pylos
To ask for Nestor's help and rumours heed
For news of my dear father's whereabouts."
(Rumours seem to come from Zeus himself.)
His declaration made – the prince sat down
And Mentor rose instead – Odysseus' friend –
To whose care entrusted the wily king
Belovèd kingdom, household, wife, and son
Ere sailing off to Troy to join the war.
  "I'll go along with him – " wise Mentor said
" – To keep him company. A journey's tiresome.
We'll tell old tales – one to another –
And while away the months 'til our return."
The Ithacans made jests about the plan –
And mock'd Telemachus for playing the fool.
But I – Pallas Athena – was the one
In Mentor's form who urged the young man on
With winging words. "Telemachus –" I said
"– You'll not lack courage, energy, or sense
From this day on – not while your parents' blood
And – yes – my words run coursing through your veins.
Nor will Imagination fail you now.
You do not shun hard work – and so there's hope

That you will reach your goal."
    Ever the Grey-Eyed One,
Remaining Mentor still in form and voice,
I urged him on – "Telemachus, your friends
Await your word to launch. So move ahead.
Waste no more time. On with your voyage."
And I in Mentor's guise sped on ahead
And Telemachus follow'd my footsteps in the sand –
'Til side by side we sat – mortal and immortal –
Together in the pilot's seat, exchanging tales
To pass the time en route to Nestor's home.

    The new-claim'd Writer took me as Her Guide.
I urged her on, in antique Teacher's guise:
"No more excuses, Pupil! Do not yield
To hesitation! Carry on your work!
Make what's at hand respond to your command –
Press on – and trust Imagination's force
To serve you well."
    The Writer – procrastinating still –
Modestly replied: "How can I write?
Teacher – I'm not adept. I hesitate,
Uncertain – "
    "Pupil – " (I hid my voice and face
But not my bright-eyed words, still in the garb
Of that Teacher from her bookish past)
" – Some of the words you'll find within yourself,
The rest some force will show you how to write.
You were not born or rear'd or school'd
Without the gods' good will." (I nearly show'd
myself just then – but scarcely did she note –
so enwrapt in doubt of self was she.)
    "So many are more favour'd in this craft
than I," the Writer counter'd cautiously.
"Could it ever come to pass for me?
What you say dumbfounds me – staggers

My weak imagination! I scarcely think
The day will ever dawn when I – "
Just so lamented Odysseus' son Telemachus
On setting sail from Pylos – Sparta-bound.
And so – my eyes aflame – as Pallas Athene
(Yet in Mentor's guise) I sharply said –
"What is this nonsense slipping through your teeth?
Let deterence come from only one –
Death, that leveler whom no one may stop!"
And thus chastis'd, Telemachus replied:
"Mentor – speak of this no more. I will
Press on."
  So the new-minted Writer and I contended –
I for daring, she for hesitation –
As night drew on – and dreams and darkness swept
Across the black-streak'd sky. But surely I –
The Grey-Eyed One – child of Zeus All-Knowing –
Was bound to win the day.

  And now when morning breaks
And Dawn's bright light in streaky colours paints
The wide-stretch'd sky – the Writer wakes with dreams
Still fresh in mind much fresher and more bright
Than ever were before. And morning after morning
A bright-eyed Guide fills the Writer's head
With tales envision'd clear on newly waking.
And now, from such remember'd dreams she draws
Fresh strength and daily draws from them
Belief in self to do the daylight work.
Just so – return'd to Ithaca and striving
To retake his hall – Odysseus himself
Grew bold from my own words on Mentor's lips –
My rousing cries in his: "Come forth – dear friend –
And stand by me! You'll feel my wingèd power
and see that I and Mentor – son of Alcimus –
take up your cause!" My hearty words alone

Help'd turn'd the tide and set Odysseus on –
Telemachus his son as well – and both
Did put their very souls and hearts to proof.
So I – in many guises (not the least
Of which are dreams) – give strength and valiant hope
For every honest, worthwhile task at hand.

And thus the Writer's will is energiz'd –
The gift unfolding that she promisèd
At the start of her high solemn pledge.
So again – shape-shifting – I return
To that unseen and private inward voice
I us'd in the Library on that former day.
I sit quiet – still – invisible – where once – my eyes
Ablaze behind my many guises – I urged
The Writer on. As Mentor – Guide – and Teacher –
Stranger – Goddess – Memory – and even Self –
As one-in-all – and also all-in-one.
My work is done. The Writer's work's begun.

Subject:	Closing the Mail Box
Date:	6/22/2003 11:45:57 AM EDT
From:	dndyoung2@owl.com
To:	dndyoung1@owl.com

> I want to speak to you.
> To whom else should I speak?
> It is you who make
> a world to speak of.
> In your warmth the
> fruits all ripen – all the
> apples and pearls that grow
> on the south wall of my
> head. . . .
> Speak or be silent: your silence
> will speak to me.
>   – Denise Levertov. "The Marriage (II)."

Beloved Dan,

Like writing these messages to you, reading in the Library has been a

lovely habit. Last week I busied myself with Cicero's *De Senectute*, reading
the Latin and English side by side, copying down passages that pleased me,
translating slowly for myself alone. The exercise steadied and calmed me.

Here are some apt passages I worked on last week:

- *Litteras Græcas senex didici, quas quidem sic avide arripui quasi diuturnam
  sitim explere cupiens.* In my old age I taught myself Greek, seizing
  upon it as eagerly as quenching a long-suffered thirst.

- *Mihi quidem ita iucunda huius libri confectio fuit, ut non modo
  omnes absterserit senectutis molestias, sed effecerit mollem etiam
  et iucundam senectutem.* Composing this book has so
  delighted me, erasing all the annoyances of old age and
  even making it seem sweet and agreeable.

- *Cuius sermone ita tum cupide fruebar, quasi iam divinarem, id
  quod evenit, illo exstincto unde discerem neminem.* I used to be
  so eager for [your] conversation but hardly foresaw what
  has indeed come to pass: When [you are] gone I will
  have no one to teach me.

Can I trust my own self to be my own true teacher?

And one more question: We've known all along, haven't we, what that
word was in "The Snow Queen"?

Te amo, carissime,

Dee

June 17, 2003

> There are, after all, so many books. . . . We struggle to write books that do
> not change the world, despite our gifts and unstinting efforts, our most
> extravagant hopes. We live our lives, do whatever we do, and then we sleep
> – it's as simple and ordinary as that. . . . There's just this for consolation: an
> hour here or there when our lives seem, against all odds and expectations,
> to burst open and give us everything we've ever imagined. . . .
> – Michael Cunningham. *The Hours.*

Dear ~~Bathsua,~~ Self and Reader,

My *annus horribilis* has become my *annus mirabilis*. Remember Chekhov's
Uncle Vanya? "It's a mad world," he says. "I have lost all feelings of control
and responsibility! What shall I do? What shall I do with the rest of my

life? Tell me what to do?" he begs. "Tell me what to do to begin to feel worthwhile again!" Vanya gropes wildly at the papers on his desk. "To work," he tells himself, "to work, to work, to work." And again he repeats, as he shuffles about in the old papers, "To work, to work, to work." I have become my work. I have become myself.

Yours faithfully,

Dee

Commonplace Book Entry: June 30, 2003

> . . . Here are books, paper, and my little knife,
> The walls of solitude from which I came,
> Here is the sobering, meditative night,
>
> The quiet room where it is dark and cool.
> After the intense green and the flame,
> The flat white walls, the table are each good.
>
> Long hours of work and the imposed rule:
> That was the time of the tremendous rain,
> The place of lightning, of the great flood.
>
> This is the time when voyagers return
> With a mad longing for known customs and things,
> Where joy in an old pencil is not absurd. . . .
> — May Sarton. "Return."

To do:

- Buy a new computer with a huge memory.
- Give up the reader's shelf at the Library.
- Clear my desk.
- Write a satiric political mystery in emails. Call it *E-Pistolarity*.

References

Dedication: *That things are not so ill with you and me. . . .* George Eliot, *Middlemarch* (Boston: Houghton Mifflin, 1956), 613.

4: *a wildly comic send-up. . . .* Flann O'Brien [Brian O'Nolan], *At Swim-Two-Birds* (Normal IL: Dalkey Archive Press: 1998), back cover.

5: Ἐξίσταται γὰρ πάντ' ἀπ' ἀλλήλων δίχα. *Ibid.*, 8.

8: *Posted by Arthur L./August 5, 2001. . . .* "John and Belle Have a Blog: The Obtuse and the Impenetrable." No longer available online.

11: *O'Brien asked his boss in the civil service. . . .* Flann O'Brien [Brian O'Nolan], *The Flann O'Brien Reader* (NY: Viking, 1978), 2. *Daughter, a fair wind course.* . . . Euripides, "The Madness of Hercules," in *Euripides: Bachanals – Madness of Hercules – Children of Hercules – Phoenician Maidens – Suppliants*, Loeb Classical Library, trans. Arthur Sanders Way (Cambridge MA: Harvard University Press, 1971), Vol.3: 137, ll. 95ff.

12: *Hush, peace. . . . Ibid.*, 210f., ll. 1042ff.

17: *I drag my table. . .* Eugenio Montale, "Notizie dall'Amiata" ["News from Mount Amiata"] trans. Robert Lowell, *Imitations* (NY: Farrar Straus & Giroux, 1990).

18: *a space of connection. . . .* James How, *Epistolary Spaces: English Letter Writing from the Foundation of the Post Office to Richardson's Clarissa* (Burlington VT: Ashgate: 2003), 4.

19: *An odd thought strikes me. . . .* How, 166, citing James Boswell, *Life of Johnson*, ed. George Birkbeck Hill, vol. 4 (Oxford: Clarendon Press, 1887), 413. *It was my hiding place. . . .* Paul Auster, "The Locked Room," *The New York Trilogy* (NY: Penguin, 1990), 232.

25: *from my Lodging in Long Acre. . . . .* Bathsua Makin, Letter 22 November 1675, to Dr. Baldwin Hamey. The Royal College of Physicians, MS 310 no. 84 (folio 119), reproduced in Frances Teague, *Bathusa Makin, Woman of Learning* (Lewisburg, PA: Bucknell University Press, 1998), 92.

28: *[E]t timide verba intermissa retemptat. . . .* Publius Ovidius Naso. *Ovid's Metamorphoses Books 1-5*, ed. William S. Anderson (Norman OK: University of Oklahoma, 1997), I.746.

30: *I drag. . . .* Montale/Lowell, "Notizie dall'Amiata" ["News from Mount Amiata"].

32: Τρὶς δέ μοι ἐκ χειρῶν. . . Homer. *The Odyssey.* Oxford Classical Texts: *Homeri Opera*, Vol. 3. Ed. T.W. Allen (Oxford: Oxford University Press, 1922), XI:180.

33: *three times she flitted . . . . Ibid. Her memory speaks more. . . .* Bathsua Makin, "Upon the Much Lamented Death of the Right Honorable, the Lady Elizabeth Langham," in Letter 2 May 1664) (San Marino CA: Hastings Collection, Henry E. Huntington Library.)

34: Τόν τε γὰρ οὐρανον εἶδε. . . . Maurice Balme and Gilbert Lawall, *Athenaze: An Introduction to Ancient Greek,* Book I (NY: Oxford University Press, 1990), 91.

35: **And for ther is so gret diversite.** . . . Geoffrey Chaucer, "Troilus and Criseyde" V:1793-1799, *The Works of Geoffrey Chaucer,* ed. F.N. Robinson (Boston: Houghton Mifflin, 1961), 479.

37: **Πολλὰ ἔχων ὑμῖν γράφειν.** . . . . *I have many things to write to you.* . . . Second Letter of John, 12. *The Student's New Testament. Greek Text and American Translation,* trans. Edgar J. Goodspeed (Chicago: University of Chicago Press, 1954).

38: **'Like' and 'like' and 'like'.** . . . Virginia Woolf, *The Waves* (London: Hogarth Press, 1931), 176.

42: **To make women learned.** . . . Teague, *Bathsua Makin,* 43, citing Barbara Kiefer Lewalski. *Writing Women in Jacobean England* (Cambridge MA: Harvard University Press, 1993), 341, referring to *Memoirs Relating to the Queen of Bohemia by One of Her Ladies* (n.d.). **But can she spin?** Teague, *Bathsua Makin,* 43, citing John Collet's *Commonplace Book* (1633), *Anecdotes and Traditions,* ed. William Thoms (London: Camden Society #5, 1839), 129.

43: **lying heavily upon me. . . under your wing.** Bathsua Makin Letter 24 October 1668, Henry E. Huntington Library Manuscript Collection, MS., HA 8801. *[E] ncouragement of Learning. . . Literitissima Mulier.* Dr. Baldwin Hamey (1600-1676) Letter to Bathsua Makin, Collection of The Royal College of Physicians, MS, 310 no. 84 (folio 119), in Teague, *Bathsua Makin, Woman of Learning,* 103. **Prosperity and adversity. . . practicall Philosopher.** Bathsua Makin, Letter 22 November 1675, to Dr. Baldwin Hamey. The Royal College of Physicians, MS 310 no. 84 (folio 119), reproduced in Teague, 92. **I could rather wish.** . . . Boccaccio, *Decameron,* trans. John Florio (London: Isaac Jaggard, 1620), http://www.brown.edu/departments/Italian_Studies/dweb/florio/index.dhtml/ (20 April 2005).

46: **Pish! A woman might piss it out!** Attributed to Sir Thomas Bloodworth [Bludworth] (1666). Museum of London Permanent Exhibit: "London's Burning – The Great Fire of 1666," http://archive.museumoflondon.org.uk/Londons-Burning/People/record.htm?type=person&id=150763/ (8 November 2013).

47: **Time counted.** . . . Thomas Stearns Eliot, "The Dry Salvages," *Four Quartets,* ll. 39-43. *Norton Anthology of Poetry,* 4th ed. (NY: W.W. Norton, 1996), 1250.

49: **Sun up: work.** . . . Ezra Pound, *The Cantos* (NY: New Directions: 1996), Canto XLIX: 40-45.

50: **Try to remember.** . . . "Try to Remember," *The Fantasticks,* music Harvey Schmidt, book and lyrics Tom Jones, 1960.

52: **Τρὶς μὲν ἐφωρμήθην.** . . . Homer, *The Odyssey, ibid.*

53: **The memory is sometimes so retentive.** . . . Jane Austen, *Mansfield Park* (1814), *The Complete Novels of Jane Austen* (NY: Modern Library, n.d.), 595.

54: **The mere habit of learning.** . . . Jane Austen, *Northanger Abbey* (1817), *The Complete Novels of Jane Austen* (NY: Modern Library, n.d.), 1160.

59: **When thou feel'st no grief.** . . . Ann Bradstreet (1612-1672), "Before the Birth of One of Her Children," *Norton Anthology of Poetry,* 4th ed. (NY: W.W. Norton, 1996), 419.

60: **May it be Thy will.** . . . . Reb Nechuniah ben HaKanah (~90C.E.), *Talmud Tractate Berachot*, 28b. **Hear, my child.** . . . . Proverbs 1:8-9.

62: Engraving captioned *"Forsake not ye Law of thy Mother. . . ."* Harleian Manuscripts. The British Library (Harleian 5974/121).

63: **She looks well to y^c ways.** . . . . Proverbs 31:27. **It doth appear out of Sacred Writ.** . . . . Bathsua Makin, *Essay on Reviving y^c Antient Education of Gentlewomen* (1673), transcribed in its entirety in Teague, 114.

72: **If our last decade or two.** . . . . Barbara Tuchman, *A Distant Mirror* (NY: Knopf, 1978), xiii.

73: **He wept the flames.** . . . . John Dryden, "Annus Mirabilis: The Great Fire of London," http://www.bartleby.com/337/563.html (11 November 2013). **We enter upon a stage.** . . . . Alasdair MacIntyre, *After Virtue: A Study of Moral Theory* (London: Duckworth, 1981), 213.

74: **September 2, 1666. The Lord's Day.** . . . . Samuel Pepys, *Diary* http://www. pepysdiary.com/diary/1666/09/ (November 11, 2013).

75: **She lives in you and in me.** . . . . Virginia Woolf, *A Room of One's Own* (London: Hogarth Press, 1929), 171.

76: **My mother was a part-time lamed-vovnik.** . . . S.L. Wisenberg, "Sheets" (Courtland Review, August 1999), http://www.cortlandreview.com/issue/8/wisenberg8f. htm (11 November 2013).

79: **According to tradition.** . . . . André Schwartz-Bart, *Le Dernier des Justes. The Last of the Just*, trans. Stephen Becker (NY: Atheneum, 1960), 4.

82: **blessings of fruitful fields.** . . . . Abraham Lincoln. Presidential Thanksgiving Proclamation, 3 October 1863. **Why this sudden restlessness.** . . . . C.P. Cavafy, "Waiting for the Barbarians," *Collected Poems*, ed. George Savidis, trans. Edmund Keeley & Philip Sherrard (Princeton, NJ: Princeton University Press, 1992), 18.

83: **'Tis all in pieces.** . . . . John Donne, "An Anatomy of ye World. Y^e First Anniversary" (1611), http://www.bartleby.com/357/169.html (11 November 2013).

93: **To reconstruct is to collaborate.** . . . . Marguerite Yourcenar, *Memoirs of Hadrian*, trans. Grace Frick (Paris: Librairie Plon, 1959), 126. **And gladly wolde he lern.** . . . Geoffrey Chaucer, "General Prologue, l. 308, "The Canterbury Tales," *The Works of Geoffrey Chaucer,* ed. F. N. Robinson (Boston, MA: Houghton Mifflin, 1961), 20.

94: **Suddenly the smell of a particular flower.** . . . . Emily Herring Wilson, *Two Gardeners: A Friendship in Letters* (Boston: Beacon, 2002), viii.

96: **As plants in gardens excel.** . . . . Bathsua Makin. *Essay on Reviving y^c Antient Education of Gentlewomen* (1673). Reproduced in Teague, 113.

97: **Parmi necessario.** . . . . Galileo Galilei, *Letter 19 March 1610 to Grand Duke Cosimo II Medici,* In Galilei, Galileo, *Sidereus Nuncius [Starry Messenger]*, trans. Albert Van Helden (Chicago, IL: University of Chicago Press, 1989), 92.

102f.: *Πρῶτον μεν φύεται ἑκαστος. . . The one who's φιλόσοφος. . . one of the philosopher's well-bred hounds.* . . . Plato, *The Republic.* Loeb Classical Library, trans. Paul Shorey (Cambridge MA: Harvard University Press, 1930), II:372.

105: *Vivitur parvo bene.* . . . Horace [Quintus Horatius Flaccus], *Odes and Epodes,* II.16 (NY: Benjamin H. Sanborn & Co., 1960), 51. [Author's translation. *Multa petentibus.* . . . III.16 *Ibid.,* 79. [Author's translation.]

105f.: *Quis multa gracilis.* . . . I.5 *Ibid.,* 6. [Author's translation.]

106f.: *O Regina, sublimi flagello.* . . . I.5. David Ferry, *The Odes of Horace: A Bilingual Edition.* (NY: Farrar, Straus & Giroux, 1997), 17. *There was something comforting. . . .* Anne Tyler, *The Amateur Marriage,* (NY: Knopf, 2004), 82.

110: *I felt unanchored and strange.* . . . V.S. Naipaul, *Enigma of Arrival* (NY: Knopf, 1987, 15. *Familiar and unfamiliar.* . . . Wallace Stegner, *Angle of Repose* (NY: Doubleday, 1971), 124.

112: *I went to the woods.* . . . Henry David Thoreau. *Walden,* ed. J. Lyndon Shanley (Princeton, NJ: Princeton University Press, 1971), 90.

115: *Oh, how stupid.* . . . Edith Wharton. "The Other Two" (1904). *The Collected Stores of Edith Wharton* (NY: Carroll & Graf, 1991), 22.

119f.: *the temperate zone. . . I must apologize. . . pacing the room. . . She set down the coffeepot.* . . . *Ibid.,* 16-22 *(passim).*

124: *For whom am I writing this?. . .* Margaret Atwood. *Blind Assassin.* (London: O.W. Toad Ltd., 2000), 43. *Domus sua.* . . . Anonymous Latin epigram.

125: *May it be Thy will.* . . . Reb Nechuniah ben HaKanah, op. cit. *And she remembered.* . . . Vita Sackville-West, *All Passion Spent.* (NY, Carroll & Graf, 1931), 150f.

126: *That our sons.* . . . Ps. 144:12.

127: *Νῦν οὖν Ὀρεστα – so now Orestes.* . . . Sophocles, "Electra," *Sophocles, Vol. I. Ajax. Electra. Oedipus Tyrannus.* Greek Text with English Translation, Loeb Classical Library, trans. Hugh Lloyd-Jones (Cambridge MA: Harvard, 1994), 126ff., ll. 16-19. [Author's translation.]

128: *Invention, Nature's child.* . . . Sir Philip Sidney, "Astrophil and Stella" (1591) 1.10-14, *Norton Anthology of Poetry,* 4th ed. (NY: W.W. Norton, 1996), 192f.

130: *The Princess Elizabeth was aforetime sad.* . . . Sir Theodore Mayerne (1573-1655), "Ephemerides," 12 March 12, 1649. In Mary Ann Everett Green, *Lives of the Princesses of England: From the Norman Conquest,* vol. 6 (London: Henry Colburn, 1855), 372.

131: *A fair beginning.* . . . *O pure sunlight.* . . . Sophocles, *op. cit.* [Author's translation.]

134: *Without ceasing.* . . . *O Erinyes.* . . . *Ibid.* [Author's translation.]

135f.: *ὀτε ὁι παγχάλκων ἀνταία. . . From excess wrath against them.* Sophocles, *op. cit.,* 140ff., ll.195-236, *passim.* [Author's translation.]

140: *Keep silence.* . . . Sophocles, *Ibid.* [Author's translation.]

141: *ἀλλὰ συγ' ἔχουσα πρόσμενε.* . . .*Ibid.*, 224f., ll.1236ff.

143: *Right now, this is the place.* . . . Eva Hoffman, *Lost in Translation* (NY: Penguin, 1989), 280.

144: *'Tis all in pieces.* . . . Donne, "Anatomy."

145: *On certain streets various eccentric or vulnerable people.* . . . Peter Ackroyd, *London: A Biography* (London: Chatto & Windus, 2003), 3.

146: *Es raro que los libros* . . . Jorge Luis Borges, "Tlön, Uqbar, Orbis Tertius" *Ficciones* (Buenos Aires: Emecé Editores, 1944; NY: Harper Collins/Edición Rayo, 2008), 19. *Books are rarely signed.* . . . Jorge Luis Borges, "Tlön, Uqbar, Orbis Tertius," trans. Andrew Hurley, *Collected Fictions* (NY: Penguin, 1998), 76f.

148: *I sit cross-legged staring at the sun . . .Thar region of Pakistan.* "Alex" [pseud.]. "The Manuscript," unpublished manuscript, National Cathedral School, 1990.

149: *Rafael pulled up at his first stop.* . . . "Alex" [pseud.]. "Mirror of Worlds." Unpublished manuscript, National Cathedral School, 1990.

150: *I owe the discovery of Uqbar.* . . . Borges, trans. Hurley, 68. *While we sleep here.* . . . Borges, trans. Hurley, 74.

151f.: *This ink! . . . what can I offer to make you understand?* Seo-Young Chu. "Cannot." Unpublished manuscript, National Cathedral School, 1994.

152: *She stares at her mother's hands.* . . . Seo-Young Chu. "On the Art of Keeping Dead Moments." Unpublished manuscript, National Cathedral School, 1994.

153: *There are no nouns in the conjectural Ursprache of Tlön.* . . . Borges, trans. Hurley, 73. *I closed my eyes. . . The world suddenly made impeccable sense.* Ashley Evans. "Inescapable Maze." Unpublished manuscript, National Cathedral School, 2002.

154: *Almost immediately, reality.* . . . Borges, trans. Hurley, 81. *The city.* . . . Evans, *op.cit.*

155: *Lie you easy.* . . . A.E. Housman, *A Shropshire Lad*. LIX. "The star-filled seas are smooth to-night," http://www.bartleby.com/123/59.html (11 November 2013).

156: *The Devil comes to the writer* . . . . Margaret Atwood, *Negotiating with the Dead: A Writer on Writing* (Cambridge, UK: Cambridge University Press, 2002), 101f.

157: *Nothing could have been done* . . . . Leon Wieseltier, *Kaddish.* (NY: Knopf, 1998), 59.

160: *I would like to hear your life.* . . . Stegner, 20.

161: *This was always a crucial moment of the day* . . . . Auster, 232. *To go where?*. . . Allen Ginsberg, "Kaddish, Part I," http://www.poets.org/viewmedia.php/prmMID/15307 (11 November 2013).

163: Σπονδαὶ δ' ἐς τὸ πᾶν ἐκ μετοίκων. . . . Aeschylus, "The Eumenides." *Oresteia: Agamemnon, The Libation Bearers, The Eumenides, The Persians*. Greek Text with English Translation, Loeb Classical Library, trans. Herbert Weir Smyth, (Cambridge, MA: Harvard University Press, 1926), 370, l.1044.

164: *Grief fills the room up.* . . . William Shakespeare. *King John*, III.iv.93-98.

165: *Have you ever seen a cornfield.* . . *against the vast unreason.* Tom Stoppard, *Invention of Love*. (NY: Grove Press, 1998), 72f.

166: *Many things, for aught I know, may exist.* . . . George Berkeley, "Three Dialogues between Hylas and Philonous in Opposition to Sceptics and Atheists," dial. 3, *The Works of George Berkeley, Bishop of Cloyne*, eds. A. Luce and T. Jessop, (London, Thomas Nelson and Sons Ltd., 1957), 232.

167: *It is useless to try to adjudicate.* . . . Wendell Berry, "A Citizen's Response to the National Security Strategy of the United States of America," Advertisement: *The New York Times*, 9 February 2003. Abridged text: http://www.commondreams.org/views03/0209-11. htm (11 November 2013).

174: *But how can I explain it.* . . . Thomas Stearns Eliot, *The Family Reunion* (NY: Harccourt Brace, 1939), 27.

175f.: *I have often maintained.* . . . Pablo Neruda, "Nobel Lecture: Towards the Splendid City," 13 December 1971, http://www.nobelprize.org/nobel prizes/literature/ laureates/1971/neruda-lecture.html (8 November 2013).

176f.: *Strange now to think of you.* . . . Allen Ginsberg, "Kaddish," *op. cit.*

178: *Now I sit at my open window, writing.* . . . Hjalmar Söderberg, *Doctor Glas (1905)*, trans. Paul Britten Austin (NY: Anchor, 1963), 16.

179f.: *I dip down, my pen a net.* . . . Rhoda Trooboff. "Writer's Block: Dreaming," *Ginseng* (Oakland, MD: Garrett County Arts Council, 2011), 40.

181: *And the one woman said.* . . . 1Kings 3:17.
182: *John Pell, mathematician.* . . *Dictionary of National Biography* (Oxford UK: Oxford University Press, 1998), XV: 706.

183: *And Rachel said.* . . . Genesis 30:8.

184: *As we see in water.* . . . Thomas Hobbes, "Of Imagination," *The Leviathan* (1668), ed. Edwin Curley (Indianapolis, IN: Hackett, 1994), 2:8.

203: *Give us not to think.* . . . Robert Frost, "A Prayer in Spring," *Collected Poems, Prose and Plays* (NY: Library of America, 1995). Cited in http://writersalmanac.publicradio.org/ index.php?date=2012/03/26 (11 November 2013). *[T]he tendre croppes.* Chaucer, *The Canterbury Tales*, General Prologue.

204: *Just like a Bird.* . . . Margaret Cavendish, Duchess of Newcastle, "An Apology for Writing So Much Upon This Book" (1653), *Norton Anthology of Poetry.* 4th ed. (NY: W.W. Norton, 1996), 455.

206: **You hope to have one gone shortly. . . .** John Pell. Letter 30 April 1654. British Library Additional Manuscripts 4280.243, quoted in Teague. 82.

207: **Y tal vez hay . . . .** Miguel de Cervantes de Saavedra, *El Ingenioso Hidalgo Don Quijote de la Mancha*, Primera Parte, (Leipzig: F.A. Brockhaus, 1866), 77 [Author's translation]. **Curae leves loquuntur. . . .** Seneca, "Hippolytus," *Seneca's Tragedies*. Trans. Frank Justus Miller. Loeb Classical Library. (NY: G.P. Putnam's Sons, 1927), Vol. I: 366 (line 607).

208: **Clos'd lips hurt no one. . . .** M.Tullius Cicero, Letter 4 (I.8), *Letters to Atticus,* ed. and trans. D.R. Schackleton Bailey, Loeb Classical Library (Cambridge, MA: Harvard University Press, 1999), I: 36.

210: **I write all day. . .** M.Tullius Cicero, Letter 251 (XII.14), *Ibid.* III: 280.

211: **En duplex ænigma. . .flere. . . silere, satis.** Bathsua Makin, "Elegy on the Occasion of the Death of Henry Lord Hastings" Uncatalogued Huntington Library manuscript, reprinted in H.T. Swedenberg, "More Tears for Lord Hastings," *Huntington Library Quarterly* XVI:1 (Autumn 1952). [Author's translation.]

213: **My son lying very heavy. . . .** Bathsua Makin Manuscript Letter 1667, "Thanking the Countess for her bounty. . . ." *The Huntingdon Papers (The Archives of the Noble Family of Hastings* (London: Maggs Bros., 1927) Henry E. Huntington Library and Art Gallery, San Marino CA. V: 175. **La dimanda onesta. . . .** Dante Alighieri, Inferno, *Divine Comedy.* 24:78. [Author's translation.]

214: **Each bud. . . .** Mary Oliver, "Goldfinches," *Owls and Other Fantasies* (Boston: Beacon Press, 2003), cited in http://writersalmanac.publicradio.org/index.php?date=2004/08/05 (8 November 2013). **The narrative of this shared memory. . . .** Rachel Hadas, "Frog Doctor," *American Scholar.* Summer 2000: 69: 3.

216: **He was aware of an immense load. . . .** Graham Greene, *The Power and the Glory* (NY: Penguin, 1990), 66.

217: **Try to remember. . . about to billow.** "Try to Remember." *The Fantasticks. Op.cit.* **But with childeren. . . .** "The Vegetable Song." *The Fantasticks.* Music Harvey Schmidt. Book and Lyrics Tom Jones. 1960. **The kind of September. . . . .** "Try to Remember." *The Fantasticks. Op.cit.*

224: **His mind was full. . . .** Graham Greene. *Op cit.*, 60. **The City had rented out gaps. . . .** Evans. *Op. cit.*

229: **Soon it's gonna rain. . . .** "Soon It's Gonna Rain." *The Fantasticks.* Music Harvey Schmidt. Book and Lyrics Tom Jones. 1960.

230: **Then we'll let it rain. . . .** *Ibid.*

231: **Her only gift. . . .** Virginia Woolf. *Mrs. Dalloway.* (London: Hogarth Press, 1925), 9ff.

232: **One man in his time. . . .** William Shakespeare. *As You Like It.* II.vii.142. **[J]ealous in honour. . . . mere oblivion.** William Shakespeare. *King Lear.* II.vii.151-165. **Have I caught thee?** *Ibid.* V.iii.21. **Have I caught thee, my heavenly jewel?. . . O this blessed hour!** William Shakespeare. *Merry Wives of Windsor.* III.iii.44f.

233: *Have I caught my heav'nly jewel.* Sir Philip Sidney, "Astrophil and Stella." 2nd song. http://www.luminarium.org/renascence-editions/stella.html (11 November 2013). *Come, let me write. . . .* Sir Philip Sidney. "Astrophil and Stella," Sonnet 34. http:// www.sonnets.org/sidney.htm#034 (11 November 2013).

234: *He was a teacher. . . .* Jack Kerouac. *On the Road.* (NY: Penguin, 1976), 85. *This was the time. . . .* May Sarton. "Return." *Selected Poems of May Sarton.* (NY: W.W. Norton, 1978), 345.

235: *O me, my heart. . . .* William Shakespeare. *King Lear.* II.iv.122.

236: *foolish, fond old man. Ibid.,* IV.vii.60. *[H]ast power . . . manhood thus. Ibid.,* I.iv.319. *[S]hould be ruled. . . . Ibid.,* II.iv.150ff. *[S]ting his mind so venomously. Ibid.,* IV.iii.47f. *Speak what we feel. . . . Ibid.,* V.iii.324. *The man that makes his toe. . . . Ibid.,* III.ii.31ff.

237: *Such unconstant starts. . . . Ibid.,* I.i.304.

240: *Full of change. . . . Ibid.,* I.i.291. *[L]ong engraffed condition. Ibid.,* I.i.301. *[I] dle old man. . . . Ibid.,* I.iii.16ff. *[I]dle and fond bondage. . . oppression of aged tyranny. Ibid.,* I.ii.51f. *Sons at perfect age. . . . Ibid.,* I.ii.76. *Old fools are babes again. . . . Ibid.,* I.iii.18.

241: *'Tis our fast intent. . . . Ibid.,* I.i.39ff.

242: *Tell me. . . which of you. . . . Ibid.,* I.i.52.

243: *our largest bounty. Ibid.,* I.i.53. *Speak. . . Nothing will come of nothing. Ibid.,* I.i.90ff. *Unhappy that I am. . . . Ibid.,* I.i.93ff.

244: *dearer than space . . . what you are. Ibid.,* I.i.57-272 *passim.*

245: *Give me thy hand. . . . Ibid.,* V.ii.7ff. *We'll set thee to school. . . . Ibid.,* II.iv.68f. *When we are born. . . . Ibid.,* IV.vi.186f. *[T]o the very brim of it. Ibid.,* IV.i.78. *When you dost ask me blessing. . . . Ibid.,* V.iii.10ff.

246: *Prithee, nuncle. . . . Ibid.,* I.iv.195f. *And all beit that he had therefore bene put up. . . .* Thomas More. "Apologie," cited in Daniel Hack Tuke, *Chapters in the History of the Insane in the British Isles* (London: K. Paul, Trench and Co.,1882), 56.

247: *Saith the Psalmist. . . waspish, displeas'd with everything.* Robert Burton. *Anatomy of Melancholy.* Vol. 1(NY: Everyman's Library, 1964), 210. (1:2.v). *Γονέων δε ἀμελεῖν ούτε θεὸς ούτε ἄνθρωπος. . . ever recommended to anyone.* Plato. Trans. R.G. Bury. Loeb Classical Library Vol. XI (Cambridge, MA: Harvard University Press, 1926). Book XI: §930E, p. 446f. [Author's translation.]

248: *Ἐάν δέ τίς τινα νόσος ἤ γῆρας. . . a madman or not. Ibid.,* §929D, p. 442.

254: *I beheld till the thrones. . . .* Daniel 7:9.

258: *An old man's relatives. . . .* Plato. *Op. cit.*

259: *When the gods hear the pleading of a parent dishonour'd. . . . Plato. Op. cit.,* §931C, p. 448f.

265: **My dearly loved friend.** . . . Michael Drayton. "To My Most Dearly-loved Friend Henery Reynolds Esquire, of Poets & Poesy." *Minor Poems of Michael Drayton.* Ed. Cyril Brett. (Oxford: Clarendon Press, 1907), 108.

267: **Even if he does sit silently.** . . . Kazuo Ishiguro. *The Unconsoled.* (NY: Vintage, 1996), 59.

268: **mission accomplished.** George W. Bush. Photo accompanying speech aboard USS Abraham Lincoln, 1 May 2003 http://en.wikipedia.org/wiki/2003 Mission Accomplished Speech (8 November 2013).

269: **Thy love is such.** . . . Ann Bradstreet. "To My Dear and Loving Husband," *Norton Anthology of Poetry.* 4th edition (NY: W.W. Norton, 1998), 315.

270: **You have my attention.** . . . Denise Levertov. "The Marriage." *Selected Poems* (Newcastle upon Tyne, UK: Bloodaxe Books. 1986), 14.

271: **In the sweat of thy face.** . . . Genesis 3:19.

274: **Omnibus omnium horarum homo.** Robert Whittinton, *Vulgaria. The Vulgaria of John Stanbridge and the Vulgaria of Robert Whittinton* (ca. 1522). Ed. Beatrice White. (London: Early English Text Society, Kegan Paul, Trench, Trubner & Co., 1932) microfilm. **Morus est vir omnium horarum.** *Ibid.* **To the weak became I as weak.** . . . 1 Corinthians 9:22.

275: **Dear Sister. . . end of this year.** John Pell Letter 30 April 1654. Passim. John Pell. Letter 30 April 1654. British Library Additional Manuscripts 4280.243, quoted in Teague. 82.

276: **For a hen. . .the house in which he finds you.** *Ibid.*

278: **Præceptoris filia mihi.** . . . Whittinton. [Author's translation.]

279: **Unde quo familiariter.** . . . **Mihi adeo aspera et acerba viditur.** . . . **Pauperum itidem filii gratia et virtute.** . . .**Citius medullam a ligone expellas.** . . . **Ubi hæ duæ lineæ exarentur.** . . . **Hei antique felicitatis recordatio.** . . .

327: **Licet amarum, cum equanimitate.** . . . *Ibid.* [Author's translation.]

280: Μέντορι ἐϊδομένη ἠμὲν δέμας ἠδὲ καὶ αὐδήν. Homer. *Odyssey.* Trans. A.T. Murray. Vol. II. Loeb Classical Library. (NY: G.P. Putnam's Sons, 1931). XXIV:547.

286: **I want to speak to you. . .** Denise Levertov, "The Marriage II," *Selected Poems.* (Newcastle upon Tyne, UK: Bloodaxe Books,1986), 15.

287: **Litteras Græcas senex didici. . . unde discerem neminem.** M. Tullius Cicero. "De Senectute," *M. Ciceronis Opera,* vol. 10: 326ff. http://books.google.com/books?id=XDIBAAAAMAAJ&pg=PA333&lpg= PA333&dq=Litteras+Græcas+senex+didici+cicero&source=bl&ots=5oH6f6y Uxu&sig=vTwjKQsycnY3AhZkyNexLlu8r-Y&hl=en&sa=X&ei=UnawUv- HNsXisASX4IGICw&ved=0CEkQ6AEwBzgK#v=onepage&q=Litteras%20Græcas%20senex%20 didici%20cicero&f=false (16 December 2013). [Author's translations.] **There are, after all, so many books.** . . . Michael Cunningham, *The Hours* (NY: Farrar, Straus and Giroux, 1998), 225.

288: **It's a mad world.** . . . Anton Chekhov. "Uncle Vanya," Act 4, http://www. gutenberg.org/files/1756/1756-h/1756-h.htm#link2H_4_0006 (11 November 2013). **Here are books, paper.** . . . May Sarton. "Return," 345.

Acknowledgments

I owe special thanks to authors Virginia Woolf, Antonia Fraser, and Frances Teague, whose books – *A Room of One's Own*, *Weaker Vessel: Woman's Lot in 17th-Century England*, and *Bathsua Makin: A Woman of Learning* – have been by my side throughout this project.

Many friends have endured my yammering about this project for years and encouraged me to see it to completion. I am grateful in particular to the following:

Mary Carpenter, Kay Dunkley, Harriet Dwinell, John Glavin, Justine Kenin, Larry Lesser, Leslie Mott, Jessica Neely, and Rebecca Wolsk, whose bracing insights eased this project through its many stages of revision.

Elizabeth Jenkins-Joffe and her colleagues, who transformed the daunting grandeur of the Main Reading Room of the Library of Congress into a welcoming, peaceful haven for study and writing.

Kathryn Brake, David Ferry, Peggy Parker, Sally Rieger, and the late Carol Eliot and James Tibbetts, whose loving dedication to their students and their disciplines has informed all stages of my work.

Laura Carns, Jeremy Dy, and Elizabeth Rosenbaum, who provided valuable technical and editorial assistance.

Anna Nazaretz Radjou (J.A. Creative) and Wayne Magoon (Beacon Printing), whose impeccable, imaginative craftsmanship has turned my raw material into a handsome affirmation of the book and paper arts.

I am forever indebted to my family – to my late parents, to my daughters Hannah and Abby and their husbands and children, and above all to my beloved husband Peter – whose steadfast wisdom, good humor, and loving generosity make possible and worthwhile everything I do.

This book is set mainly in Garamond, an old-style serif typeface named after the Parisian publisher and punch-cutter Claude Garamont (c. 1480–1561), one of the first to specialize in type design as a commercial service to others, thereby spreading new typefaces throughout the world of European-language printing. The adoption of Garamont's type by the French court for its printing influenced printing across Western Europe. Garamond's letterforms are said to convey a sense of fluidity and consistency. Considered to be among the most legible and readable serif typefaces, Garamond has also been noted to be one of the most eco-friendly major fonts when it comes to ink usage.

Also used in this book is Arial, a sans serif font drawn in 1982 by Robin Nicholas and Patricia Saunders for the Monotype Foundry (now Monotype Imaging, based in Woburn, Massachusetts). Designed originally for IBM and early laser printers, it was adopted in 1992 by Microsoft for part of its suite of Windows system fonts and since then has been a staple of most computers, textual applications, and laser printers. Also used widely in newspapers and advertising, Arial is described as versatile, contemporary, universal, and authoritative.